I0645304

TEMPTING THE DRYAD

REBECCA RIVARD

WILD HEARTS PRESS

Tempting the Dryad: A Fada Novel

The Fada Shapeshifter Series

Copyright ©2016 by Rebecca Rivard

Sea Dragon's Hunger: A Fada Shapeshifter Story (excerpt)

Copyright ©2018 by Rebecca Rivard

This book is a work of fiction. The names, characters, places, and incidents are products of the author's imagination, or have been used fictitiously and are not to be construed as real. Any resemblance to actual persons living or dead, locales, or events is entirely coincidental.

Cover art and design by Laura Gordon/The Book Cover Machine

Editing by Katherine Teel

All rights reserved.

No part of this book may be reproduced in any form or by any electronic or mechanical means, including information storage and retrieval systems, without written permission from the author, except for the use of brief quotations in a book review.

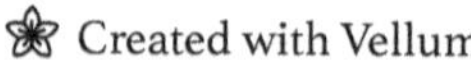 Created with Vellum

THE FADA SHAPESHIFTER SERIES

The fada.
Shapeshifters created during Dionysus's infamous bacchanals from a mix of fae, human and animal genes.
They're ruthless, untamed—and when they love, it's forever.

Stealing Ula: A Fada Shapeshifter Prequel (Nisio & Ula, set in Ireland)

The Rock Run River Fada
Seducing the Sun Fae (Dion & Cleia)
Claiming Valeria (Rui & Valeria)
Tempting the Dryad (Tiago & Alesia)
Sea Dragon's Hunger (Cassidy & Nic)

The Baltimore Earth Fada (The Darktime Trilogy)
Saving Jace (Jace & Evie)
Charming Marjani (Marjani & Fane)
Adric's Heart (Adric & Rosana)

Fada Shapeshifter Short Reads
Lir's Lady (#3.5—Lir & Isleen)
Shifter's Valentine (#3.6—Jenny & Chico)

Find out more and read exclusive excerpts: https://rebeccarivard.com/shapeshifters/

To stay informed and be eligible for giveaways and sneak peeks of upcoming novels, go to rebeccarivard.com or sign up for my newsletter (http://www.subscribepage.com/i6x3j1).

1

The argument erupted out of nowhere.

One moment the Rock Run River Fada were eating breakfast in the spacious cavern that served as the clan's dining hall, and the next moment Cleia was on her feet and slapping her hands on the plank oak table.

"I will not," she told her mate, her lovely face set.

Dion do Rio, clan alpha, rose as well, facing her across the table. He placed his own hands on the surface.

"Excuse me?" he asked in a soft voice that sent a tremor up the spine of everyone nearby.

At the next table, Tiago exchanged a look with his younger sister Rosana. When their oldest brother took that tone, a smart person ran for cover.

But not Cleia. A queen in her own right—of all seven sun fae clans—she allowed Dion to push her so far and then she shoved right back.

"I *said*," she repeated, "that I will not sit at home crocheting baby booties or whatever you think a pregnant woman should be doing. I'm going and that's final. Artan and Grady"—her long-time bodyguards—"can come too, if it makes you happy."

Dion speared his fingers through his shoulder-length black hair. "It will not make me happy," he gritted. "Those Baltimore fada are sneaky *filhos da puta*. I don't trust them worth a damn."

"Look, I know you've had trouble with them in the past."

That's an understatement, Tiago thought. The Baltimore Earth Fada Clan wanted Rock Run, and they'd done everything short of all-out war to get it.

"But there's no harm in listening to what they have to say," Cleia continued. "If they try anything funny, I can always 'port myself out of there."

Dion snorted. "You can't teleport instantly. And in the few seconds it takes, they could have a knife in your heart."

"But why would the earth fada want to hurt me? We sun fae aren't their competition—you are. We have something Lord Adric wants and we're more than happy to take his money. We're not using that quartz for anything."

"Damn it, Cleia, you know what that SOB is like. He doesn't negotiate, he takes. He'll sweet-talk you into letting his men on your lands and then steal the damn quartz right from under your nose."

"Then I'll ask for a large payment up front."

"What if it's just a cover to infiltrate and then attack you? You're going to have to let your wards down to allow them to enter."

"I'll hire your men as guards. Everyone knows they're the best there is."

"*Claro.*" He flicked his fingers in a dismissive gesture. "*Mas—*" Dion had slipped into Portuguese, never a good sign.

"It's a win-win situation," his mate shot back. "Rock Run will get a hefty fee for protecting us and my clan will—"

Her words ended in a small shriek as Dion rounded the table in two big steps and scooped her up in his arms. "*Basta.* Enough." He strode toward an exit. "No more arguments."

"Put. Me. Down." The sun fae slammed an elbow into his chest.

Tiago winced. That had to hurt.

Across the table, Rosana pressed her lips together, trying not to laugh.

"*Acalme-te*." Dion brought a big hand up and smacked his mate's round bottom.

Uh-oh. The entire room held its collective breath.

Cleia's breath hissed out. Her exotic amber eyes narrowed. "You like water so much. Why don't you go jump in a pond, you slimy green frog?"

Her lips moved. Magic shimmered in the air.

"Like hell," growled Dion. His mouth descended on hers in a hard kiss, preventing her from completing the spell.

The men hooted, while the women yelled encouragement to Cleia. "Keep fighting, my lady. Don't let him win."

But the two had disappeared in the direction of their quarters.

The clan adults exchanged knowing smiles. Dion and the sun fae queen had a fiery mating, but they were crazy in love. Everyone knew how this latest fight would end.

Only Tiago felt no mirth. Face blank, he slapped butter on his whole-grain roll. It had been almost five years since his oldest brother had mated with Cleia. The pair had at last conceived a much-wanted child, news that had been received with great joy by both Rock Run and the sun fae.

Cleia was elated and his badass brother couldn't stop smiling.

And Tiago was eaten up by jealousy.

Because he'd had Cleia first. She'd lured Tiago with a glamour, keeping him for one wild, never-to-be-forgotten week, then tossing him back like a too-small fish when she learned he was barely twenty-one, a child to a fae of Cleia's two hundred-plus years.

But he hadn't been a child even then, and he certainly wasn't one now, five years later. He was a full-grown fada male with all the needs that ran in the hot, part-animal blood of his kind.

From the bench beside him, Fausto, his otter friend, tilted his silky brown head and regarded Tiago, small mouth pursed. Lifting onto his hind legs, the otter snatched a walnut from a bowl on the table, cracked it between strong jaws and offered Tiago the meat.

Tiago gravely accepted the offering. "*Muito obrigado, meu amigo.* Thank you, my friend."

Although he and his friends spoke English among themselves, his Gift for communicating with animals worked best when he spoke in Portuguese, the clan's native tongue.

Fausto chittered a cheerful reply. As far as he was concerned, food was the cure for just about anything.

Rosana leaned across the table. "Be happy for them," she murmured. "Dion was alone for a long time before he met her."

His jaw clenched. "I know."

His eldest brother had changed since he'd mated with Cleia. He smiled more easily and had learned to delegate authority so he could spend more time with his family. Tiago had been too young to realize it, but Dion had been lonely. A brother and sister weren't enough—a man needed a woman.

And damn if he needed his younger sister to point it out to him.

Tiago jumped to his feet. He had to get out of there. Once it had been enough simply to be around Cleia. To talk with her, laugh with her, gaze on her long golden body.

But now, he wanted more, his beast a restless pressure beneath his skin. At night he burned for her, tossing on the mattress as he spun dark fantasies in which he stole her from his brother. Fantasies that by day caused his gut to twist with shame.

The mate bond was for life. Only death could sever it.

It was time for Tiago to leave—permanently—before he committed an act so vile, he avoided naming it even in his mind.

He jerked his head at Fausto. "Let's go."

THE ROCK RUN base had been carved from a system of underground caverns bordered on the north by Rock Run Creek and to the east by the Susquehanna River, a large, fast-flowing river that drained into the Chesapeake Bay. The base's main exit was six fathoms beneath the surface at the confluence of Rock Run Creek and the Susquehanna.

To leave the base, you had to pass through a hidden grotto accessible only by a narrow underwater tunnel. Tiago went first, swimming through the tunnel and then up through the icy creek to surface in the Susquehanna. It was early April and a light rain was falling. The river was only a shade above freezing, a temperature that would've been dangerous for a human. But to a river fada, it was invigorating.

Tiago lifted his face to the rain and paused to wait for Fausto. Ordinarily Tiago would've been either on sentry duty or training with the other warriors, but he'd just returned from an overseas mission and had several days leave coming to him. Maybe he should just get the hell out of here—go down to Baltimore, maybe.

Fausto popped to the surface nearby, blinking his round black eyes against the raindrops.

"*Onde agora?*" Tiago asked. "Where to now?"

The otter shrugged and treaded water nearby. It was clear he didn't care; he was just along for the swim.

"Okay, then."

Tiago glanced around. To the north was Rock Run territory, with most of the land for the first few miles on either side of the Susquehanna owned by the clan. To the southeast was the Chesapeake Bay and the human town of Grace Harbor. The river in that direction was controlled by humans.

The last thing Tiago needed right now was to run into a human boater. In his current mood, if the man pissed him off, he just might snap his neck, setting fada-human relations back several decades.

"*Vamos.*" He jerked his chin at Fausto and struck out upriver, deliberately staying as a man. Best to work his muscles until they screamed...anything to calm the beast.

Fausto kept up for the first quarter mile or so, gamely propelling himself forward with his webbed paws and tail. When he grew tired, Tiago had him climb on his back and continued north.

It was another mile before they came upon a trio of small, densely wooded islands. The humans hadn't found it worth their while to harvest the relatively minor stands of trees, and eventually the islands had passed into Rock Run's hands. The islands' only residents were three dryads, sisters who'd agreed to tend the forest and its animals in return for a home and Rock Run's protection.

Tiago tread water near the center island, the one occupied by the middle sister. Alesia.

Deus, he needed to see her. He supposed this was where he'd been heading all along.

Fausto had already slipped off his back to swim to the island. The otter loved visiting Alesia.

Tiago followed suit. He kept spare clothes in an oilskin bag stored in a tree near the beach. After donning a pair of shorts, he strode into the woods, Fausto loping alongside him.

The island was covered by an old-growth forest of oak, hickory, walnut, beech and maple. As they followed the familiar path to the center, the rain increased. Tiago raised his face to the chill drops. Water was his element, necessary to him in the most basic, primal way. The easiest way to harm a water fada was to keep him from his river or lake or sea.

He and Fausto entered a clearing presided over by a large pin oak surrounded by daffodils in full bloom, a present from him to Alesia. With her Gift for making things grow, the bulbs had rapidly multiplied and now the clearing was carpeted in sunny drifts of yellow and orange and white.

He wasn't a flower kind of guy, but he liked seeing them here. They seemed—right. His shoulders eased and for the first time since returning to Rock Run last night, he felt like he was home.

He glanced toward the oak's crown. "Alesia? You home?"

No response. But he sensed her in the tree, watching him. He narrowed his eyes at the uppermost branches.

From above came a chuckle, cut short.

His lips peeled back in a feral grin. Backing up, he took a running jump and caught the first branch, and hauled himself up. Fausto chittered a greeting to Alesia but remained safely on the ground.

Dryads were born at the same time as their host trees. As Alesia and her oak had grown, the tree had shaped itself into a cozy abode with quirky furniture formed from its branches and trunk, and clever nooks for storage. Alesia had added cushions woven from grass, and at the oak's sturdiest point, she'd strung a wide hammock between two branches.

Tiago had never seen a home that so perfectly matched its inhabitant's personality. He could almost envy Alesia the connection she had with her oak.

Near the crown, he halted and sniffed. As a dryad, Alesia had the ability to blend into the bark, making her almost impossible to detect with the naked eye. But her scent filled the air, wild and green, with a tantalizing overlay of woman. To his animal-enhanced sense of smell, it was as if she'd waved a bright flag.

He followed his nose until he located her on a seat formed from a branch, her back against the trunk. She'd become one with the oak—literally—her skin, hair and clothing hardening to a gray, bark-like substance.

He scaled the last branch to crouch before her. "Change."

The air shimmered. Gradually her skin softened and her color returned to its usual smooth ivory. She had a heart-shaped face with exotically tilted eyes and a pointed chin. Her hair was next. He watched, fascinated, as it changed from gray to a sun-streaked brown that tumbled over her shoulders. A pointed ear poked out of the curls, the mark of a pureblood fae.

The last to change was her dress. The green cotton was spattered with rain drops. His gaze caught on where the damp material clung to her breasts, hardening the nipples into inviting points. Her chest began to rise and fall, and her lips parted.

He drew in a slow breath and reminded himself that Alesia was a friend, not a lover. Still, he couldn't help brushing a thumb across her soft, rose-colored lips as he waited for her to finish.

By the time her eyes opened, she was smiling. "Hello, Tiago." She pressed a quick, bashful kiss to his cheek, and her wild forest scent washed over him.

He clenched his fists and wished for—hell, something he couldn't put words to. That things were different.

That *he* was different.

"It's good to see you," she said. "It's been too long."

"I've been busy." It wasn't a lie—he'd been away on a job with his squad. But he'd also been avoiding her.

She flinched and he swore under his breath.

The gods knew he wanted Alesia. They'd met five summers ago when a den of half-feral fada had taken a cavern beneath her oak as their lair. The den's leader, an old Greek sea fada, had kidnapped and drugged a Rock Run woman named Valeria and forced her to take part in a dark, forbidden bacchanal. Worse, they'd sold Valeria's adopted daughter to the Baltimore earth fada.

It was only by chance that Tiago had witnessed the abduction. When he'd realized what was happening, he'd gone back for Rui do Mar, Dion's second-in-command and Valeria's mate.

During the rescue, something had sparked between Tiago

and Alesia. He'd returned a few days later, thinking to drown his craving for Cleia in the dryad's taut little body.

But it hadn't been that easy. Like most fae, Alesia had been raised to think of the fada as little better than animals. Men who'd as soon as slit your throat as talk to you. Men who lured women to take part in their wild rituals as the Greek sea fada had done to Valeria.

It had taken weeks to coax Alesia into trusting him. By then Tiago *liked* her—too much for the no-strings fuck he'd sought. It seemed wrong to take her as a substitute for the woman he really wanted.

But he couldn't keep away. She was unlike any female he knew. She made things grow. She made him laugh. Even the beast calmed in her presence.

Sometimes he believed she was the only thing keeping him sane. He'd cut off his own arm before he hurt her.

So he kept visiting—and somehow, they'd become friends, he and this shy, half-wild dryad who trusted almost no one.

Now she touched his arm, her fine dark brows furrowed. "What's wrong?"

"Nothing."

"Nothing?" She tilted her head, her eyes knowing and a little sad.

His chest squeezed. He was afraid that despite his good intentions, he'd hurt her anyway. "I shouldn't have come. Not today."

"I hear Queen Cleia's going to have a baby."

"Yeah." His voice was gruff. He cleared his throat. "I mean, yes, she is."

"Tiago. This is me, Alesia. I know you're upset."

He glanced away. "She and Dion are so damn happy. The whole clan is so damn happy. And I—" He grimaced. "I want to rip someone's head off. Some brother, huh?"

She regarded him steadily.

Foolish woman. She should push him out of the tree and

conceal herself so well he'd never find her. Because he was this close to shoving her up against the trunk and sinking himself into her, deep and hard, whether she wanted it or not.

Anything to mute the pain, the clawing need to show Cleia and Dion what he could do...if he chose.

When Alesia spoke, her voice had a thread of steel. "You're a good man, Tiago do Rio."

That thin line tethering him to good behavior snapped. Alesia might think she knew him, but she didn't. He'd held back, careful to show her only his best self.

He came onto his knees and leaned into her, allowing his barely leashed lust to seep into his voice. "You think so, *querida*? Why don't I show you just how good I am?"

He brought his hand to her nape, curving his fingers around the slim column a bit too firmly. Not enough to bruise—but enough so she'd have to work to escape him.

He *wanted* to frighten her, even as he felt a spike of shame. He shoved it aside, allowing the restless black beast to rise to the surface.

Her big golden-brown eyes grew even larger. A pulse leapt in the soft skin beneath his fingers. When he spoke, the darkness tinted his voice.

"Talk to me, Lesia." He stroked his thumb down her throat. "I know you want me. Say yes. I'll make it so good..."

She swallowed, a deer caught in headlights.

His lips twisted. *Deus*, he was a bastard. She *was* afraid of him.

And even though the beast reveled in that, the better part of him—the part that still fought the darkness—was ashamed. He was opening his fingers to release her when she touched a moist pink tongue to her lower lip.

His entire body went rigid. It seemed even the forest stilled, waiting for her answer.

"All right."

2

____

$\mathcal{A}$lesia knew the instant Tiago stepped onto her island. The forest kept her informed of any visitors, but with him, she always *knew*.

Something changed in the air, stirred within herself.

It had been over a month since his last visit. He'd told her then he was going on another mission. Goddess, she dreaded them. He left abruptly to return weeks later with a set face and burning eyes. He never said where he'd been or what he'd been doing, and she didn't ask.

After the first couple of weeks she found herself walking the beach, scanning the river for him. When she realized what she was doing, she gave herself a shake and headed back to work.

Spring was a busy time for a dryad. Not only was she cultivating her own garden, she was inspecting every tree on the island, making sure they'd come through the winter undamaged and disease-free and that the forest and its creatures maintained a healthy balance.

But she couldn't help worrying. If Tiago was hurt, would anyone at Rock Run think to tell her? Her hands tightened on a sapling she was nursing back to health. It could be months before she heard. No, if she wanted to find out how Tiago was doing, she'd have to go to the Rock Run base.

She swallowed sickly.

Because she did *not* want to go to Rock Run. Fada males were the assassins and mercenaries of the fae world. Even the women were scary. Alesia had as little to do with them as possible.

But for Tiago, she'd do it. She wasn't the swimmer the river fada were, but as a dryad, she could 'port herself to any tree within a five-mile radius, and from there she had only to walk along Rock Run Creek and a sentry would investigate. No one got close to a fada base without their permission.

She'd almost made up her mind to it when she sensed him on the island.

The trees passed the news, a whisper in their leaves. *He's here, he's here.*

Her heart leapt. She dashed through the rain to her oak. Scurrying up the trunk, she settled onto a branch and willed her skin to change color and harden until she blended, chameleon-like, into the bark. It was a game the two of them played. Before Tiago, she hadn't even known the fada had a playful side.

Now she blinked at him. Had she heard him right?

She'd wanted him for so long, had pictured him doing just this during the long winter nights while the forest slept as she kept a solitary vigil.

She curled her fingers into her palms. *Please Goddess, don't let this be another dream.*

But he was very real, very male. She could breathe his rich scent, hear his inhale as he waited for her response. See the water dampening his wavy black hair, carelessly pulled back and tied with a leather thong.

He leaned closer, dominating her with his body, his startling silver-blue eyes boring into hers. He'd grown taller and broader in the five years since they'd first met. At twenty-one, he'd still been in late adolescence, since fada and fae matured later than humans.

But he was a man now, with a warrior's wide shoulders and hard muscles. A sexy strip of black hair arrowed down his abdomen to the waistband of his shorts, and one big bicep was encircled by a Celtic knot tattoo.

"Talk to me, Alesia." His thumb caressed her neck. "I know you want me."

She moistened her lips. Around them the rain sheeted down, but the oak enclosed them in their own private shelter.

Speak, Alesia. Or he's going to leave.

Blood pounded in her ears, slow and heavy. "All right."

He rocked back on his heels as if she'd slapped him. "All right?"

She gulped. Okay, that wasn't the reaction she'd been looking for.

She'd told herself that if all he wanted was a friend, then she was okay with that. But she'd lied.

Because sweet Goddess, she wanted him. For Tiago, she just might beg.

"Yes," she said more strongly. *Please...*

He set a hand on her thigh and leaned closer. "I'm not sure you understand. I want you, Lesia." His voice thickened. "Hard and fast. Slow and deep. I want you pleading for me to take you—any way I want. Do you think you can take that? Because if not, tell me now and I'll leave this island and never come back."

A fine tremor ran through her. Her stomach knotted, a tangle of want and need and yes, a touch of fear. He was a large, powerful man and she'd seen firsthand how brutal the fada could be.

The hand on her thigh tightened, then released. "Hell. Don't be afraid. I'd never—look, I'm in a godawful mood today. I should never have come." He started to withdraw.

"Don't leave." She caught his arm, knowing that if he left now he'd honor his promise and never return. She'd never have another chance with him.

"*Te quero*," she said in the language of his clan. She didn't have the Gift of tongues like some fae, but he'd taught her some basic phrases. "I want you too. So, yes. I'm saying yes to all that."

His nostrils flared. Then his lips curved in a slow smile. "All right, then."

He slid his fingers into her hair and brought his mouth to hers in a kiss. Not the hard, demanding kiss she'd expected, but slow and sweet. Rubbing his lips over hers. Sliding his tongue along the seam of her lips and then into her mouth.

Tasting her as if she were a rare and wonderful treat.

She made a sound low in her throat and sucked on his tongue. His breath quickened and his bicep hardened beneath her hand.

He slanted his mouth over hers, deepening the kiss. His fingers tightened on the base of her skull while his other hand moved to her breasts, weighing and caressing them, pinching her nipples into hard points beneath the damp cotton.

Desire stabbed from her breasts to her womb. He slid his hand down her abdomen to cup her mound through the dress.

She moaned and pressed against him. "Tiago. Please—"

He rotated the heel of his hand over just the right spot. She sucked in a breath and he chuckled darkly. "You like that, baby?"

"Yes. Oh, yes."

But she wanted to touch him, too. She ran her hands over his body, exploring the hard muscles of his shoulders and back. Smooth olive skin, slick and cool from the rain.

Her fingers followed the dark trail of hair to his waistband, dipped inside.

The muscles of his stomach jumped. "Alesia." He gripped her shoulders and drew a jagged breath. "By the gods, I need this. Need *you*. Watching the two of them together...it drives me mad."

She briefly closed her eyes. Even now, he was thinking of

Cleia. She'd swear the sun fae queen had Siren blood, the way men made asses of themselves over her—even now, when the woman was happily mated.

"Fuck." Tiago passed a hand over his face. "Sorry. I—"

She stopped his words with a kiss. "Forget her," she said against his lips.

She waited until he gave a jerky nod and then she pulled back enough to undo the metal button of his waistband. She trailed her fingers across the firm flesh. His breath sucked in and she smiled.

Right here, right now, he was hers, not Cleia's. And she was going to make the most of it.

"If you want me," she husked, "then have me."

His gaze was on her hand, inching its way lower. His throat worked. "I shouldn't," he said without much conviction.

"No?" She eased his zipper down. His cock sprang free, darkly flushed and eager. She encircled it with her thumb and first finger. He was hot and hard beneath her palm. She worked him slowly. "This is what you came for, isn't it?"

"Damn it, Alesia." He caught her wrist. "You're not making this easy. I came to see *you*. Not for this."

"No?" She squeezed him. "But you want it. Or was that little speech about how much you want me just talk?"

His lashes lowered, forming dark fans over his cheekbones. Then he growled and reached for her. "Come here."

He shifted their positions so he was against the trunk with her on his lap. He speared his fingers in her hair and drew her head back to expose her throat. She swallowed noisily, and his nostrils flared.

"I want you." He skimmed his mouth down her throat and nipped the sensitive skin at the base. "Fuck, yeah, I want you."

Hot liquid spread through her veins, settled in her belly as a low ache. He licked the small wound, and her eyes closed in pleasure.

He moved his mouth to her ear, tracing the delicate whorls with his tongue, tugging gently on the small gold hoop in her earlobe. She squirmed in his lap, and he drew a sharp breath.

She grinned. "Something's poking me, fada." She wiggled her bottom again.

He clamped a hand on her thigh, holding her still. "You"—he nipped her earlobe—"look like one of those naughty fairies in the human storybooks. One who plays pranks like stealing your shoes or tying your hair into knots while you're asleep."

She let her head fall back against his shoulder. "Maybe I feel naughty."

He pushed her hair away from her neck and pressed small, biting kisses to the turn of her shoulder. "I'll tell you a secret," he said, his mouth warm against her skin. "I like naughty fairies. It makes me want to...punish them a little."

His hand had somehow made its way under her skirt. He pinched her clit, just hard enough. Sensation raced through her. She stifled a moan. Goddess, the man was going to drive her crazy.

He looked down at her, mouth curved.

She ran her tongue over her lower lip, enjoying how his eyes darkened. "I—I'd better be careful then," she managed to say.

He nudged her thighs further apart. "Open for me."

When she obeyed, he pushed up her skirt and eyed her mound. "No panties, hm? You *are* bad. Who were you expecting?"

She met his eyes. "You, Tiago."

"Good answer." He worked her skirt up further, baring her to the waist. "Ah...pretty. So damn pretty."

He dipped his finger into her and then out again, circled her needy sex, building her arousal in slow, knowing increments. Way too knowing, as far as she was concerned. But then, in the past few years, Tiago had had more women than she cared to think about. If he couldn't have Cleia, he'd apparently decided to work his way through the available fada females—and a good number of humans as well.

His other hand tightened in her hair, bringing her close so he could kiss her, hard and deep, his tongue moving in time with his fingers until she was dizzy with arousal. A gust of wind spattered them with rain. His mouth moved to her shoulder, tonguing a stray drop.

He trailed his lips over her collar bone and then sank his teeth into the sensitive flesh at the turn of her neck, slowly, gently —and with unmistakable possessiveness.

A thrill raced down her spine. She gripped his shoulders. "Tiago. I—" Her voice sounded high and needy in her ears.

Suddenly, there was a scrabbling in the tree below them. Fausto heaved himself onto a nearby branch and launched into a scold.

Tiago muttered a curse and jerked her dress down over her thighs.

"Fausto?" Alesia looked dazedly from him to the irate otter. "What—"

Tiago raised a hand. "Okay, okay," he muttered in Portuguese. "I'm sorry, all right? But we're busy, damn it."

Alesia blinked. "Was he waiting in the rain all this time?"

"It won't hurt him," Tiago returned, but he was careful to switch to English so Fausto wouldn't understand. "He's a fucking otter. His fur is waterproof."

Alesia pushed off his lap and crouched beside Fausto. "You poor thing," she said in her rudimentary Portuguese. "We're so sorry. But aren't you a clever one?" She smoothed a hand down his slick fur. "I didn't know you could climb trees—and so high, too."

Fausto unleashed another round of infuriated chatter. Alesia didn't have to understand otter to realize he was complaining that he only had to climb trees when his so-called friends deserted him.

Behind her, Tiago expelled a breath. "I said I was sorry."

Alesia scratched Fausto behind the ears. "Don't be cross, *belo*. Here, have a treat." She offered him a bit of the dried fish she kept in a container for him.

The otter took it in both paws and gobbled it down. Mollified, he rubbed his head against her leg. Tiago growled, a low, feral sound.

Both she and Fausto started. The otter cast Tiago a look, and then back at her.

Fausto muttered an apology and then, with a courtly nod to Alesia, began making his way back down to the ground. It was hard going—she could hear him chittering grumpily to himself, and once there was a thud that vibrated through the whole tree.

She caught her breath, but Fausto would be insulted if she offered to carry him down. Besides, at twenty-some pounds, he wasn't exactly a lightweight.

Tiago remained against the trunk, long legs stretched before him, regarding her through hooded eyes. He'd pulled his fly together to cover himself, but the air was thick with unsatisfied desire.

She shot him a rueful look. She knew how he felt; her breasts were full and tender and there was an empty ache between her thighs.

"Fucking otter has a crush on you," he muttered.

"You think?" she asked, charmed. "Well, he's gone now."

She started back to him, but he looked away. "Maybe it's for the best."

She watched, stunned, as he rose to his feet and zipped up his shorts. "You're leaving?"

"Yeah. You're a friend, Lesia. I shouldn't have—"

"Why not? I want it. You want it. We're both unmated. I don't see the problem."

"Because, damn it. You mean something to me. I can't do it with you. Not when I'm in lo—" He broke off and shook his head.

Something clenched deep in her chest. "I see."

"Hell, Lesia. I'm sor—"

"*Don't.*" She came to her feet as well. She could take anything but him apologizing. "Just—don't."

Tiago scraped a hand through his wavy black hair. "I'm sorry. Maybe you don't want to hear that, but I am."

She swallowed over the boulder in her throat. Then she lifted her chin. Because when it came down to it, she *was* too proud to beg.

"I understand. And why should you be sorry? You can't help how you feel."

To her horror, hot tears pricked her eyes. She sucked in a breath and leapt to the branch below, blindly making her way back to the ground. Tiago's daffodils drooped under the heavy rain, their bright heads bowed. She knuckled the tears away and stared at them as he dropped to the forest floor beside her.

"Alesia—" He reached for her and then brought his hand back to his side. "I'll see you. Okay?"

She closed her eyes. Then she stretched her lips into a smile and turned to face him. "Yeah, sure." When he still didn't move, she said, "I'm okay. Really."

"All right." With a jerk of his head, he strode out of the clearing, the daffodils shivering in his wake.

Fausto appeared from wherever he'd been hiding. He rose up on his hind legs to gaze after Tiago with an expression of utter disgust. It would've been comical if she wasn't feeling so bad.

She crouched down to wrap her arms around him and nuzzle his neck. He rumbled comfortingly.

"*Adeus, belo,*" she said over the constriction in her chest. "Come visit any time—you don't have to wait for Tiago. *Compreende?*"

The otter nodded. He pressed a bunch of leaves into her hand before loping after his friend.

Alesia inhaled raggedly. She bit her lip and concentrated on breathing until she had herself under control.

Her fingers tightened on the leaves. The crisp scent of watercress filled the air. She glanced down. Fausto had given her a handful of early greens.

She let out a half-sob, half-laugh. "Oh, *belo*. Food isn't going to make *this* better."

3

Cleia collapsed on top of Dion and waited for her breath to settle.

He wrapped his arms around her. Beneath her cheek, his chest rose and fell, his heart beating hard and fast from their loving.

She let out a contented sigh. Stars, but she adored her big, hard-bodied shifter, even when he was at his dominant, overprotective worst. He was finding it even more difficult to back off now that she was carrying their first child. Goddess help her when she actually started showing.

"Mm." She pressed her lips to the underside of his jaw and lifted off his chest to curl up next to him, head on his shoulder. She smoothed a hand down the taut muscles of his abdomen. The sun fae had a hot, fast metabolism. Dion always felt so wonderfully cool to her, like a rain shower on a summer day.

"*Amo-te,*" he murmured. He turned his head to nuzzle her ear.

"Love you too." She tucked a lock of wavy black hair behind his ear. "Why don't you come with me?"

"I figured you'd tell me no."

She lifted her head. "And that would've stopped you?"

"No." Two fingers traced the edge of her jaw. "But I'd rather you didn't go at all." When she simply gazed back at him—they'd already had this argument—he dropped his head back onto the pillow. "Fine. If you insist on going, I will too."

Already he was acting as if it were her only option. Still, he'd made a concession; she could, too. "I'd feel safer if you were there," she admitted.

"*Sim*?" His tone was skeptical.

After all, she had a cadre of loyal bodyguards, headed by Artan and Grady, who were so protective they even kept an eye on Dion, even though it was almost impossible for one mate to truly hurt the other. Even an argument like the one they'd just had was unpleasant, since you felt not only your own anger but your mate's.

And she was powerful in her own right. Not only did she have the Gift of teleportation, she had the ability to draw on the sun's energy. If she wanted, she could fry a man to ashes. But of course, Dion knew her better than anyone, and he knew she'd never actually done it.

And unfortunately, like teleportation, she couldn't do it instantly; she needed time to access the energy, let it build.

"Yes," she stated. "I know Artan and Grady would die for me, but you're my mate, and besides, you have fada senses—nothing gets by you. And frankly, you think like a fada—you've got that twisted, Machiavellian mind. That's what's needed here."

"*Obrigado*," was the wry reply. "Thank you. I think."

She grinned and snuggled closer. "And you have to admit the Baltimore clan has kept their word regarding Merry."

When Valeria and Rui's adopted daughter turned out to be the niece of one of Adric's lieutenants, the earth fada had tried to steal her back. But after they saw that Merry had bonded with Valeria, Adric and the lieutenant, Jace Jones, had agreed to allow the little girl to remain at Rock Run. In return, Dion allowed Jace to meet regularly with his niece. He was her dead mother's only brother, after all.

"True. Adric surprised me there. I thought he'd use Merry to worm his way into Rock Run."

"He loves Merry."

"Jace Jones?"

"Yes, of course. But Adric does too. He's like you in that, Dion. As alpha, he treats all the clan's children as if they were his own."

"Mmph."

Cleia smothered a smile. Dion didn't like being compared to the Baltimore alpha, but that didn't mean it wasn't true. Both men were equally smart and ruthless when it came to advancing their respective clans. If Adric wasn't the alpha of an earth fada clan, Dion would probably be his mentor.

But instead, he was a thorn in Dion's side.

Maybe allowing the earth fada to mine for quartz was a mistake, but Cleia figured that if Adric had a legitimate way to increase his clan's wealth, he'd stop trying to muscle in on Rock Run territory.

Apparently the north edge of the Rising Sun compound sat atop a rich vein of quartz. To the sun fae—and water fada—quartz was just a pretty rock, but earth fada could do amazing things with the mineral.

Cleia was well aware that she held the upper hand. She wouldn't say no to a good offer, but her clan had no real need for the Baltimore shifters' money. On the other hand, Rising Sun didn't need the quartz, and allowing the earth fada to mine would improve relations between the two clans.

And even better, she'd have an excuse to pay Rock Run a generous fee for protection during the mining. Before meeting Dion, she'd taken one Rock Run warrior after another as a lover, unknowingly seeking what she'd eventually found in their alpha. But she'd inadvertently been draining her lovers' life energy, causing the clan's downward spiral. It may have been unintentional, but it was she, Cleia, who was responsible for Rock Run's decline.

Fortunately, that had ended with her and Dion's mating and these days the clan was doing much better. Still, the fee she'd pay them would be welcome, especially since Dion stubbornly refused to take any money from her.

"I still don't like this," Dion said. "Why is Adric so eager to mine up here? Sure, he wants the quartz. But it's damn convenient that half of it happens to be located under your territory. Not only that, it puts him right across the river from Rock Run."

She stifled a sigh. "What does it matter? Your people will be in charge of security. If I know you, a mouse won't be able to squeak without you knowing. And if one of them does slip past you, my warriors will be patrolling as backup."

He expelled a breath. "All right. I have to admit, Rui's for it." Rui do Mar was Dion's second, but the two had grown up together and acted more like joint commanders than alpha and subordinate.

Dion's fingers sifted through her hair. She wasn't just the sun fae queen, she was the Conduit, drawing energy from the sun for her people's use. The exposure streaked her hair into gleaming ribbons of gold and platinum and copper. Her mate, coming as he did from a dark-haired, olive-skinned clan, found her bright locks fascinating.

When he spoke again, his voice was so soft she had to strain to hear him. "It's just that if I lost you, I don't think I could go on."

Her heart turned over. "You're not going to lose me. I promise."

His large arms wrapped around her. "I'm going to hold you to that." He brought his mouth down on hers, hard.

He didn't stop until she was making needy moans and rubbing herself against him. When he lifted his head, his smile was arrogant and very masculine.

Something about that smile always brought out the devil in her.

She slid her hand down his belly, found his rapidly growing erection and wrapped her fingers around it.

His breath jerked in. "*Sim, querida*. Touch me. Just like that."

She worked her hand up and down his cock. He wasn't cool here; he was hot and stiff. She increased the pressure and he groaned.

"*Deus*, woman, have mercy."

She stilled. "You want me to stop?"

"Hell no." He closed his eyes, the lashes thick and black against his cheeks. She could sense his rising need through their bond.

They were still on their sides, his arms loosely around her. She curved around him, one knee between his legs, her face buried in his neck, while she worked him slowly and deliberately. Breathing in his scent, a cocktail of river and salt and man.

A spurt of fluid coated her fingers. She spread it around the smooth cap.

He muttered something dark and sexy and tilted her chin up so he could kiss her. She released him to sink her fingers into his long, wavy hair and sucked his tongue deeper inside.

He broke the kiss and, turning on his back, lifted her up to straddle his thighs. She braced her hands on his chest and smiled down at him.

He gazed back, eyes molten, exploring her body as if it were brand-new to him: playing with her nipples, caressing her hips, stroking her wet, aching core.

His hands shaped her waist. It was too early to feel the baby yet, but each in their own way had sensed the new life before the healers confirmed it.

Cleia felt a tiny, vibrant energy a few inches below her navel. For Dion it was her scent, and other subtle changes such as the increased blood flow to her abdomen.

Just yesterday, Dion had laid his head on her stomach and stilled. "I can hear his heartbeat." He'd looked at her with wonder.

"Hers, don't you mean?" And they'd grinned at each other.

Now he hesitated, one long-fingered hand over her womb. "You're not too tired?" he asked, his hard face so warm with love her breath snagged.

She leaned forward to press her lips to the sensitive skin below his ear. "Never, sweetheart."

4

Fausto's intrusion splashed over Tiago like an icy shower. He scowled at the otter but Fausto had eyes only for Alesia. She left Tiago's lap to soothe the irate animal and he was left to gaze at them both, his blood still thrumming.

Damn, he wanted her. He wanted to run his hands over those long, coltish limbs, tease her nipples into aching points. He wanted to tear off the green dress, bend her over the branch and take that round, firm ass from behind. He wanted to push her down on her back, spread her legs and lick and suck her for long minutes until those exotic topaz eyes were dazed with desire. And then he'd crawl over her and—

He swallowed hard.

The beast growled that it was all right, she wanted it.

Take the female. Push her against the trunk and fuck her, hard and fast.

Make her scream. Make her beg.

Her long, tawny curls fell forward, exposing the soft ivory of her nape. He swallowed a groan.

He had taken a dark satisfaction in having his fingers around her neck, controlling her. In that moment, he wasn't sure he'd have taken no for an answer. He'd allowed the beast out, bent their combined will on her.

The beast flexed its claws. *Yes...take her. Show her who's master.*

It would be so easy. He had the means to control her, to force her to do anything he wanted.

And that was even more of a problem than the fact that he was using her to forget another woman.

He sucked in a breath and willed his raging erection to subside.

Alesia touched her nose to Fausto's and something moved in Tiago's chest. She was such a gentle soul. Fausto adored her. She fed him treats and cuddled him as if he were a pup instead of the patriarch of a large, multigenerational family. And Fausto, smart bastard, lapped it up.

She was kind, nurturing. And too damn good for a man like him. Someone with a dark Gift, one so powerful and easily misused that even his own people feared it. If word got out, he'd be a pariah in his own clan.

His eyes squeezed shut. When they opened, he was on his feet and zipping up his shorts.

Alesia's fine brows drew together. "You're leaving?"

He tried to apologize, but that made it worse. If only he were as callous as some of the older men—he'd just take what she was offering and then leave.

But he wasn't. And he couldn't.

This was *Alesia*. His best friend.

And even though she'd seemed willing enough, he couldn't swear he hadn't influenced her to say yes.

He wracked his brain for something to say but she was already on her way out of the tree, leaping nimbly from branch to branch in that way she had of seemingly ignoring gravity.

Back on the ground, she tried to act like she wasn't hurt, but he could see she was fighting back tears. He gulped. Lord, he was such a screw up.

He practically ran out of the clearing.

He told himself it was for the best. He treasured Alesia's friendship. If he left now, there was a chance they could continue as they'd been.

But if he took her, the shadowy, cold-hearted beast would win another victory. The beast that growled for him to shove her up against the tree and fuck her, no matter whom it hurt.

The beast didn't understand. If he took her, it would change everything.

He had stashed his shorts and was nearly at the river when Fausto loped up, his disapproval plain.

"You think this is easy?" Tiago snarled. "You think I want to leave?" He kicked at the soil, dislodging an acorn.

He scooped it up and stared at it, hard. *Compelling* the budding oak curled within to grow. Faster and faster, pressuring it even when it resisted, the beast gleefully egging him on. The shell exploded, torn apart by the too-rapid growth, the tiny oak in a hundred pieces.

The beast rumbled in satisfaction while Fausto scowled up at him.

Sick to his very soul, Tiago flung the pieces to the ground and dove into the water.

He took his time returning to Rock Run. It was lunchtime and Fausto wanted to eat. That was fine with Tiago; better that than sit through another meal in the dining hall, watching his brother and Cleia. So he changed to his otter and together he and Fausto gorged on mussels, clams and smallmouth bass brought to the surface by the rain. When they were done, he left Fausto at his den and changed to his dolphin for the swim back to the base.

He had himself under control now, but his mood was still edgy. Alesia had been on his lap, hot and open. He'd had merely to rearrange their bodies, spread her legs and he'd have been inside her. Giving her exactly what she wanted, what she'd all but begged him to do.

And what had he done? He'd left both her and himself unsatisfied.

His lips twisted. Hell, he was a candidate for goddamn sainthood.

But it could've been worse. He'd almost lost control of his beast. His stomach clenched at how close he'd been to unleashing his Gift on Alesia.

A fada's Gift was a special thing. It rarely manifested before puberty and a fada could be as old as thirty turns of the sun before he or she knew what it would be. The whole family eagerly awaited its manifestation. Dion was a Gifted hunter. His second brother Nic was preternaturally good at tracking, and their third brother, Joaquim, had inherited their soothsayer mother's ability to see a short distance into the future.

As for Tiago, everyone, including him, had believed his Gift was to communicate with animals.

But it seemed he'd been blessed—or cursed—with two Gifts, the second which came somehow intertwined with his beast. A Gift that was the most rare and powerful of them all.

So rare, a generation could pass without it appearing.

So powerful, it could make him an outcast among his own people.

Compulsion.

He could compel others to do his will. And he'd been tempted to use it on Alesia.

So damn tempted.

It struck him that this is what it must've been like for Petros Okeanos, the man who'd kidnapped Valeria and Merry. Okeanos had had a Gift similar to Tiago's. But unlike Tiago's Gift, which allowed him to compel obedience through a kind of mind control, Okeanos could take control of people's bodies and force them to do his will as if they were puppets and he the puppet master.

The man had gone mad with the power.

Tiago shuddered. It was his worst nightmare—that he'd turn into the same kind of monster.

The river nearby rippled and a sentry in dolphin form popped to the surface and shifted to man. It was Chico Nobrega, one of his best friends. Tiago shifted to man as well and the two of them swam closer to shore and stood up in the waist-deep water.

The son of a Rock Run man and a Rhode Island sea fada, Chico had his father's Mediterranean coloring and his mother's clean-cut features and easy-going personality.

"What's up?" he asked Tiago with a grin.

"Not much. I just came from upriver. Everything's quiet."

"Visiting Alesia?"

The beast stirred at another man's use of her name. "Yes," he said shortly.

Chico's smile was very male. "She's a hot little piece, no?"

"She's just a friend."

"Then you won't mind if I try my luck—"

Tiago's hand was clamped around Chico's throat before he realized he'd moved. "Stay the fuck away from her. Understand?"

Chico swore and grabbed Tiago's wrist. Several heartbeats passed as the two of them stared at each other, locked in a silent contest. Then his friend stilled. "Okay, okay," he gasped. "I didn't know. She didn't say—"

Tiago forced his fingers to release Chico's throat. "When? When did you see her?"

Chico dragged in a breath. "A week ago. Maybe more. When you were on that mission in Portugal."

He nodded. His squad had been in Portugal to help their ancestral clan, the Douro River fada, in a territorial skirmish with some earth shifters. "And?"

"And nothing. The alpha sent me to check on all three dryads, make sure they were all right. Alesia was polite, nothing more. But I thought maybe—"

"She spoke to you?"

"Actually," Chico admitted, "she hid from me. I traced her by her scent, but she didn't come out until I told her I was your friend and that Lord Dion had sent me."

That sounded like Alesia. Tiago relaxed a bit. "She's shy."

"But you know what they say about the quiet ones. And damn, there's something about her. She's got the tightest—" Chico's hands shaped a woman's ass in the air. Tiago's lips peeled back and Chico hurried to say, "Okay, okay. I get it—she's off limits. But you said yourself she's just a friend."

"She is," Tiago said, not caring that he was being unreasonable. The beast refused to allow Alesia to go to anyone else, even if he couldn't have her himself. "But that doesn't mean she wants you sniffing around her. She's a solitary and on top of that, she's afraid of fada. It took months before she'd really talk to me. If Dion wants to know how she is, he can damn well ask me. I'll make sure he knows that. Stay away from her from now on. Got it?"

He was the dominant among the younger males. He didn't often pull rank on his friends, but this time he caught and held Chico's gaze until the other man averted his eyes.

"Sure, Ti. Whatever you say."

AFTER LEAVING CHICO, Tiago continued to the base's main entrance, passing back through the narrow underwater tunnel and into the grotto. As he hauled himself out of the water onto the stone floor, a trio of fae lights winked on, bathing the small cave in a soft green light. He slipped through a hidden door, found his shorts on a shelf where he'd stowed them and headed down the corridor into the base.

He checked the dining hall first, but it was empty save for people cleaning up after the noon meal. He downed a cup of the strong, dark coffee that was always left on the warmer and headed for the operations room. His brother wasn't there either, but the *tenente* on duty said that Dion was in his quarters.

The door to Dion's apartment was open, but the *sala*, a spacious living room carved from a natural cavern, was empty. Tiago glanced around. Dion's quarters abutted another apartment that was shared by Rosana and a couple of her friends. When their father had been alpha, the family had lived here—their parents, Nisio and Ula, and Tiago and Rosana. His three older brothers had had their own rooms in other parts of the base.

After their parents had been lost somewhere in the North Atlantic, Dion had become alpha. He'd moved back into the family quarters to look after Tiago and Rosana. Nic and Joaquim had helped for a while, but they'd been too dominant to accept Dion as alpha for long. Within a year, they'd left to freelance as mercenaries for the fae and the occasional filthy rich human.

Dion had done his best, but he was a warrior, not a home-maker. He'd made sure Tiago and Rosana had the basics, and that was about it.

Not that Tiago had noticed. At eleven, all he'd known was that his mom and dad were gone and his family seemed to be breaking apart. He'd felt as lost as six-year-old Rosana, but he'd sucked it up, tried to act the man like his older brothers.

In the past five years, though, Cleia had turned the apartment into a home again. The old couches had been replaced with two large, comfortable sofas flanked by end tables. The sturdy plank oak table had been polished until it shone, and more chairs added so the whole family could take meals in the alpha's quarters if they chose.

A rug woven of bright reds, golds and blues covered the stone floor, and on the walls were hangings in equally cheerful colors. Cleia had even found potted plants that could grow in the dim light preferred by the fada.

He heard Cleia and Dion in the bedroom along with Rosana. Continuing through the *sala*, he found the three of them lounging beside the large pool on one side of the bedroom.

Outside, the rain was still falling, so the ceiling shafts contributed only a small amount of illumination. More fae lights floated overhead, turning the gray cavern a muted green.

With their dark hair and olive skin, Dion and Rosana blended into the shadows in the way of river fada. Cleia, however, couldn't blend in if she tried. Not with her bright hair and love of sunny colors. Even her golden skin seemed to shimmer.

She grinned up at Tiago from where she was reclined on her forearms next to Dion. "Hey, there."

"Hey, Cleia." He smiled down at her, bracing himself for the usual punch of lust. It came, but it was almost automatic. He frowned and sat next to Rosana, idly tracing circles in the water with her foot.

She bumped her shoulder against his. "Where've you been all morning?"

"Out with Fausto."

Cleia sat up and smoothed down the skirt of her bright yellow sundress. He suspected there were times she sensed the dark turn of his thoughts; he'd caught her eyeing him with a speculative expression. But she persisted in treating him like a younger brother, as if that could somehow make it true.

"I was wondering where you were," she said. "How are you, anyway? Seems like you're never home anymore."

"I'm good. And you?" He swallowed. "And the little one?"

She patted her abdomen. "She's great," was the wry reply, "but all I want to do is sleep and eat. The healers tell me it's only for the first few months. The sleeping part, anyway."

"I'm sorry," he murmured, then made himself ask, "It's a girl, then?"

"That's what I think, but Dion's sure it's a boy. Says the do Rio men make boys, not girls." She grinned at her mate.

Dion was on his side beside her, his head propped in his hand. He just smiled, looking remarkably like a cat who'd swallowed the cream, and placed a proprietary hand over her still flat belly.

"It's too early to tell. Ask me in another month or so—I should be able to scent his gender then."

"Excuse me." Rosana gave a dramatic toss of her long black hair. "Am I not a do Rio?"

"Of course," Dion replied. "But you're the only female after four males—and we thank the gods every day for you."

"Hmph." She tilted her head and tapped a finger to her lips. "I think we should pick out a name. How about Rumpelstiltskin? Or Natsu Dragneel? If it's a boy, of course."

With an effort, Tiago dragged his gaze from the sight of his brother's fingers splayed across Cleia's abdomen.

"Natsu Dragneel." Dion's voice was neutral.

"He's a Japanese manga character."

"Comic books," Tiago added. "Chico buys them for her."

"He eats fire. And has spiky pink hair," Rosana said with a smirk.

"Only if you let me name your firstborn," Dion shot back.

She threw back her head and laughed. "No thanks." She rose to her feet. "I'd better go. I have kitchen duty for supper."

"I should head back to Rising Sun," Cleia said without moving. "Olivia wants to discuss the meeting with Adric." Lady Olivia was her cousin and the administrator of the Rising Sun clan's affairs.

Dion caressed her abdomen. "There's no hurry. Rest, *querida*."

"Don't tempt me. Olivia is waiting."

She made to stand, but Dion leapt up first to help her to her feet. He smoothed his hands over her bare shoulders, his expression so tender that Tiago glanced away. "Be back by dinner or I'll come looking for you."

"Yes, my lord," Cleia replied in tones that were anything but submissive.

Dion shook his head at her and gathered her close for a long, open-mouthed kiss.

Tiago turned to find Rosana at his side, her expression sympathetic. She gave him a hug. "You were upriver?"

He hugged her back. No matter how tightly wound he was, he always had time for his sister. Their three brothers were all so much older that he and Rosana had formed a unit, raised almost as a second family by first their parents, then Dion.

"Yeah," he said. "I went to see Alesia."

Rosana nodded. She'd tried to make friends with Alesia, but the dryad had been too shy to say much, and his sister had given up.

"You have a few days off, don't you?" Rosana asked as he draped an arm around her shoulders. They headed into the *sala* ahead of Dion and Cleia. "Wanna go somewhere? We could shift to our dolphins and swim across the bay, visit one of those little towns on the Eastern Shore."

He shook his head. "Not this time, *querida*." He loved his sister but he'd be damned if he took her along for the kind of relaxation he craved right now.

A vision of Alesia in that damp green dress flashed before his eyes. *Maybe*—

But no. He'd made the right decision. Their friendship was too precious to risk fucking things up.

His sister's face fell. "Okay. Sure."

"Next time I have some time off, we'll take a trip. Okay?" He gave her a squeeze and turned to find Cleia waiting to hug him.

He froze. There she was again, treating him like a younger brother.

For the most part, he'd learned to deal with it. The training to be a fada warrior was harsh, designed to challenge both mind and body. If you couldn't control your animal, you were toast.

Today, though, his control had been eroded to a thin edge. As Cleia enclosed him in a friendly embrace, his heart sped up and his hands came to her waist. His fingers tightened on the supple flesh he could feel beneath the thin dress. Inside, his beast came alert.

Beside him, Dion was hugging Rosana and telling her he'd see her later.

Tiago forced himself to release Cleia. She murmured something about having a good day and stepped back. Their eyes met and something in him contracted at the pity he saw there.

Did she know?

But of course, she must have some idea. He'd been her lover, after all, before she realized how young he was and sent him home.

Later, when Dion had taken her prisoner in a last-ditch attempt to save the clan, Tiago had been the one she turned to for help in escaping. And he, afraid that Cleia would die if she was kept underground without sunlight much longer, had betrayed his own brother, giving the coordinates of his quarters to Adric so that she might live.

Then it turned out that Dion had been about to free Cleia anyway.

So, yeah, he wanted this woman. Desperately.

To see her pity lashed his soul. Humiliation heated his cheeks, but Cleia had turned away.

"Wait," she told Rosana. "I'll come with you. If I can't have the sun, I wouldn't mind a snack before I head back to Rising Sun."

His sister blinked. "We just ate lunch an hour ago."

Cleia draped her arm around Rosana's shoulders. "Your point being?" The two of them strolled down the hall, laughing.

Dion watched them go, a little smile on his face. He slanted

Tiago a sheepish look. "I—it's the most amazing feeling. Knowing that we created a life together."

His throat tightened. He was happy for his brother. *He was.*

"I'll bet," he managed to say.

"But you stopped by for a reason, yes? Have a seat." Dion waved a hand toward the couches.

"This won't take long." He remained standing. "Chico told me you sent him to check on the dryads. I'd like to formally request that I be the liaison to the dryads. There's no need to send anyone else unless I'm away for more than a few weeks."

His brother rubbed his chin. "You're friends with the middle one—Alesia. Can I ask when you last saw her?"

"Today."

"I mean before that."

Tiago's jaw set. How did his brother always manage to put him in the wrong?

"A month or so ago," he admitted. "As you know, I was in Portugal. But normally I visit every week or so."

"That's what I thought. I'll consider your request—it might be good to have a more formal liaison between Rock Run and the dryads—but I'd still like the sentries to keep an eye on them. I can't have a repeat of what happened with Okeanos. He nearly took over your Alesia's island with his den. *Deus* knows what he'd have done to her if he'd gotten any more powerful."

That was true. For some reason the Greek sea fada had left Alesia alone, probably because he feared her mother, a powerful dryad. But by the time he'd kidnapped Valeria, he'd been half-feral, more animal than man. He'd wanted women for the males in his den. Sooner or later, he'd have gone after Alesia too.

But Okeanos was dead, slain by Rui do Mar during a mate-duel over Valeria.

And Tiago couldn't erase the picture of Chico flirting with Alesia from his mind.

"I can handle it," he insisted. "Unless I'm away on a mission, Alesia and her sisters are mine."

It came out more forcefully than he intended, but he didn't take it back. Dion drew a breath. Tiago knew he was a hair's breadth away from triggering his brother's dominance, a situation they'd both avoided up until now, but Dion needed to know how important this was to him.

Still, he dropped his gaze, even as inside, the beast strained to get at the alpha. To *challenge* the alpha.

We can take him.

"All right," Dion said at last. "But you'll report on the dryads to Rui."

The beast subsided, appeased. "Fair enough."

"Tell me," his brother asked, his silver eyes sharp, "what is Alesia to you?"

"A friend."

"She's not for you," Dion said bluntly. "She may be a dryad, and I'll admit they're not like most fae, but my mating aside, the fae only want us for one thing. Or make that two things—they're happy to hire us to fight their little wars, too."

"Not Alesia," he returned. "She thinks of me as a friend."

"Don't fool yourself, *irmão*. We're animals to them."

"Not Alesia," he insisted.

His brother shook his head but before he could say anything else, Rui appeared in the doorway. "Can I come in?"

"Of course. We're finished. Right, Tiago?"

Rui stepped inside followed by Miguel, one of the older warriors. "It's about the Baltimore Earth Fada," he said. "Miguel here was in Baltimore. Something funny's going on."

"What do you mean?"

Rui nodded to Miguel. "You tell him."

"I was at the Full Moon last night," Miguel told Dion. "Playing poker in the back room. I overheard a couple of earth fada talking about this deal Adric is trying to set up with you."

"And?"

Miguel scratched his buzz-cut head. A stocky man of middle height, he was like a sledge hammer in a fight, overwhelming his opponents with sheer force, making him one of the clan's best warriors. But he preferred to leave the long-term strategizing to others. "I only overheard a little. They were in the alley when the door opened. As soon as they realized we could hear them, they shut up."

"What did they say?" Dion prompted. "I want to know the exact words."

Miguel's black brows beetled. "She said, 'Adric will be up at Rising Sun all the time.' And he said, 'When the cat's away—' Then the man noticed the door was open. From where I was sitting, I could see him glance over his shoulder."

"That was it?" Dion demanded. "You're sure?"

"*Sim.*"

"Do you know who they were?"

Miguel shook his head. "I couldn't see the woman, and the alley was pitch black. All I saw was a young man with dark hair. I did notice he moved like a wolf. You know—sly, stealthy."

"That describes half of the Baltimore clan," muttered Rui.

"I had the impression the woman was a wolf, too. But she could've been a cat—like I said, I didn't get a good look at her."

Dion exchanged a look with his second-in-command.

"Sounds like Adric has some trouble," said Dion.

"Good," replied Rui. "It will keep the man busy. But what about Cleia?"

Dion fingered his chin. "I don't see a problem. If anything, it works to our advantage. Like you said, it will keep him busy. Less time for him to cause trouble for the sun fae—or Rock Run." He glanced at Miguel. "You did right to report this. Thank you."

The warrior gave a short nod and strode out of the room.

Dion started to confer with Rui. Tiago remained where he was, listening.

His brother's second was slightly larger with a broad face, and he kept his black hair cropped short where Dion wore his long and secured by a leather tie, but the two men were brothers in all but blood. Rui had even been nursed by Ula do Rio when his own mother died in childbirth.

Tiago wasn't jealous of the two men's friendship. They were both so much older than him that they'd always been Dion-and-Rui, more father figures than anything else. But just once, he wished Dion would ask *him* for advice, if only about the younger members of Rock Run.

Rui said that it wouldn't hurt to send a couple of people to Baltimore, see if they could find out anything more. "I'd go myself, but Valeria's too close to her time." His mate was heavily pregnant with their second child.

"Good idea," Dion said, "but who?"

"What about Davi?" Rui replied. "He's itching to prove himself—"

Tiago stepped forward. "Excuse me." When they turned to him, he continued, "This thing with the earth fada? I can help. I know Baltimore better than anyone."

Something about the city drew his beast, even though the rest of him was put off by the noise and smells and concrete.

Dion was shaking his head even before Tiago had finished. "It's out of the question."

Rui shifted as if he disagreed, but Dion was alpha. The final call was his.

Tiago's jaw tightened. He was a warrior, a full-fledged member of his squad, and dominant not only to the younger people, but most of the clan. But his brother still treated him like a pup.

"With all due respect, sir," he said evenly, "I know Baltimore."

"No," was the curt reply. "And you know why."

Tiago flushed. "If this is what happened with Cleia and Adric—"

Five years ago, after Dion had taken Cleia captive, Adric had been hired by the sun fae to find her. The earth fada alpha had played on Tiago's worry for her, until Tiago gave him Cleia's exact location within the base so that she could be rescued.

To Dion, it didn't matter that Tiago had believed Cleia was his mate. That he couldn't just stand by and do nothing as she grew weaker, cut off from the sunlight that was as necessary to a sun fae as food.

As far as Dion was concerned, Tiago had not only betrayed him, he'd endangered the entire clan. Tiago was lucky Dion hadn't executed him—or banished him for life.

"It is," Dion said now. "You're under orders to stay away from Adric and the Baltimore shifters—or have you forgotten?"

Tiago took a heartbeat too long to reply.

His brother growled. A reprimand—and a warning.

"No," Tiago gritted out. "Sir."

"Good." Dion turned to Rui, presenting his back to Tiago.

Tiago's eyes narrowed. It was a clear insult—unintentional maybe, but to a fada, turning your back on another male meant you considered him too far beneath you to be a threat.

He fisted his hands and stalked from the room.

5

———

*A*lesia stared down at the pieces of acorn scattered on the beach. She'd *felt* the tiny oak's pain and fear as it had been forced to grow so fast it split apart at the subcellular level. Its anguished psychic scream had drawn her to this site.

The fine hairs on her nape lifted. "Why?" she whispered.

And how? How had Tiago been able to do that? Because it had to have been him.

She knew he was a hard man, suspected that he'd killed, although he didn't share that part of his life with her. But this, this spoke of dark magic.

Fear seeped into her. Chilled, she wrapped her arms around herself, recalling every bad thing she'd ever heard about the fada.

Picturing Valeria's bruised, terrified face as the old Greek sea fada, Petros Okeanos, had forced her down the stairs to his underground den.

And seeing again Tiago's wintry blue gaze when he returned from a mission.

She gave an involuntary shudder and knelt to pick up the pieces.

A single oak produced tens of thousands of acorns. Very few

made it to seedling and even fewer to a full-grown oak. Chances were high this embryonic oak would have been food for a squirrel or a blue jay. Still, there was something terrible about the way it had died.

She curled her fingers around the shattered bits of shell and seed and rose back to her feet again.

In the forest she clawed one-handed at the soil until she'd made a small depression and then tipped the pieces into it. As she scooped the moist black loam back on top, she felt a flash of anger. The fada might own this island but by their own promise this was *her* forest, *her* trees to nurture. Tiago had been a guest. However mad or confused or hurt he was, he had no right to harm one of her oaks.

A rustle in a nearby tree made her rock back on her heels. A dark-haired dryad was agilely descending a sturdy tulip poplar.

"Mama?" Alesia gulped and quickly jumped up, brushing the dirt from her hands.

Naomi lived on an island thirty miles upriver, but she rarely visited any of her three daughters. They were expected to come to her.

That she was here now was *not* good.

Alesia darted a look at where she'd buried the acorn pieces. Naomi considered the Rock Run fada little better than thugs. She'd done everything possible to discourage her daughter's friendship with Tiago. No way could Alesia let her know about Tiago and the acorn.

"Hello, darling." Naomi leapt the last few feet to the ground. She was still a beautiful woman as she entered her fifteenth decade, with rich brown hair, perfect features and the elegant bearing of a ballerina. Her tree was a stately white oak that dominated its clearing.

"Mama." Alesia pressed a kiss to her mother's smooth, unlined skin. "This is a surprise."

Naomi nodded and glanced around. Her gaze skimmed over

the disturbed soil and Alesia held her breath, but her mother only said, "I'm here because I sensed something—something dark. Has anything happened?"

"No, no," Alesia hurried to reply. "Everything's fine." But bile rose in her throat at the lie. She swallowed hard.

Naomi narrowed her eyes. "Tell me you're not still seeing that river fada."

Alesia bristled. "His name is Tiago do Rio." She might be bruised from Tiago's abrupt departure and the discovery that he was apparently dabbling in dark magic, but deep down, Tiago was a good man—which her mother would know if she bothered to get to know him. "And he's my friend," she added.

Naomi arched a single dark brow. "He only wants between your thighs—and after he does, you'll never see him again."

"That's not true. Even if it was, why wait five years?"

Her mother dismissed that with a wave of her hand. "He's playing with you, love. What are five years to us? You can't trust a fada. They'd love to kill every last fae, because then who'd be left to keep them in check? Not the humans. The Rock Run Clan should've stayed in Portugal where they belong."

Alesia's jaw tightened. "They have as much right to be here as we do. The first dryads came from the Mediterranean—just like the first fada. And the Portuguese river fada settled Rock Run close to eighty years ago. Tiago's as American as you or me. Just because we've been here a few centuries longer doesn't make us better than them."

"No? They're beasts, Alesia. Rutting, murderous beasts. Everyone knows they have animal genes—along with human." Naomi sniffed as only a pureblood fae could. "And now their alpha has mated with the sun fae queen."

Alesia sighed. "You can't control the mate bond, Mama."

"No? Well, Cleia always had a weakness for fada. But who knows what that man did when he was holding her prisoner? Probably bound her will somehow."

Alesia opened her mouth to object that on the contrary, it had been the queen who'd been harming Rock Run, but her mother was on a roll.

"And what about the bacchanalia? Don't tell me they've banned them. Look what happened here on your island—with one of their own women. They've just gotten smarter at hiding them."

"That's enough, Mama," Alesia said sharply.

Naomi wasn't used to that tone from any of her daughters. Her mouth turned down.

"Tiago's been a friend to me," Alesia went on. "A good friend. He brings me flowers, bottles of Rock Run's best wine. In the winter, he makes sure I always have enough food. And he takes care of Phillis and Dina as well," she added, naming her sisters.

"That's kind of him, I suppose. But I didn't come here to argue about that fada"—her mom's black eyes narrowed—"unless he had something to do with the disturbance I sensed. That was it, wasn't it?"

Alesia swallowed. It was an effort not to glance at the disturbed soil. She had to divert Naomi. She wouldn't put it past her well-connected mom to report Tiago to the dryad tribune in their Greek homeland. Oaks were sacred to the dryads. A fada compelling an oak to grow until it shattered could start an international incident, ending with Tiago imprisoned—or worse.

She met her mother's suspicious gaze and hoped her voice wouldn't betray her alarm. Another lie on top of the previous one would send her to her knees, but—"I had a couple of earth fada on the island." This was true, as long as she didn't say when. "I told them to leave, that this is Rock Run territory. A couple of Rock Run sentries saw them and chased them away. Maybe that's what you sensed."

It *had* happened, although last month, not as recently as Alesia had implied. Still, Alesia had been grateful that her island was claimed by Rock Run, not the Baltimore fada. The earth people had a sardonic edge, even when they were trying to be friendly. Given the choice between the two of them, she'd choose a river fada any day. At least with them, you didn't feel as if they'd be smirking as they slipped a blade between your ribs.

To her relief, her mom accepted that. "They don't want a fight with Rock Run. I suppose you should be grateful for the river people's protection."

"I am."

Naomi's face softened. "I only want what's best for you," she said, taking Alesia's hand. "I know you're lonely. The fourth decade is when a dryad's mating urge grows strong. I recall how I was when your father came to me."

Male dryads could leave their home trees for longer periods than females, so when the urge came upon them, they set out into the world to seek a mate. Alesia's own father was from an Ohio forest. He was there now, but he visited frequently and would until either he or Naomi died. Like the fada, the fae mated for life.

"You'll find your mate," Naomi continued. "But when he finds you, what's he going to think if you're with that fada?"

Alesia stared at her, arrested. Her voice, when she spoke, sounded odd in her ears. "If he's my mate," she heard herself say, "it won't matter."

Because suddenly it all made sense: Why she always knew when Tiago was near. How she often guessed what he was feeling before he spoke a word. Why she'd wanted him from the first, allowing him to get close even though she'd been raised to fear the fada.

Her heart had reached out, connecting to his with a filament-thin line. The mate bond, tenuous, not yet complete, but *there*. And today—touching and being touched by him, breathing his scent, the simple act of saying "yes" to him—today had breathed that bond into life.

Dryads rarely mated with outsiders, even other fae. They

were too different, bound as they were to their trees, preferring the quiet, peaceful life of a solitary to the messy interaction of a clan.

"Well." Naomi squeezed her hand. "I just wanted to make sure you're all right."

"Thank you, Mama." Alesia pulled her into a hug.

Her mother patted her awkwardly on the back.

"And don't worry," Alesia said. "I'm fine. Tiago would never hurt me."

I hope.

They kissed and then her mother strode lithely back to the tulip poplar. She ascended to the first branch. The air around her shimmered greenly, and then with a wave of her hand, she was gone.

Alesia's shoulders sagged. Her stomach still hurt from the lie she'd told, but she barely noticed. Instead, she pressed the heel of her hand to her heart, her chest tight with wonder—and pain. Because the mate bond could only be completed if both people were willing.

And Tiago was in love with another woman.

TIAGO HEADED for his room in the unmated males' quarters. It was mid-afternoon, and people were returning to the base to shower and change before dinner. Several hundred adults called the Rock Run caverns home, along with an equal number of children. He passed warriors returning from the day's workout and sentries heading out for the evening patrols. The teachers who worked in the clan's creche had handed off the children to their families and were enjoying some free time before dinner. The fishers would've dropped off the day's catch in the kitchen around lunchtime, but those clan members who oversaw the vineyards or farms were just arriving back.

He was friends with nearly everyone. Ordinarily, he would've stopped and chatted, but today he just nodded and walked on.

As Tiago entered the *sala* of the quarters he shared with several other unmated males, Chico stepped out of the room next-door. His face split into a smile.

"There you are," he said as if Tiago hadn't practically choked him an hour ago. "I've been looking for you. Me and a couple of the guys are heading down to Baltimore. You in?"

"Sure." Right now all Tiago wanted was to get drunk and find a woman, lose himself between her soft thighs. "But look, I'm sorry for grabbing your throat. That was out of line."

"No worries. She's your woman. I'd have done the same if it were me."

Tiago opened his mouth to say Alesia wasn't his woman, then shut it again. Better to let Chico think he'd claimed the dryad so that he'd leave her alone.

His friend jiggled a key ring. "I snagged a Jeep. Can you be ready at five?"

A couple of hours later, they were on their way to Baltimore. Chico at the wheel, with two other men from their cohort in the back seat. The windows were down, loud music blared from the radio and the Jeep's stiff suspension was rattling Tiago's bones.

He shot Chico a grin. "Is this as fast as this thing goes?"

His friend grinned back from behind dark sunglasses and pressed the accelerator down. The Jeep jerked and then sped up.

"I'm looking to get laid," Chico said in a voice loud enough to be heard above the music. "What d'you say, my man?"

"Sounds like a plan."

Behind them Gabe and Jaxon made noises of agreement. The four of them had trained in the same cohort from the time they were pups, although they didn't see each other as much since they'd all made warrior and been assigned to different squads.

Tiago gazed at the strip of trees hurtling past. He was thinking about Miguel. The older warrior had been one of Cleia's first

Rock Run lovers. Miguel had never mated, although it had been nearly two decades since he and the queen had been lovers. After his return he'd been only half a man, his life energy inadvertently drained by Cleia. Then, like everyone at Rock Run, Miguel had been revitalized by the fresh energy that Cleia and Dion's mating had brought. He was once again the warrior he'd been. But although he was rarely without female company, he'd never had a special woman.

Had Miguel simply never met his mate—or was he still in love with Cleia? If so, damn, that was pathetic.

And he, Tiago, was no better.

He clenched the window frame.

Chico asked if he wanted to go to Spanish Town. He nodded and released his grip. "Sure."

They parked the Jeep in Upper Fells Point outside a shop selling poufy dresses for a teenage girl's Quinceanera celebration. Aside from the bodegas and the Spanish street signs, Spanish Town was typical Baltimore, long blocks of brick or Formstone rowhouses with wide marble steps, the only shade a few scrawny street trees.

The rain earlier had cleared the air, and the streets were dotted with locals taking advantage of the early spring weather. The humans they passed gave them wary looks and moved aside —and not just because they were four big, hard-looking men. It was because they were fada. Even when a human didn't know for sure, some primitive sense warned them of the predators in their midst.

Chico directed them to a nearby bar. Inside, a handful of people hunched over their drinks in the gloom as a Spanish rap song blared. The bartender, who turned out to be the owner as well, scurried to make them at home. He was a beefy Latino with slicked-back hair who reminded Tiago of a couple of his Portuguese cousins.

"Would you gentlemen like a table?" Pulling out a chair, the man jerked his head at the sole waitress, who sauntered over to ask what they were drinking. They ordered bottles of dark Mexican beer, and on Chico's advice, large platters of both the chicken and fish empanadas as well as two baskets of homemade salsa and chips.

They spent the first hour catching up with each other as they downed the surprisingly good empanadas and chips. Chico's most recent mission had been guarding a sexy fae rock star. His entire squad had been hired to guard the woman, although apparently their main purpose had been to provide hard-bodied men to do her bidding.

"It was a tough job," Chico said with a smirk, "but somebody had to do it."

As night fell, the small bar filled up. Tiago took a swig of the beer and glanced around. A table of three human females were eyeing them. Some humans got off on having a fada lover, although a mating between a fada and a human was almost as rare as one between a fada and a fae. He caught the eye of a curvy woman with a head of short black curls, and gave her a slow smile.

Her blond friend nudged her and they both giggled.

Chico rose to his feet. "Would you ladies like some company?"

"Sure," said the blonde and moved her chair to make room for him. Chico set his chair next to hers.

Tiago hesitated. Now that it came down to it, it felt somehow wrong—disloyal to Alesia. But he placed his chair next to Chico's, which left Jax and Gabe to sit with the other two women.

Chico smoothly drew the blonde into a private conversation, while Tiago, Jax and Gabe talked to her friends. The two of them were friendly enough, but it was clear they weren't interested in fada, which was a relief as far as Tiago was concerned.

An hour went by, and he went to the john. When he came back, he, Jax and Gabe exchanged glances and the other two men rose to their feet.

"Catch you later, Chico," Tiago said.

His friend glanced up from where he was toying with the blonde's earring. "What's up, Ti?"

"We're heading out—but you stay. We'll get a ride back to Rock Run from someone else." If not, they could always spend the night in the Fells Point rowhouse that Rock Run kept for any clan member who needed it.

Chico made to stand. "I'll come too."

"No—we're okay." He winked at the blonde. "I'm just restless tonight."

"Okay, sure." Chico dropped back into his seat with a smile for his pretty little friend.

Tiago tossed some money on the table, inclined his head to the ladies and strode with Jax and Gabe out of the bar.

6

Tiago contemplated the beer bottle in his hand. It was empty again.

At some point after leaving Chico, he'd become separated from Jax and Gabe. He'd walked along the waterfront for a couple of miles before heading back to Fells Point, where he'd ended up at the Full Moon Saloon, a cave-like bar that catered to serious drinkers. The Full Moon was owned by Claudio, an Amazonas river fada from Brazil who'd chosen to live as a solitary, i.e., without a clan. Humans were tolerated, but the saloon was mainly for fada.

After a nod at the big bouncer—a Baltimore shifter, because Adric wouldn't have stood for a river fada in a security position—Tiago had found a stool at one end of the oak bar and settled into drinking.

Midnight came and went. The bar was filled with shifters, along with a sprinkling of humans looking for a walk on the wild side. On the tiny stage a band was playing rhythm and blues. Tiago had been drinking steadily for a couple of hours with only the empanadas he'd eaten earlier to soak up the alcohol. He wasn't exactly shitfaced, but no one would call him sober, either.

The bartender, Sophie, was a motherly Tunisian sea fada whom everyone fell over themselves to please. Tiago wasn't sure where Claudio had found her, but since she'd started working at the Full Moon, there'd been a dramatic drop in bar fights. Something about the maternal Sophie calmed their animals.

Now she took the bottle from him and without asking, set a glass of ice water in front of him.

He frowned down at it. "I'm not drunk."

"Sure, *habibi*. But drink it anyway."

He shrugged and obediently drained the glass. He *was* thirsty. And if he didn't drink it, Sophie would refuse to bring him another beer.

He glanced around the bar again. An earth fada female in tight leather pants was taking a seat at a table with a couple of friends. He was buzzed enough to stare boldly, uncaring that the earth shifters in the bar outnumbered river fada by more than two to one.

He wasn't the only one checking her out. The woman was serious eye-candy: big dark eyes, a short Afro that set off long, high cheekbones and a tight gold tank with a plunging neckline that showcased killer breasts.

She caught him looking and flashed him a knowing smile before deliberately turning her back on him to say something to her girlfriends.

But unlike with his brother, Tiago didn't take it as an insult. No, the woman was daring him.

And he was in the mood to take her up on it.

He ordered another beer from Sophie and sipped it, taking his time before he glanced back at the earth fada woman. She'd shifted her chair so he could see her profile. She darted a glance at him and toyed with the cat-shaped earring dangling from her earlobe.

His blood started to hum. She was interested, all right.

But there were too many Baltimore shifters in the bar. A Rock Run fada couldn't just approach one of their women. Yeah, fada females had the right to choose their own mates, but their males could make it damn difficult to get close enough to initiate the dance.

He turned around on his stool and gazed out at the crowd. His back was to her now but he could feel her studying him.

The band switched to a slow, sexy number and several couples got up to dance. He thought of the three pretty humans. Chico was probably cuddling with the blonde in some dark corner now, while he, Tiago, was sitting here alone, getting drunk.

He probably could've had the curvy dark-haired one if he'd put his mind to it. Sure, she'd been wary of him, but he'd seen the looks she'd been sending him. But he hadn't even tried, and now he wondered what the hell was wrong with him, because if he wanted a woman, why should he feel guilty about it?

Alesia might have ten years on him, but compared to him she was an innocent. Hell, the woman spent most of her time on an uninhabited island with only trees and forest creatures for company. He knew she'd only had a few lovers.

He recalled her rubbing noses with Fausto and his chest knotted.

His feelings for Cleia aside, he was all wrong for Alesia. He was a creature of water and dark caverns, while she needed sunlight and open air and fresh green leaves. She was a nurturer, someone who made things grow—and he was a member of a fada warrior squad, a man who had killed.

More than once.

She might think she wanted him, but if she knew about his Gift—what he could do with a thought, a wish—she'd be terrified of him.

But a human wasn't the answer either.

From now on he'd stick to his own kind. Fada women had the

same hot, wild blood as the males. They understood when a man wanted a good fuck and nothing more.

He took another sip from his beer and turned to face the bar again. The woman cast a look at him and toyed some more with her earring, a smile playing on her full lips.

He kept his gaze straight ahead. Don't do it. You'll just get your ass kicked.

A man settled on the stool next to him. An earth shifter with the rangy build and amber eyes of a wolf.

The other man ordered a beer from Sophie. While he waited for it to arrive, he nodded at Tiago. "You're one of the Rock Run alpha's brothers."

"That's right." He wasn't surprised the man knew who he was. He was a younger copy of Dion: same wavy black hair and light blue eyes, same Mediterranean features. "Name's Tiago."

"Luc," the other man returned.

Tiago nodded and turned his attention to the TV over the bar, which was broadcasting a replay of an Orioles game with the sound off. Sophie brought their beer and for a few minutes, the two of them watched the baseball game in silence.

Tiago eyed Luc covertly. Like Dion, he was suspicious of Adric's sudden desire to mine quartz at Rising Sun. Rock Run and the sun fae compound shared a border marked by the Susquehanna River. Even though Rock Run was on the opposite side of the river from Rising Sun, the Baltimore shifters would still be damn close.

Luc had the scent of a dominant, and he carried himself like someone high in the hierarchy. Tiago would bet a month's pay the man was one of Adric's lieutenants.

But the Full Moon was neutral ground and from further down the bar, Claudio was eyeing them both, clearly wondering why a Rock Run man was drinking with a Baltimore wolf.

Tiago sipped his beer, thinking. Even if he got Luc talking, the man was hardly likely to share his clan's plans for Rock Run.

Not unless he was compelled to.

Tiago stared at the TV without seeing it. The more he used his Gift, the more it frightened him—and *not* because it drained energy, although that was part of it. No, it was because every time he used his Gift, it became a little easier, a little more tempting to compel someone...just because he could. And worse, with each use, the beast gained power—and his beast was a dark, feral thing.

He'd vowed not to use his Gift except when absolutely necessary.

Still, the compulsion wouldn't have to be much, just a question and then a little pressure...

He spun the beer bottle slowly back and forth between his palms. It was risky. If Luc realized Tiago had used compulsion on him, he'd report it to Adric and the Baltimore alpha would come gunning for him.

And worse, everyone would learn what Tiago was.

The fada were a long-lived race with the memories to match. The people of his clan hadn't forgotten that Tiago had betrayed the base's location to an earth fada. Oh, Dion had kept it quiet, but all the *tenentes* knew, and word had spread, at least among the upper hierarchy. If they learned about his dark Gift, he'd be shunned.

No. It wasn't worth it.

Tiago turned his attention to the game but his skin was prickling. This was how he'd met Adric. He'd been sitting on almost the same stool when the Baltimore alpha had sat down beside him, although Tiago hadn't realized whom he was talking to. The game on the TV had been soccer, not baseball, but otherwise it had been eerily similar.

He and Adric—or Ric, as he'd introduced himself—had fallen into a discussion about the game. Pretty soon, a couple of other earth fada had joined them, the four of them tossing back shots and trading stories about women. From there, Adric had played on Tiago's worries about Cleia like a maestro.

It had ended with Adric handing him a quartz that had been engineered into a smartphone. "Call me," he'd said. "If your woman is in trouble—"

And Tiago had been drunk enough to accept it.

Not that Tiago blamed Adric for taking advantage. Sure, the Baltimore alpha had played him, but he'd also kept his side of the bargain, helping the sun fae to rescue Cleia. If Adric had intended to use the information he'd obtained to attack Rock Run, well, he'd never admitted it.

He glanced at Luc.

Hell, if Tiago was smart, he'd leave. But something kept his ass on the stool and when Sophie returned, he indicated Luc and said, "I've got the next round."

They both slanted him a suspicious look. Then Luc shrugged. "Thanks." When the beer arrived, he nodded at Tiago and turned his attention back to the TV.

Ordinarily, Tiago would've left the man to his baseball game, but something was egging him on—and this time, he couldn't blame his beast. No, it was the very human part that needed to prove himself to his brother.

He jerked his chin at the TV. "The O's might go all the way this year."

"Could be."

Tiago persisted, and they exchanged a few comments about the game. Meanwhile, to his left, the sexy earth fada glanced at him from time to time until Luc scowled in her direction and the looks stopped. So he *was* someone high in the Baltimore hierarchy. In fact, the man was barely holding himself back from testing Tiago's dominance. Tiago could feel it; fada males had a sixth sense about these things.

His beast sensed it too and bristled beneath his skin, which increased Luc's tension. He shifted on the bar stool, took a gulp of his beer.

That edginess worked to Tiago's advantage.

His heart sped up. The beast was fully awake and eager: *Yes. Talk. Ask. Protect the females...*

The beast had a point. Cleia might be in danger or even Rosana. Even Alesia wouldn't be safe in an all-out war between Rock Run and the Baltimore shifters. Somehow that made it better.

Tiago met Luc's eyes and started to push. "Your alpha is going to meet with Queen Cleia."

"That's right." The other man answered readily. He wouldn't even feel the compulsion yet, although it would make him answer without thinking it through.

"What do you know about it?"

Luc opened his mouth. "Me? I—" He halted and frowned. "Thanks for the beer," he said as he set the empty bottle on the bar, "but that's clan business."

Ah. The man was stronger than Tiago had guessed. But then he'd never attempted to work on such a delicate level.

"Of course not," he murmured and pushed harder. "But my brother doesn't want to let your clan on sun fae land. He's going to stop the mining if he can. So it's to your benefit to talk to me. I can talk to Dion, explain why it's so important."

Luc nodded.

A fine sweat broke out on Tiago's brow. The few other times he'd tried to compel another fada, it had been under extreme conditions. Other than that, his main practice up until now had been on animals. It was a hell of a lot more difficult to compel a man without him knowing.

"Talk to me," he crooned.

"We need that quartz," Luc said simply.

"Why?" Tiago held his breath and pressed a bit more.

He felt Luc start to give in, but then a pretty earth shifter strolled by, and Luc glanced at her and the moment was lost. Tiago released the compulsion; it was too risky to hold any longer.

Luc gave him a sharp look and drew a slow breath, checking his scent.

Tiago turned his attention back to the baseball game, willing his heartbeat to slow. He was fucked if Luc realized what he was doing.

But damn, he hadn't learned anything Dion didn't already know. And he'd been so close…

Luc growled. "Look," he said in a subvocal voice for Tiago's ears alone, "I don't know what the hell you're up to, but I know damn well you of all people have no reason to help us."

Tiago shrugged. "So you say."

It was an evasive answer—not a lie, but not the truth, either—and Luc knew it. He growled again, loud enough that Claudio frowned their way.

Luc lowered his voice but his tone was hard. "I don't like you Rock Run shifters. I don't like your brother, and I especially don't like that he mated a fae. But he's kept his word to my friend Jace and allowed him to see Merry. He even lets Jace bring her home now and then."

"Merry's home is at Rock Run," Tiago returned. "She's a member of our clan now. But," he added grudgingly, "I know that Valeria and Rui want her to know her uncle. And they appreciate that Jace, too, has kept his word."

Luc nodded. "That's why I'm telling you to get the hell out of this bar. Now."

Tiago bristled. "This is neutral territory. You can't tell me to leave."

"No," Luc agreed. "But if I were you, I'd leave anyway. Because no one is going to answer your questions—and because I'm not the only one who saw you checking out Shania."

Tiago darted an involuntary glance in the woman's direction but she was no longer at the table.

"Yeah, her," Luc said grimly. "I don't know about Rock Run, but here in Baltimore, we watch out for our women. So if you want to keep that pretty face of yours, hit the road. *Now.*"

Tiago's hand fisted around his beer. *Pretty face?*

Hell, the man had no fucking idea. The only way he could take Tiago would be to first knock him unconscious, and even then, his beast, residing as it did in a more primitive area of his brain, would probably remain conscious long enough to fight back.

Sophie bustled up. "Something wrong, gentlemen?"

"Just having a friendly conversation," Luc replied and with a nod at Tiago, he got up and sauntered toward the back room and its perpetual poker game.

The bartender pressed her lips together and raised a brow at Tiago.

"You heard the man," he told her.

"Friendly conversation, my ass. I could smell the testosterone from three yards away." She cast a pointed look at the door. "Bar's closed as far as you're concerned. Claudio's orders."

"All right." With a shrug, Tiago got to his feet. He'd crash at the clan's rowhouse tonight and then swim back to Rock Run tomorrow. First, though, he had to make a pit stop.

The bathrooms were located in a tiny hall behind swinging doors. When he exited the men's room, the earth fada woman—Shania—was waiting to enter the ladies' room. She slanted him a glance from where she leaned against the wall playing with the chunk of quartz hanging from her neck.

Tiago looked her over, lingering on those long, leather-clad legs.

When he raised his gaze, her dark eyes challenged him. "Like what you see, river man?"

He thought of Luc, warning him away from her. He thought

of his brother, ordering him to stay away from the earth shifters. And deliberately set a hand on the scarred wood paneling beside her head.

"Very much. You're a beautiful woman, Shania."

"Smooth." Her lips curved. They were painted scarlet, a bright splash against her ginger-brown skin. "I like smooth."

"Then we have something in common."

The smile increased. She gave him her hand. "You know my name, but I don't know yours."

"Tiago." He clasped her fingers in his. The fingernails were blood red to match her lips and so long they curved, claw-like, from her fingertips. As he released her, he wondered what her animal was. Something sleek and predatory—a cougar, maybe.

She traced one of those long fingernails down his bare arm, sending a flash of heat directly to his groin. "Buy me a drink, Tiago?"

He shook his head regretfully. "Sorry, but I was on my way out."

"Too bad. Although we don't have to drink—"

"True." Tiago curved a hand around her nape. He leaned in so his mouth was a breath from hers. "I can think of something a lot more...fun."

"I like how you think, sugar. But not here. The men in my clan—"

"I understand." He brushed his lips over hers. "Why don't I meet you behind the bar?"

"I'll find you."

He gave her neck an approving squeeze and headed for the swinging doors.

Outside, a couple of other bars were in the process of emptying. Tiago rounded the corner and made his way down the alley to the back of the saloon, where he leaned against a building on the other side of the alley.

The brisk spring air felt good after the confines of the bar. He could hear voices and cars on the nearby street, but back here it was silent save for the rustling of a rat in a nearby garbage can. He tipped his head back against the wall and drew in a deep breath, gazing at the few stars that had managed to break through the smog and light pollution.

Alesia probably had a great view of the stars tonight. Her island was in the center of the Susquehanna, an hour from Baltimore and several miles from the nearest town. No place on the I-95 corridor was free of light pollution, but she could at least see more than the handful above him.

His chest constricted. What the hell was he doing?

But, by the gods, he needed a woman—and right now any woman would do. He wasn't proud of that but it was the truth. In a way, he was doing it for Alesia. This way the two of them could stay friends. Sex between them would ruin everything.

He shoved his hands in his pockets. Where was that woman —Shania—anyway?

Then she appeared from around the corner. She sauntered down the alley, a sleek, two-legged cat in tight pants and a short black-and-gold jacket.

"Come on." She took his hand. "There's an afterhours club just a block away. It's after one o'clock. It should be open."

He tugged her to a halt. "I said I've had enough."

"But I'd like a drink." She came up on her toes to brush her lips over his. "Please, Tiago?"

His groin snapped to attention. Maybe another drink wasn't a bad idea.

7

The afterhours club was shoehorned into a dank basement beneath a rowhouse. It reeked of beer and smoke, the stony-faced humans who patronized it apparently not giving a damn that Baltimore had banned cigarettes in public places.

"Welcome to the Wildcat," Shania said.

"It's owned by your clan, then?" And if so, why bring him here if she was trying to keep this a secret?

She shook her head. "The owner's a human. But she doesn't discriminate."

She pulled him to a table in a dark corner, set her chair so close to his she was practically in his lap and ran a hand down his shirt. One long nail scratched his nipple through the material.

He dragged in a breath and tugged at his pants to accommodate his hardening cock.

His companion smiled.

Their waitress arrived. Shania ordered a martini and he a whiskey, straight up. While they waited, her busy fingers moved lower, testing the bulge beneath his zipper.

"Mm," she murmured, her mouth warm against his ear. "I

can't wait to take this out and play." Her hand closed on him, the nails sharp against his hard flesh even through the cloth.

His breath rasped in. He gave her ass a squeeze through the leather and probed her ear with his tongue.

Wrong, growled his beast. *She's wrong.*

The voice was so unexpected that Tiago pulled back before he realized what he was doing. Fortunately, the waitress had returned with their drinks, so Shania didn't notice.

She removed her hand from his lap to raise her martini to him. He touched his glass to hers and tossed the shot down. The warmth filled his belly.

What the fuck? Usually his beast was more than eager for sex.

Still, no fada ignored their animal without a damn good reason. They might overrule it, but they didn't ignore it. The animal worked on instinct and often knew things before the man.

Shania's hand was on his fly again. "I always wanted to fuck a river shifter."

He shoved his grumbling beast back into whatever black corner of his soul it occupied and placed his hand over hers, pressing it against his erection.

"Yeah?" He gave her a slow smile. "I might be able to help you with that."

Her response was a throaty purr. Then her gaze flicked past him and at the same time, a hand descended on his shoulder.

"*Boa noite*, Tiago."

He took one look at the grizzled face looming over him and started to his feet. "Jorge?"

What the hell? Jorge was supposed to be on the other side of the ocean, banished to the Sahara along with his friend Benny and two Greek sea fada, where they'd been sentenced to work for the Sudanese sun fae for their part in Valeria and Merry's abduction.

Tiago shot a look around the club, because where Jorge was,

Benny wasn't far behind. But all he saw were humans and a handful of earth fada.

"Sit down." Jorge pressed his shoulder.

Tiago let himself be guided back into his seat, and the older man sat down heavily in the chair next to him.

Tiago tried to conceal his shock. Jorge looked like he'd aged a hundred turns of the sun in the five years since he'd been banished. He'd been an imposing barrel of a man, but now he looked like all the life had been sucked out of him. His skin was sun-burned and wrinkled as a dried apple, he'd lost weight and his brown hair was peppered with gray. His gaze darted from Tiago to Shania and then around the room as if he was having trouble remembering why he was in the club.

Still, the real mystery was why Jorge was in Baltimore at all. He and Benny had once been members of Rock Run, but five years ago they'd secretly joined the small den that Petros Okeanos and two other Greek sea fada had started on Alesia's island. Okeanos may have been the ringleader, but all five of them had been behind Valeria's abduction—and probably that of other women as well

Okeanos was dead, killed by Rui in a mate-duel. But rather than executing the other four, Dion had extracted a promise from them: they were to labor for the rest of their lives for the Sudanese sun fae in the hottest, driest part of the Sahara. For a water fada, it was almost worse than a death sentence.

Jorge, Benny and the other two men had sealed the vow by speaking their true-names. To a fada, such an oath was as binding as a literal imprisonment. Jorge shouldn't have been able to leave the Sudan without becoming deathly ill.

Tiago forgot all about Shania. His heart started to thump, slow and hard. This was his chance to show his brother what he could do. If he could capture Jorge, or at least find out what he was up to...

Jorge was studying him in turn. "How are you, *irmão*?" he asked in Portuguese and stuck out a hand.

Tiago looked at it without taking it. "I'm not your brother," he replied in a hard voice.

"*Não*?" Jorge lifted a finger at the waitress. "Well, have a drink on me anyway. For old times' sake, *sim*?"

Tiago hesitated. Much as he'd love to show Dion he could handle something like this on his own, the sensible part of him noted that Benny was probably around somewhere, too, and while he could probably take either of them on his own, together they might be too much.

But like most water fada, he didn't carry a cellphone. Something about their biochemistry shorted out small electronic devices, even the so-called waterproof ones. And payphones had gone the way of the eight-track and the desktop computer. To get a message to Dion, he'd have to return to the clan's rowhouse and use the landline to call the base.

"If Dion won't mind, that is," Jorge added slyly.

Tiago bristled. "Leave my brother out of this. And speak English," he added, belatedly recalling Shania, "the lady doesn't understand Portuguese."

"Of course." Jorge switched to heavily accented English and smiled at Shania. "And such a lovely lady."

She inclined her head, amused. "*Obrigada, senhor.*"

Tiago raised a brow. Apparently she knew at least a little Portuguese.

The waitress arrived with a whiskey bottle and a shot glass. After she poured Jorge's drink, he had her refill Tiago's glass as well, and ordered another martini "for the senhorita."

Tiago looked at the whiskey without moving. He should leave, call the base. Jorge had crossed the line when he'd joined Okeanos's den. Drugging women so you could use them sexually was the act of a savage, not a man.

But something kept him planted on his seat—and not just the chance to prove something to Dion.

Jorge had once been Tiago's mentor. After his mother and father went missing, Rock Run had been in an uproar. Dion's main focus had had to be the clan. It was Jorge who'd stepped up to take Tiago's eleven-year-old self under his wing. For that year, the gruff older warrior had been merciless—but the best damn teacher a boy could've asked for.

Then Jorge and Benny had been ensnared by Cleia and her powerful glamour, and had left to live at the sun fae compound. When they returned five years later, Tiago was a warrior in training and Jorge was a different man—bitter, cynical. He and Benny had left soon after to ride the waves, giving in to their animals and traveling the world's oceans in the way fada did when old or traumatized. Nothing was heard of them for years until they reappeared as members of Okeanos's den of renegades.

"So." Jorge ran his eyes over Tiago. "I see you are a man now."

Tiago couldn't help a treacherous spark of warmth at the praise from the man he'd once admired more than anyone except Dion. But that didn't mean he wasn't suspicious.

"What do you want? And how the hell did you escape the sun fae?"

"Can't a man buy an old friend a drink?"

"He could. But we're not old friends. You were my teacher, Jorge—and that was almost fifteen years ago."

Beside him, he was aware of Shania's gaze darting between him and Jorge. Something about her interest struck him as odd, but he didn't have time to sort it out before the waitress returned with her martini.

Shania lifted the glass, her scarlet nails wrapped around the stem. She took a sip and then set the glass down. Her fingers came to her quartz, toying with it. Tiago stared at it. The crystal was fascinating, a milky gray with a swirl of black running through the center. And was that a flame burning deep inside?

He swayed toward her and then caught himself.

Ass. Everyone knew the earth fada could use their quartz to manipulate you. He dragged his gaze away and caught her wrist. "Stop it. Now."

She struggled to free herself. "Let. Me. Go."

"Not until you tell me what the fuck you were doing with your crystal."

"Tiago." Jorge set a heavy hand on his shoulder. "Let the lady be."

He shook him off and glared at Shania. "Tell me, you bitch."

Shania snarled and rose to her feet. She clawed at Tiago's hand, but he tightened his grip and jerked her close. "Try that again, and you'll be sorry."

Her eyes flashed angrily and he gave her a little shake. "Understand?"

"Yes," she hissed. "Now let me go or I'll scream murder."

Across the room, he heard the earth shifter men get to their feet. He was still angry, but it wasn't worth a bar brawl. Besides, there was still Jorge to worry at. He snarled back and released her.

Her lip curled. "Serves me right for thinking a river fada was anything but a cold fish." She stalked off as Jorge smothered a laugh.

Tiago glanced at the scratches on his hand and cursed. "The woman was trying to hypnotize me."

"Earth fada," Jorge returned with a shrug.

Shania disappeared into a dark corner with the earth fada men. Their heads came together, and a couple of them shot glances at him.

Great. He was probably going to get jumped the instant he set foot back outside.

He turned back to Jorge. "You know you're a dead man, don't you?"

His former mentor moved a shoulder. "Have a drink, and then

you can tell me how long I have before Dion sends someone after me."

"Cut the crap, Jorge. You must know I'll tell him you're back. How long do you think you have?"

A man dropped down on the seat vacated by Shania. "Tiago." It was more a snarl than a word.

"Benny," Tiago returned, unsurprised. "I was wondering where you were."

Benny had long since abandoned any loyalty to the clan, his only allegiance to Jorge, his friend and sometime lover. Now he had the raw stench of a feral, his animal clearly running the show. His brown hair fell in matted coils around his shoulders and a scar slashed its way down one dirty cheek.

Benny moved his chair closer so that Tiago was sandwiched between him and Jorge. His coal-black eyes burned into Tiago's. "You think we'll let you tell him?"

Tiago nearly snorted at the other man's attempt to establish dominance. Benny didn't know who he was dealing with. Beneath his skin, the beast flexed its muscles, growled lowly.

He straightened his spine, his gaze never leaving Benny's. "You don't have a choice."

"Hey," Jorge said with a frown at Benny. "This is just a friendly conversation." At Jorge's look, Benny eased off, although he kept his chair where it was.

The drinks came, including a shot glass for Benny, and the other two men tossed theirs down. Tiago found himself following suit, even though he knew he should leave.

Fuck that. He could handle these two and another two besides. *Besides...*

He lost track of his thought and frowned. That was some strong whiskey. His brain felt as if it had been soaked in molasses.

"Why?" he asked Jorge.

"Why what?"

Tiago forced his sluggish mind to concentrate. "Why—you

here? Forget Dion. If Rui finds out you—you're here, he'll kill you. Won't matter that you're not—not in our territory. You ashaulted—*assaulted*—his mate."

Benny leered. "She liked it. She was begging—" He halted as Tiago's head swung toward him.

"You lie. I was there. I shaw—saw what you did to her."

Okeanos had drugged Valeria with an aphrodisiac that made her nearly crazed with lust. When he and Rui had burst in on them, Okeanos had Valeria down on her knees, sucking his cock, while Jorge and Benny slapped her around.

"You make me—shick."

He made to stand up but Jorge reached behind his back to slap Benny on the head. "*Idiota. Cale a boca.*"

Benny shot his friend a resentful look but obediently shut his mouth.

Jorge placed his arm on Tiago's shoulders, holding him in his seat. Tiago blinked woozily at his glass. Damn, that last shot had been strong. He had the uneasy feeling the other man's arm was the only thing keeping him from sliding to the floor. Forget about leaving. It was a struggle just to remain upright.

"As for why we're here," Jorge said, "this is our home territory. It calls us."

"Mmph." Alesia's face swam into his mind. *Yes. That was why he was here. To protect his woman.* He forgot about Rosana, Cleia, Valeria. It was Alesia who was important.

"Stay away from her," he gritted out.

"Stay away from who?"

"Her. Alesia."

"Who is this Alesia?"

Not a lie, but an evasion. But as quickly as the thought occurred, Tiago lost it again.

Jorge called for a refill. Tiago shook his head, but the bartender poured the whiskey into his glass anyway.

He didn't have to drink it though. He pushed the glass away. His arm didn't seem to be working right and the glass teetered.

Benny caught it and pressed it into his hand again. Tiago stared at it, entranced. The light from a nearby wall sconce was reflected in the amber liquid. It reminded him of rising to the river's surface from deep below on a summer day, the sunlight streaming through the dancing current.

Beside him, Jorge spoke. "You ever wonder what it's like? A baccha?"

"No," he muttered, irritated at the interruption.

But he did. His beast wondered—and he did, too.

"No? A man of your...talent?"

Tiago stilled. *Nobody knew about his Gift.* Not even Dion.

He sobered enough to shake Jorge's hand off his shoulder. "What d'you mean?"

"Just that I was a young man like you. Strong. Smart. I only wanted a fair chance. Instead, the old lord changed everything. We moved with him to America and then what did he do? He banned the bacchas, made sure only his son had a real shot at becoming the next alpha. And now his son has mated with a fae." Jorge spat on the floor. "Must be even harder for you. Knowing you're stronger than your brother in every way."

He couldn't know. Could he?

"I don't have to listen to this." Tiago turned sideways on the chair, giving Jorge his back. But that left him facing Benny.

He came to his feet. Dizziness swept through him. He put both hands on the table, hoping they hadn't noticed.

The other two men rose up as well. Jorge leaned closer. "But don't you wonder what it's like?" His voice was a seductive croon. "I know you do. The blood of Dionysus flows in your veins, same as us. The baccha is our birthright."

"Go to hell." Tiago took a step back. "You're d—dead men. And I'm leaf—leaving."

"*Sim, sim, irmão.* Whatever you say."

Faces rushed at him.

Shania and another earth shifter.

Benny, his dark eyes gleaming with malice.

Jorge with his arm around a slim, black-haired woman in a bright tunic. He wrapped his hand around her nape, tugging her close for a long, lascivious kiss, while two other men whom he didn't know watched.

Tiago blinked. Where had all these people come from?

The floor swelled under his feet and then dropped, like the deck of a ship. He shifted his feet, trying to keep his balance.

An arm came around him, holding him up. Benny spoke from the other end of a long, dark tunnel. "Come with me."

8

$\mathcal{D}$ion took a stance behind Cleia's chair and folded his arms.

The Baltimore fada had arranged to meet in a large, sunlit conference room in a hotel overlooking Baltimore's Inner Harbor. The wall-to-wall windows were out of consideration for Cleia, the sun fae being partial to bright, open spaces. The room definitely wouldn't have been the first choice of the earth fada, who, like Dion's people, made their homes in underground dens and caves.

Dion suspected the harbor location was an attempt to appease him, and he did like knowing the water was just yards away. If he turned his head he could see the sparkling blue expanse, view boats moving to and fro. One of those boats held several of his men, in fact. Just in case.

Still, if it had been up to him, he'd have forced Adric to come to them, make it clear he was the supplicant. But Cleia had nixed that. "When dealing with fada, neutral territory is best."

"*Ah, sim?*" he'd said.

"Yes," she'd stated firmly. "Otherwise either you or Adric is going to feel at a disadvantage, and next thing I know you'll be locked in a dominance contest and we won't get anything accomplished."

He shot her an irritated look. Then his lips twitched. Sometimes he forgot his mate was more than two hundred years old and damn smart.

"All right," he told her. "It's your show."

"Thank you." She caressed his cheek. "I know this is hard for you."

"Damn right," he muttered.

He enclosed her in his arms and buried his face in her bright hair. He might be half her age, but a hundred turns of the sun was still a long, lonely time to be without a mate. He'd rip his own heart out if that's what it took to keep her safe. And knowing a child was on the way...

The meeting was about to begin. He settled his face into stern lines, his gaze on Adric. They'd already greeted him and his second—a man named Zuri whom Dion knew was one of his lieutenants—and exchanged the kind of meaningless pleasantries that made Dion's neck itch. Adric had asked why Dion was here, and Cleia had explained that Rock Run was going to handle security on the project. Adric had nodded impassively, but Dion scented his displeasure.

Adric also hadn't liked that outside the conference room, two Rock Run *tenentes* were standing guard along with Artan and Grady. *Tough.* If Adric wanted to deal with Cleia, he'd better get used to the fact that she and Rock Run were a package deal.

Now Adric took a seat across from Cleia, while Zuri took a stance behind his alpha, mirroring Dion.

Adric was young for an alpha—thirty turns of the sun or so—with the taut, edgy physique of the big cat he was. Like Dion, he was wearing a button-down shirt and black pants, but in Adric's case, the pants were jeans and the shirt a shimmering gray silk with the top three buttons undone to display a good portion of his dark bronze chest. A chunk of quartz hung from a leather cord around his neck and his spiky dark hair was bleached yellow at the tips.

He looked exactly what he was: a cocky SOB.

But the man was also damn smart. Dion might not like the other alpha, but he respected what he'd accomplished. Before Adric had wrested control of the Baltimore clan five years ago, it had all but imploded, wracked by an internal battle for control that wiped out most of its leadership.

Rumor had it that Adric had quietly and methodically executed anyone who stood in his way on his march to becoming alpha, including his own uncle. Dion didn't doubt it for a second.

"You have everything you need, my lady?" Adric asked Cleia. "Is there anything we can offer you? A drink? A more comfortable chair?"

Dion's hackles raised. So what if Cleia was a powerful fae queen? A pregnant female was a vulnerable female. He'd seen Adric's nostrils flare when she entered the room. His animal rumbled lowly, unhappy that this rival male knew his mate was with child.

Cleia shifted and he glanced down. She was wearing a sun fae's version of business attire—a sleeveless dress in a summery yellow with a slightly scooped neck and a pleated skirt. Her hair fell in a thick plait to the midpoint of her back, a strand of diamonds intertwined in the shiny strands. She was beautiful, glowing with health—and too damn exposed, her bare nape a slim, breakable column.

He widened his stance. Outside the closed door, he could hear Artan and Grady muttering to each other. The guards were pissed off that their queen had ordered them to wait in the hall. He wondered if they'd sensed his agitation; they were fae, not fada, but their family had guarded Cleia's for centuries and they had a preternatural sense where her safety was concerned.

Adric's odd bronze eyes cut to Dion. As usual, the bastard was smirking. He'd been an irritant in Dion's hide practically from the day he'd become the Baltimore alpha. His clan was composed mainly of cats and wolves. They needed room to roam, and Rock Run owned one of the last large tracts of private land in the mid-Atlantic. It was no secret that Adric wanted Rock Run's territory.

Dion glared back at the younger man. The tension ratcheted higher, neither of them willing to give an inch.

"Dion," Cleia murmured and brought her hand to her shoulder. He dragged his gaze from Adric's to lay his hand over hers. She turned her fingers to squeeze his. He released a slow breath and reminded himself that he was here to protect her, not engage in a pissing contest with the other alpha.

"Thank you, my lord," she told Adric. "I'd appreciate a glass of water."

"Of course." The earth fada nodded at Zuri, who went to the door and spoke in low tones to someone waiting on the other side of Artan and Grady. Dion knew one of the big blond guards would personally taste the water before allowing Cleia to imbibe it. Rival fae had been known to poison one another at just this sort of meeting.

"Let me explain why I asked for this meeting," Adric said as Zuri resumed his place behind him. "As you know, our surveyors found a vein of quartz that is partially on Rising Sun land. We would like your permission to mine it. As a sign of our good faith, we have refrained from mining the part of the vein that is not on your land, although we bought the mineral rights from the farmer who owns it."

Smart, thought Dion. The man was making it clear the mining would happen either way. If the sun fae didn't allow them to mine, they'd still have the noise and environmental effects to deal with right on their north border. But at the same time, in seeking Cleia's consent, the earth fada showed they were prepared to be courteous.

"For your rights," Adric continued, "we are prepared to pay an amount equal to what we paid the farmer." He named a figure that made Dion's brows lift.

Cleia inclined her head. "An impressive sum, my lord. But as you know, we sun fae have little need of money. Everything we touch seems to generate riches."

And, Dion reflected wryly, it didn't hurt that a few of her people had the Gift of spinning straw into gold.

"The payment can be in precious stones—rubies, emeralds, diamonds."

Cleia's interest sharpened. Like all fae, she had a weakness for bright baubles, yet couldn't tolerate the long hours underground required to mine them. They could buy them, of course, but the fae loved to barter.

She fingered the diamonds glittering in her braid. "I'll admit, that's appealing. But if you have that kind of money, why can't you just buy the quartz you need?"

For the first time Adric's self-assurance slipped. "I—we don't have it." He glanced at Dion, clearly unhappy at being forced to admit how poor his clan was in front of his chief rival. "I had hoped we could work out a payment plan—a portion upfront, the rest to come as we mine the quartz."

"It's that valuable?"

"No. Its value is in what we can do with it once it is mined."

"A payment plan might be acceptable. But I warn you, the first payment will be a large one. My mate doesn't think you can be trusted."

The earth fada's mouth tightened, but he replied in even tones, "We'll do whatever it takes."

Cleia inclined her head, and he said, "Then we have a deal—"

She raised a hand. "Not so fast. We are stewards of our land, not simply the owners. There's no deal unless you agree to keep the effects of the mining to a minimum. You will also return the land to its original state when you are finished."

"Of course."

He was interrupted by a knock on the door.

Zuri stepped into the hall to accept a tray with glasses and a pitcher of ice water. Dion was amused to see Grady holding the door for him. Zuri was frankly beautiful, with a hard body and the black hair and warm brown skin often seen in earth shifters.

But the bodyguard was a professional; he used the opportunity to scan the room, even though he and his cousin, as well as Dion, had checked it thoroughly before allowing Cleia to enter. Behind him Artan had his back to them, gazing out into the hall. Dion allowed himself to relax slightly. He and Cleia's guards didn't always see eye to eye, but they'd protect her to their last breath.

Zuri set the tray on the table and took his place again as Adric offered Cleia a glass of water. Dion intercepted it and took a taste before handing it to his mate.

Just to be sure.

Adric's eyes glinted, half amused, half irritated. Not that Dion gave a damn.

"You have my personal guarantee"—Adric smoothly picked up the thread of the negotiation—"that your land will be as beautiful as it ever was when we are finished. We pride ourselves on returning the land to its natural state. And our mining techniques are very advanced—we don't strip or blast the earth. We mine beneath the surface, entering through narrow shafts. You won't even know we're there."

"That sounds acceptable."

"About security," Dion said.

Adric raised a brow. "He speaks for you?" he asked Cleia.

It was an insult, as if Dion were her boy toy rather than alpha of his own clan. His jaw tightened.

"He's my mate," Cleia replied in a hard voice. "His concerns are my concerns."

"I beg your pardon," Adric said to Dion.

He jerked his head in acknowledgment. "The queen has hired

Rock Run to provide security while you're on-site. Your people will be confined to the area in which you are mining. If any earth fada is discovered elsewhere—no matter what the reason—the deal will be immediately terminated. Is that understood?"

"Yes," Adric replied without hesitation.

Interesting. The man must be desperate for that quartz.

Cleia rose to her feet, hand extended. "Then we have a deal, my lord. Lady Olivia will contact you to work out the details about payment and so forth."

Adric shook her hand. "Thank you, my lady." With a sly glance at Dion, he kept hold of her hand as he came around the table and raised her fingers to his lips.

Dion's hackles rose. But the man had been a pup when Dion was one of his father's most trusted warriors and advisors. He simply stared back expressionlessly.

The Baltimore alpha released Cleia's hand and stepped back. "Peace to you and yours." He included Dion in the ritual goodbye. "I'll contact Lady Olivia as soon as possible. We'd like to begin work in early May."

"That should be fine," Cleia replied. "Peace to you and yours." She inclined her head and headed for the door.

Dion allowed her to pass before turning back to Adric. "Just so we're clear: my people will be under orders to execute anyone who sets even one toe outside the agreed-upon perimeter. No excuses. No second chances. Understood?"

"Understood." He flashed Dion a cocky smile.

"Good." Dion stepped closer and lowered his voice. "And know this, too, you *filho da puta*. If you ever put your lips on my mate again—for any reason whatsoever—I'll break every bone in your goddamn body."

He met Adric's smile with his own and strode after Cleia.

9

Twin gremlins crouched on Tiago's shoulders and hammered gleefully on his skull. A red-hot shaft of light burned his eyeballs through closed lids. He covered his face with his arm.

It helped. Barely. He swallowed a groan.

Breathe in. Out. In.

Again.

His mouth was dry, his tongue as gritty as sandpaper. He tried to swallow but he had no spit. *Water. He had to get water.*

He raised his arm and forced his lids open.

He lay on a mattress on a dirt-encrusted floor. To his left, dawn light streamed in through two uncurtained windows. He squinted and shifted sideways out of the sunlight.

The movement caused his stomach to heave. He rolled onto his side and spewed its contents onto the dirty wood floor. When he was done, he pushed himself up to sitting and rested his arms on his bent knees, breath rasping in and out. It felt as if he'd lost an argument with a semi. Every bone in his body ached.

Gradually he became conscious of another sound. A slight,

quick inhale from a corner of the room. Underneath the pungent smell of his vomit, he scented fear.

Female fear.

And death.

He lifted his head and peered into the corner. A naked woman sat on another mattress. A young, slim woman with short black hair. Her thin arms were wrapped around her knees, her eyes wide and scared, and an ugly bruise marred the smooth skin of her cheek.

At his look, she shuddered and averted her gaze.

Tiago became aware he was naked as well. And hard as a metal spike.

She darted a glance at his groin and whimpered. "*No—*"

"For God's sake. What do you think I am?"

She lifted a shoulder without looking at him. Not exactly a vote of confidence.

He cut a glance sideways and located the source of the death he scented: Benny. Sprawled naked near the only door, his long hair spread out in a ragged brown fan and a look of sheer horror on his face.

Tiago passed a hand over his eyes. *What the hell had happened here?*

He glanced back at the woman to find her staring at him. "He's dead," she said unnecessarily.

"Yes." His voice was a rasp. He had too little spit even to moisten his lips. "I—is there something to drink? Water?"

"Just wine." She indicated a wineskin a few feet from him. "It should be okay to drink."

His stomach turned at the thought of alcohol, but he desperately needed moisture. He picked up the skin and took a cautious sip. It helped, enough that he could take in his surroundings.

They were in the front room of a rowhouse. Other than the two mattresses, the furniture consisted of a couple of stools and an upended crate which held the remains of a meal—half-eaten shrimp and risotto and a roasted vegetable salad. The walls were chipped and missing chunks of drywall, and there was the sickly-sweet smell of rotting wood.

His stomach heaved but it was too empty to do anything but contract painfully. He waited until it passed and then tentatively moved his limbs, fingered his ribs. He touched a deep, dark bruise that made him wince, but by some miracle he didn't seem to have any broken bones.

He turned his attention back to the woman and lifted the wineskin. "Would you—?"

"Yes, please." But she didn't move.

He came to his feet. The room swung dizzily around him and he had to wait until he had his balance, before shuffling across the floor to sink down on the mattress next to the earth shifter. She took the skin and drank, but he didn't miss how she shrank from him.

He was afraid that if he tried to stand up again, he might end up face-down on the floor, but he edged to the other end of the mattress. Then her words registered.

"What do you mean, the wine should be okay?"

She hugged her knees again. "They drugged you," she told her bare toes. "And me. But not here. Before. Then they brought us here. To…" Her voice faded but he could guess why they'd brought her here.

Him, he wasn't so sure.

"Son of a bitch." The meeting in the bar came back to him. Not just Benny, but Jorge as well. And Shania—and another woman, the one Jorge had been kissing. "You were there, too—in the club." It was a statement, not a question, but she answered it anyway.

"Yeah. They took some as well, but not as much."

"Some of what?" Tiago shot a look at his insistent erection, fearing he knew the answer.

"An aphrodisiac. It made you—" She shook her head. "They

said you'd drunk too much whiskey already, that was why it made you crazy."

His jaw hardened. He cursed, long and low. "And Jorge? Where's he? And the others?"

"I don't know. There were four men. All water *fada*. After Benny—after you killed Benny—the others ran out of here."

"I killed—"

Tiago eyed the dead man, his gut twisted with foreboding. Benny had a few marks on him but nothing that should have been fatal. Tiago refused to feel guilty for his death; the man had obviously gone feral and would have continued kidnapping and drugging women for his pleasure. He'd needed to be stopped.

But *how* had he died?

Tiago's gaze stopped on Benny's horror-stricken face. "Hell."

He felt rather than saw the woman flinch. He turned back to her, his chest squeezed so tight he could barely force the words out.

"And you? What did I do to you? And the other woman —Shania?"

She bent her head, her hands gripping her bent knees as if they were a lifeline. He stared at the bruises on her arms and legs, dark splotches against her butterscotch skin.

Bile rose in his throat. He swallowed sickly. "Tell me," he demanded in hoarse tones. "I have to know."

She closed her eyes. "I—it's not what you think."

"Just tell me the truth. I won't hurt you, I swear on my *avó's*— my grandmother's—grave."

"I don't know about Shania. I never saw her, not after we left the club. Maybe she got away—I hope so. But me—" Her breath shuddered in, the delicate blades of her shoulders rising and falling. "All four of them. You were out of it, passed out on the floor. You didn't know—" She halted. Two tears squeezed from beneath her closed eyelids.

Tiago shut his eyes as well. *Deus and all the gods*. It was as bad as he'd feared.

"After—when they were through—they laughed to see you on the floor. Benny—he started kicking you, shouting at you to get up. Jorge forced open your mouth and poured wine into it." She saw him glance at the wineskin and shook her head. "You were already drugged. It was just wine, something to bring you around. Anyway, it worked. You woke up enough to come to your feet, but you were out of your head."

Tiago groaned. But he was starting to remember.

Fists.

Feet.

Slamming into his head, his legs, his belly.

The painful thump of his head as Benny banged it against the hard floor. *Thump. Thump. Thump.*

No wonder he ached all over.

Others had joined in. That's when he'd realized there were four of them. They'd been relentless, each blow thudding through him as if multiplied a hundred times until he had to bite his hand to keep from screaming with pain.

And all the time he was distracted by a raging hard-on, until he'd realized what must have happened. They'd drugged him with the same aphrodisiac they'd used on Valeria. It increased every sensation, both pleasure and pain. It had nearly driven her mad.

He'd gone a little crazy then.

The woman regarded him warily. "You were furious. Started shouting you were going to beat them bloody."

He cursed under his breath.

Red-hot anger had blurred his vision. The drug simmered painfully in his blood. He'd come to his feet swinging, catching first Jorge, then Benny in the face. They wavered on their feet. Recovered.

The other two men—sea fada, by their scent—took one look

at him and scurried out the door, but Benny—or was it Jorge?—taunted him. "Take us, little brother. Take us."

The beast erupted. Tiago bellowed a wordless challenge and charged, uncaring that it was two against one. He wanted to rip their heads from their bodies.

And he could.

Suddenly he halted, focused. Their eyes widened as he ordered them to lie on the floor at his feet—and they found themselves obeying.

He reached for Benny, closed his hand around his windpipe. Lifted him like a rag off the floor.

A furious growl. His.

"*Tu vais morrer*," he told Benny, instinctively switching to Portuguese.

You will die.

Benny's face was a mask of terror, the scar a red slash against his cheek. His eyes widened, then rolled back in his head. His heart stuttered, stopped.

And just like that, he was dead.

Tiago tossed him aside and turned to Jorge.

The other shifter's chest heaved. He strained against the floor, his face purple, trying but unable to move, as helpless as a bug pinned to a board.

Tiago's lips stretched into a dark smile. He reached for the helpless, straining man.

"Oh, Goddess." A woman's voice. Soft, nearly inaudible.

He swung his head to look at her. He could scent Jorge on her. In his crazed state, she was the enemy's woman. She came to her feet and looked at him, a hand to her throat, her eyes huge with fear.

"You," he grated. "Sit down."

In that moment of inattention, Jorge twisted from his grip and scrambled to his feet.

Tiago swung back. "Halt." The force of compulsion was behind his words.

Jorge halted. A shudder ran through his body. The compulsion held him in place, but he could still talk.

"Tiago." He stretched out a hand, palm out. "*Acalme-te, irmão.* We didn't know—"

"I'm not your fucking brother."

Tiago started forward but the simmering pain erupted, liquid fire eating a path along his nerves as the aphrodisiac reached its full force. He staggered and lost his ability to focus on anything but the agonizing sensation of being burned alive from the inside out.

Jorge escaped into the hall, slamming the door behind him. A lock clicked in place. A moment later the front door slammed as well.

Thwarted, the beast raged. *Chase. Kill.*

Tiago started after him. One kick and the door swung open, half off its hinges.

A whimper halted him. He swung toward the woman curled up on the mattress.

Take.

The enemy was gone, but *she* was still there. Smelling like them.

Tiago clenched his fists, his chest working like a bellows. The pain receded but in its place was the primal urge to fuck.

He took a step toward the woman. She whimpered again and scrambled backward, landing on one of the bare, stained mattresses.

"Stay there," he growled. Compelling without meaning to. "You're not going anywhere until I'm finished with you."

She froze, her hand on her throat. He stalked toward her.

By the gods, he needed to fuck. Craved it. Burned to have it, urged on by the wildfire scouring his veins.

But more than that, he required revenge. And she represented both. Now that he was closer, he scented Jorge, Benny and the other two men on her—and that she hadn't been unwilling.

She hissed at him, claws sprouting from her fingertips. But he could tell she lacked the energy to complete the change.

He pushed her down onto the mattress.

"No." She struggled to get away but he easily controlled her. "It's not what you think. I didn't want this. They tricked me, drugged me. Brought me here, same as you. Don't. Please—I'm begging you."

But her body said otherwise. He scented her arousal, mixed with fear and an odd, dizzying aroma that both drew and repelled him.

She saw his nostrils flare and drew a breath as well.

"It's the aphrodisiac," she explained frantically. "Don't give in to it. Don't make *me* give in to it. Please, Tiago."

She was an earth fada. It was there in her scent and warm Caribbean coloring. Which meant she could scent him as well as he could scent her.

His hands tightened on her shoulders, the need to fuck wrenching his balls. The beast slashed at his skin, urged him to take her.

She wants it. She needs it. Look, she's hurting, same as you.

He kneed her legs apart.

"No," she moaned. "Please. Listen to me." A tear slid down her cheek.

He halted and stared at her, his breath loud in his ears. Then he touched a finger to her tear-streaked cheek. Another tear slid over his finger. Hot and wet. His senses were so jacked up he could practically taste the salt.

He jerked back his hand and came to his feet, back arched, fists at his side. His head dropped back on an agonized groan. "Damn, woman. You don't know what you're asking."

She stared up at him, crying those silent tears.

He flung himself away from her and fell on another mattress, curled into a ball and shaking with a desire so strong it was torture. The woman remained still. He wondered why she was still there and then the fire flared again and sent him into a dark, blessedly pain-free void.

Now Tiago slanted a look at the woman from where he sat on the mattress. She was still gazing at him warily.

He scraped his fingers through his hair and sat straighter. He felt marginally better, although weak; vomiting had probably helped rid his body of the last of the drug. And the damn hard-on had finally subsided.

His internal clock was out of whack but from the height of the sun, it was around nine in the morning. Too much daylight to do anything about Benny's body. Tiago was lucky Jorge hadn't come back for it while he was still unconscious—he'd be dead, more than likely.

What a frigging mess.

"Can I go now?" the woman asked. "Please?"

He moved a shoulder. "Sure."

"Say it. Tell me I can go."

He gave her another look and then it dawned on him why she was still there. He'd put a compulsion on her powerful enough to keep her where she was all this time.

"Sorry," he muttered. "You're free to go, whenever and wherever you like."

She placed a hand on the wall and dragged herself to her feet. She took a step forward and then hunched over, an arm to her stomach. A small, hurt sound escaped her lips. He forgot his own battered body and struggled up as well, but when he started toward her, she thrust out a hand.

"*No.* Stay where you are."

He froze. "I'm sorry—I just wanted to..."

She drew herself upright and tilted her chin at a proud angle. "I'm fine." She headed toward the door, taking short, stiff steps like an old woman—or one who'd been hurt in the most basic way possible.

He squeezed his eyes shut. When he opened them, she was at the door.

"Miss, please." He spoke in the same calm tones he used with skittish animals. "You can't go out like that. Not without any clothes."

She glanced down at herself. She was a fada, and nakedness was unremarkable among shapeshifters. But they were in Baltimore, and although the house appeared to be on a little-used side street, people were out and about.

She crossed her arms over her stomach. "I thought I'd shift. I can change to my cat, keep to the side streets. But first I need water—and to pee."

"But Jorge and the others could still be around somewhere—"

"They're not."

"How do you know?"

"I was listening for them."

Hell. She must have been up all night, huddled on the mattress, wondering if the men would come back—or if Tiago would wake up and she'd have to fight him off.

He expelled a breath.

She hunched a shoulder and waited—still wary of him, he realized with a stab of shame—and when he didn't say anything further, slipped out of the room and into a bathroom across the hall.

Well, at least he could make sure she was safe. His nose and ears told him that she was right, they were alone in the house. Jorge and the other two men had probably gone into the water to heal. But just to be sure, he did a sweep of the first floor, confirming that it was empty save for a few sticks of furniture.

The upstairs held another bathroom and two bedrooms, also empty except for a broken chair and a pile of blankets in one of the rooms. It was clear that Jorge and Benny, and maybe the other two men as well, had been squatting here. Tiago was surprised the Baltimore shifters had allowed it.

He returned to the bathroom and stuck his head under the tap, drinking the water in great gulps. It tasted of chemicals, but it was nectar to his parched throat. His most pressing need taken care of, he used the toilet and then glanced at the shower, hoping against hope it worked. He smelled rank, and he was smeared with dried blood and *Deus* knew what else. Stepping into the bathtub, he turned on the faucet and sent a prayer to the water gods.

They must've taken pity on him, because it came out in a decent stream. Ice cold, but that was fine with him. He took a sliver of soap from the sink and stepped into the chilly spray. He winced and then heaved a sigh. It was heaven.

For a minute he stood there, letting the water wash away the blood and sweat and the acrid scent of alcohol and the drug still working its way out of his system. But he was afraid the woman would leave without him, and even though that might be for the best, he felt responsible for her. He scrubbed the soap over his head and body, rinsed it out and then reluctantly turned off the water.

The only towel was encrusted with grime. He ignored it to shake himself like a dog. As he squeezed the excess water from his hair, he caught sight of himself in the cracked mirror above the sink. It wasn't pretty: a black eye, split lip and a mass of reddish purple bruises on his abdomen and thighs. If he didn't have a fada's strength, he'd be in the hospital.

He scowled. One way or the other, Jorge was going to pay.

To his surprise, the woman was waiting in the hall.

"I found our clothes." She thrust a bundle at him and slipped into the bathroom, shutting the door behind her. If there had been a lock, he was sure she'd have turned it. "You can go," she told him through the closed door. "I'll be okay."

"I'll wait," he growled back.

He was damned if he was going to leave her to make her own way home. Not just the honor of his clan was at stake, his own personal honor was as well. If he hadn't gotten so drunk that Jorge and Benny had been able to drug him without his knowledge...

His shirt and pants smelled almost as rank as he had, but he didn't have anything else, so he put them on. While he waited for the woman to finish her shower, he found a shoestring in a drawer and tied his wet hair back, before checking the front- and backyard.

There was still no sign of Jorge or the other two. He did find his sandals, though, where they'd been tossed out the back door into the bushes. And the SOBs had taken all his money. He went back into the front room and glared down at Benny. Even though he hated that he'd lost control of his beast, the scum had deserved what happened.

He picked up a pair of pants and searched them. No money, but he did find a switchblade, which he shoved into his back pocket.

The woman was in the shower for a long time. He went to the base of the stairs and looked up, wondering if he should check on her, but while he was debating, the water shut off. When she came back downstairs, he was at the kitchen counter, tearing the remains of a loaf of Italian bread into pieces.

She appeared in the doorway, black hair slicked down and dressed in a wrinkled tunic, loose-fitting pants and a pair of sandals. Despite their rumpled state, the clothes were of a rich fabric—silk, he guessed—and the sandals were of a soft, expensive-looking leather. She obviously had a high status among her own people.

Tiago swallowed uneasily. The Baltimore shifters would love an excuse to war with Rock Run.

"You're still here," she said flatly.

"Don't worry—I swear I won't bother you. All I want to do is make sure you're safe."

She acknowledged that with a slight nod.

He offered her a share of the bread, got them each a glass of water and invited her to take the only stool in the room. As she walked toward it, he was relieved to see she was moving more easily. He closed his eyes against a fresh wash of shame. If only he'd been in a condition to stop those bastards from hurting her.

The bread was stale. He took a drink and chewed mechanically. He had to get some food in him. He was still too weak. There was no way he'd be able to fight off Jorge right now, let alone two additional men.

The woman was studying him surreptitiously. He glanced at her, then away. Now that his head was clearer, he had the uneasy feeling he should know her name.

He set down his glass of water. "My name's Tiago, by the way. Tiago do Rio."

"I know."

He recalled then that she'd called him by name last night. He waited for her to introduce herself in turn, but when she didn't, he said, "Okay—you don't have to tell me who you are. But please allow me to escort you back to your den. It's the least I can do."

"The sentries wouldn't let you within a mile of it."

"Then I'll leave you when we see them. Please, miss—I want to make sure you're okay. Let me do that much, at least."

He left his greatest fear unspoken, that Jorge was somewhere nearby, waiting. Jorge didn't like to lose.

"What about him?" She jerked her chin in the direction of the front room.

"Benny? He can rot for all I care. But I'll contact my—Lord Dion, let him know. He won't want to bring the human police into it. This is Rock Run business."

The police didn't like the local fada—water or earth. The Baltimore commissioner's hands were tied by the treaty the fada had made with the federal government, but he hated that they were a law unto themselves. He'd jump at the chance to crack down on them, curb their comings and goings.

The earth shifter eyed him another moment, then inclined her head. "Marjani. My name is Marjani Savonett."

Hell. No wonder she looked familiar. "Adric's sister."

"And you're the youngest brother of the Rock Run alpha. Interesting, hm?"

10

———

The street outside the rowhouse was empty save for a woman pushing a stroller on the opposite sidewalk. Tiago inhaled, testing the air for any sign of Jorge or the others. Nothing, save the stale spoor left behind when they'd passed through hours ago.

He glanced at Marjani, who was sniffing the air herself. He couldn't believe he hadn't recognized her sooner. True, the only time he'd seen her had been five years ago at Cleia and Dion's mating ball, but she hadn't changed that much. On the other hand, he'd been so upset that day that he hadn't registered much besides the fact that he'd lost Cleia to his brother.

"Where to?" he asked.

Yesterday's rain had washed everything clean, leaving the sun shining in a bright blue bowl of a sky. While he waited for her answer, he took another deep inhale. They were in southeast Baltimore, just yards from the water. He could scent the Patapsco River, the last ten miles of which was a tidal estuary that formed Baltimore's harbor. A biting wind blew off the water and overhead, seagulls wheeled and screeched.

The rich, fertile mix of salt and fresh water tugged at him like an umbilical cord. No matter that this water carried an unhealthy measure of pollution as well. In the past twelve hours, he'd been drunk, drugged and beaten. Like a wounded animal, all he wanted was to go to ground until he healed. He glanced toward the harbor and promised himself that as soon as Marjani was safely with her own people, he'd change to his dolphin, swim out to the clean, open waters of the Chesapeake and spend a few days floating with the currents and dining on fresh fish.

"That way." Marjani pointed west toward the Inner Harbor. "Adric is meeting with Queen Cleia today. I—I want to go to him."

He nodded and fell into step with her. So the meeting was today. He hadn't heard the results of Cleia and Dion's argument, but he was sure Dion would be there, too. There was no way his brother would let his mate meet with another alpha, especially Adric, without him.

He scowled. Dion was the last person he wanted to see right now. He'd want to know what had happened and Tiago's secret was bound to come out. Too many people knew about it now—Marjani, Jorge, the other men in the room last night.

And besides, there was Benny. Dead, with no marks on him to explain why he died—and that look of horror on his face.

Tiago squared his shoulders. Maybe it was for the best. He couldn't hide what he was forever.

Marjani touched her throat as if feeling for something that wasn't there and he realized her throat was bare.

"Your quartz," he said. "Where is it?"

"They took it."

He frowned. An earth fada could focus the energy in a quartz crystal, use it to amp up his or her Gift. But it was more than that; they were attuned to their particular quartz in some odd way. He knew that little Merry needed it to help her shift, too.

"You're not hurting?"

"No." But she couldn't conceal a grimace.

He'd have known it was a lie anyway from the bitter spike in her scent, but he didn't call her on it. If he were in her shoes, he wouldn't want to betray a weakness either.

"That doesn't mean I'm powerless," she added, seeming to read his mind. "I still have my claws. And I can use any quartz to focus my Gift."

"But that one was special."

"Yes. That one was special."

"I'm sorry," he said. "And for the record, I'm not the enemy. I'm guessing you must be hurting. If there was anything I could do to help, I would."

She blew out a breath. "Sorry. I know you were under the influence of the drug as much as I was."

They walked another few yards. "I am hurting," she admitted in a low voice. "It's like they ripped out a part of me. And they did it deliberately. He—Benny—forced me to give it to him and then he—he smashed it into pieces in front of me and threw them in the harbor."

She said it as if they'd killed a living thing. And perhaps, for an earth fada, they had.

"Bastards," he muttered.

"Yeah. They wanted to make sure I couldn't be traced—or call for help." She dragged in a breath before continuing, "My brother must know by now that I'm missing. He probably has people out looking for me. I only hope he didn't call off the negotiations because of this."

"Cleia's pretty reasonable. I'm sure if he explained what happened to her, she'd reschedule."

"Would she?" She shot him a hopeful look. "I've heard she's not like most fae, not, you know—"

"An arrogant, self-centered dickhead?"

"Yeah." She gave him a tiny smile, the first he'd seen from her. "Adric won't want to take the chance, though." She shook her head. "He's going to go ballistic when he finds out what happened. The two of us—we're all that's left. Our parents died before he became alpha."

"Those were rogues, Marjani. Make sure your brother knows that. Dion banished Benny and Jorge five years ago. And those other men, they're sea fada. They're not from Rock Run."

Two sea fada. He hadn't gotten a good look at them, but they must've been the two Greek sea fada Dion had banished to the Sahara. Nothing else fit. *How the hell did they escape—and why hadn't Dion and Cleia been informed?*

She nodded. "I'll tell him."

They turned onto a busier street. They were in Canton now, a fast-growing neighborhood of loft apartments and well-kept brick rowhomes scattered among upscale restaurants, shops and other businesses. People glanced at their grim, bruised faces and steered a wide path around the two of them, which was fine as far as Tiago was concerned.

Marjani was flagging. He went to put his arm around her shoulders and then halted, recalling how she'd flinched when he tried to touch her before.

"Maybe we should call a taxi." His hand went to his pants pocket before he remembered that Jorge and his friends had ripped him off. He swore under his breath. "The pricks didn't leave me any money. But we can pay when we get to the hotel."

She hesitated and then nodded. "Okay." It was the first she'd admitted to any weakness; she must be feeling even worse than she was letting on.

"Look," he said. "You're exhausted. If you don't let me help you, we'll never get there." He set an arm around her back, keeping the touch light but supportive.

She stiffened, but when he lifted his arm, she said, "No. Keep it there, please. I need touch."

"Okay, then." He stepped to the curb and raised a hand. A taxi swerved in their direction, but as soon as the driver got a look at them, he swung back to the middle lane and continued by, his gaze resolutely straight ahead.

Tiago let loose a vivid curse but Marjani just shook her head.

"Hey, we're fada—and we look like hell."

Tiago slanted her a wry look. "We do look pretty damn bad, don't we?"

She tilted her head. Her lips lifted in a ghost of a smile. "I don't know; that purple bruise under your eye adds a certain something. I'm not sure about the split lip, though."

He shook his head at her, but he smiled, too. "Let's go to the corner," he said and started walking again. "They'll have to stop at the light and then I'll be damned if they ignore us. If I have to, I'll stand in front of it and refuse to let it move."

Unfortunately, when they reached the corner, there were no cabs to be seen. Marjani's shoulders slumped.

"Hey." He gave her a squeeze as he scanned the street for the familiar yellow vehicles. "Just another few minutes. Can you do that?"

She lifted her chin. "Of course," she said and slid him a look. "Sorry. I'm not usually so weak."

"I can tell that." In fact, she reminded him of Rosana: slim, almost delicate in appearance, but with a rock-solid core. "And you have nothing to be sorry about."

Deus, when he thought about what they'd done to her—what *he'd* almost done. The woman had been through hell: drugged and assaulted, then on top of that, spent the night frozen in place by the compulsion he'd put on her—and terrified he was going to wake up and attack her, too. It was a wonder she was holding up as well as she was.

Another taxi approached. Tiago gave an imperious wave, but the driver took one look at them and continued past. Tiago growled.

"Maybe we should just keep walking," Marjani said.

"Give me a couple more minutes. Here, why don't you sit on

the bench?" He guided her to a nearby bus stop and helped her sit, staying close by as he continued to scan the street.

She looked down at her hands. "All I wanted was to have some fun with my friends. I wasn't drinking. I never have more than a beer or two. One of them knew this Greek guy—Orius. We talked, had a dance. I didn't see his friend. Not then. But it was another Greek sea fada. He must have drugged my wine while I was dancing with Orius. I—they pulled me over to meet you and Jorge and Benny. The next thing I knew we were in that room. You were on the floor and the two of them pushed me down—" Her voice broke. She raised her hand toward her throat again, dropped it back to her side.

"Marjani—"

"I'm glad you killed him," she said in a hard voice. "I just wish you'd gotten the others, too."

He swallowed. "Look, I'm sorry. For everything, especially my part in it."

"It wasn't your fault. You were drugged, the same as I was."

"Yeah, but I knew better. I knew Jorge was bad, but I thought I could handle him. I promise, he's a dead man. I'll kill him myself if I have to."

She nodded jerkily.

Suddenly every hair on his body stood on end. He swung around, but he was already surrounded by four large, growling earth shifters. He snatched the switchblade from his back pocket and flicked the catch.

"No, wait," Marjani cried. "I know these men."

Tiago hesitated, and in an instant, they were on him, two of them taking hold of his arms while the third got him in a choke-hold from behind. The fourth pressed a pistol to Tiago's temple.

He froze. It was the shifter from the bar, Luc, his eyes a night-glow orange, his animal to the fore.

"Drop the knife," he ordered in guttural tones.

Well, Tiago thought wryly, at least Marjani was safe.

But the other man was enraged. Sparks of light shimmered around him, his animal trying to force a shift. "Drop the knife," he repeated, "before I put a bullet through your skull."

"Okay, okay. Take it easy." Tiago let the switchblade clatter to the sidewalk, but Luc wasn't appeased.

He pushed the gun harder into Tiago's skull. "What the fuck did you do to her? And I want the truth."

Tiago opened his mouth, but Marjani pushed herself between him and Tiago. "No, Luc. It wasn't him. He didn't do anything. He was helping me, damn it."

"Stay out of this, Jani." Luc used one hand to set her gently but firmly aside without removing his gaze from Tiago's.

Around them, a small crowd of humans was gaping at them, mouths open. A few had their smartphones out, filming the encounter, and in the distance sirens sounded.

Great. Not only was this going to be on YouTube, somebody had called 911. Dion was going to kill him.

If Luc didn't first.

Tiago forced himself to stare calmly into the earth shifter's glowing eyes. It didn't help that his own beast was still agitated from last night. It moved angrily beneath Tiago's skin, itching to take on all four men, especially the wolf who dared threaten him.

Blood.

Kill.

And Tiago was on a thin-enough edge today that he was tempted to allow the darkness out to play.

But he knew that would be the final straw as far as Dion was concerned. His brother would have no choice but to banish Tiago.

And even though it might be for the best if Tiago left Rock Run, he couldn't quite make himself do it. No other clan would welcome a man with his Gift; he'd be forced to either hide it or live as a solitary. He'd had a taste of the solitary life five years ago, when he'd run away rather than face Dion after betraying

Cleia's location to the earth fada, and he'd hated it. Without the brakes on the beast exerted by his brother's dominance and the clan's calming influence, he'd nearly gone feral—in a very short time.

"What did you do, river fada?" Luc asked. "I can smell the sex on her. And I know she wouldn't have given herself to you willingly."

The man at Tiago's neck tightened his grip.

Tiago concentrated on breathing as best as he could and ordered his beast to stand down. "She didn't. And I didn't. If you'd just give me a chance, I can explain."

"Who then?"

Marjani shoved herself back between Luc and Tiago again. "Damn it, Luc, will you listen to me? You've got the wrong man. He saved me from them. I swear to God, if you hurt him, I'll—" She drew a sobbing breath.

"From who?"

"I—don't make me tell you here in front of everyone. All you need to know is that Tiago helped me. He was taking me to Adric."

Luc glanced at Marjani. "This is true?"

"Yes. I swear it."

Tiago moistened his lips. "You heard her," he said in even tones. "I didn't hurt your female. Put down the gun and I'll explain, but you need to calm down." He wasn't deliberately trying to tap into his Gift, but in the stress of the moment, he couldn't help pressing a little.

The sparks dissipated. Luc slowly lowered the gun and shoved it into a holster beneath his arm. The other man eased up on the chokehold and Tiago gulped in some much-needed oxygen.

Then Luc growled. Knocking the other man's arm out of the way, he grabbed Tiago's throat. His claws had sprouted. They dug into Tiago's skin and he scented his own blood.

"You—you're trying to hypnotize me somehow. What the hell are you?"

"Let. Him. Go." Marjani grabbed his arm. "It doesn't matter. He saved me, I'm telling you."

She'd finally gotten through to the man. His grip eased and he darted a glance at Marjani. "He saved you?"

"Yes. That's the truth, Luc—you'd know if I were lying."

He nodded, then growled again. "You let him touch you. I smell him on you."

"It was only his arm, and that was because I needed help to walk. He was taking me to Adric. I'm—I need to get to him, Luc. Please?"

Luc scowled but released Tiago, and his men did the same. "You can explain this to the alpha," he told Tiago.

Tiago rubbed his throat ruefully. "That was the plan, to take your female to her brother. But you don't need me now. I'll—"

The three men surrounded him, making it clear he wasn't going anywhere without their say-so.

"You're coming with us," Luc said evenly. "If what you say is true, you have nothing to fear."

"Sorry," Marjani told Tiago, "but he's a stubborn SOB. Just come along. Please. Adric will want to talk to you anyway."

Luc bared his teeth. "Or I'll rip your fucking throat out."

The three men shoved Tiago forward without waiting for a reply. Luc took Marjani's arm and kept her on his other side, making sure both he and another man were between her and Tiago.

"Look," Tiago said, "I was trying to call a cab when you found us. She's hurt, exhausted—I'm not sure how much farther she can go."

Luc scowled, but turned to the nearest man. "Call Beau. Tell him we need transport for five people."

The man nodded and, touching his quartz, relayed the message.

The sirens grew to an ear-splitting pitch and three patrol cars skidded to a halt on the road next to them. Two men and a woman exited, shouting, "Freeze." Three Glocks were trained on them.

"Raise your hands," the woman ordered. "Now."

Tiago sighed and obeyed.

11

———

Marjani raised her hands, and, summoning what must have been her last ounce of energy, called, "I can explain. I'm Lord Adric's second in command."

"His sister," the female officer said.

"Yes."

The woman motioned Marjani forward. "Talk. The rest of you keep your hands where we can see them."

Tiago watched in admiration as Marjani handled the police officers with a mixture of charm and diplomacy. She assured them it was all a mistake, and it wouldn't happen again.

"Lord Adric would apologize personally if he were here," she added. "But I promise, he'll deal with these men. He's ordered that there be no public altercations."

"I'm glad to hear that," the woman replied, "but you tell your brother to get his house in order. The captain won't be happy to hear we got called out for a pack of rutting shifters."

Marjani stiffened but inclined her head. "I'll make sure he knows."

By then, Beau had arrived in a roomy gray sedan. He was a beefy, slow-talking man; Tiago would bet good money his animal was a bear. The police left and Beau ushered them into the car, Luc and Marjani in the front seat, the other three men in the back seat with Tiago. They made sure he was in the middle, of course.

Before Beau could start the car, Marjani said, "Shania. Is she all right?"

"I don't know. Why?" But Luc already had his quartz out. He tapped it a couple of times. "Shania? You there?"

She answered in the affirmative and Marjani heaved a sigh of relief.

"We found Marjani," Luc told her.

"Thank the gods. Where was she?"

Marjani shook her head.

"She'll explain when she sees you." Luc signed off and put an arm around Marjani. She let out a small breath and rested her head on his shoulder. "So Adric's going to deal with us, hm?"

"I had to say something to get them off your asses. But you know the rules. Adric's not going to be happy, especially since you're a lieutenant."

Luc grunted. "You should see your face, Jani. If Adric had found you first, that river fada would already be dead."

"And that would've been a big mistake," she returned, "because that river fada happens to be Tiago do Rio. Dion's brother."

"I know. I met him last night at the Full Moon—when I told him to stay the fuck away from our women." Luc turned his head to glare at Tiago. "Maybe next time you'll listen."

Tiago stared back. He was fed up with Luc's posturing. He was the man's equal in dominance, and it was time he acknowledged it. "This had nothing to do with the woman."

"Tell it to Lord Adric."

They held each other's gazes for another moment and then Marjani shifted, her breath hitching as if even that small movement was painful, and the earth shifter's attention snapped back to her.

"And I'm telling you, Luc," she said, "that he helped me. So lay the fuck off."

He grunted again, clearly not convinced, but stopped trying to out-stare Tiago. "You're hurting, baby. Why don't we drop you off at Suha's? I can handle this."

She shook her head. "I need to see Adric, make sure he understands what happened."

"If you're sure—" He smoothed a hand over her hair, then stilled. "Where's your quartz?"

"They smashed it. The men who kidnapped me."

"Christ," muttered Luc. He pressed a kiss to her temple. "I looked for you after you left the bar last night. I thought you were doing something to block me again. If I'd known where you were—"

"I *was* blocking you. You and Adric both. And yeah, go ahead and tell me how stupid that was. I deserve it."

He shook his head. "Oh, Jani. I—"

The three men in the backseat with Tiago murmured agitatedly among themselves.

Tiago ignored them to lean forward, forearms on his knees. Now that he didn't have Marjani to worry about, his own aches and pains were making themselves felt again. It didn't help that he was stuffed into a car with five earth shifters itching for vengeance, and that his own beast was still edgy and lashing its figurative tail.

He gritted his teeth and told himself that it was only for a few minutes.

Right about the time he decided he either had to bust out of there or lose it, Beau stopped the car in front of the hotel, a concrete-and-glass edifice overlooking the Inner Harbor, and the six of them piled out. It was getting on lunchtime and the streets were crowded with a mix of tourists and office workers, but just as last night in Spanish Town, the crowd parted for them like water around a cluster of massive boulders. Even if you didn't know they were fada, nobody was going to mess with five large, stony-eyed men.

Luc sent one of the men with Beau to park the car, ordered the other two to follow with Tiago and headed up the wide marble steps with Marjani.

She glanced over her shoulder at Tiago. "The meeting is on the second floor."

He nodded as the five of them entered the lobby. A large, well-dressed clerk appeared from behind the mahogany desk and planted himself in their path. "Pardon me, sirs, madam. How may I help you?"

"You can't," Luc snapped. He gave the clerk a look that made him blink, and kept moving so that the man had to step aside or be bowled over.

Marjani made a sound of exasperation and tugged Luc to a halt. "We're here for the meeting in the Harborview Room," she told the clerk. "I'm Lord Adric's sister."

"Excellent," the man said with a wary look at Luc. He did a double-take at Tiago's face. "Go right ahead," he said, and with an elegant bow took refuge behind his desk.

"Damn it, Luc," Marjani said as they mounted the stairs to the second floor, "how many times do I have to tell you to play nice?"

"The human should know to stay out of my way."

She shook her head and Tiago grinned, even though it hurt his cut lip.

As they reached the second floor, two earth fada sentries stepped forward, halting them. Beyond them, Tiago saw Artan standing shoulder to shoulder with Grady in front of a door that led to what he assumed was the meeting room, and a few feet away, two Rock Run *tenentes*, Ed and Davi. The sun fae males took in Tiago's battered state but remained at their stations, but Ed and Davi rushed forward.

Meanwhile, the earth fada sentries were greeting Marjani and

Luc. "Marjani," the taller one said with a sidelong look at Tiago, "Adric has men out looking for you."

She didn't stiffen her spine or visibly raise her chin, but suddenly she was every inch the alpha's second in command. "Does he? Then let me pass."

"Of course." But he shot another look at Tiago, clearly wondering what a river fada was doing with his alpha's sister—and why he looked as if he'd been in a brawl.

Marjani made an impatient sound. "This is Lord Dion's brother. Now, get out of the way, Corban."

The sentry's cold dark eyes narrowed, but at that moment Ed and Davi came up on either side of him and the other sentry.

"What's the problem?" Ed growled.

Before Tiago could explain, the door to the meeting room opened and Dion exited, checking that the hall was safe for Cleia to enter. He saw Tiago and put a hand out to stop Cleia.

"Wait here," he told her and strode toward their little group.

Adric was right behind him. "Marjani. Where the hell have you been? I've got half the clan out looking for you." He pulled her into a tight hug. She stiffened and he released her, frowning. "What is it, Jani? What's—"

He halted and lifted one of her hands, staring at the bracelet of fingerprint-sized bruises marring her skin. Tiago had been too out of it back in the rowhouse to understand their full import, but now he realized someone had held her down by the wrists.

Adric's gaze traveled to the ugly splotches higher up her arms. "What the *fuck* happened?" Without giving his sister a chance to answer, he shot a dangerous look at Tiago. "And why the hell are you with do Rio?

"I'd like to know that, too," interjected Dion. "What's going on, Tiago?"

And then Cleia came up, flanked by Artan and Grady, and suddenly everyone was talking at once, demanding to know what had happened.

Marjani passed a hand over her face. "I—"

"For God's sake," Tiago interjected, "leave her alone. Can't you see she's hurt? She needs to sit down, not—"

Adric swung toward Tiago. "What the fuck business is it of yours?"

Tiago's nostrils flared. Beneath his skin, the beast bristled. He glared back at Adric. He was injured, hung-over from that damn aphrodisiac—and sick unto death of the Baltimore shifters trying to push him around. The beast clawed at his insides, demanding blood.

And, by the gods, he was tempted.

"Enough." Cleia's low voice cut through the hubbub. She turned to the hurt woman. "What would you like to do, Marjani?"

Marjani shot her a grateful look. "I'll answer your questions, Ric. But please, not in the hall."

The earth alpha's face softened. "Of course, babe. Why don't we use the conference room?"

"All right. But not everyone—just you and them." She indicated Cleia, Dion and Tiago. "I don't...I can't—" Her face crumpled and she turned into his shoulder.

Luc made a movement toward her, but checked himself.

"Jani?" Adric rubbed her back, his expression taut. "Calm down. We'll do anything you say." He jerked his head at his men and they withdrew a few feet.

Cleia moved to Marjani's other side and slid an arm around her waist. "It's all right. You're safe now." She and Adric steered Marjani down the hall to the conference room.

Dion gave Tiago a searching look, then jerked his head for Tiago to precede him down the hall.

Inside the room, Adric guided his sister to a seat at the large black table, then removed his quartz pendant. "Here, kitten. Put this on." He stepped behind her chair and hung it around her neck.

"Thank you," she whispered, wrapping her fingers around it. "They smashed mine. It's—the pieces are in the harbor now."

Adric's fingers closed on the back of her chair, white-knuckled. "Who?"

His bronze eyes flashed an eerie metallic blue and narrowed on Tiago. It was like looking into the heart of a flame. Tiago had to lock his knees to keep from taking a step back.

Dion moved in front of Cleia, instinctively putting himself between her and the furious man.

"Ric," said Marjani. "It wasn't him. I swear it."

Adric inhaled, visibly regaining control of his animal. Removing his hands from the chair, he took the seat beside Marjani with Cleia on her other side. Dion sat at the end of the table next to his mate, which left Tiago opposite Adric and Marjani.

"Talk," the Baltimore alpha barked at him.

Tiago glanced at Marjani, who gave him a small nod. "I was out drinking at the Full Moon and I ran into a Baltimore shifter. A woman. She invited me to an afterhours club. The Wildcat."

"Who? I want her name."

Tiago hesitated. He hadn't forgotten that Shania hadn't wanted the men in her clan to know that she was flirting with a Rock Run male. But there had been that odd interest in him and Jorge, as if she'd deliberately brought the two of them together.

Marjani spoke up. "It was Shania. But she didn't leave the Wildcat with us."

Adric nodded without saying anything, but Tiago knew he must be wondering what Shania had been up to.

"At the club," Tiago continued, "I ran into some river fada I know." He met his brother's eyes. "Jorge and Benny."

Dion's expression didn't change but Tiago could see him absorbing the implications. "How?" he asked coldly.

"Hell if I know, but it was Jorge and Benny all right. I had a couple of drinks with them—that's when they drugged me. The next thing I knew we were in a rowhouse on the east side." He gave the name of the street. "There were four men by then—Jorge and Benny and two others. I didn't get a good look at them, but I'm betting they were those two Greek sea fada—the ones who were part of Okeanos's den. Anyway, I passed out. Apparently they gave me too much of the drug on top of the drinking I'd already done. And Marjani, well—"

He cut his eyes at Marjani and halted. Across the table, her breath shuddered in.

Adric turned his head to glare at Dion. "You know these men? They're yours?"

"They were. At least, Jorge and Benny were—I don't know about the other two, but I suspect I know who they are. I banished all four of them five years ago."

"Why?"

Dion's mouth flattened. "For attacking Valeria and Merry," he admitted.

"It was them? And you left them alive?"

"Four of them. Rui killed the leader in a mate-duel. I sentenced the other four to live out their lives in the desert. Jorge and Benny—we were friends, once, and Jorge was one of my *tenentes*. So like an idiot, I showed them mercy."

"But for a water fada," Cleia interjected, "that was a harsh punishment—to be kept from the water like that...it's a living death."

Both men ignored her. "Still, somehow they escaped," Adric said in a neutral tone. "In less than five years."

"Yes." Dion's jaw clenched so hard Tiago feared he'd crack a tooth.

"Orius." Marjani spoke into the fraught silence. "I don't know the other's name, but Orius is the one I met at the Wildcat."

Dion cursed. "It's them all right. The four men I banished were Jorge, Benny, and two Greek sea fada named Orius and Mys." He turned back to Tiago. "Did they—"

"Yes. They must have drugged us with the same aphrodisiac, the one Okeanos used on Valeria."

"An aphrodisiac?" Adric repeated. "You mean a love potion?"

Marjani pressed a fist to her mouth. "I didn't even want to fight back," she said lowly.

"Oh, sweetheart." Cleia rubbed the younger woman's back. "Don't be so hard on yourself. It wasn't you; it was the drug."

Adric's hand went to where his quartz should've been. When he didn't find it, his fingers curled into a fist which he set back on the table, softly, menacingly.

"I want the truth, Jani." He jerked his chin in Tiago's direction. "I don't care if he was fucked out of his mind. Was he a part of it?"

"No." Marjani had been looking down at the table, but now she lifted her head and met her brother's eyes. "He's telling the truth. They drugged him, too—put it in his whiskey while they were still in the club. I heard them boasting about it. When he came out of it, he fought back. If it wasn't for Tiago, I'd still— they'd still have me. He saved me."

Tiago tensed, waiting for her to get to the part where he'd turned into a beast, but all she said was, "He didn't lay a hand on me. And I know he wanted to." She swallowed noisily. "But he didn't."

Adric speared his fingers through his hair, leaving the bleached spikes sticking straight up. "Then I owe you my thanks," he told Tiago.

Tiago jerked his head in acknowledgement, although he didn't deserve the man's thanks.

"If it would help," Dion told Marjani, "I could send a man to retrieve your quartz."

She shook her head. "I appreciate the offer, but no. They broke it into pieces too tiny for me to use."

"So let me understand," Adric said to Dion. "These men are outcasts."

"That's right."

"And you had a chance to kill them and you let them go."

"I banished them, *sim*." Dion gazed back steadily, refusing to meet the challenge Adric was all but flinging in his face, but not backing down either. Tiago knew how hard it must be for his brother to allow a man a third his age to reprimand him. "A mistake—one I'll never make again."

"A mistake," Adric repeated scornfully. "My sister was drugged and raped, you sonofabitch. Because of your fucking *mistake*."

Dion ignored him to look at Marjani. "All I can say is that I'm sorry. Believe me, *senhorita*, if I'd known this was going to happen, I'd never have let them leave Rock Run alive."

She gave a jerky nod.

Adric rose to his feet. "Let's get out of here, Jan—"

"There's more," Tiago interjected. "Benny's dead."

The earth alpha retook his seat. "You?" He eyed Tiago with something like respect.

"Yes. We fought, and I—killed him."

"Then I owe you doubly."

Tiago felt a wave of self-loathing. Hell, he'd come close to raping Marjani himself. If he hadn't thought about Alesia at that moment...

"You don't owe me a damn thing. If I hadn't been so drunk, they'd never have hurt your sister."

"But she might still be there if you hadn't fought them off."

Tiago moved a shoulder. "I suppose."

"They're mine." Adric shoved away from the table and stood up. "I claim them."

"No." Dion rose too. "This is my problem. I'll clean it up."

"Yeah?" Adric's lip curled. "Will you have the balls to execute your friend Jorge this time? Or will you just slap him on the wrist so he can keep hurting women?"

Marjani placed a hand on his arm. "Adric, please—"

He covered her hand with his own but continued to glare at Dion. "Tell me. How would you feel if she were your sister —Rosana?"

Tiago stiffened. They'd certainly done their homework. Dion kept Rosana close, rarely letting her leave Rock Run. But then he recalled how Adric had stared at Rosana five years ago at the mating ball. The man had actually had the balls to ask her to dance. Tiago had been gone by then, but a couple of Rock Run males had run him off.

Dion's mouth tightened. "I'd want to rip off their goddamn *colhões* and feed them to the fishes."

"Then we understand each other. It's my sister. My territory. I claim them. Let's go, Jani." Adric helped his sister to her feet. She couldn't conceal a wince, and anguish flashed across his face.

But when he spoke, his voice was soothing. "Oh, baby. I'm sorry we kept you here so long. First thing we'll do is call a healer."

Tiago and Cleia stood as well. The sun fae queen touched Marjani. "I'd be happy to help. I'm a healer as well."

Marjani shook her head. "Thank you, but I just want to go home."

"Again," Adric said to Cleia, "peace, and our thanks. But I'd prefer to get her to our own healer." He set a hand on the small of his sister's back and started for the door.

"Wait," Dion said.

Adric halted. "What?" he asked without turning around.

"I haven't agreed to your claim. Jorge and the others are my problem. I'll take care of them."

"Like you did before?" Adric twisted his head so they could see his sneer. "No thanks."

Dion went rigid. His expression didn't change, but everyone in the room stilled, even Adric, the scornful look fading from his face. Tension thrummed in the air like a struck tuning fork.

A beat passed. Two.

"That was a mistake," Dion replied evenly. "One for which I accept full responsibility. But since it's my mistake, I'll take care of it. Jorge's life is mine, as well as the other two. For one thing, if they're in the water, you'll have the devil of a time tracking them."

Adric glanced at his sister, then scowled. "Three days—that's all I'll give you. After that I'm going after the bastards if I have to follow them into Hades itself."

Dion inclined his head. "Fair enough."

Adric helped Marjani from the room.

Grady appeared in the doorway. "My queen?"

"Give us a few minutes," she said with a glance at Dion, and he withdrew.

As soon as the door closed, Dion slammed his palm onto the table. "Damn Jorge and Benny anyway. I should've slit their sorry throats when I had a chance. And how the hell did they escape? They swore an oath on their true-names. Breaking a vow like that should be tearing them up from the inside out."

"That's something I'd like to know myself," said Tiago.

"And why haven't I been contacted?" Cleia added. "I expected Lord Okot to keep me updated about all four of them."

Dion growled. He sliced a glance at Tiago and switched to Portuguese. "What I don't understand is why? Why you, Tiago?"

"Easy pickings," he said bitterly. "I happened to be there and I was stupid enough to drink with them. But I'm also your brother."

"Maybe they were trying to disrupt today's meeting," Cleia said.

Tiago nodded. "Jorge hates you," he told Dion. "He's got to be pissed at seeing how the clan is doing so much better since you and Cleia mated. He'd do anything to cause trouble for you."

"Well," said Dion, "as far as I'm concerned, this is war. All three of them are dead—by sunset if I have my way."

"Maybe I could help," Cleia started to say.

Dion was by her side in two large strides. He grasped her

shoulders and gave her a little shake. "Don't even think of it. I don't want you within a mile of him—especially now. *Entendes*?"

She blinked up at him. "Yes, of course. But—"

"I mean it, woman. If he somehow got hold of you—"

"Hey." She cupped his cheek in her hand. "Don't worry. I'm stronger than him, remember?"

"Maybe. Maybe not. But that's not the point. Promise me, Cleia. I want to hear you say it."

She rolled her eyes but did as he asked. "I promise."

"*Bom*." Keeping an arm around her, he turned back to Tiago, taking in the bruises, the wrinkled, pungent T-shirt, the day-old growth of beard. "*Deus*, Tiago. They worked you over, didn't they? What the hell were you doing in that bar anyway?"

"Not now," Cleia said. "He's hurt, Dion. Let me help him."

"I'm fine," gritted Tiago.

His brother just shook his head. "Where's Benny, anyway? I'd better send some men to clean that up—unless Jorge got there first."

Tiago gave him the address. Dion called Ed and Davi into the room and explained what needed to be done. Benny would be feeding the fish by the evening.

With them gone, Dion turned his attention back to Tiago. "Now talk. I want to know exactly what happened. I believe I ordered you to stay away from Baltimore and the earth shifters."

"You said stay away from the earth shifters, not Baltimore."

"And having a drink with an earth shifter female is your idea of staying away from them?"

"No." Tiago met his brother's angry scowl. "I disobeyed a direct order. I spoke with an earth shifter at the Full Moon, too. One of Adric's *tenentes*—Luc. I saw a chance at finding out what the earth shifters were up to, and I took it. And you know what? I'd do it again. Because if I wouldn't have had the run-in with Jorge and Benny, I might have gotten some useful information."

Dion brought a hand up and squeezed his nape. "*Deus, irmão.*"

Tiago squared his shoulders. "I have no excuses. I deliberately disobeyed you. I'm ready to take the consequences."

"What about Jorge? How did he get involved?"

"He came to our table, wanted to buy me a drink. I told him no but he did it anyway."

"And? Did he have you tied to your seat so you couldn't haul your ass out of there?"

"Dion, please." Cleia placed a hand on her mate's arm. "This can wait, can't it? He needs healing."

Dion stared at Tiago, his jaw tight. But what cut deep was the disappointment shading his eyes. "Fine." He stalked across the room to stare out at the harbor.

Cleia pointed Tiago to a seat beside a window on the other side of the room. "Sit down and I'll see what I can do."

He sank into the chair she indicated. The adrenaline that had sent him across Baltimore in order to see Marjani safe had completely dissipated, leaving him drained and aching. His head was pounding and his body felt like one big bruise. Even breathing hurt.

Cleia had, of course, set him in a shaft of sunlight. As a sun fae, she drew energy from the sun; it would boost her Gift of healing.

He closed his eyes against the brightness and let his chin sink to his chest. Cleia's hands settled on his shoulders. He gave an involuntary sigh as energy undulated through him in slow waves, seeking out his bruised and battered places. Warming...soothing...repairing.

She couldn't heal him completely, but she could speed the process. A sense of well-being spread through him, like sunbathing on a river bank after a hard swim.

When she released him, he fingered the bump on his head in wonder. It had shrunk to half its former size and the pain had faded to a dull ache. He moved a hand to his ribs. They felt as if they'd had a week to heal.

He caught Cleia's hand. "Thank you."

The sun was behind her, making a halo of her multicolored hair. She inclined her head, her smile kind. She appeared beautiful yet remote—like the sunrise or a far-off star.

She glanced at Dion, still gazing out at the harbor, hands behind his back. He turned around as if she'd called his name. Their eyes met and her smile broadened. Tiago could almost feel the electricity arcing between them.

And in that moment, he knew he'd never have her. She was his brother's, body and soul.

He released her hand and looked away. *Deus*, he was an ass. Because even though he'd known the mate bond was rare and special—fae and fada seldom mated twice, even if one of the pair died young—he'd stubbornly held out hope.

"You all right?" His brother's gruff voice broke into his thoughts.

He came to his feet. "Yeah." His body, anyway.

"*Bom*. Now what the fuck happened in that rowhouse? And I want the whole story this time."

12

———

"The whole story?" Tiago repeated.

Like all fada—water or earth—he could trace his lineage back to the god Dionysus himself. The fada had been born in the god's wine-soaked bacchanals, and the ancient lusts called to them like a siren's song, dark, enticing, the god's blood a seductive midnight ribbon weaving through the braid of fae, human and animal genes.

Tiago didn't attribute his beast to his animal heritage. He placed the blame for it squarely at the god's door: Dionysus, born from the seed of a god and a human. Dionysus and his reckless, raw carnality. Dionysus and his tart purple grapes and rich red wine and wild orgies that lasted until the participants slumped to the ground unconscious.

From Dionysus had come the god's touch, a black beast of a power that was tempting, so goddamn tempting—

"Yes," Dion replied. "I know damn well there's more than what you told Adric. I want the truth, Tiago. The whole truth."

Tiago squeezed his nape. The truth was he could kill a man with a thought.

But how did you tell your brother that? And not just your

brother—the man who'd raised you from the time you were a pup.

Dion and Cleia scrutinized him: his brother with growing impatience, the sun fae queen thoughtfully.

"Well?" Dion demanded.

Cleia took a seat. "Whatever you say won't leave this room. I promise you that."

The first he'd known of his second Gift had been three years ago. He'd been on a mission, his first as a fully invested Rock Run warrior. He and a squad of four other men had been sent to Mexico to wipe out a nest of rogue night fae who were kidnapping and torturing the local sea fada.

Tiago had cornered the last, most vicious night fae. The man had fought hard and dirty—trying to generate enough negative emotion in Tiago to incapacitate him—but Tiago was ready for that. He fought back, cold and merciless. When the night fae saw he'd lost, he'd muttered a spell to 'port out of there.

Something raw and very primitive awoke in Tiago: the beast, enraged that the prey was escaping.

Tiago narrowed his eyes and ordered the man to freeze—and the night fae had, to his astonishment.

Tiago had moved in and slit the man's throat—a quick, clean death. The other man had never moved. It had been easy, like shooting fish in a barrel.

Too damn easy.

Shaken, Tiago stared down at the dead man as the beast, coldly satisfied, settled back into whatever shadowy corner in Tiago's soul he called home.

The squad leader ran up and clapped him on the back. "Good job, do Rio."

"Thanks," Tiago replied automatically. Numbly, he helped the others clean up, knowing he could tell no one, not even Dion. *Especially* not Dion.

This was more than the animal that was a part of all fada. This was dark. A beast.

If word got out, he'd be an instant outsider, feared and likely shunned. The fada knew what his Gift did to a man—and it was nearly always men who inherited it. He might start out with good intentions, but a fada male was a hard, ruthless creature to begin with. The temptation to use such a Gift was damn near irresistible.

After experimenting enough to understand how the Gift worked, Tiago had decided not to use it again unless absolutely necessary. For the most part, he'd kept to that decision, using compulsion only when his safety or that of the clan was threatened. But each time he called on it, he lost another piece of his soul to the primitive black beast.

He was terrified that sooner or later he'd break and use his Gift for less honorable purposes.

Just because he could.

Dion was speaking. "May I remind you," he said, "that I'm not just your brother, I'm your alpha. And I want to know what in Hades is going on. You're a strong, promising fighter, but there's no way you can take on four grown fada and win."

"No?" Something snapped in Tiago. He was tired of hiding what he was. He was tired of his brother treating him as if he were still wet behind the ears. He was tired, period. "Fine," he snarled. "You want to know how I killed Benny? Come here. *Now*."

He let the beast rise, bent their combined will on his brother.

Dion's eyes widened, then narrowed. He cursed and gritted his teeth, resisting with everything he had. His chest heaved, the powerful muscles straining against his shirt. A button popped off and flew across the room.

Cleia gasped and came partway to her feet, hands on the chair's armrests. "Stop it, Tiago. *Now*."

"He asked," Tiago replied, his gaze locked on his brother. He beckoned with his fingers. "Come, *irmão*. To me."

Dion growled low in his throat. "No, damn you."

A blood vessel beat in his temple. His face was beaded with sweat. A part of Tiago couldn't help being impressed at his brother's strength of will.

Dion almost succeeded in throwing off the compulsion. Then his foot slid forward.

One step. Then another and another.

Tiago was dimly aware that Cleia had come to her feet and was muttering to herself. Energy crackled at the tips of her fingers. He knew she could knock him out—or for that matter, stop his heart for good—but he didn't care. She raised her hands and he tensed, but for some reason she held her fire.

Dion glared at Tiago, his eyes the icy, feral silver of his animal. He had a Gift for drawing on energy himself, but he was using everything he had to resist the compulsion. "Let. Me. Go."

Tiago held him for another heartbeat. Then he flicked his fingers and released the compulsion.

Dion's breath whooshed out. For a moment, the two of them stared at each other. Then Dion had Tiago by the throat.

"Don't *ever* do that again," he gritted. "Not unless you're prepared to challenge me for alpha." He gave Tiago a shake. "Understand?"

Tiago kept his eyes down, acknowledging his brother's dominance. For now. He forced himself to reply calmly. "Yes. But you asked."

"*Deus*." Dion thrust Tiago from him. He paced away, then back. "How long have you known?"

"Three years."

"Three fucking years? When were you going to tell me?"

"I don't know. I—" Tiago sank into a chair, head in his hands. All Cleia's energy had gone into healing his body, and after the night he'd had, a confrontation with his alpha was the last thing he needed. He felt weary to his very bones. "I'm not sure I was ever going to tell you."

"Does it work on anyone?" asked Cleia. "The fae, for instance?"

Tiago nodded. "I've used it on both fae and fada, although never anyone from Rock Run. Mainly I used it when I was out on a mission. And animals—that's how I learned to control it."

"Three years." His brother scrutinized him. "And you've controlled it all that time."

"Yes."

He flashed to that acorn on Alesia's island. He'd been closer to losing control that morning than he'd ever been. A seemingly small thing, to force it to grow. It hadn't even been a seedling, merely the possibility of one. But his stomach twisted, remembering. The acorn had been pure potential, innocence at its most basic—and he'd destroyed it.

He *was* turning into a monster.

"You've never used it on anyone in the clan?" Dion asked.

His head snapped up. "No. I swear I haven't."

Dion inhaled, no doubt testing his words for truth, then nodded. "You can use it to kill? That's how Benny died?"

"Yes. I don't remember everything that happened, but I ordered him to die—and he did. And there was a night fae that time my squad was in Mexico. I told him to halt and he froze. That's when I slit his throat."

"Suppose," said Dion, almost to himself, "that you *could* control it. What a warrior you'd—"

"No," Tiago interrupted. "You still don't understand."

"Dion," Cleia murmured.

He glanced at her, then jerked his chin at Tiago. "So tell me. Help me understand."

"This isn't something I can turn on and off like a fucking switch. It's like a dark beast, chewing on my soul. Every time I give in to it, every time I use it, it takes another piece of me. That's the kind of weapon it is. One that eats the user from the inside out—and grows stronger each time." Tiago scrubbed his hands over his face. "Hell, I can barely keep it in check now. If I call on it regularly, *invite* it out, God knows what'll happen."

His brother's expression held a mix of pity and compassion. "I'm sorry, *irmão*."

The last thing Tiago had expected was pity. It seared him to the bone, especially coming from the man he most wanted to impress.

He rose abruptly to his feet, afraid that if he remained here much longer, he'd do something he'd regret, like challenge his own brother for dominance. "Look," he said, "I feel like frigging shit warmed over. I need to get into the water. I'll see you back at the base in a day or two. Okay?"

Dion nodded. "All right. You have twenty-four hours, but only because you'll heal more quickly as your animal. You're to report to me by noon tomorrow. Is that clear? There's still the matter of your disobeying orders."

"I'll be there."

"Tiago." Cleia rose from the chair, hands outstretched. "Please—"

He swung around to face her. Something in his face made her recoil.

He smiled grimly. "Yes," he said. "You, at least, understand."

13

$\mathcal{A}$dric half-led, half-carried Marjani through the blighted neighborhood he called home, Zuri on her other side. There were plenty of good people here in East Baltimore, but they stayed inside where it was safe. They passed a couple of moms with children, but also a pimp snarling at one of his girls and a well-dressed man strung-out from heroin and slumped on a cracked marble stoop.

Adric barely glanced at them. Not even the most broken, feral human was stupid enough to mess with three fada, and his underground den was concealed from the magical world by a fae ward.

They picked their way around two plump rats gleefully rooting through a trash bag. Marjani stumbled over a break in the sidewalk and sagged against him. He could feel the rapid flutter of her heart, hear her short, shallow breaths. She was going into shock.

Rage sucked the air from his lungs. His cougar rose up and nearly took control. But even the animal knew that would just make things worse. It subsided to pace agitatedly beneath Adric's skin.

The hell with this. He swung his sister into his arms. "Hang on, Jani. We're almost there."

"I'm sorry, Ric." A tear slid down her bruised cheek. "I—"

"Stop it. Nobody blames you."

He nuzzled her neck like when they were cubs, and was rewarded by her slight smile. Even better, the wild beating of her heart slowed, grew less erratic.

"That's it," he murmured. "Calm down. Everything's going to be all right."

Luc had called Suha, their head healer, from the hotel, and left to pick her up. Beau had taken the rest of them to a place a few blocks from his den—its actual location was on a need-know-basis only—and then he, Zuri and Marjani had gone on alone.

They reached the run-down house that hid his den's entrance. Adric rented the house to a couple of baby-faced drug dealers—more camouflage. Luc and Suha were waiting in the backyard next to the basement entrance that led to his den.

He set Marjani down and, keeping an arm around her, greeted Suha and Luc. "Where's Jace?" Jace Jones was his fourth lieutenant and the other member of his inner circle along with Marjani, Zuri and Luc.

"He was on the east side near the rowhouse where they took Marjani," Luc said. "He's going to start at the house and then check along the waterfront, see if he can sniff out the bastards."

Adric nodded. It was the logical place to start looking—water fada didn't like to get too far from their rivers and oceans. He intended to keep his word to Dion, but that didn't mean he wasn't going to do some investigating on his own.

Turning his attention back to his sister, he muttered the words that removed the ward guarding the entrance. No one but Marjani could enter without his express permission.

Marjani started gamely down the steps, but he could feel her trembling. With a muttered curse, he swept her back into his arms and carried her down the two flights of stairs, Suha and the two men close behind.

As they entered the living room, they set off motion detectors that triggered the quartz wall sconces. The sconces glowed on, casting a soft amber light over his few pieces of furniture—a second-hand couch, a coffee table liberated from a dumpster and the plush rug that was his one luxury because his cat had wanted it.

He'd furnished the apartment five years ago when the clan was living hand-to-mouth. They were doing well enough now that he could've bought some new furniture, but frankly, he couldn't be bothered. And it sent a message that as alpha, he wasn't enriching himself at the clan's expense like his uncle had.

Suha came up beside them to take Marjani's hand. "How are you, honey?" she asked in a low, tranquil voice. Her animal was a deer, and she had a doe's liquid brown eyes and soothing presence.

Marjani managed a wobbly smile. "All right, I guess." That was his sister. The woman wouldn't admit she was hurting if she were sprawled on the floor bleeding out.

"Let's get you into bed, and then I'll see what I can do."

Adric led the way to his sister's old bedroom. She'd lived with him during his first, rough years as alpha, but two years ago she'd insisted on moving to her own place, saying she needed to get away from the politics always swirling around him. He'd agreed, but only because she'd moved into a group den with several of her girlfriends and a couple of his toughest males, including Luc.

So he hadn't even known she was missing until he'd arrived at the meeting to find she wasn't there. He'd immediately sent word to Luc, told Zuri he was acting as second and then done his best not to worry. The quartz deal was too important to let himself be distracted. The rich lode beneath the Rising Sun fae's lands would keep the clan supplied for the next century.

An earth fada's personal quartz was special, a high-grade

crystal keyed to their own particular energy pattern, a unique vibration that fed both owner and quartz. But in the peace that had followed the Darktime, some of his young, hungry and tech-savvy clan members had developed ways to engineer all sorts of electronic toys from quartz—smartphones, surveillance hardware, even weapons.

The beauty of quartz was that it was waterproof and damn near indestructible. Unfortunately, though, the technology burned through energy at a rapid rate. They'd figured out how to get the energy from low-grade quartz, but at the rate they were going through their own supplies, they'd soon run out. They desperately needed the large new supply the clan's miners had located on the border of Rising Sun.

Now he looked down at his sister's wan, bruised face and swallowed against a dark wash of guilt. What did all the fucking quartz in the world mean against her safety?

She was his only family, the kid sister who'd given him a reason to keep going after their parents had been brutally executed by their dad's own brother, an alpha bent on wiping out all opposition. He should've called off the meeting immediately to go looking for her.

He set Marjani on her feet next to the bed. The walls were still a warm yellow from when Marjani had lived here but the mattress was bare save for a pair of thread-bare pillows. Adric scowled, but hell, he was an unmated male. If he had a woman over, she damn well didn't sleep in the spare room.

Marjani sank down onto the bed, her expression stoic, but she couldn't conceal a flinch as her bottom touched the mattress. She was hurt in the worst sort of way a man could hurt a woman.

The anger he'd felt up to this point was nothing to the killing fury that raged in him now. He automatically brought his hand to his chest, seeking his quartz to calm himself, but he'd given it to Marjani.

He closed the hand into a fist and started barking orders. "Get the sheets," he told Zuri, pointing to a cedar chest at the end of the hall. "And you," he told Luc, "get her a glass of water or juice. *Something.*"

They weren't simply his top lieutenants, they were two of his oldest friends. But they didn't take offense at his tone, just hurried to obey.

"And a couple of blankets," added Suha. "We need to keep her warm."

Marjani tugged at her tunic. "I want to get out of these clothes."

"Of course." Suha helped her across the hall to the bathroom. "Get her a T-shirt," she mouthed at Adric, and then closed the door.

Adric had to dig to find something clean—laundry was not one of his favorite chores—but he managed to unearth an old shirt. He gave it to Suha and then helped Luc make the bed.

Meanwhile Zuri produced two glasses, one water, one orange juice. "So she has a choice," he said as he set the glasses on the nightstand.

"Good," Adric said. "A choice is good."

"Yeah," chimed in Luc.

As one, they looked toward the bathroom. The door was still closed and the shower was running, but they could hear Marjani crying, softly, hopelessly.

Adric's fists clenched.

Beside him, he heard Zuri's low growl. His lip curled to reveal his wolf's fangs.

Luc's eyes were a pure, animal gold. "It was a Rock Run fada?"

"Four renegades, possibly feral," Adric said. "Two originally from Rock Run and two Greek sea fada. One of the Rock Run shifters is dead, killed by Tiago do Rio." He filled them in on what he'd learned at the hotel.

"So we owe Tiago do Rio," Luc said.

They all scowled. None of them liked owing a Rock Run shifter—and the alpha's brother to boot.

"Well, hell." Luc blew out a breath. "I guess I'm thankful he was there."

The bathroom door opened and the two women emerged.

Marjani seemed calmer, but it was the flat affect of someone who's been deeply traumatized, a state Adric was all too familiar with from the Darktime. She plodded into the bedroom, the gray T-shirt hanging loosely around her slim body.

Adric's whole body went rigid at the bruises high on her thighs. Beside him, Luc and Zuri's breath hitched.

Adric's cougar rose up, so agitated it tried to force him to shift. Usually they were so in sync he didn't feel the cat as a separate entity, but now it was furious, mainly at Marjani's attackers, but also at Adric. The cat hadn't wanted Marjani to move away; she was family and should stay close, under Adric's protection.

Now it tried to force the shift so it could go hunting—with the water fada—any water fada—as prey. Adric's claws slid out.

Blood.

Kill.

He drew a slow breath and ordered it to stand down. But it was difficult, especially since the part of him that wasn't an alpha but a brother wanted to go hunting, too. The cat snarled but obeyed, retracting its claws.

Luc nudged Suha aside to help Marjani to the bed. "Are you thirsty? Would you like something to drink?"

"Juice, please."

While she drank the orange juice, Zuri turned back the covers as Suha looked on with a slight smile. It *was* a little amusing seeing his badass lieutenants cluck over Marjani like a pair of broody hens, but Adric just thanked the gods they were his friends.

Marjani finished drinking and handed the glass back to Luc.

"Get into bed now," he told her.

She nodded and lay down. Adric found her ready submission almost harder to take than the bruises. His sister's spirit might be housed in a slight body, but she was as tough and battle-hardened as the rest of them. She'd had to be, to survive the Darktime.

Luc pulled the covers up to her chin, his hard face inscrutable, but Adric scented the fury coming off him in hot, pungent waves. But his hands were gentle, tucking her in and then stroking her shoulders through the blankets.

Luc had been in love with Marjani for years. Unfortunately, Marjani thought of him as a good friend, nothing more. "I'm waiting for her to grow up," he'd told Adric the one time they'd talked about it. "She's my mate. She just doesn't know it yet."

Adric had shaken his head. Mates usually recognized each other on some level, but Marjani showed no interest in Luc whatsoever. Adric just hoped that Luc wouldn't cause problems when she did find her mate.

"Comfortable?" Luc asked Marjani now.

She nodded and he stepped back so that Suha could pull up a chair next to the bed.

Adric crouched down on the bed's other side and took his sister's hand. She clutched his fingers. When she spoke, her voice was so soft that he could barely make out the words. "I'm fine, Ric. Really."

"Sure, kitten. And Suha's going to make you even better. Okay?"

"Okay," she said in that same almost-soundless voice. "But—can it just be Suha and you?"

"Of course." Adric jerked his head at Zuri and Luc, who had taken a stance at the foot of the bed, both of their faces dark with the same impotent rage that he was feeling. "Wait in the living room—I'll be out in a few minutes."

He shut the door behind them and returned to the bed. Taking Marjani's hand again, he eyed her bruised cheek and silently vowed that if it turned out more than a couple of Rock

Run renegades had been involved, he wouldn't rest until the river clan was on its knees. The hell with the agreement he'd made with Dion—and to hell with the quartz. This was personal now.

Suha sent him a sharp look. "Calm yourself, my lord."

She was young and pretty, not unlike Marjani in looks, although taller and with darker skin. Adric had known her since they were both children. They'd even had a hot hook-up or two a couple of years ago. The formal "my lord" was to remind him what was at stake.

"Don't worry about me," he snapped back. "Just make her better."

"I'll do my best."

"I know." He passed a hand over his face. "I'm sorry, Suha. I—"

But she had turned her attention to his sister. "All right, sweetheart." She placed her hands on either side of Marjani's face. "Take a deep breath and let it out slowly. Let yourself relax."

Marjani closed her eyes. Her face softened so that she looked like a teenager, especially with her cropped hair. But then she *was* young, not even out of her twenties.

Too young to be an alpha's second, just as Suha at twenty-six was too young to be a clan's head healer. This was what had come of their elders' vicious jockeying for power. Even his parents hadn't been immune.

Not for the first time, he wished his uncle and his cronies a hot, merry time in whatever hell they inhabited.

"That's it," Suha murmured. She glanced at him. "You too, Ric. Breathe. She needs your energy."

Marjani touched the quartz he'd lent her. "You need this—"

"No. Keep it." He wouldn't—in fact, couldn't—have shared his quartz with just anyone, but Marjani was a close relative. It wouldn't be as attuned to her as it was with him, but it would still boost her healing. "You can give it back to me when Suha is done.

And then we'll see about getting you a temporary one until you feel up to finding one of your own."

"All right." She shut her eyes again.

"Breathe," the healer said.

Marjani's breath whooshed out and Adric realized that she'd been holding it.

"That's it," said Suha. "In and out. Picture yourself in a safe, warm place. You too, Ric."

Adric nodded and entwined his fingers with Marjani's. He kept his eyes open, because when he closed them, all he could think about was what she'd undergone last night, and that just fed his fury, which was bad. He was barely maintaining control of both himself and his cat as it was.

"Breathe, Adric," Suha prompted.

He obediently inhaled.

"You're warm and comfortable," the healer told Marjani. "Your body is already beginning to heal itself."

The tension eased out of Marjani. His own breathing slowed. Picturing himself in a safe place was out of the question, but he was one of the most powerful earth fada alive. He could add his strength to Suha's, help heal his sister.

Keeping her hand in his, with the other he cupped the crystal resting on her upper chest. It responded instantly to his touch. Energy swirled through him. He directed it toward Marjani, felt the current join with the warm golden light that was Suha's healing energy.

"That's it," muttered Suha. "Keep it up—just like that."

He closed his eyes and poured his heart and soul into visualizing his sister healthy and whole again.

He felt her body absorb the energy, begin to heal. He only prayed that her spirit would heal as well.

~

Long minutes later, Suha heaved a sigh and sat back. Marjani was in a deep sleep, the bruises on her face and arms already fading.

Suha turned her soft brown eyes on Adric. "I've done what I could. Her body's well on its way to being healed, but—" She moved a shoulder.

He released Marjani and came to standing. His legs were cramped, and when he consulted his internal clock he was surprised to realize more than thirty minutes had passed. He took a moment to stretch before coming around the bed and drawing Suha to her feet.

"Thank you, love. You're fucking amazing. Anything I can do for you—anything at all—just let me know." He dropped a grateful kiss on her mouth.

"Hey." She touched his face. "You don't owe me a thing. I'm a healer. This is my job. And you know I love Marjani like a sister."

"Even so, I mean it. You'll let me know if there's anything you need. That's an order." He waited for her nod before continuing, "You'll stay the night?"

"Of course. I brought my things." She indicated a colorful cloth bag in the corner.

He left her watching over Marjani and went into the living room. Zuri had left but Luc was pacing impatiently, waiting to report.

"Zuri left to help Jace," Luc said. "Jace called to say that Rock Run's already taken care of the dead body. The other three men had split up, but Jace tracked the Rock Run man—Jorge—to the harbor. He must have gone into the water because Jace lost his scent. A couple of Rock Run's trackers were already there so Jace laid low."

"Rock Run went after him?"

"Yes. They had a boat, but the bastard had too much of a head start. And even if they shift to their animals they can't track in the water much better than we can. That shark they have for a second might be able to—Rui do Mar—but he wasn't there. So the SOB is safe for now unless the river trackers can find him." Luc growled. "But why aren't we the ones hunting them down? Marjani's ours."

"But they're river fada—and Lord Dion swore he'd take care of it." Adric brought Luc up to date on his agreement with the Rock Run alpha. "They might not be able to use scent to track him in the water, but don't forget, they can shift to dolphin and search for him through echolocation."

"I know, I know," Luc grumbled. "And they can follow him underwater where we have to stick to the surface."

"If do Mar is around, he'll go out looking as his shark. These were the same men who kidnapped his mate. He's got as much skin in this game as we do."

Luc nodded but Adric could tell he wasn't happy. If he'd been in his wolf form, he would've been bristling with outrage. It wasn't just that one of their own females had been attacked. It was that it was Marjani, the woman Luc thought of as his.

Well, he couldn't be any more pissed off than Adric. He reached for his quartz, and when he didn't find it, shoved his fingers through his hair instead. "How the fuck did this happen, anyway?"

"She was at the Full Moon last night, playing cards in the back room. I was there, keeping an eye on her."

Adric nodded. Marjani might not return Luc's interest, but to his sister's irritation, Luc had appointed himself her bodyguard. When she'd complained, Adric had simply replied, "If it's not him, it's me," and she'd subsided, although not without muttering that she was a lieutenant, not a five-year-old.

"And?"

"She slipped out the back when I was in the john. I traced her to that afterhours club up the street—the Wildcat—but after that, nothing."

Adric scowled. He should've known Marjani would find a way

to ditch Luc. She'd done it before, after all. But as she'd pointed out—multiple times—she was his second and a damn good fighter besides. He had to allow her a certain amount of freedom or her position in the clan would be undermined.

He jammed his hands into his pockets and stared into the fireplace he'd installed so he could curl up as his cougar, soaking up the heat. Not that he spent much time enjoying it. His clan was in much better shape than when he'd taken control five years ago, but getting the various factions to work together still took too damn much of his time and energy.

Right now, there was wood laid, but it wasn't lit. He'd set a fae light to flicker at the back, though. Give the illusion of a warm, welcoming hearth.

Luc growled and Adric's gaze snapped to him. His friend's wolf-gold eyes bored into his. "She should've had a bodyguard assigned her."

"That was your job," he returned.

Luc shifted uneasily, but he didn't back down. "Unofficially, yes. But she's your second—and above me in the hierarchy. I have no authority over her." And damn if that didn't chafe the other man.

"If I assigned her an official guard, I might as well announce she's no longer my second. You know that as well as I do."

Luc shook his head, but let it go. "There's something else," he said. "I saw Tiago do Rio at the Full Moon. I sat next to him at the bar to make sure he wasn't up to anything."

Adric's brows shot up. "And?"

"And nothing. Oh, he tried to find out why we want to mine that quartz, but hell, in his place, I'd have done the same thing. To tell the truth, he seemed more interested in getting laid. He had his eye on Shania, but I told him to stay the hell away from our women."

"What did he say to that?"

Luc moved a shoulder. "He didn't like it, but he left. I went into the back room to keep an eye on Marjani."

"Who else was there?"

Luc named several people, all of them men and women who'd fought with Adric from the start. He couldn't—wouldn't—believe that they were traitors.

"I sat in for a couple of hands," Luc continued. "Everything seemed calm enough, so I went to the john. When I came back, she was gone."

"Damn it." Adric paced across the floor. "It all seems too neat—do Rio and Marjani at the bar the same night—but I suppose it could just be coincidence. Or someone saw an opportunity and went for it. I want you to talk to Shania. See if she knows anything."

"All right." Luc glanced toward the hall that led to the bedrooms. "Can I see her?"

"She's sleeping."

"I won't bother her. I just want to see her."

"Go ahead, then. But when you come out, I want you to find out exactly what happened at the Wildcat. Who was there, who saw Marjani last? Start with Shania, and then talk to your other den mates. Somebody knows something."

"You think this wasn't just some feral water fada?"

"Hell if I know. But it's damn suspicious that the two people who got caught up in their games were my sister—and the brother of Rock Run's alpha."

Luc nodded. They both knew this incident could've easily provoked a war between their clan and Rock Run.

Adric paced around the room. The cat wanted out. It wasn't as easy to shift without his crystal, but all he had to do was relax and let it come through. His body warmed, and there were a few lost seconds, and then he was a cougar.

He waited until Luc left and then settled down in front of the fireplace, his head on his paws. He hadn't mentioned his deepest fear to Luc. That someone was trying to start a personal war between him and Dion. The other alpha was strong, but Adric had the power of his quartz. A duel between them could end with both of them dead, leaving a vacuum at the top.

His cousin Corban, for instance, would love to step into that vacuum.

And maybe there was someone at Rock Run who felt the same.

14

Cleia watched from the couch as Dion paced back and forth across the stone floor of their *sala*.

After Tiago had left, she'd 'ported the two of them to the Rock Run motorboat stationed in the Inner Harbor. There, Dion had sent a message to Rui do Mar and the base, then put his third, Luis, in charge of the search for Jorge and the two Greek sea fada. Meanwhile, Dion and Cleia returned to Rock Run so that he and his second could work out a plan for dealing with the three rogue fada.

Rui had been waiting in their apartment. This time nothing, not even his mate's pregnancy, could stop him from joining the search.

"It's not just about Valeria," he'd said, his face set in cold, hard lines. "This is a deliberate attempt to set Rock Run and Baltimore at each other's throats."

"My thoughts exactly." Dion's expression was equally grim. "If Tiago had raped Marjani under the influence of that damn drug, Adric would have been out for blood. He wouldn't have given us a chance to explain. He'd have gone after Tiago—and then I'd have gone after him."

"And if Adric harmed you or Tiago," Cleia had said with dawning horror, "I'd have blasted him to kingdom come. All three of our clans would've been feuding."

The two men glanced at each other. Cleia had the distinct feeling a question had been asked and answered.

"Jorge's in the water?" Rui had asked.

Dion nodded. "We traced him to the Inner Harbor, but that was early this morning."

Rui was already at the door. "Then he could already be up here. I'll change to my shark. If he's within a mile of Rock Run, I'll know."

"I'll put a guard on Valeria and the girls at all times. Just in case."

"She'll be in our apartment along with Merry and Noela," Rui said. Noela was Valeria and Rui's toddler. "I'll make sure of it before I leave."

Cleia winced on Valeria's behalf. The two of them weren't exactly friends—Valeria had never forgotten the year Rui spent at the sun fae compound ensnared by Cleia's glamour—but Cleia knew how much the fada woman hated being cooped up in the base. However, it was clear Rui wasn't going to let either her or the children poke a toe outside the caverns until they'd caught Jorge.

"I'll start with the creek," Rui said, "then I'll make sweeps of the Susquehanna."

"Double up the sentries and take a couple of warriors with you," Dion told him. "And Rui? Don't forget he may have the two sea fada with him."

His second's smile was savage. "I haven't." And with a curt dip of his head to Cleia, he was gone.

Now Cleia watched as Dion smacked a fist into his palm. "Damn it, anyway. I should've executed those bastards when I had a chance. Adric's right. I was weak and look what happened."

"Stop it." She rose to her feet. "You loved Jorge like he was family. We both thought he'd been turned by Petros Okeanos, that he'd never have gotten involved in something like that on his own. And Benny was a member of your clan, someone you'd known almost as long as Jorge."

He passed a hand over his face. "I keep asking myself one thing. How many other women have they hurt?"

"Oh, sweetheart." She crossed the space between them and took hold of his shoulders. "Don't do this to yourself. Don't forget, they weren't on the loose all this time—they were in the Sudan. I know how you feel—that poor young woman. But the important thing is she's safe now. You just have to find Jorge and make sure it never happens again."

"I don't blame Adric for being so pissed off. If it had been Rosana—"

"Stop it." She gave him a little shake. "You're not the only one with regrets—I was there that day, too, you know. I agreed that sending them to the Sudan was a suitable punishment."

He cradled her face in his big hands. "It was my territory, my business. It wasn't your decision to make."

She bit her lower lip. He was right. They had an agreement to never interfere in each other's clan affairs. They might talk things over, offer advice, even combine resources for joint projects, but they maintained a bright, clear line between his responsibilities as Rock Run alpha and hers with Rising Sun and the other six sun fae clans she ruled as queen. Their mating would never have worked otherwise.

She moved away from him. "What I'd like to know is how in Hades did they escape—and why wasn't I contacted?" She found her tablet—powered by fae electronics—and sent a curt message to Lord Okot of the Sudanese sun fae clan asking just that.

Okot was a tall, regal man with short dark hair and skin touched with gold. He replied almost immediately. "We don't know how they escaped, my lady," he admitted, his handsome face chagrinned, "but it appears they had some help from the outside. I was just about to contact you. I assure you I have my best people out looking for them."

Cleia's scowl made Okot flinch. "That's not good enough. This involves my mate's clan. You should've informed me immediately."

"Forgive me, my lady. I'll leave immediately for Baltimore—"

"Don't bother. One of the men is already dead, and there are two clans of shifters looking for the other three. If they can't find them, no one can."

Okot inclined his head. "As you say."

"However, I expect a report on exactly how they escaped."

"Of course, Cleia. They must have had help—our wards were smashed to bits. Unfortunately, both guards are dead so it's difficult to determine exactly what happened. But I promise I'll look into it personally and get back to you as soon as I know more."

"You do that. And Okot"— Cleia glanced at Dion's forbidding expression—"they won't be back."

"Very well, my lady."

"Peace to you and yours," she said and ended the call.

A knock sounded on the partly open door and Isa, Dion's former nurse, bustled in carrying a large tray of food. As Dion rushed to take it from her, she frowned at Cleia.

"I've brought you lunch," she said in a voice heavy with disapproval. She was officially retired, but she'd helped raise all five do Rios and considered them her family. "It's past time you ate."

"*Obrigada*." Cleia helped herself to a strawberry as Dion placed the tray on the table. Her own mother had passed to the other side nearly fifty years ago; if Isa wanted to coddle her, she was happy to oblige. "I *am* hungry."

Appeased, Isa pointed to the various dishes. "We have cod cakes, just how you like them, and those are some of the first strawberries from the new greenhouse. I know how you like your fresh fruit. And some salad and bread, of course."

"You're a treasure." Cleia bent to kiss her. "I don't know what we'd do without you."

To her delight, a flush touched Isa's round cheeks. "Eat. The child needs it—and so do you." She crossed her arms and waited until Cleia sat down and picked up her fork, then with a satisfied nod, wished them both a good day and bustled back out the door.

"*Me desculpe, minha querida.*" Dion's expression was remorseful as he took a seat catty-corner to Cleia. "I should've remembered you hadn't eaten." He smoothed a hand over her womb.

She nudged the other plate at him. "I had a big breakfast. And I was absorbing energy from the sun the whole time we were at the meeting. That went well, don't you think?"

Dion nodded and picked up his fork. She kept the discussion light, moving from the meeting to her plans for decorating the baby's nursery. Dion nodded and agreed, but she could tell his mind was elsewhere.

He finished his lunch and sat back. He'd cleaned the plate, but she'd have bet a handful of her favorite jewels that he had no idea what he'd eaten. She touched his hand. "Tiago will be fine, Dion."

He shot her a bleak look. "What am I going to do with him?"

"I'm not sure you have to do anything *with* him, love."

He shook his head. "My own brother has the Gift of compulsion and I didn't even know."

"It's not your fault. It's no one's fault. Tiago is what he is. And he would've told you sooner or later."

"You don't understand. If the clan finds out, he'll be shunned. *When* they find out. Because they will."

"But why would he be shunned?"

"We're fada," was the grim reply. "We're already controlling SOBs. Imagine a fada male who can control you with a word, a look. Look what it did to Okeanos. Would you want that man anywhere within a mile of you? No one will trust Tiago not to take advantage."

"But Tiago's different. Everyone knows he's basically a good man. He's struggling now, but he's strong. He'll figure out how to control it—I'd stake my life on it. Actually, from what he said, he's *been* controlling it—for three years."

"I just hope you're right." He rose to his feet and put the dishes in the sink to soak before resuming his restless pacing. "Damn it, I'm his brother. I should be able to help somehow."

"Dion." She stood up as well. "He's not a boy anymore. This is his Gift, his burden. He has to deal with it himself."

"I suppose you're right." He scraped a hand through his hair. "I'm going to lose him, Cleia. Just like Nic and Joaquim."

"No." She crossed to him and took his hands. After the do Rio parents had been lost at sea, it had fallen to Dion to raise Tiago and Rosana. He considered them more his children than siblings. "That won't happen. You won't let it."

"How am I going to stop it?"

"Love him," she said. "Show him he has your support. He's terrified his Gift is going to take over. I know how he feels—the first time I channeled the sun's energy for my clan, I was so scared my knees felt like jelly. I knew if I wasn't strong enough, I'd go up in flames."

He shot her a wry look. "Is that supposed to make me feel better?"

"The point is I *was* strong enough, and so is he. But he could use training. There has to be someone who can work with him, teach him the control he needs."

"But who? His Gift hasn't appeared in our clan for seventy-five years. I remember the man—we grew up together. He couldn't have been much older than Tiago is now when he challenged my father for alpha. But he couldn't resist trying to control him, and that voided the challenge. It took my father and two other men to kill him."

"Perhaps someone in New England?" A large Portuguese river fada clan had settled the coast of Rhode Island and Massachusetts along with the human Portuguese immigrants. "Or in Portugal or one of the other European clans?"

"It's worth a try." He enfolded her in his arms. "I'll get someone on it. Thank you, *querida*."

She hugged him back. She wasn't sure even Dion knew how much he loved Tiago. Losing him would be worse than losing his other two brothers, hard as that had been. For Dion, it would be like losing a son.

"Meanwhile," she said, "you have to be prepared for the clan to find out."

He lifted his head to look at her. "*Sim*?"

"The clan will take their lead from you. If you make it clear Tiago has your trust, that you're not afraid he'll use his Gift against you, they'll come to accept it."

"That just might work. Tell me"—his fingers toyed with her braid—"how did you get so wise?"

"It's simple common sense." But she smiled up at him.

"Hm. Is that a gray hair I see?" He pretended to examine her braid. "Because I think that extra hundred years you have on me has someth—"

She elbowed him in the ribs and he grinned and gathered her closer. She slid her hand under his T-shirt and caressed his abdomen.

He gave a low, contented growl. "*Amo-te*."

"Love you too." She pressed a kiss into the warm hollow beneath his ear.

Dion drew her to the couch and pulled her onto his lap, her head against his shoulder. They were silent for a time. Cleia didn't know what Dion was thinking about, but she was hoping she was right about Tiago. Because if she was wrong, he could use his Gift to tear the clan apart. Even she might not be able to stop him.

He might even turn it on her.

Not that she thought he would, but she wasn't one hundred percent sure. Once or twice, she'd caught Tiago considering her in a way that was decidedly unbrotherly....

She was strong, but so was he. And if he caught her by surprise, who knew what would happen? His Gift apparently worked on the fae, otherwise he wouldn't have been able to kill that night fae.

Dion's low voice rumbled in her ear. "I'll have to tell Rui and Luis. As my second and third, they need to know. We'll have to make a decision about Tiago. I can't let him go out with his squad until he has this thing under control."

She bit her lip and decided to go with her instincts. Yes, Tiago had a dark side, but as she'd said to Dion, he'd clearly been controlling it for years.

"That would be the worst thing you could do. He'll think you don't trust him, and that will only make it worse. You have to show him he has your complete trust, that you know he can do this. Because he has to take control—or it will destroy him."

"I don't know, love." He shook his head and she sensed his denial through their bond.

But he had to understand what was at stake. "He's on a knife's edge, Dion. Push too hard and he's going to break. And there's a good chance it won't be you he attacks. He loves you too much."

"Who then?"

She moved a shoulder.

His whole body went stiff. "You think he'd kill himself?"

"If it was for the good of the clan. You'd do the same yourself." What Dion didn't seem to understand was how similar he and his brother were.

"Hell." His head dropped back against the couch. "I'll have to think about this. I just don't want to lose him—but better that than a challenge from my own brother. Maybe I should just send him to Nic or Joaquim. At least then he doesn't have to deal with being the alpha's youngest brother on top of everything else."

"Oh, Dion." She could hardly bear the sadness emanating from him through the mate bond. She gave him a hard hug. "It will work out. You'll make the right decision. I know you will."

He shook his head, and then giving her a last, lingering kiss, lifted her off his lap and set her on the couch. "You rest now," he said as he rose to his feet. "I'm going to the operations room to see if there's any news about Jorge or the sea fada."

"I can rest later." She stood up as well. "I should go back to Rising Sun and tell Olivia how the meeting went."

He snagged her braid and tilted her head back. "And if I say you rest first?"

She slid her fingers around his nape and slanted him a look up from under her lids. "I'd say yes, my love."

"And do whatever you damn well please." He gave her a hard kiss and released her hair. "I'll save my breath. But promise me you'll come straight back—or you *will* have a fight on your hands."

She smiled into his eyes. He was learning to bend; she could too. "It's a date."

15

---

*A*lesia crossed her arms over her stomach.

Tiago was hurting. She'd *felt* it last night, waves of pain and fury that left her curled into a ball on the hammock, her tree rustling in distress. Terrified her mother would sense her agitation and return, she'd forced herself to remain calm, keep her breathing even.

With the morning, the pain had eased. She'd gone about her day, weeding the early spring vegetables like peas and lettuce. But she couldn't help wishing she had some way to contact him.

She stabbed her trowel into the soil, cursing her isolation. It was a dryad's way, to live alone and close to nature without the technology other fae relied on, but her mate needed her and she had no idea where he was.

He wasn't in physical distress anymore—at least, not much— but his mood was so bleak it scared her. If the man was hurt, why didn't he come to her?

But she knew the reason.

It was up to her to go to him. She was still hurt and angry about yesterday, but the mate bond wouldn't let her rest until she knew what was the matter. She'd always had a special radar where he was concerned, but now she could home in on him from anywhere, following that tenuous bond to his current location.

She grabbed a waterskin and a sack of walnuts, climbed to the top of her oak and concentrated.

East. He was east and a little south, somewhere in the middle of the bay but closer to the other side.

She closed her eyes, visualizing where she wanted to go. In an instant, she'd 'ported several miles down the river to another oak. Then another, this one taking her across the top of the bay where it was only a few miles wide. Then another and another, skipping down the Chesapeake's eastern edge until she landed in a massive white oak a little south of the Sassafras River.

She exited the tree and looked around her. She was at the edge of a thick stand of trees. The area appeared to be deserted, a wildlife sanctuary, perhaps. Before her was a narrow beach, a tumble of sand and round black stones.

She walked to the water's edge. A brisk wind blew off the bay, whipping her hair around her face. She caught it with one hand, glad of the thick wool sweater she was wearing over her jeans, and squinted toward the horizon. Tiago was out there, somewhere in the vast, sun-silvered expanse of water.

He wouldn't be in his human form, not if he was injured. The fada healed more quickly as their animals. Most likely he'd be a river dolphin.

But how to contact him?

She paced up and down the beach. Noon came and went and she left the beach to forage for food. The pickings were slim this early in the year, but she made a meal of her walnuts and some wild watercress she found along a nearby spring.

When she returned, she remained on her feet, staring out at the water. The tie between her and Tiago had grown stronger. She could almost see where it stretched toward the horizon, not quite visible and yet hooked firmly into her heart.

She brought her hand to her chest, considering. *Why not?* She gave a tentative mental tug on the bond, pulling until she felt resistance. She held her breath and tugged harder.

She felt the instant Tiago became aware of the tug. As she'd guessed, he'd taken the form of a dolphin. She sensed the streamlined shape of his body; the fast, easy glide as he moved through the waves.

The bond tickled. His muscles twitched. He frowned and then flicked his head, snapping the bond in half.

She sighed and sent it out again. This time she cupped her hands around her mouth and called to him as well. "Tiago? It's me, Alesia."

Even if he wasn't close enough to hear her voice, perhaps the bond would carry the sense of who was trying to contact him.

The bond touched him again, tugged. She held her breath, but this time the connection remained steady. A minute passed, then another. She rose to her toes, eyes narrowed against the sun. He was getting closer, she was sure of it.

Then a dolphin appeared, flashing in and out of the water in graceful arcs. It was large, with a river dolphin's elongated snout and dark gray body. The dolphin glided to a halt a few yards from shore and studied her with Tiago's silver-blue eyes.

He didn't appear happy.

She swallowed. "Hello."

Power rippled over the dolphin's smooth gray skin. The color changed from a dark charcoal to warm olive. The head rounded and shaped itself into Tiago's hard, sensual features, his jaw shadowed by a night beard. Fins elongated into limbs, and a broad back and shoulders emerged. The last thing to appear was the black tattoo encircling his upper arm.

He rose from the water, unashamedly naked, hair falling to his shoulders in dark, wet whorls. "Alesia. What in *Deus*'s name are you doing here?"

She ignored him to gape at his bruises. "Good grief, Tiago. What happened to you?"

His lips curved in a sardonic smile. "Would you believe I ran into an old friend?"

"No," she replied baldly.

"Well, I did—two of them. I made the mistake of having a drink with them. Things went downhill from there."

"So I see. But what happened?"

"Never mind that." He put his hands on his hips and raised a single black brow. "You called me here for a reason, right?"

She moved a shoulder. "I was worried about you."

He moved a shoulder. "As you can see, I'm okay. Cleia gave me a dose of healing energy, and swimming as my dolphin helped."

Of course, Alesia thought. The sun fae queen *would* be the one to help Tiago. Then she was ashamed of herself. The important thing was that Tiago was better. Now that her first shock had passed, she could see that he was already healing; the bruises were yellowing and the cuts were scabbed over.

He closed the few feet between them. "Why are you here, Alesia?"

"I told you. I was worried about you." Her hands raised almost of their own volition, running over his face and body, assuring herself that he was all right.

A tremor ran over his skin, but he remained still, allowing it.

She rubbed his upper arms. "You're cold. I—"

"I'm not cold."

"No?" She took his hand. "Come onto the beach anyway."

She drew him toward a log in the sun and sat down. He took a seat at the other end of the log. "How'd you do that, anyway?" he asked. "Call me here?"

He didn't sense it then, not the way she did. He didn't realize it was the mate bond. The knowledge slashed her heart.

She smoothed her hands over her jeans. "I can do that with

friends sometimes," she prevaricated, and then gulped as her stomach rebelled against the small lie.

"Yeah?" He slanted her a skeptical look. She'd forgotten that fada could scent a lie, but it wasn't entirely false—she could do it with him, and he *was* a friend, even if she wanted him to be more. "How did you know something was wrong? I've been hurt before and you didn't know. Or did you?"

"No. This was the first time."

"So what's different now?"

She moved a shoulder. "I just had this feeling you were hurt. Last night—it wasn't just a fight, was it?"

He stared out at the bay without replying. Several seconds ticked past before he blew out a breath. "You may as well know. Jorge and Benny and a couple of their friends worked me over. You remember them—the four men from Okeanos's den."

She angled her body so she could see his face. "The ones who hurt Valeria?"

"Yeah. There was a woman this time too, an earth shifter. They hurt her pretty bad. I was too fucked up to stop them."

"But aren't they supposed to be in Africa?"

"Apparently they escaped." His lips twisted. "At least Benny won't be hurting any more women."

It took her a few seconds to realize what he meant. "He's dead?"

"Yeah."

"You?"

"Yeah."

She furrowed her brow, trying to read his mood. She wouldn't have expected him to be overjoyed at having killed someone, especially a former member of his clan. But Benny had been a bad man, and from what Tiago said, he'd only gotten worse. So why this inner revulsion, as if he'd slain an innocent?

"They attacked you, didn't they? You had to defend yourself— and the earth shifter woman. No one could blame you for that."

He turned his head to glare at her. "You want to know every last freaking detail, don't you?"

"Yes." She set her jaw. "And I think you need to tell someone."

He looked back at the water. A minute passed, and then his chest heaved. "I was at a bar in Fells Point, drinking. I'm sorry about how I left things with you, by the way. I can be an ass sometimes."

"I know. But thank you."

He gave a humorless chuckle. "You do know, don't you? Sometimes I think you're the only person who really knows me. And even you don't know the worst of it."

She scooted down the log and placed her hand on his back. It was rigid under her palm. "Go on."

"Like I said, I was at a bar. There was this woman—an earth shifter. She invited me to an afterhours club."

It was her turn to go rigid.

Tiago shot her a look. "Told you I'm an ass."

She moved a shoulder without saying anything, and he continued, "Jorge was at the club. He sat down at our table, which is when I should've gotten the hell out of there, but I didn't. I knew Dion would want to know what he was up to, and I wanted to be the one who reported it. You know, show Dion what I can do. Then Benny showed up, and the woman got pissed at me and left. One of them must've slipped that goddamn aphrodisiac in my drink—the same one they gave Valeria."

"Oh, Tiago." She rubbed his lower back.

"Yeah." He drew in a breath. "The next thing I knew, we were in some dirty, broken-down rowhouse. But it wasn't just me. There was a woman, too. An earth fada, but not the same one from the bar."

She stilled. She'd seen what that aphrodisiac had done to Valeria. "Did you—"

"No. God, I wanted to." He gave a mirthless laugh. "I was crazy for sex, craving it like the worst drug. Anyone would've done—woman, man. Hell, I was so hard I'd have fucked a knot-hole. And to make it worse, they'd already taken a turn with her. I could smell them on her, smell how much she still wanted it. But it was the drug, not her. She was terrified, begging me not to touch her. So I didn't. I couldn't." He slanted her a crooked smile. "First you, then her. I'm a frigging saint, huh?"

"Oh, Tiago." She let out a breath she hadn't known she was holding. "But me—that was different. I wanted you. You know that."

He lifted a shoulder. "Anyway, before all that happened, I passed out—I don't know how long—maybe an hour, maybe more. That's when the four of them had their fun with that poor woman. Well." He inhaled jaggedly. "It seems Benny got tired of waiting for me to wake up and perform for them like some kind of goddamn trick dog. He started to rough me up. I woke up, all right—half out of my mind from alcohol and the drug—and fought back. The others got away, but not Benny."

She brought her hand to his cheek. The black stubble was rough under her palm, his whole face tight. She smoothed her fingers over the clenched muscles of his jaw.

"It wasn't your fault, Tiago. He brought it on himself."

"That's what I keep telling myself." He gazed out at the water. "I think of that woman and how they hurt her—and not just physically. She's strong, but between them and the drug, they damn near broke her."

Alesia bit her lip. "She's all right?"

"As well as can be expected. Turns out, she's Lord Adric's sister. I went with her to the hotel where he was meeting with Cleia and my brother. Cleia offered to help, but he took her to his own healer."

"Lord Adric's sister?" She gulped. "Goddess, Tiago. What did he do?"

"He wanted to cut off my balls and shove them down my

throat, but his sister—Marjani—convinced him I wasn't to blame. You know what I think?"

A chill went down her spine. "That it wasn't a coincidence."

"Hell, no. Those bastards were trying to provoke an incident. Get Dion and Adric gunning for each other and who knows what would happen? At least Marjani was able to vouch for me. *Deus* knows what Adric would've done if he thought Dion's brother had raped his sister." Tiago shook his head. "On top of that, Jorge tried to stir up trouble between me and Dion—said it must be hard for me, knowing I'm stronger than him. I told him to go to hell, and that's the last thing I remember until I woke up in the rowhouse. With that poor woman shut in there with me."

He shuddered like a great horse and she leaned her head against his shoulder. "It's all right, Tiago. At least you got her away from them."

"I *am* cold, Lesia. So damn cold. Oh, not my body—but there's a block of ice where my soul should be." He turned to face her. His eyes bored into hers, the pupils dark with need, the irises a thin silver rim. "I don't have any right to ask this, especially after yesterday, but I need you."

She could've resisted anything but that naked admission. The hurt that still lingered from his rejection yesterday eased. She didn't understand why he'd left so abruptly, but this was her mate —and he needed her.

"It's all right." She brought her free hand to his cheek. "I need you too."

He inhaled slowly and released her hand to slide his fingers around her nape, and then his mouth was on hers. His lips were firm and cool. He ran them over hers, softly, gently.

Closing her eyes, she brought a hand to his shoulder and opened her mouth. His tongue slipped inside and his taste filled her mouth, dark, luscious. And so right.

She sucked his tongue deeper. A wave of heat undulated down her spine, blooming in her belly like the slow unfolding of a flower. Her fingers tightened on his shoulder. She moaned, a wordless plea for more.

He skated a hand down her leg, his large fingers cupping her ass. "Ah, baby."

He slid his hand lower to where she was already slick. His breath hitched and he scooped her onto his lap so her breasts pressed his chest through the sweater, his erection hard against her bottom.

"Alesia," he said against her mouth. "I need to be inside you. So bad. Tell me it's okay."

Goddess, couldn't the man tell how much she wanted him? "It's okay," she murmured. "It's okay."

She angled her mouth to kiss him again, but her fingers touched a hard lump on the back of his head and he flinched.

"They did this?" she asked.

"Yeah. Slammed me against the floor."

"Oh, sweetheart. Maybe we should wait. You're hurt—you need time to heal." She tried to pull away but he tightened his arms around her, keeping her on his lap.

"It's not so bad. And we can take it slow, right?" His voice was smoky soft. "Slow and easy. I ache for you, baby. I can take a little pain if it means I can have you."

"But—"

"Enough." He touched two fingers to her lips. "You called me, remember? And you already said it's okay. So don't try to back out of it now." His voice was hard but she could see the uncertainty in his eyes.

She nodded mutely.

He pulled her sweater over her head and tossed it aside. She was wearing a sky-blue ribbed tank beneath. "Pretty," he said as he slid the straps down her shoulders, exposing her breasts and trapping her arms by her sides.

She moistened her lips. "Tiago?"

"That's better." He tipped her over one arm and eyed her bare upper body with a wicked smile that made her inner thighs clench. "Now you don't have anything to do but enjoy."

"But—" She lifted her hands and dropped them again. "I want to touch you, too."

"You'll have your chance. But right now this is all for you. You don't mind, do you, sweetheart?" A work-roughened fingertip teased her nipple, sending warmth streaking from her breasts to her belly.

Her head fell back against his shoulder. "No," she agreed. "I don't mind."

"I promise I'll set you free...when I'm ready to." He pinched the other nipple and she moaned. "But you have to trust me. You do, don't you, *querida*?"

He stilled, waiting for her answer. Her brain whirled. How had he switched so rapidly from needy to the one calling the shots? But this was who Tiago was—a strong, dominant man. And maybe this *was* what he needed after last night—to be the one in charge. To know he could give pleasure. To know he wasn't merely—or even mostly—a killer.

Still, this wasn't just about him. It was about her, too. And Goddess help her, she wanted it however he wanted to give it to her.

She wanted *him*.

"Yes," she said. And then more strongly, "Of course I do."

His smile was dark with anticipation. "Oh, Lesia. This is going to be good...so good."

16

Tiago looked at Alesia's small, firm breasts, the pretty peach points thrust high by her position over his arm. She licked her lips, her expression excited and a little uncertain. Her hair fell over his arm in a wild, sun-kissed mass.

He speared his fingers into her hair and gently pulled her head back so he could nuzzle her neck. Marking her with his scent and taking hers on him in return. His head and ribs still ached but it was a dull pain, easily ignored.

He inhaled deeply, drawing in her subtle, woodsy fragrance and reveling like a pup in the peace he drew just from being with her.

He hadn't lied. He did need her. Bad. Maybe it was a side effect of that damn aphrodisiac, but he didn't think so.

Something inside had shifted. He wasn't quite sure what or why, but he had an overwhelming need to take Alesia, to make her his. His woman.

The beast agreed whole-heartedly.

He released her hair so he could cradle her in his arm. His other hand was still on her breast, the fingers olive brown against her creamy skin. She wasn't that much lighter than him—she had those Greek ancestors, after all—but here, on her breasts, she was ivory-smooth, her skin untouched by the sun.

She made a small sound and he glanced back at her face. Her tip-tilted eyes met his, the pupils large and dark. Then her head dropped back against his shoulder, her neck bared in erotic submission.

He swallowed hard. He knew the gesture didn't mean the same thing to her as it did to a fada, but damn, it brought out the dominant in him. Although wrapped up in that was the urge to protect and care for her.

He squeezed her breast. It was petal-soft and cool under his fingers. "You're cold," he murmured, massaging the nipple with his palm. "I'll have to warm you up."

She shuddered with pleasure. He smiled and brought his mouth to her other breast, drawing on one nipple while playing with the other. She squirmed and tried to free her hands. He caught them and pulled them behind her back, clasping her wrists in one hand.

"Not yet, sweetheart. Remember who's in charge here."

"Tiago," she scolded breathlessly. "Stop teasing."

He grinned. He should've known she'd push back. She might be shy but that didn't mean she was weak or lacking in courage.

"I don't think so," he said and slid his mouth over her breasts, swiped his tongue through her cleavage. She tasted fresh and a bit salty, like the upper bay in spring. "I think you like it." He pressed love-bites to the top of her breasts, her throat. "Tell me, Lesia. Tell me you like it. I want to hear you say it." He lifted his head and waited.

Her chest heaved, raising those pert breasts in a way that had his pulse speeding up. "Yes, damn you. I do like it—a lot."

A growl rose from deep in his chest. He released her wrists to spear his fingers in her hair and gave her a hard, deep kiss. Thrusting his tongue between her lips, sweeping it over hers. Showing her what he wanted, what he was going to have.

She wriggled on his lap, pressing against his erection and sending a punch of sensation to his lower belly. He dragged his mouth from hers and took a deep breath. He was close, so close to being deep inside her hot, wet cunt. But he didn't want their first time to be like that, fast and furious.

When he had himself under control, he said, "That's good." He played with one of her hard little nipples. "Because I like teasing you. I'm going to be doing it a lot."

She blinked up at him. "You are?"

"Oh, yeah. This isn't a one-time thing, Lesia." There was no way they were going back to being friends after this. They weren't even going to be friends with benefits—not if he had anything to say about it.

He set her on the log to take off her heavy canvas work boots and then skimmed off her jeans. . No panties again. The woman must always go commando. By the gods, if he'd known that all these years...

Pulling her back on his lap, he toyed with her soft curls, enjoying the needy little sounds she made. "Ah. You're nice and wet down here. Now why is that, hm?" His finger slid deeper, inscribed a circle around her clitoris. "I think you can hardly wait to have me inside you. Is that it? Tell me, baby."

Her breath was ragged but she shook her head. "Your head's too big as it is, at least where women are concerned."

"That's because I'm good to my women." He slid a finger into her, stroked slowly. "Would you like to find out how good?"

Her breath hissed out. She squirmed beneath his hand. "Maybe."

"Maybe?" He lifted a brow. "Let's see if I can change that to a 'Hell, yeah.'"

Setting her on the log, he knelt on the beach and spread her legs so he could see her slick pink center. Her arousal scented the air, rich and enticing. His nostrils flared. His balls tightened and his cock, already rock hard, swelled even more.

He took hold of her thighs and set his lips to that pretty pink flesh. It pulsed beneath his mouth.

"Yes," she breathed. "Ah Goddess, Tiago. That's it...yes."

His lips curved against her skin. He licked her, slow and deep, then again. She squirmed and got her arms free of the tank. She pulled it off and dropped it on top of her jeans. She slanted him a look and then, bracing her hands on the log, deliberately spread her legs a bit wider.

"Bad girl." He slapped the side of her ass. "Did I say you could do that? Next time I'll have to tie you. You won't get free until I allow it."

Her eyes rounded. He chuckled and brought his mouth back between her thighs, licking and tasting her.

Her hands clutched the back of his head, pulling him closer. Her breath came in short, aroused huffs. "Tiago." She rocked her hips into him. "I—"

He slid a finger into her. "That's it," he encouraged. His voice sounded thick in his ears. "Come for me, sweetheart. My pretty little fawn. Let me hear you scream."

He swirled his tongue around her clit and then sucked it deep into his mouth. Her hips jerked and her inner muscles clamped on his finger. He removed it and she whimpered.

"Don't worry," he soothed. "I know what you want."

He slid two fingers into her this time. Her breath hitched and he felt the first waves of pleasure moving through her. He continued stroking her while he teased her clit with his tongue. She called his name and arched her back as she came with a wild, uninhibited sensuality that had him growling in pleasure. Maybe she was a match for a fada male after all.

He stayed with her until she collapsed forward, her head on his shoulder. Then he gentled his touch, bringing her down with slow, easy strokes until she lifted her head.

"Yum." It was almost a purr.

He gave her a cocky smile. "It was good, yes?"

She pursed her lips and tilted her head to one side. "Not bad."

So she still wanted to play? His smile widened. "Not bad, huh? I'll give you not bad."

He stood up and lifted Alesia so that he was straddling the log and she was straddling him with her feet on either side of his legs, his cock pressed against her center. She was warm and wet from her climax. He stilled, his hands on her breasts.

She sucked in a breath, waiting for him to do something, but he held motionless, toying with her nipples, his gaze on hers.

"Tiago? Aren't you going to move?" She rocked against him.

"Me? I'm just enjoying you, Lesia. We can stay like this as long as you like."

She regarded him through half-closed lids. "But what if I want to move?"

She lifted her hips and slid up and down his cock. Up and down...slowly. Then again, and again. Not taking him inside, but exploring his entire length with her slick, hot tissue.

He stifled a groan. The woman was killing him. But he was damned if he'd break first.

"Then," he replied, his eyes never leaving hers, "you have to admit that it was better than not bad. That it was, in fact, the most amazing fuck you ever had." He pressed against her.

She giggled. "And if I don't?"

"Then we can stay right here. I'm comfortable, aren't you?" He leaned back, hands on the log behind him, lips curved.

She considered him. "You do look comfortable. Too comfortable." She enfolded his cock in her fingers and squeezed.

Pleasure shot through him. He jerked and tightened his grip on the log, his gaze on the long, tanned fingers encircling him. "Damn, woman. You fight dirty."

"You think?" She grinned.

Then she forgot to tease, absorbed in exploring him. Her hand slid over the smooth, sensitive skin of his cock, stretched tight over the engorged flesh beneath. She traced a thick vein to the root, brushing her fingertips over his balls, heavy with arousal. A drop of fluid glistened at the tip of his cap.

She shifted onto her stomach and stretched out along the log facing him, her round, firm bottom in the air. Her tongue flicked out to taste him.

Pleasure flashed through him, hot and electric.

"Alesia," he gritted. His hands were fisted on his thighs now. "Please. Have mercy." He looked at her raised ass and had to close his eyes against the lurid pictures flooding his mind. The things he'd like to do to her...

But she'd only had a handful of lovers—although you wouldn't know it from the skillful way she was teasing him with her tongue.

She lifted her head and narrowed her eyes at him as if she guessed his thoughts. Then she swirled her tongue around his cap and sucked him inside.

His hands jerked up from his thighs and then fell back again. "*Sim, menina*," he said, falling back on the language of his birth as his mind blanked with pleasure. "That's it, baby. Take me. Take all of me."

She sucked harder, her tongue gliding over his hard flesh in a perfect rhythm. He brushed her hair back and grasped her head, holding her where he wanted her. He began to move his hips, slowly fucking her mouth.

She swallowed on him and he made a low sound of enjoyment. "*Tão bom*," he said in hoarse Portuguese. "So damn good."

She hummed her agreement and he felt it in his balls. Hell, all the way down to his toes. All he could do was groan.

She dropped to her knees on the beach. Wrapping her hand around the base of his cock, she took him even deeper, swirling her tongue over him, sucking him to the back of her throat, working him with her hand.

He opened his eyes so he could watch her mouth on him. It

had to be the sexiest sight in the world, seeing her on her knees before him, his cock thrusting between her moist red lips.

He tightened his grip on her head and pumped into her mouth, slowly and carefully so as not to go deeper than she could take.

"Lesia—" His voice was gritty. "You're so damn good at this. I should—" His head dropped back and he forgot to think, just let himself feel.

ALESIA SMILED against Tiago's flesh.

He tasted so good, hard and slick against her tongue, his flavor a mix of salt and spice. She had to grin at how he couldn't help taking control, positioning her how he wanted, but still taking care with her in a way that made her heart contract.

Right now, his mind was on only one woman—her, Alesia—and if she had her way, that was how it would be from now on. She was tired of waiting for the man to come to his senses.

He was *hers*.

It was time he acknowledged it.

"Lesia. Sweet Lord. I'm going to come."

She sucked harder. He dragged in a breath and gripped her head, pressing deep. His hips jerked and his seed spurted into her mouth, briny as the sea. He stilled and groaned with pleasure, his cock jerking until he was drained.

He released her head and put his hands on his thighs, gulping air. "Hell, woman. I saw stars."

She grinned and pressed a kiss to his thigh before coming to her feet. Picking up her waterskin, she filled it at the nearby spring. As she drank, Tiago leaned back on his elbows and watched her through heavy-lidded eyes, his expression holding a gleam of ownership that sent a frisson up her spine.

It wasn't going to be easy, mating with a shifter. But something in her—something deep and primal—wanted his possession, craved it.

Still, that didn't mean he got to have things all his own way. If the man owned her, she was going to demand some rights, too. Starting with no more trolling in bars for women. She was going to have to make it clear that this exclusive thing went both ways.

She offered him the water. "Want some?"

"Thanks." He took a long drink, then reached for her hand. "Come—you're getting goosebumps. Let's get out of the wind."

He led her into the woods to a natural hollow protected from the chilly breeze that was blowing off the bay. It was late afternoon, the sun already low in the sky. Here in the trees everything was green and gold shadows. Together, the two of them fashioned a comfortable nest from leaves and dried grass. When they were finished, Tiago lay down and reached a hand to her.

She lay next to him, head on his chest, taking care so as not to press on his bruises. Beneath her cheek, his heart beat slow and steady. She snuggled closer, breathing him in, and traced a finger over the black knots of his tattoo. His bicep bulged beneath her fingertip. The man's arm was probably twice the size of hers.

She remembered how uneasy he'd made her, the summer they'd first met. But even then, she hadn't been afraid of him, just wary. Maybe she'd known even then that someday she'd be lying here with him in this cozy nest.

He stroked her hair. "Thank you, *querida*," he murmured.

"For what?"

"The gift of yourself."

Touched and bit amused, she threaded her fingers through the soft mat of black hair on his chest. Tiago might have been born in America but he could be very old-world European at times. She supposed it came from growing up in the insular world of the Rock Run Clan. It was only after Dion mated with Cleia that Rock Run had started to socialize with the local sun fae, and the Rising Sun compound was less than ten miles from Rock Run.

"No thanks necessary."

"You liked it, hmm?"

Her lips curved. Nobody could say the man lacked self-confidence. But she was too relaxed to tease him about it, and besides, his hand was sliding between her legs.

"Next time, sweetheart," he said against her ear, "I want to be inside you when you come. You'd like that, wouldn't you? A big, hard man, deep inside you?"

Hot moisture pricked between her thighs. His middle finger found it, dipped inside, rubbed suggestively. At the same time he tongued the sensitive point at the top of her ear.

Her breath snagged. "That would be nice," she managed to say.

"Oh, I promise it'll be more than nice. But"—he removed his hand and rolled onto his back—"there's something you need to know first."

She sensed his uneasiness through the mate bond, weak as it was. She lifted her head to look at him. "Tiago?"

"You know I killed Benny, but what I didn't tell you is how." His throat worked. "My hand was around his throat, but that wasn't how he died. I compelled him, Alesia. I told him to die and his heart stopped."

She felt the color drain from her face. She sat up. "You *compelled* him?"

"Yes."

"But—I didn't think fada could do that. Only witches and vampires can put a compulsion on someone."

He sat up as well and moved a few feet away. "The fada can't," he said flatly. "Only the monsters."

"Monsters? What do you mean?"

"Do you remember Petros Okeanos? The leader of the men who kidnapped Valeria?"

She swallowed. "You—you're like him?"

"Not exactly. But his Gift was a kind of compulsion. He had the power to bind people in an invisible net and then order their bodies to move like they were his puppets—that's what he did to Valeria. It's very rare—maybe one per clan in each generation, and maybe not even that many. He's the only other fada I've ever known with a Gift even close to mine."

She slowly shook her head, taking it in. Then she stilled. "That acorn on my island? That *was* you. I—"

He nodded, shamefaced. "I compelled it to grow—too fast—until it just blew apart. I'm sorry, Lesia. I was pissed off—not at you, at myself—but that's no excuse. I shouldn't have done it."

She recalled the primal scream the tiny oak had given and felt a little sick. "Are you sure? Maybe you're wrong about Benny. Maybe he had a weak heart anyway."

He glanced away. "It wasn't the first time. Well, it was the first time I actually killed someone with my Gift, but once I forced—compelled—a man to freeze. Then I slit his throat."

She stared at him, chest tight. This was Tiago, she reminded herself. Her mate. Her friend. The man who brought her flowers and candy. The man who'd just given her one of the best orgasms of her life.

But suddenly the stories she'd heard about the fada were running through her head. And those missions when he'd come back with a hard face and burning eyes...

This wasn't dark magic. No, this was worse—it was *part* of him.

She swallowed hard. "I'll have to think about this."

"Of course," he replied, his face expressionless. "I understand."

She rubbed her hands over her upper arms. "I'm cold. I—let me get my clothes." She rose to her feet.

He stood up as well. "I'll come with you."

"No. Please don't. You need to heal—and I need to get back

home. Okay?" She touched his chest apologetically and started backing up.

He remained where he was, hands fisted at his sides.

But as she turned away, suddenly he was in front of her, blocking her way.

She blinked. "Tiago?"

He didn't say anything, just took hold of her upper arms and scrutinized her with eyes a bright, pure silver. His expression was hard, watchful. She knew she was looking at his animal—and it was staring back as if she were prey.

"Don't go." His voice was guttural. His will beat at her with a force that made her stagger. He gripped her more tightly but kept up the pressure.

With an effort, she gathered her own resources and pushed back. "Stop it, Tiago."

He ignored her to cup her jaw. "Don't go," he repeated. "Stay with me, Lesia." His voice softened into a seductive croon that slid over her skin, teased at her breasts, made her womb clench. "You know you want me."

She tilted her head, leaning into his warm palm. Every part of her body prickled with awareness.

It would be so easy to give in to him. So damn easy. After all, it would only be what she wanted, too. She closed her eyes, tempted. So tempted.

"That's it." A soft, persuasive murmur. "You're mine, little fawn. We both know it."

No. Not like this. Even through the lustful haze he'd induced, she knew it was wrong. She opened her eyes and removed his hand from her face.

His nostrils flared, but he didn't try to stop her as she stepped back. The pressure on her dissolved as if it had never been.

She felt oddly bereft. Then her brows snapped together. "Did you just use it on *me*?"

He moved a shoulder. His eyes slowly regained their blue tint, but he still had that watchful expression.

"Damn you," she said through clenched teeth. "What's the matter with you? You have no right to try and force me to stay. You—"

"Go," he barked.

She jumped and took a step back, gaze locked on his face. "I—"

His growl ripped through the clearing.

She gulped. "I'm going, I'm going." She took another few steps back and then turned and hurried through the trees. Walking at first, and then moving faster and faster until by the time she reached the beach she was running.

17

———

*H*ell. Tiago listened as Alesia crashed through the trees with none of her usual grace. The sounds halted, and then everything was still, save for a lone robin scolding nearby.

He scowled and scraped his fingers through his hair.

Maybe he shouldn't have told Alesia about his Gift. But Dion, Cleia and Marjani knew. Jorge and Benny had seemed to as well, although he didn't know how. Maybe Okeanos had sensed it in Tiago, although five years ago, he hadn't even known himself.

But now that it was out, word would spread, and he'd wanted Alesia to hear it first from him. He owed it to her, as both a friend and a lover.

But he should've given her time to absorb it. Hell, they'd only just become lovers, and then he'd dropped a fucking bombshell on her.

Man, he was an idiot. He lowered himself into the grassy nest they'd made for themselves and sat with his head in his hands.

He'd been right to tell Alesia about his Gift; in fact, he probably should've done it before now.

But what in the name of everything holy had induced him to

let it loose on her? Because that had been all him. Sure, the beast had freaked when it saw her backing away and instinctively tried to stop her, but Tiago hadn't even attempted to interfere. No, he'd been a willing partner. In that moment, he'd have sold his own soul to keep her with him.

Which come to think of it, was pretty much what he'd done.

He dropped onto his back to stare bleakly up at the sky. He'd never felt so alone in his life. Even after his parents had been lost at sea, he'd had his brothers and Rosana and the rest of the clan. But now his Gift was a wedge between him and the rest of the world. Even Alesia was afraid of him.

He shook his head and curled up on his side. The beast stretched and pushed beneath his skin, urging him to shift and go after their woman, but he gritted his teeth and ignored it and after a while it subsided.

He must have slept then, because when he opened his eyes again, it was pitch black. He came to his feet and gave a tentative stretch. Thanks to Cleia, he was healing even more rapidly than normal. He was still sore, but nothing he couldn't handle.

He debated spending the night on this deserted stretch of shore, but his animal was still agitated at the loss of Alesia. It would be happier in the water, and so would he.

A few minutes later he was swimming as his river dolphin. His belly rumbled, reminding him he hadn't eaten for hours. He sent out a series of rapid clicks to scan for food and with a few minutes had located a school of bluefish.

His hunger satisfied, he started across the top of the bay. About halfway back to Rock Run, he met up with a couple of wild bottlenose males, and after some posturing and tail-slapping, established that he was their dominant. He spent the night with the bottlenoses, dozing in the way of a dolphin, one side of the brain awake while the other slept, so that he could surface every few minutes to breathe.

His dreams were dark, restless. He was back in the rowhouse

with Benny and Jorge, the blows raining endlessly on his body, and then Benny's face changed to Dion's, furious at being compelled, until Tiago wrenched himself awake and shot to the surface, sucking in air through his blowhole.

He fought sleep until his still-healing body overcame him. This time, he caressed his way down Alesia's taut little body, and saw her flinch and turn away when she realized just how dark he really was. Then she was darting through the trees and he knew that if he didn't catch her, *compel* her, he'd lose her forever.

No. By the gods, no.

His whole body shuddered. He awoke to find himself once more at the surface, gulping oxygen through his blowhole.

He would *not* lose Alesia—but neither was he going to compel her, ever again. Right then and there, he swore a binding vow, the kind that would cause him serious damage if he broke it.

But on the other hand, he wasn't going to give her up. He'd allow her some time to cool down, to absorb what he'd told her and then he was going after her. She'd started this and he was damned if he'd let her back off now. She'd just have to deal with what he was.

Hell, who was he kidding? He'd go down on his knees and beg if that's what it took. Because a life without her in it didn't bear thinking about.

It was as if a fog had lain over his heart, a fog that was one part youth and one part sheer stubbornness. Yeah, Cleia was a fucking sex goddess and he'd never forget the week he'd had with her, but the two of them would never have had the equal relationship she had with Dion.

No, to a powerful fae like her, Tiago had been little more than a shiny new toy.

But Alesia was different. She saw him as himself, Tiago. And he was pretty sure she was in love with him.

Which was good, because he cared about her. Now the fog had lifted, he realized just how much. So what if she wasn't his mate? Hell, Dion had seen one hundred turns of the sun before he found Cleia.

You didn't have to be mated to want a woman—and he wanted Alesia, very much.

He was going to have to apologize, though, explain that he'd panicked because he'd been afraid to lose her. And then he'd do whatever it took to win her back. He'd worked hard to gain her trust. One mistake couldn't blow that completely—could it?

The bottlenoses circled him, clucking in agitation at his odd behavior. The more aggressive dolphin nudged Tiago with his beak and Tiago lunged back, raking his teeth over its back.

The dolphins backed off, but he could tell they were upset, and a few minutes later they slipped away. He started swimming too, but west across the top of the bay toward Rock Run. It was nearly dawn. The sky was slowly lightening into a hazy pink and gold. He waited until the sun was above the horizon and then snacked on a couple of mouthfuls of herring before setting out in earnest.

As he entered the mouth of the Susquehanna, he wondered why he was returning so tamely. He could head south down the bay to Baltimore and then just keep going. Sign on with a freighter or the merchant marine; water fada were always in demand in the shipping industry. He couldn't hide from Dion forever, but he wouldn't have to. He hadn't done anything bad enough to get himself banished. He was a grown man; he had the right to leave if he chose.

He could even go looking for his brothers, Nic and Joaquim, and hire out as a mercenary as they had.

But he'd given Dion his word. He wasn't going to turn tail and run at the last minute like the half-grown pup his brother seemed to think him.

And if he left now, who knew when he'd seen Alesia again? By the time he returned, she might be with another man—even mated.

His jaw hardened. *Over my dead body.*

No. He'd stay and face Dion.

He turned up Rock Run Creek. Chico was on duty as a sentry along with a friend of theirs named Eliana, both of them patrolling as their dolphins. The two of them whistled a greeting, then Eliana slid up alongside Tiago, sending out a stream of worried clicks.

You okay, Ti? I heard you were in a fight.

You should see the other guy, he shot back. Then he remembered that the other guy was dead and grimaced.

Eliana had been in his cohort along with Chico, Jaxon and Gabe. Everyone liked her; she was hard-working and sweet without being too girly. Now she gave a dolphin chuckle—which was more like a snort—and then sobered.

What happened? People are saying it was Jorge and Benny, that they've gone feral.

It was them. And two sea fada from Okeanos's den.

It's true about Benny? You—

Yeah.

She clucked in sympathy.

Chico had been circling and listening. Now he said, *The base is on alert. Security's doubled. Rui was out all night looking for Jorge and the other two. He just got back.*

He shifted to human, and Tiago followed suit. The two of them glanced at Eliana, who rolled her eyes but took the hint. She gave a slap of her tail that drenched them both and resumed her sweeps of the creek.

Chico took in Tiago's still-healing black eye. "So what happened?"

Tiago gave him a short version of what had happened, leaving out the part about his Gift. He intended to tell Chico—soon—but right now he was still too raw from Alesia's reaction. As he talked, the two of them swam slowly upstream to where the water was shallower until they were standing waist-deep in the creek.

He finished his story, and Chico put his hands on his hips and shook his head. "Damn, bro. You're lucky you got out of there alive. And what's with Jorge and Benny? So what if they're not officially members of Rock Run anymore? That's on them, not you. But to drug you and a woman?" He spat into the water. "That's fucking messed up on so many levels. I only wish I'd known you were in trouble—I'd have helped kick their asses. But I was with that human."

"Good, huh?" Tiago asked to change the subject. He appreciated that Chico was pissed—he'd have felt the same in his place—but he was done talking about last night. All he wanted was to get through his interview with Dion and then go try to fix things with Alesia.

His friend just smiled.

Tiago shook his head, but he was smiling too. He thought of telling Chico about how he'd almost had an earth shifter, but that was probably best forgotten. And he was *not* going to talk about Alesia.

"Look," he said, "I'd better get going. Dion wants to see me for an ass-chewing. I was under orders to stay away from the earth shifters. I promised to report back by noon."

"What's the hurry? It's not even nine o'clock yet."

"Might as well get it over with." Tiago ran a hand over his chin. "Besides, I could use a shave and some breakfast." Those few mouthfuls of herring seemed a long time ago.

"Okay. We'll talk later—I'm on duty until four o'clock. And Tiago?"—Chico pulled him into a hard hug—"do me a favor, okay? Next time you go investigating, take me along."

"You got it."

They nuzzled each other, exchanging scents in the way of longtime friends. Chico's skin carried the sharp bite of worry, telling Tiago he was more upset than he was letting on. Tiago swallowed and hugged him back.

Eliana glided up. *Well?*

He gave her a lopsided grin. "Sorry, Eli. Chico can tell you what happened."

She nudged him affectionately, and he hugged her back before heading downstream to Rock Run's deep water entrance.

Most of the clan was already at work. He made it to his room without running into anyone else, but barely had time to shed his shorts when Rosana knocked on his door.

"Tiago? You back yet?"

He stifled a groan, but wrapped a towel around his hips and let her in.

She grabbed him by the shoulders. "I've been so worried." She gave him a little shake. "Why didn't you come home with Dion?"

"I needed to heal."

She narrowed her eyes. "You *are* hurt. What happened, anyway? Dion wouldn't tell me anything, just that you were in a fight with Jorge and Benny, and that Benny's dead."

Tiago pulled her close for a hug and a kiss, and then set her gently but firmly aside. He loved Rosana, but as the only girl in a family of four older males, she'd been petted and spoiled since the day their mother first brought her into the world. It was even worse now that she was a woman, and damn pretty—for a sister. Half the clan's unmated men were after her.

He, however, was her brother, not some lovesick, horny male.

"Sit, Rosie." He pointed to one of his two chairs. "I need a shower and a shave. If you want to talk to me, you're going to have to wait."

"Don't call me Rosie," she returned automatically, but obeyed. "Did you really kill Benny?"

"Yes," he said shortly, and before she could ask anything else, grabbed a pair of shorts and went into the bathroom. "Fifteen minutes," he said and shut the door.

When he returned, he felt much better. He'd showered and shaved, and combed the tangles out of his hair.

Rosana bounced out of the chair. She looked more like their Irish sea fada mother every day, right down to the stubborn look on her pretty face. Tiago felt a pang. He still missed his ma, even after all these years.

"Well?" she demanded.

He sighed and once more gave the short version of what had happened.

Her fine black brows furrowed. "You fought off four men? Without any help? I heard Dion say something to Cleia about your Gift. But your Gift is talking to animals, right? How could that hurt anyone?"

Tiago dragged a hand over his wet hair. Rosana might be spoiled, but she was smart—and she knew how to keep a secret. And he was done hiding what he was from his closest friends and family.

"I have another Gift," he said.

THE DINING HALL was nearly empty. Breakfast had already been cleared but the gruff head cook, Gabriela, had a special fondness for Tiago, and produced a basket of rolls, cheese and a plate of salted cod, which he washed down with a large espresso.

Fausto trotted into the big hall. He was welcome to come and go in the base as he pleased, but somehow he only showed up when Tiago was eating.

He headed across the room to where Tiago sat at a table by himself and set his paws on the bench beside Tiago. "Up," he said in his otter-flavored Portuguese.

Tiago boosted him onto the bench. "I guess you heard."

Fausto grunted, his gaze on the last piece of cod.

Tiago waved a hand. "Help yourself."

The otter wrapped his paws around the fish and made short work of it. Tiago tipped some of the espresso onto the plate for him and handed him a chunk of bread. Fausto had developed a taste for caffeine, which was probably as bad for him as it was for canines, but hey, he was a big boy.

The otter dipped the bread in the bitter brown liquid and downed it in a few quick bites, standing on his hind legs to lap up the last of the espresso from the plate. He lowered himself back to the bench and tilted his head to consider Tiago with his round black eyes.

"You okay." It wasn't a question.

"*Sim*. Pissed off that those guys got ahold of me, but I'll live." Tiago leaned closer and lowered his voice. "They're not going to get away with it. I don't care what Dion says, I'm going after Jorge and the other two."

Fausto made a doubtful sound. "See Dion. Then see."

Tiago scowled. "I knew you'd say that."

Fausto just shrugged. "Come. Get me."

"When I go after them?"

Fausto nodded.

"*Obrigado*," Tiago said without saying yes or no. Fausto was a tough bastard in his own world, but at twenty-five pounds or so, he wasn't a match for a fada. Still, he appreciated the offer.

"Get me," the otter repeated and then flowed off the bench to the floor in his boneless way. "Later," he said and headed for the door.

Tiago shook his head. Sometimes he thought the only reason Fausto put up with him was for the food.

He came to his feet. Time to get this over with.

He found Dion in the operations room with Rui. They were with two sentries, but Rui immediately dismissed them. "You have your orders. Report directly to me if you see any trace of them."

They nodded and left, and Dion and Rui turned to him.

Rui knew. Tiago could tell from the look on the older man's face. He should've expected it, but this was a secret he'd kept from everyone, even his family, for three years. His whole body went taut. He felt exposed, and let down by Dion.

"Good morning." He knew he sounded stiff, but damn it, that's how he felt.

Dion opened his arms. "Come here, *irmão*."

Tiago hesitated, and then went to him. His brother's arms closed around him and they hugged for a long moment. At least his beast accepted it. Tiago had been half-afraid it would challenge Dion again.

Dion released him and looked him over. "You're better?"

"Yeah."

"Good." His brother folded his arms over his chest. "So, Tiago—what the fuck? You go behind my back, conducting what amounts to an unauthorized investigation. You hide a Gift from your alpha. You're my brother and I love you, but you're subject to the same rules as anyone else in the clan."

Tiago glanced away. "I know. And I'm sorry—there's no excuse. I just thought—"

"Go on," Dion prompted. "I want to know. What the hell were you thinking?"

"I suppose I wanted to prove myself. Show I could be trusted. After that thing with Adric five years ago, I know you've never really been sure of me."

Dion frowned. "That's not true—"

"No?" Tiago met his eyes. It was his brother's turn to look away.

"But I don't blame you," Tiago continued. "I deserved it. Hell, I gave Rock Run's location to a Baltimore shifter. I did it for Cleia, but we both know Adric would've taken you out in a heartbeat if he'd had the chance. So I've worked my ass off to show you I can be trusted. I've obeyed you without question, followed my squad leader's orders to the letter, done my damn best to make every mission a success. But it never seems like enough."

"That's where you're wrong," Rui interjected. "We noticed. You're under consideration as a squad leader yourself."

"I am?" Tiago felt a flash of pleasure, until he realized that was another thing he'd probably screwed up. "I admit that coming on to an earth shifter female was a dumbass idea. But I won't apologize for trying to find out what Jorge and Benny were up to. You and Rui are always telling us to think on our feet. Jorge came to me—I didn't go to him. The man's smart. If I'd have left even for a few minutes to contact Rock Run, he'd have disappeared."

"Okay," Dion said. "I'll give you that. But this Gift of yours—" He blew out a breath. "I need proof you have it under control."

Tiago stiffened. "I've controlled it for three years."

"*Sim*? From what you said earlier, I'm not sure who's controlling who. Sounds more like a tiger you have by the tail. Can you swear to me you can control it in every situation?"

Tiago stared at him. His hands wanted to fist but he forced them to remain loose at his sides. Losing his cool would only count against him.

"No," he admitted. "I can't."

Dion and Rui exchanged a look. Then his brother shook his head. "I'm sorry, Tiago. I can't clear you to go out with your squad until we're sure—until *you're* sure. You can train with them, but you're to stay close to base for the next month. Meanwhile, I'll contact the Rhode Island sea fada. They may have someone who can help you with your Gift."

"No," he blurted. "Let me go after Jorge. Give me that much."

"Absolutely not," his brother returned. "And that's an order. Any questions?"

Tiago's stomach churned. But he bit back his anger to say, "No, sir."

Dion dragged a hand through his hair. "Look, *irmão*, take a couple of weeks. Relax, swim, allow your body to heal. You're on medical leave as of now."

Tiago gave a tight nod.

"This is only a precaution," Dion added. "I believe—no, I *know* you can do this. You appeared in complete control at the hotel. If it were only you and me, I'd take a chance, but I have the rest of the clan to think about."

It was too little, too late. Tiago's hands fisted. This time he didn't try to unclench them. "Do I have permission to leave the creek?"

"Of course. You're not confined to base. Feel free to travel anywhere in our territory. You can even go into Grace Harbor." Dion named the nearest small town. "Just stay out of Baltimore— and that's for your own safety."

Tiago jerked his head in assent.

Dion studied him, a worried frown between his eyes. "You sure you're okay?"

"I'm fine. Can I go now?"

Dion put a hand on his shoulder. "I love you, Tiago. You know that, don't you?"

"Yeah. Sure."

Dion waited for him to say more, but Tiago kept his mouth stubbornly shut. His brother could protest all he wanted, but it was clear he didn't trust Tiago worth a damn.

Dion let out a small breath. "Okay. Here's what I want you to do: think this over for a week. Then come to me with a plan. Explain how it works and what you're doing to control it, and we can go from there."

"Thank you," he said stiffly. That was something, at least.

Dion waited another few moments and then said, "That's all."

"*Obrigado, meu senhor,*" he repeated in that same stiff voice, and with a nod to Rui, stalked from the room.

18

———

dric sat at the kitchen table and watched as Marjani downed a plate of jerk chicken, rice and plantains with single-minded determination. She'd spent most of the last twenty-four hours asleep, waking just once to eat and use the bathroom before crawling back into bed again. He'd stayed close, alternating with Suha in watching her.

Sometime after midnight, she'd gotten so restless that he'd changed to his cougar and climbed into bed with her. She'd awakened enough to take off the T-shirt and change to her cat as well, then settled next to him with a sigh. He licked her jaw until her eyes closed and she fell back asleep.

They slept the rest of the night curled together. He woke to find she'd burrowed her head and part of her body under his so that he was draped over her back. His stomach clenched. She hadn't done that since they were cubs and she'd been afraid to sleep because both their parents were gone on missions and they'd been left with their uncle Leron, a man who'd been quick and brutal in his punishments. His own three cubs were as afraid of him as Adric and Marjani, but that didn't stop them from tormenting their two younger cousins when the adults weren't around.

Shortly after dawn, Zuri had arrived to update him on what he and the other lieutenants had discovered. To Adric's frustration, it wasn't much. Tiago do Rio had left the Full Moon shortly before closing and reappeared a short time later at the Wildcat. He'd had a drink with Shania, but she'd left soon after he'd started drinking with the two river fada. After that, Tiago hadn't been seen again until Luc and his men had come across him and Marjani trying to hail a cab in Canton, a neighborhood on Baltimore's east side.

Adric had frowned. "He wasn't seen after he left the Wildcat?"

"No. It was late, remember—and a Wednesday, a work night. Not too many people out."

"What about Jani? No one saw her, either?"

"The waitress thinks she might have seen her leave with a man—maybe one of the Greek sea fada—but she wasn't sure. She's new—doesn't know your sister. But after that, no."

"Could they have been using a glamour?" A glamour could be used to change a person's looks.

Because it was damn strange that no one had seen either Tiago or Marjani after they'd left the club. The cats in his clan outnumbered the wolves and other animals two to one, and while they weren't truly nocturnal like cats in the wild, they were often up late into the night.

"It's possible," the lieutenant replied. "But they'd have to have a fae cast it, and a glamour doesn't come cheap. I don't know where four clan-less fada would get the cash."

"Unless they traded it for something the fae want, like a war between the local fada. And even better, this war would involve the sun fae, too."

"The Virginia night fae." Zuri lifted a single black brow. "You think this might have something to do with Jace's niece?"

"Hell if I know. But it's damn suspicious." The Virginia night fae were the closest fae clan other than the Rising Sun fae. But unlike Cleia's fun-loving, sociable clan, night fae were nasty, energy-sucking creatures that even other fae avoided.

Worse, the Virginia prince's son and heir, Tyrus, had it out for Merry Jones, the mixed-blood who was both Jace's niece and Valeria and Rui do Mar's adopted daughter—and Tyrus's half-sister. She'd be dead right now if her grandfather the prince hadn't personally seen to her protection.

"What about Shania?" Adric asked. "Did she see anything?"

"No one's seen her since yesterday morning. I tried to track her through her crystal, but it's gone dead. Either she's blocking us—or it's been destroyed like Marjani's."

The hairs on his nape raised. This was all connected, he was sure of it. "I want her found ASAP."

"I've got several men looking for her."

"Hunter," he said between clenched teeth. He exchanged a look with Zuri.

Five years ago, he'd had to execute Hunter after he'd stolen Merry Jones for Tyrus. Fortunately, the Rock Run fada had gotten the girl back before Hunter could pass her to the night fae.

At the time, Adric had suspected that Hunter had been turned by his cousin Corban, who was every bit as sly as his father Leron had been. Corban believed that as Leron's eldest son, he should've been the next alpha, but after losing to Adric in a challenge after his father's death, he'd accepted a position as a high-ranking sentry.

Shania had been Hunter's lover, but she'd seemed to accept that he deserved what he'd got. The man had turned traitor; Adric couldn't let him live. But executing Hunter had been one of the hardest things Adric had ever done. He'd grown up with the man and considered him a friend.

Zuri nodded grimly. "I always suspected she was in on it with him. The woman's got a dark side beneath that party-girl face."

"Find her," Adric snapped. "I want that woman—yesterday."

"I'm on it," Zuri said, and left.

Adric allowed himself one long, vicious snarl before returning to Marjani. He'd snatched some sleep during the night, and he wasn't going to be able to rest until they'd found Shania, so he sent Suha to sleep in his bedroom and took up his vigil at his sister's bed again.

WHEN MARJANI finally woke for good, it was afternoon. She bolted upright, looking wildly around.

"Hey, hey." Adric straightened from where he was sprawled in a chair. "Take it easy. Everything's cool."

She blinked and slumped back onto the pillow. "You look like hell, Ric."

Normally, he'd retort that if anyone looked bad, it was her— she had dark shadows under her eyes and her skin was tinged an unhealthy yellow—but instead he just took her hand.

"How are you, kitten?"

"Better."

"Good." He squeezed her fingers. "Here—I have a quartz for you."

While she'd been asleep, he'd gone through a stash of quartz that he kept for situations like these. Now he held out the one he'd selected, a beautiful conglomeration of amethyst crystals ranging from smoky gray to purple. Something about it had said Marjani to him.

"Thanks." As her fingers closed around it, she expelled a small breath. Then her lips curved in an infinitesimal smile. "It's perfect, Ric. I don't think I'll need to search for another."

She handed his own quartz back to him. As it settled onto his chest, the energy relinked with his, giving him a much-needed boost.

He handed her a leather cord. The less he touched her new

quartz, the better; the tiny crystals needed to attune themselves to her energy. She wrapped the cord several times around the gray-and-purple chunk, secured it with a square knot and hung it around her neck.

"That's better." She wrapped her fingers around the amethyst and gave him another slight smile, which seemed to be all she could manage right now.

"Ah," Suha said from the doorway. "You're up. And hungry, I'll bet."

Marjani moved a shoulder. "I'd like another shower first."

"Anything you want, babe."

"I'll get lunch," Adric said, and left them to it.

Luc arrived with a duffle bag of Marjani's clothes that Adric had asked him to pick up. Adric wasn't letting his sister out of his sight until she was completely healed, and maybe not even then. He left Luc to guard the women while he picked up a large order of jerk chicken and several side dishes from their favorite Caribbean restaurant, comfort food from their childhood with a Jamaican mother.

Marjani was at the kitchen table with Luc and Suha when Adric returned with the food. She watched, expressionless, as he set a plate before her. But once she picked up her fork, she didn't stop eating until she'd cleaned the plate. She listened with that same expressionless face when Adric told her she was going to be rooming with him for the foreseeable future, and then agreed without argument.

Adric's heart sank. What had they done to his kick-ass, take-no-prisoners sister?

Suha laid a hand on his arm and mouthed, "Give her time."

Zuri called to say that Shania was still missing. Marjani stared down at the table but he could tell she was listening.

When Adric cut the connection, she asked, "You think Shania was helping those men?"

Adric expelled a breath. "Look, I know she's your friend—"

"No," Marjani returned flatly. "She's not."

He came alert. "Why do you say that?"

"Because I remember now that I gave her my drink to hold while I was dancing. I think she put the drug in it. But even if she didn't, she was there when they took me out the back door. I don't remember much, but she didn't do a thing to help me. She just stood by and watched while they shoved me into a car."

Adric's jaw tightened. "I see."

"Can you tell us what kind of car?" Luc asked.

"Sorry." Marjani shook her head. "I was too out of it. It was dark, that's all I remember—black, or maybe dark blue. I'm not even sure it was a car—it could've been a small SUV."

"Any unusual scent?" said Luc.

"No." Marjani jumped to her feet. "I'm telling you, I don't remember. I was drugged and they had their hands all over me. And they'd smashed my quartz, so I felt like hell. So no, I wasn't paying attention to the damn car."

Luc rose with her. "No worries, baby. Here, why don't you lie down?"

Marjani deflated. "No," she said listlessly. "I'm not tired. I think I'll just sit in the living room."

"Can I come with you?" he asked.

She shrugged. "Sure. Why not?"

With Marjani out of the way, Suha pulled Adric into his bedroom and closed the door. "You have to be patient," she hissed. "Her body's healing, but it's going to take a while before she feels safe again."

"You think I don't know that? But this is my sister. When I became alpha, I promised she'd never be hurt again."

"Oh, honey." Suha clasped him in her arms. "You can't keep a promise like that."

He heaved a breath and for a few seconds, let her comfort him. Then he gently set her away from him. "Don't worry. I'll give her whatever time she needs."

"You're a good brother, Ric." Suha touched his cheek. "And the best alpha a clan could have. Just—don't be too hard on yourself, okay? Things happen. You're just one man. You can't be everywhere, protecting everyone."

"You think I don't know that?" he returned. "But this is my fucking sister."

"I know. I know. But she'll get better. I promise."

He jerked his head in acknowledgment and opened the door. "I'll take you home now. You must be tired. If anything changes, I'll let you know."

Suha hesitated and then agreed. "I *am* tired. I feel like I could sleep for twelve hours straight."

LATER THAT AFTERNOON, Adric crouched in his cougar form on Rock Run territory. He'd had to get outside—do *something*—before he exploded. So he'd left Marjani with Luc, and starting at the shabby rowhouse near the Patapsco River, had done some tracking of his own. Searching for something—anything—that would lead him to Jorge or Shania or even the Greek sea fada.

But he found nothing that they didn't already know. Jorge and the sea fada had taken to the water, and Shania had disappeared without a trace. So he got his motorcycle and expanded his search north. As anxious as he was to find Shania, Jorge was the more urgent problem right now, and Adric would bet good money the man was somewhere on or near Rock Run territory. It was the man's home ground, and a smart fada could change his scent so as to escape detection.

Jorge probably had a hidey-hole that no one else knew about, like the one Adric had maintained when his uncle was alpha.

Adric left his bike in a state park a few miles from Rock Run, walked into the trees and shifted to his cougar. In a few miles he was at Rock Run's border. He paused. For any fada to cross onto another clan's territory without permission was a punishable offense, but if you were an alpha, it just might get you killed. Not that he'd ever let that stop him before; he and his soldiers had been slipping on and off Rock Run's land for years. He had no doubt that Dion and his people did the same in Baltimore.

This part of Rock Run was heavily forested. He darted into the trees, keeping out of sight of the Susquehanna River and the sentries who patrolled there.

About a half mile in, he found a ledge overlooking the river and leapt onto it. He was at the forest's edge. To the east were Rock Run's vineyards, and beyond that another, smaller stand of trees which concealed Rock Run Creek and the underground caverns that made up the river clan's base.

It was nearly dusk. He scooted back on the ledge so that he was in the shadows and fixed his gaze on the river. Something told him Jorge was out there somewhere, but he had no way to track him. Damn the river fada anyway, and their ability to change into water animals. Still, they didn't spend all their time underwater.

He stared out at the fast-moving river and considered his next move.

A raindrop splattered on his nose. *Great.* It was starting to rain now. His cat rumbled unhappily. Suddenly, the scent of a young female teased at his nostrils. He forgot about the weather to rise partway up, nose twitching.

It was her. He was sure of it. Coming toward him on the path that ran along the river. He forgot about Jorge as his heart sped up.

The young woman was in sight now. And he was right, it *was* her: the youngest do Rio and the only female, Rosana.

He kept files on all the key Rock Run fada, but he had *her* file memorized: Rosana do Rio, just twenty-one years old, which was barely mature by fada standards, since shifters matured later than humans. Black hair, blue eyes. Well-liked, but a bit of a smart-aleck. Closely protected by her brothers and everyone else in the clan.

Too damn closely protected. Adric hadn't seen her since Cleia and Dion's mating ball five years ago—and he'd tried.

Back then she'd been all long legs and promise, with a cloud of black hair and big blue eyes in a heart-shaped face. Now she was coming into her womanhood, still slender but with curves he literally ached to touch.

And the long-sleeved black T-shirt and short white shorts showed them off to perfection. His gaze moved down her body, fixing on those long legs. She was wearing black leather sandals with straps that wound around the lower part of her calves. His mind swam with salacious images of her in those leather sandals and nothing else.

She halted fifteen feet away and looked straight at him. He stilled. She shouldn't be able to see him in the shadows, and the wind was blowing in the wrong direction for her to scent him.

"There's a sentry twenty yards up the river," she said calmly. "If I call out, you're dead."

Adric considered that for about two seconds. Then he gathered his muscles and leapt off the ledge, landing so close to her that the air he displaced caused her hair to lift from her shoulders, then settle back down.

She didn't even twitch an eyelid.

Impressed—and more intrigued than ever—he shifted to man, standing before her naked, his only adornment the quartz around his neck.

He crossed his arms over his bare chest and met those rich blue eyes. "Go ahead. Call them."

She drew a slow breath. Beneath the shirt, her breasts shifted. His gaze flicked down. Damn, she had nice tits.

He jerked his gaze back up, prepared to clap a hand over her mouth or run like hell. But she let out the breath. Her eyes flickered and he watched as her gaze traveled down his body, catching on his cock, already half-hard.

His cock twitched and grew, enjoying the attention. She stared at it for a long moment, and he found himself grinning.

She scowled at him. "You're Lord Adric. The Baltimore alpha."

"And you're Rosana do Rio."

"How did you know?"

He shrugged. She didn't need to know he'd never forgotten her, not since that first glimpse at the mating ball. She'd fascinated him—her face, her body, the graceful way she'd danced—but most of all, her innocence. It was a powerful aphrodisiac to a man who'd been brought up in a warring clan and forced to fight for everything—food, respect, and on the darkest days, his very life.

His hand went to his quartz, playing with it. Almost without his volition, it started to glow. He had an unusual Gift for an earth fada. He was so in tune with his quartz and so powerful personally, honed as he'd been in the crucible of a vicious civil war, that he could use his quartz to hypnotize.

Most earth fada had a slight ability to hypnotize, but his Gift allowed him to hypnotize practically anyone—and in a few short seconds.

Now he toyed with the quartz. Tempted. Because by the gods, he wanted this river female. He could hypnotize her, take her somewhere off Rock Run territory and enjoy her—for hours. He wouldn't harm her. He'd even make sure she enjoyed it in return.

And the best part was he could fix it so she wouldn't remember who or how it happened.

Rosana was looking at the quartz, her soft red mouth slightly open. Temptation seethed in him, so powerful his hand trembled.

She stretched out a hand. "Can I touch it?"

With an effort, he closed his fingers over the quartz. The energy warmed his palm, then receded. "No."

She blinked. "I'm sorry. I should know better. Merry told me that no one can touch an earth fada's quartz except a close relative—and even then you need to be careful."

"Or a lover," Adric said.

Her fine black brows drew together.

"A lover can touch it," he clarified. "If you ask first."

"Oh." He watched, fascinated, as her soft lips pursed.

"I'd let you touch it," he murmured. "If you asked me nicely."

She gulped and then took a step back, a faint flush on her cheeks. "Why are you here, anyway?"

Belatedly, he remembered Marjani and dropped the quartz. It was his turn to redden, but his was due more to guilt than embarrassment. "I'm looking for the man who hurt my sister."

"I heard what happened." She moved closer again, touched his arm. "I'm so sorry. Is she going to be all right?"

Lord, he liked having her hand on him. He ached to bend down and taste her pretty lips. She was just a few inches shorter than him; the two of them would fit together perfectly. Her breasts against his bare chest, his cock nestled in the curve of her belly...

And because he wanted it so badly, his reply was a growl. "Yes."

She removed her hand, but her smile was sincere. "I'm glad. Tell her we were asking about her, all right?"

He nodded. "Thank you," he said, more gently this time.

Rosana cocked her head like a blue-eyed robin. "Is that why you're here? To find Jorge and the others? Because my brother has everyone out looking for them, too. If they're here, we'll find them."

"If you say so."

"But you need to be doing something, don't you?"

He thought of Marjani and briefly closed his eyes. "Yeah."

When he opened them, Rosana was still standing temptingly close. He gazed down at her, knowing he should shift back to his cougar and leave. He had no business with the sister of the Rock Run alpha.

Hell, after what had happened, Dion would think Adric was deliberately messing with his sister. Add that to his being on Rock Run territory without permission and the other alpha would be justified in beating him within an inch of his life.

But he wanted a touch. Just a touch.

A single wavy black lock had fallen over her eye. He reached out and rubbed it between his thumb and index finger. It was so soft, like a cat's underbelly. He moved closer and speared his fingers into the silky mass, sliding his other arm around her waist.

A hundred yards downriver they heard two men talking.

Rosana shot a nervous glance over her shoulder. "Go," she said in a low voice. "Now. If they find you with me, they'll tear you apart."

His gaze was on her mouth. "It might be worth it." He moved his hand down to that tight, sweet ass and gave it a squeeze.

"Stop it," she hissed but her eyes were half-closed, her body straining toward his.

His face was just an inch from hers now. "Stop it?" He inhaled. She was aroused, and they both knew it.

But they were even, because his cock was prodding her belly.

The rain was falling in earnest now, drenching them both. Her eyes shut, the curly black lashes dark crescents on her damp cheeks. A raindrop rolled down her temple and he caught it with his tongue, then moved down her face to her throat.

Her head fell back. "Mm," she said, so low it was almost a purr.

He nipped her sensitive underjaw and she gave a wriggle that sent heat straight to his balls.

The voices came closer. Rosana's eyes flew open. "Get out of here," she whispered and shoved at his chest.

"In a minute." He jerked her up against him for a hard kiss. When she gasped, he slipped his tongue inside her mouth.

She moaned and sucked on his tongue. Her hands were caught between them, but she wasn't trying to push him away. No, she had a leg wrapped around his hip and was digging her nails into his skin, practically climbing his body in her effort to get closer.

He gave her a last, hard kiss and then reluctantly released her. He couldn't afford an incident right now. But it was damn difficult when everything in him was clamoring to shove down those tiny shorts and take her right here in the woods.

He tapped her on the nose. "See you around," he said with a lopsided grin.

She stared back at him, her chest heaving. "I—"

He touched his crystal and shifted to his cougar. A few seconds later he was loping back the way he came. Just before he disappeared into the trees, he glanced back.

Rosana was gazing after him, eyes narrowed, hands fisted on her hips.

He gave a cheeky twitch of his tail and went to a full-out run.

19

———

*T*iago finished packing his messenger bag. He stood up and nervously wiped his hands down his T-shirt. Should he put on something nicer? But Alesia liked him in this shirt—said the blue matched his eyes.

He slung the canvas bag over his shoulder and headed for the clan marina.

The young female manning the desk glanced up as he approached. "Hello, Tiago. What can I do for you?"

"I'd like to check out a kayak."

"Help yourself." The woman—a friend of Rosana's whose name escaped him at the moment—glanced curiously at his bruised face, but all she did was make a notation on a sheet of paper.

"Thank you." He grabbed a paddle and headed to where a dozen kayaks were stored in a small shed at the end of a pier. He set one in the water, stowed his bag in the cockpit and headed upriver—to Alesia's island.

He should be feeling like shit. In the past twenty-four hours, he'd been beaten, killed a man—and even though Benny had deserved it, it had still left Tiago shaken—and come within a hair of challenging his own brother for alpha. To top it off, he'd confessed his darkest secret to Alesia and then proceeded to demonstrate that she was right to be afraid of it—and him.

So yeah, he felt pretty damn bad, and that meeting with Dion and Rui hadn't helped.

But he also felt strangely lighter. Like that weightless feeling you get at the end of the day after setting down a heavy backpack you've been lugging around for hours.

He hadn't realized how much his secret was weighing him down. It was a relief to have it out, at least to his family and Alesia.

He still might be shunned when the clan found out, but he was starting to think he should be the one to tell them. For one thing, it would be better coming from him, rather than having it spread through rumors and whispers. And for another, he was tired of hiding what he was. If people he'd known his whole life couldn't accept his Gift, then maybe he'd be better off somewhere else.

He passed Chico and Eliana, patrolling the Susquehanna as their dolphins, and saluted them with his paddle, but didn't stop.

It was good to be out on the river. He paddled steadily, gazing around him. The trees on both sides of the river were leafing out, and as he passed Rock Run's main vineyard he could see workers moving among the vines. His still-healing ribs twanged from the pulling motion and he eased off. Even so, it took him less than a half hour to travel the mile or so upstream.

As he approached the middle island, his stomach tightened.

Stop it, he told himself. Alesia would want to see him. They'd been friends for five years, for *Deus*'s sake. That couldn't all be for nothing. Hell, she probably already regretted running out on him yesterday.

But just in case, he was bringing gifts. He glanced at the bag between his feet. Alesia loved surprises. If there was one thing he'd learned in the past few years, it was how to tempt his dryad.

And then there she was on the narrow beach. Overnight, the temperature had dropped twenty degrees and a brisk April wind was blowing. She was bundled up against the cold in the green wool sweater, slim jeans and work boots from yesterday. She'd jammed a green-and-blue striped cap onto her head and her curls were whipping around her face, and she couldn't have looked any sexier.

He gave her a tentative smile. "Hey, *querida*."

She gazed back, unsmiling. Panic sliced up his spine.

The beast murmured: *The female is yours. Take her. You can make her do anything—anything you want.*

Tiago growled. *Like hell.* If he couldn't have Alesia of her own free will, then he'd live without her.

The beast considered that, then subsided. Not convinced, but allowing Tiago to win—for now.

Sooner or later, the two of them were going to have a reckoning. But not today.

He turned the kayak toward shore.

ALESIA WATCHED as Tiago dragged the kayak onto the beach. When she'd left him, all she could think was that she had to get away. Back to her island and her oak. She was safe there.

Teleporting so many times in a short period was tiring work. By the time she reached the island, it was dark out and she was exhausted. She 'ported directly to the oak, where she lay along a thick branch, her cheek on the solid, comforting bark. Hot tears slid down her face.

Her oak rustled consolingly. It didn't judge. They were bound together for life, but it wasn't a jealous relationship. The oak knew she required a mate, just as she needed food and water and occasional ventures into the larger world. If and when she found her mate, the tree would rejoice with her.

At first, Alesia was sure this was one huge, cosmic mistake. Tiago *couldn't* be her mate. She couldn't possibly be bound for life to a man with such a dark Gift.

Which meant this thing she was feeling couldn't be the mate bond.

She wrapped her arms around the branch and cried herself to sleep.

With the dawn came shame. It hadn't been easy for Tiago to tell her about his Gift. He'd been hurting, afraid she would think he was some dark, terrifying freak, and what had she done? She'd run away—like he was some dark, terrifying freak. He shouldn't have tried to use it against her, but he'd been scared, too.

Goddess, she was a coward. Even if she wasn't Tiago's mate, she was his friend. She should've been more understanding.

Now she watched as Tiago took a canvas messenger bag from the kayak's cockpit. "I brought you something."

He'd obviously been back to Rock Run. He'd shaved and put on clean cargo pants and her favorite periwinkle-blue T-shirt. He stood tall, shoulders back, and if you didn't look too close, you'd think he was strong and self-assured. But his eyes were wary, and instead of coming closer, he stayed where he was, hands clenched on the messenger bag.

Guilt twisted her stomach. She'd done that to him.

He'd said he was a monster and she hadn't even argued. She'd known he sought reassurance, but she'd been too shocked to give it. She told herself that anyone would've reacted in the same way, but she wasn't anyone.

She was Tiago's mate. And even if she wasn't, she *knew* him, knew with a bone-deep certainty that he was *not* a monster.

She tried to smile back, but her lips were trembling. "Hey."

"I brought you something," he said again.

And just like that, she gave in. It wasn't that he'd brought her a gift. It wasn't even that he was her mate.

It was the guarded look on his face, as if he was steeling himself for rejection.

This was *Tiago*, the man she loved—and he needed her.

"A present?" She crossed the short space between them. "What is it?"

She wasn't pretending to be interested. She loved gifts. She hadn't even known how much she loved them until Tiago started bringing them. Sure, her family exchanged presents at birthdays and the winter solstice, but Tiago's were special.

He grinned and relaxed. "Let me see..." He handed her a gold box encircled by a deep brown ribbon.

She instantly recognized the logo. "Chocolate." She bit her lower lip.

She couldn't produce chocolate on the island, and she didn't often go into town for supplies because even a small town like Grace Harbor was too crowded for a solitary like her, and besides she didn't have much money, just a small yearly payment from Rock Run for her contribution to the clan.

But Tiago had discovered how much she liked chocolate, and he'd started bringing her a big box every few weeks.

She removed the ribbon and lifted the lid. It was an assortment of dark chocolate. Her mouth watered just looking at all those lovely pralines and ganaches and caramels—and were those truffles?

"You didn't have to bring me anything. I shouldn't have run away like I did." But her fingers tightened on the gold box. No way was she giving it back.

He gave a crooked smile. "It's customary when you're courting a woman."

Surprise slammed into her. For a moment, she couldn't breathe. Had he finally realized they were mates?

"Is that what you're doing?" she managed to ask. "Courting me?"

"Yeah. You're mine, Alesia—no more running away."

No, he hadn't realized.

She pressed her lips together. She could tell him, but she wanted him to come to it on his own. "I wasn't the one who ran away the other day."

"No," he agreed. "Like I said, I was an ass. Two times over. I'm sorry, Alesia. You were right—I shouldn't have tried to use my Gift on you. I promise on the grave of my *avó* that it will never happen again. I won't use it on you—not even in fun." He spoke his true-name to bind himself even further.

"Thank you. I know you won't, but—thank you."

He flashed her a grin and then reached into the box for a truffle dusted with a reddish-brown powder. "Here, *querida*." He held it to her lips. "Have a taste."

Goddess, she loved it when he called her *querida* in that husky voice. Keeping her gaze on his, she bit into the truffle. It was delicious: a bite of heat followed by lush chocolate. She hummed with pleasure and rolled it around on her tongue, savoring the flavor.

Tiago's mouth quirked. "Have the rest." He urged the other half on her.

"What is it?" she asked when she could speak again.

"Chili chocolate. They dust it with chili and cayenne powder."

"No kidding." She licked the last bit from her lips.

"I thought you'd like it." His gaze was on her mouth, his eyes very blue.

He leaned closer and she thought he was going to kiss her, but instead he pulled back and reached into the canvas bag for a second, smaller box, this one white with a teal bow. "I brought you something else, too."

"You did?" She set the gold box of chocolate on his bag and took the white one from him. It looked like jewelry. He'd never brought her jewelry before.

She held it to her heart.

He guided her to sit on the kayak and then watched as she

undid the pretty bow. Inside was a delicate silver willow leaf suspended from a thin black leather cord.

"Oh, Tiago." Her throat clogged. She touched the silver leaf. "It's...beautiful."

"You like it, then." The corners of his eyes creased in a smile.

"I love it." She picked up the necklace to examine it. The pendant was beautiful, the silver obviously worked by hand, and the fine black cord suited it perfectly.

Tiago took the necklace from her and motioned her to turn around. "Let's see if it fits."

She set down the box and obeyed, lifting her hair out of the way so he could place the cord around her neck. He fastened the silver clasp and pressed his lips to her nape. One hand toyed with the willow leaf where it nestled a few inches above her breasts.

"I love it." She craned her neck to get a better look. "It's beautiful. Where did you get it?"

"In Grace Harbor, at a shop a few doors down from the candy store. I saw this a few months ago and thought of you."

"Thank you," she said and turned her head to kiss him. She lifted the leaf so she could admire it. "But I should change, put on something prettier." She tugged self-consciously on her sweater. It was a muddy heather green and fraying at the elbows.

"No. You're perfect." His hand slid under the sweater and the cotton tank she was wearing beneath, found one of her breasts. He toyed with the nipple and her head dropped back against his shoulder.

"You could lose the hat, though." He pulled it off and tossed it onto his bag. "There now." He pulled her up against him again, his hands on her abdomen beneath the tank top, and nuzzled the back of her ear. "What do you think? Could you be with a man like me?"

She tried to twist to see his face, but he held her where she was, facing away from him. "A man like you?"

He nodded against her hair. "You know what I am now. And

I'll be honest, I've done some things. Bad things. But I'm working to control it. What I did last night—that wasn't me. I swear I've never used it on a woman before."

"I know." She squeezed his hands. "And I'm sorry I ran away last night. It wasn't just that you tried to use your Gift on me. Even before that, I was afraid. I saw what you did to that acorn, and..." She trailed off.

"I'm sorry, too. It was wrong of me. I lost control." He expelled a breath. "I guess after the past few days, you may not believe me, but I swear I can control it. Especially when I'm around you. There's something about you that calms my animal—the beast."

"Your beast?"

He moved a shoulder. "That's what I call it. My animal's pretty dark—a beast. But being around you calms it, makes it easier for me to control it."

She pressed a kiss to the side of his mouth. "Then I'm glad."

But she must have sounded doubtful, because his arms tightened on her. "Damn it, Alesia. Tell me you're not afraid of me. You know I'd never hurt you."

She wriggled from his grip and swung around to face him. "I'm *not* afraid of you, Tiago do Rio. For one thing, I *know* you can control it. For another—"

"How?" he interrupted. "How do you know I can control it?"

She gripped those big shoulders and gave him a shake. "I just do. Because you did last night, for one thing. And because I know *you*."

He enfolded her in a hard hug. "Thank you," he said, then added in a voice so low she had to strain to hear it, "Dion doesn't think I can."

"He said that?"

"Yeah. He said he's not sure who's controlling who. He put me on medical leave. I'm not allowed to go out with my squad until he's sure of me. He's got everyone out searching for Jorge and the two sea fada, and I can't help."

"Oh, Tiago." She wrapped her arms around his big body. "He's your brother. How can he not know—"

"I used my Gift against him."

Her mouth snapped shut. "Oh."

"Just to show him what I could do," he hastened to say, and explained what had happened at the hotel. "But I can't blame him. Hell, if I were alpha, I wouldn't want someone like me around either."

She smoothed a hand down his nape. "Give him time. He'll come around."

"He wants proof I can control my Gift. How the hell am I supposed to give him proof?"

"Give him time," she repeated.

Tiago pressed his lips together and then nodded. His hands came to her face and suddenly, they weren't talking about Dion anymore. His thumbs caressed her cheeks and his gaze held hers so that she couldn't have looked away even if she'd wanted to.

"Come with me," he said. "I want to take you out. A date. Okay?"

A date? She'd never been on a date in her life. Sure, she'd had what humans called hook-ups. But a date? No.

She was so stunned that all she could do was nod.

"But not here." He brushed his mouth over hers. "Too many sentries. I want to take you upriver; that's why I brought the kayak. There's a little waterfall at the edge of the state park that no one ever goes to."

"A waterfall?" Her voice sounded throaty in her ears. "I'd like that."

They moved at the same time, meeting in the middle. His kiss was hard at first, but as it spun on, it became tender. She felt his need through the mate bond, stoking her own arousal.

When he lifted his head, his irises were pure silver.

Her heart skipped a beat, but somehow she wasn't afraid. "Tiago?" She tilted her head to one side.

He drew a slow breath. For a few seconds his eyes remained a hot, molten silver, and then they gradually returned to their normal color.

He gave her a last, hard kiss and then came to his feet, pulling her up with him. "Let's go."

20

————

Tiago guided the kayak onto shore. They were a few miles upriver in a strip of woods on the opposite side of the river from Rock Run. Human territory, but five miles from the nearest town. Sure, they could've picnicked on Alesia's island, but he'd wanted to take her someplace special.

And even better, they'd be totally private, somewhere no one would think to look for them. Even Fausto couldn't interrupt this time; it was too far away from his den.

He stowed the kayak in the trees near the river, picked up the messenger bag and a plaid blanket and then took Alesia's hand and led the way to a deer trail that wound its way through the strip of woods. The farmers who owned this land had left the trees as a natural barrier to suck up fertilizer run-off from their fields.

They followed the trail until they came to a slender creek, then continued along the water another few hundred yards until they reached a small waterfall tumbling over large black boulders. The rain clouds had dissipated and the afternoon sun streamed through the trees, bathing everything in a golden haze.

"It's beautiful." Alesia gazed around her.

He smiled, pleased. "I thought you'd like it. You're the first person I've brought here."

"Really?" Her eyes crinkled.

He nodded. This was his special place. Even Fausto had only been here a few times.

He guided Alesia across the stream to a grassy hollow on the other side. She spread out the picnic blanket while he set out the food on a nearby rock: crusty peasant bread, a wedge of sharp cheddar, olive tapenade, pickled vegetables, a couple of apples and a bottle of the clan's own red. The box of candy went in the center along with the wine and two glasses.

Alesia sat cross-legged on the blanket and poured the wine while he sliced the cheese and bread. He put it on a wooden plate along with a sampling of the other food, and then reclined on his elbow next to her, the plate between them.

"Mm." She handed him a glass of wine, her gaze on the sliced cheddar. For a dryad, cheese was like catnip—and Alesia especially loved sharp cheeses.

He touched his glass to hers. "*Saude.*"

"To your health," she repeated and took a sip of her own wine. Her gaze flicked to the cheese again.

He stifled a grin. "Go ahead. Have some." He held a slice to her lips.

She grinned back and took a healthy bite. Her eyes closed in pleasure. "It's. So. Good."

He watched, enthralled, as she chewed slowly and reverently. Feeding Alesia was better than eating himself.

She swallowed the last of the cheese and chased it with a sip of wine.

He leaned in to run his tongue over the seam of her lips. She tasted good—sweet and a bit spicy from the wine.

She dipped a finger into her wine and traced his lips. He touched his tongue to the fingertip and watched her eyes widen at the jolt that went through them both. He sucked the finger into his mouth, and she moaned, her fingers tightening around the wine glass.

He set his own glass on the rock and kissed his way down the side of her neck. When he reached the soft skin above her collar bone, he nipped, sucking the skin between his teeth to give her a love-bite.

She moaned and pulled him closer. "We can eat later."

"Or I can feed you." He lifted his head and brought an apple slice to her wine-stained lips.

She ate it slowly, her gaze on his. He could swear he tasted it along with her: the burst of tartness, the sweetness that followed. The different textures—crisp flesh and smooth peel. The scent of the apple mixed with her own summery green aroma.

When she finished, she picked up another slice and held it to his mouth. "Now you."

They took turns feeding each other the apple and cheese, with occasional bites of bread and sips of the dry, fruity red. By the time they were both sated, they were lying on the blanket facing one another, and his cock was straining against his pants.

Part of him wanted to finish this, to drag off Alesia's jeans and take her. But another part was enjoying the slowness, the hot simmer in his belly.

She lifted her head to down the last of her wine. "More?" he asked. When she said no, he set the glasses on the rock along with the plate.

When he'd turned back, she was removing her sweater. Underneath she was wearing a hot pink tank that made her skin glow. But what made him swallow hard was the way the stretchy cotton clung to her breasts. They were exactly as he remembered: high and round and perfect.

She saw him looking and misunderstood. "It was a gift from Dina. She says this color looks good on me." Dina was her younger sister, the one who somehow managed to be a fashion-ista even while living in a tree on a secluded island.

"Yeah?" He dragged off his T-shirt and propped himself on a forearm next to her so he could run his hand over the soft cotton. The tank had a self-bra that was basically just another thin layer of material. He could pinch her nipple through it, make it stand up. "Your sister is right. I like it."

"Really?" She plucked at the material and made a face. "It's not too...pink?"

"I like you in anything. But no, it's not too pink—it's pretty."

A corner of her mouth turned up. "Good answer."

He knew she was recalling that day they'd almost made love in her oak. He pinched her other nipple in retaliation. "I'm not just saying that just to get into your pants."

"No?" She slanted him a look up from under her lashes. "Why not?"

He blinked, then grinned. "Okay. I *am* saying it to get into your—"

She sat up, took the hem of the tank and dragged it over her head. He halted, the rest of the sentence caught in his throat. She came back down on the blanket and gave him a slow smile that would've done a siren proud.

Somehow he got his thick tongue to form words. "*Deus,* Alesia"—he smoothed his palm over one dusky peach nipple—"you're so damn beautiful."

"So are you." Her hand came to his bare chest, found one of his nipples, played with it.

"No. I—"

She curled her fingers around his neck and stopped him with a kiss, her tongue seeking entrance. He opened his mouth and sucked her tongue, then he was on top of her, his fingers tangled in her hair, his body pressing hers into the blanket. The simmer in his belly boiled over, erupting through his veins like a fireball.

Slow down, he told himself, but his hand was already cupping her ass and pulling her closer. He ground himself against her mound and she gripped his hips, egging him on, those high, round breasts crushed against his chest.

With a groan, he dragged his mouth from hers and started moving down her body. However ready she seemed, he didn't want to fall on her like an animal. He knew what the fae said about the fada. Besides, he wanted to enjoy her, starting with those soft peach nipples.

But as he lowered his mouth to her breast, Alesia slid her hand between them and undid the button of his pants. He gave her nipple a hard suck and then came to his knees, straddling her. She reached for his zipper and eased it down over his erection. He was wearing cotton boxers beneath. She slipped a finger through the opening and caressed him.

He hissed and her lips curved in a wicked smile. Her hand closed on him and she squeezed. He curved his body over hers, his hands on the blanket on either side of her ribs, and pushed into her soft, cool fingers. At the same time, he caught her other nipple in his mouth, teasing it with his tongue and then pulling strongly.

Her grip on him tightened. Heat jolted through him. His balls clenched and he thrust into the welcoming circle of her fingers. They stayed like that for a minute, he licking and sucking her breasts, she working his cock.

Then he lifted his head and took a deep inhale. "Too many clothes."

She gave one last squeeze and then released him. They worked together, no fumbling despite their hurry. She undid her jeans and lifted her hips; he pulled them off.

His hands went to her panties and then he halted, as he took in the fact that this time she was wearing panties. Plain white briefs that were about the most erotic thing he could imagine. They hugged her hips, the material sheer enough that he could make out shadowy curls and the outline of her plump lips.

He framed her hips with his hands and pressed a kiss to her

center, finding her sweet little button and blowing hotly on the fabric just above it so that it was her turn to hiss.

She raised her hips and demanded breathily, "Do that again."

He inched the material down, exposing the top of her pubis. The curls were sable brown, darker than the honeyed brown on her head. He brushed his lips over the soft skin just above.

Her stomach sucked in. She held herself still, not even breathing. He slipped his tongue deeper, beneath the panties, flicking her clit.

Her breath rushed out.

He smiled and moved lower, pursing his lips and again blowing hot air against her through the white briefs.

She moaned. "Goddess, that feels good."

He lifted his head. "Let's get these off." He dragged off the briefs, then kicked off his own clothes before coming back on his knees between her bent legs. "There now."

She was slick and hot and beautiful. He smoothed his hands over her thighs, drinking her in with his eyes, inhaling her salty woman scent.

She made a small, needy sound. "Tiago—"

He pressed a kiss to the inside of her thigh. "What do you want, baby? This?" He dragged his tongue through her glistening folds.

"It's a start."

His brows shot up. He raised himself up enough to see her teasing smile.

"Hm. Let's see if I can do better." He drew her clitoris into his mouth and suckled.

Her hips lifted. "That's pretty good," she said in a strained voice.

He spread her with his thumbs. "No more talking," he growled, and then proceeded to lick and tease her until she was pleading with him to take her.

"Not yet," he said, and sliding a finger inside her, swirled his tongue around her plump little nubbin until her breath sobbed out. He slid a second finger inside her and she came in a series of small shocks, her inner muscles convulsing around his fingers. He continued stroking and lightly tonguing her until she went limp, then rose up to straddle her.

Her eyes were closed, her cheeks flushed, her hair a tawny fan over the green-and-blue plaid.

He brought his hands to her rib cage. She was narrow but strong, a woman who did the physical labor of caring for her trees and garden. Still, she'd be no match for a man like him—or like Benny. His stomach tightened as he realized that Jorge and Benny might very well have gone back to her island this week. Sure, the Rock Run sentries kept an eye on the dryads, but Jorge and Benny knew this area as well as any of the sentries—maybe better. And Benny had been so far gone into his animal that he'd have taken any woman he happened upon like a rutting beast...

"Tiago?" Alesia had opened her eyes and was gazing up at him. "Is something wrong?"

He smoothed his hands over the delicate curve of her torso. "I'm worried about you and your sisters alone on those islands. If Jorge and Benny had come up here first—"

"They'd have to catch us first—and that's not easy. Even Okeanos never got ahold of me, and believe me, he wanted to. Now come here. I'm cold." She tugged on his shoulders.

He lowered himself onto her, careful to keep some of his weight on his forearms. He was still uneasy, but right there and then he decided to stay with her until Jorge and the other two men had been captured. After all, he was on medical leave. He didn't even have to train with the other warriors if he didn't want to.

And if he stayed, he could fuck Alesia any time he wanted to.

He rubbed his body against hers. Her skin *was* chilled; he had to keep in mind that she didn't have a water fada's metabolism.

He enfolded her in his arms, sharing his heat with her. "I could start a fire," he said against her neck.

"I don't need a fire. You can keep me warm." She undulated against him.

"Mm." He nudged her with his cock.

She shifted so the tip slid inside her. He stilled, practically shaking with need. He didn't want this to be hard and fast. He wanted to take care with her, show her how special she was.

She hummed low in her throat and lifted her hips to take him deeper.

He growled. His beast rose in him, dark and eager. He shoved it back down and started to move, slow, easy thrusts that took him just a few inches inside her, and then back out again. But she was so damn tight and hot. He tensed, afraid he might literally break if he didn't maintain his control.

And if he broke, the gods knew what he'd do to Alesia. He thought of the promise he'd made her and clenched his jaw.

Her fingers dug into his buttocks. "Tiago—" she said in a strained voice—and then nipped his neck.

He lifted his head. "What the hell was that for?"

She gave him a fierce look that would've done a fada woman proud. "I want you—now. All of you." She rocked her hips and he slid all the way in.

Oh, yeah. She felt like home—the cradle between her thighs hot and wet and welcoming, somewhere he could sink into and stay for the next hundred years or so.

Yes... The beast had risen again. For a moment, Tiago was worried, but unlike with Marjani, the beast wasn't threatening. No, it was as absorbed as Tiago in the sensation of being inside Alesia.

She inhaled sharply and wrapped her arms and legs around him. The fierce look changed to pure pleasure, her eyes half-closed, her teeth sunk into her lower lip.

He thrust in again, both parts of him—man and beast—reveling in bringing that look to her face.

Mine.

He didn't even bother to consider what that meant, just lowered his head to nuzzle her neck. "Talk to me, baby. Is this what you want?" He flexed his hips and thrust in again, a little harder, going deep inside her.

"Yes," she gasped. "That's it."

She urged him into her, her fingers clenched on his ass, heels digging into his thighs. He gave a few slow, deep strokes. Then, spurred by her soft cries of encouragement, he increased the rhythm, moving harder, faster.

She tightened her inner muscles around him. He changed the angle of his thrusts and circled his hips so that he was stimulating her clit. Her eyes widened, the pupils so dilated they appeared almost black, and then she threw her head back and clenched down on him—hard—her muscles opening and closing on him in rhythmic waves.

Heat slammed up his spine. He thrust into her again and again, frenzied now, and then groaned and followed her over the edge.

When he could think again, he was on his back, Alesia's head on his shoulder. He played with her ear, fingering the sensitive point at the top. She moaned and his lips curved. *Deus*, he loved the sexy little noises she made.

"That was—awesome." She stroked a hand down his abdomen. "Why did we wait so long?"

"Because I'm a frigging idiot."

She chuckled and rested her hand on his chest, her fingers spread over his heart, a warm, pleasing weight. "When you first started coming around, I thought all you wanted was a piece of you-know-what. Then when nothing happened—"

"You were right." He slapped one firm buttock. "I wanted this."

"Yeah?" Her tone was pleased.

"Hell, yeah." He pressed a kiss to her temple. "Why do you think I kept coming around? But then we became friends and—" He moved a shoulder.

"I'm glad," she said. "That we were friends first."

"Me too."

"But I wanted you too."

"I know."

She made an embarrassed sound and closed her eyes. "You smelled it on me, right?"

"Yeah." He nuzzled her ear, licking a slow circle around that cute little point. "But if it makes you feel any better, you smell very, very good. Green and a little spicy...like a vineyard in summer."

She gave a spurt of laughter. "If you say something about wanting to plow me, I'll—"

He rolled on top of her. "What?" He rubbed against her mound. "What will you do, woman?"

She wrapped her arms around him. "This," she said—and took him inside her again.

A LONG TIME LATER, Alesia opened her eyes. She was curled into Tiago, his arms around her. They must have dozed off, because it was almost dusk, the shadows slanting through the trees as the sun slid out of sight.

She tangled her fingers in the hair on his chest and gave a contented sigh. Goddess, she felt good. A bit sore—it had been a while—but in that replete, I-saw-fireworks way.

She lay there for a few minutes, listening to the rhythmic sough of Tiago's breath before she reluctantly wriggled out of his arms.

He opened an eye. "Alesia?"

"Back in a minute."

She grabbed her clothes and headed into the trees to pee, then crouched in the creek to clean herself. The water was barely a few degrees above freezing. She hissed as she lowered herself into it. You'd think she'd be used to it, living as she did in the forest, but she liked her baths hot, thank you very much. At home she'd rigged up a tub in the hollow of a large rock which she filled with buckets of steaming water so she could bathe in comfort.

Oh, well. She gritted her teeth and splashed the icy fluid over her face and chest.

Something made her turn her head. Tiago had rolled on his side to watch her.

She arched a brow. "Like what you see?"

His mouth quirked. He circled an index finger in his direction. "Turn a little more this way."

She shook her head at him but she was grinning as she continued washing. As her hand went between her thighs, he spoke again, his tone a caress in the deepening shadows.

"You don't have to do that for me. I like how you smell—my scent and yours, together."

Her sex clenched at the possessiveness in his voice. The man could get her going with just a few short sentences.

She finished and rose from the stream to face him. "I'll remember that." It came out huskier than she'd intended. Inviting.

"See that you do."

He was on his feet now, the setting sun behind him, his strong, beautiful body outlined against the dark trees. His eyes glowed silver, and she knew he was using his night vision to look her over. Her skin tingled.

She was used to running wild on her island, but she was also a solitary. She'd only had a few lovers, and she'd never felt completely comfortable with any of them. With any other man, she would've already been dressed.

But this was Tiago. She liked having him look at her. The heat in his eyes made her feel powerful...sensual. She lifted her hair from her shoulders in a deliberate movement that raised her breasts. Might as well give the man something to look at.

His gaze zeroed in on her nipples, puckered from the cold. They pricked and hardened even more.

His eyes flashed. When he spoke again, it sounded as if his teeth were clenched. "Get dressed, Alesia."

"Why?" But she stepped out of the water. "Are you worried about Jorge?" She'd seen the Rock Run sentries: a pair of river dolphins patrolling the river, and two more hard-faced men in a speedboat.

"I wouldn't have brought you here if I was. But you'll be safer back in Rock Run territory, especially with me there."

She sat on a log to pull on her jeans. "So you're going to stay the night?" she asked casually.

"Hell, yeah. I'm not leaving you alone until we catch Jorge."

Her heart skipped a beat, started to sing. Sure, Tiago was on edge after what had happened in Baltimore, but he didn't have to guard her personally. The extra sentries would keep her safe enough.

If he was coming back with her, it was because he wanted to.

As she reached for her tank top, Tiago crossed to her and knelt on the grass. He cupped her breasts and placed a soft, reverent kiss on each of her nipples.

"You are so fucking sexy," he gritted against her throat. "I'm always hard around you." He moved between her thighs, one large hand palming her ass, and ground himself against her jeans.

The tank top slipped from her fingers. She gripped his shoulders to steady herself. He nuzzled her neck and her head fell back. He ran his lips over the hollow below her ear. His tongue flicked out, tasting her. Tiny stars of sensation danced over her skin.

A gust of wind rattled the trees. She shivered as it passed over her damp body, and Tiago ran his hands over her back.

"You're cold—you should finish getting dressed. When we get back to your island, I'll get a fire going."

"All right."

But neither of them moved. Instead they remained there, arms wrapped around each other, indulging themselves in light, sweet kisses: on the mouth, the face, their earlobes. His body heated hers. A few yards away, the waterfall played a quiet song over the stones.

Tiago exhaled and released her. "We need to go, babe."

He handed her the tank top and then stepped into the trees to relieve himself. Meanwhile, she finished dressing and then returned to the blanket to pack up their leftovers. When he reappeared, he went into the creek to wash. It was too dark now to see much, but she got some nice glimpses of hard wet shoulders and a taut ass.

He had pulled on his pants and T-shirt when he stilled and sniffed the air. "Hurry up. Someone's coming." He slung the messenger bag over his shoulder, grabbed her hand and started down the path toward the kayak.

They'd only gone ten yards when he paused and took another deep inhale. Then he shoved her toward the trees. "It's Jorge," he hissed. "Get out of here—*now*. I'll be all right."

Her heart stuttered. She could see them now, too: two dark shapes, coming rapidly upstream toward them.

"*Now*, Alesia," Tiago rapped out. And then he was pounding down the path toward the men.

She cast an anguished look after him, but what could she do? If she stayed, they'd only catch her as well. Better to return to her island and hail one of the sentries. They'd get the whole base out to help him.

She darted toward the nearest tree large enough to hold her weight. Suddenly, a dark shape loomed in front of her. A big, naked man.

She shrieked and skidded to a stop, her heart pounding so hard it felt as if it would explode out of her chest. In an instant, the man had an arm locked around her neck and something sharp pressed to her throat.

His growl raised every hair on her body. "Do exactly what I say," he gritted against her neck, "or you're dead."

21

As he closed in on the two men, Tiago cursed himself. Damn it, he should've been paying more attention. But the Jorge he'd known would've been smarter than to turn up this close to Rock Run.

He caught a whiff of the second man's scent. It was Orius, one of the Greek sea fada. *Good.* With Alesia safe, he could take out these bastards for good.

He slowed and bunched his muscles.

"Stop." Jorge flung up a hand, palm out. "Unless you want your woman to die."

Tiago froze. His gaze went from Jorge to Orius.

One sea fada.

He swung around. Thirty yards upstream, another man had Alesia in a tight hold and was urging her toward them.

Mys—and he had a knife to Alesia's throat. Her eyes met Tiago's, her face ashen.

His bowels iced.

Behind him, Jorge said, "I've been looking for you, *irmão.*"

Tiago turned sideways and backed away so that he could keep

Jorge and Orius in his vision. Mys and Alesia came closer, and he saw the thin red line the blade had cut in her soft skin.

His fists clenched, his every instinct clamoring to go to her aid. But a wrong move could result in her death.

He could scent her blood now. Beneath his skin, the beast awoke. A growl tore from his chest and wicked claws sprouted from his fingertips.

"Let her go," he gritted in a voice he barely recognized as his own.

Alesia stiffened. "Tiago—look out!"

A stick snapped behind him. He started to swing around, but an arm wrapped around his neck.

"Don't move," Jorge snarled in his ear. A knife pricked Tiago just above his right carotid.

Like hell. He slammed an elbow into Jorge's ribs.

Jorge grunted but held on. The movement pressed the blade deeper. Something warm trickled down his neck.

Jorge's breath was hot against his cheek. "I said *don't move.* Not a single fucking muscle. I know what you can do, but Okeanos said you need your eyes to do it. So keep your gaze on the ground —or the dryad dies. Understand?"

Tiago stiffened. The SOB was right.

Before he'd realized that using his Gift made the beast more powerful, he'd experimented on various animals, trying to learn what he could and couldn't do. To compel another to obey him, he needed to be looking at them—and it helped if he issued a verbal command, too. Something about the synergy of voice and eye fueled his ability. Even then, if his target had an exceptionally strong will, like Dion, it could take ten or twenty seconds for the compulsion to kick in.

Too damn long.

"Okay," he ground out, reluctantly keeping his gaze on the ground. "But let the woman go. She has nothing to do with any of this."

"Maybe not. But you care what happens to her, *sim*? That makes her worth keeping."

"No, damn you." Tiago's eyes snapped up. He dragged in a breath. There was no way he'd let these bastards get ahold of Alesia.

Both Jorge and Orius were restraining him now while Mys kept the knife to her throat.

She gulped, eyes big in her too-pale face. "It's all right," she told him in a strained voice. "I'm fine. Really."

Tiago glared at Mys and flexed his claws. This man was one of the bastards who'd forced Valeria to take part in Okeanos's dark games and helped kidnap Marjani. He could hardly bear to see Mys breathing the same air as Alesia, let alone touching her.

Inside, his beast writhed, its fury dark, primal. But the anger was mixed with terror, that Alesia would be hurt as the other women had been.

Kill. Now.

Protect the female.

Ours.

The beast was practically bursting out of Tiago's skin, willing —no, eager—to die if that's what it took to save Alesia.

The mate.

The knowledge slammed into Tiago like a fist to the gut: *Alesia was his mate.*

He went hot, then ice-cold. He must've gone rigid with shock, because Jorge growled a warning and tightened his grip.

Tiago ignored him to narrow his eyes at Mys. The rage and fear churning in him like a dark cyclone coalesced, and he and the beast merged in a way they never had before, the beast ceding control to Tiago while adding its own elemental, untamed energy.

Tiago grabbed that energy and directed it at Mys with every-thing he had. "Let her go," he ordered, mouthing the words so that Jorge didn't hear. "*Now.*"

The other man bared his teeth in challenge. Then a look of astonishment spread across his face. His arms opened and he released Alesia.

Yes. Tiago wasn't sure if it was him or the beast who hissed the word.

Alesia's eyes went wide as pie plates. Her fear saturated the air, sharp and acrid. He just prayed it wasn't him she was afraid of, but he couldn't worry about that now.

"*Die,*" he hissed at Mys, but at that instant a dark cloth descended over his eyes, breaking the compulsion before it could take effect.

He jerked and tried to tear it off, but Jorge's knife pressed deeper. "Put your hands down and hold still—now. Or I'll let Mys have her right here in front of you. Believe me, he wants to."

He forced himself to release the cloth. The man meant it. Both his scent and his tone held truth. Tiago could fight, but Jorge's blade was millimeters from slicing his artery. And if he died, the gods knew what these men would do to Alesia.

"Try that again," Jorge growled, "and we'll take your woman and use her every way known to man, and then drop her in the deepest part of the bay. *Compreende?*"

Tiago's jaw clenched, but he had no choice but to agree. "Yes."

The other man made sure the blindfold was tight around Tiago's eyes, and then they pulled his hands roughly behind his back and bound his wrists together with a leather thong.

Jorge removed the knife and stepped to one side. Tiago stood proudly, head up, legs braced apart. "You've got me now. Let her go. I promise I won't fight—"

The air behind him shifted. He instinctively ducked, but it was too late. He heard Alesia moan, "*No,*" and then a light exploded behind his eyes and everything went black.

~

THE GREMLINS WERE HAMMERING on Tiago's skull again—loud rat-a-tat-tats that reverberated painfully through his brain.

He swallowed a groan. Gradually, he became aware that he was lying on his side on a damp stone floor, his wrists bound behind his back. For somewhere nearby came the trickle of a stream. His tongue was thick in his mouth. He moistened his lips and tried not to think about water.

He opened his eyes but everything remained dark. His heart gave a hard thump before he remembered he was blindfolded.

He drew a steadying breath.

Then he realized he couldn't scent Alesia and his heart started pounding in earnest. What had those SOBs done with her? He thought of Marjani and his whole body went taut.

He forced himself to relax and take in what he could of his surroundings. Somehow he knew he was still on the opposite side of the river from Rock Run. The air smelled of damp earth and something oily, like kerosene or another fuel. A cave, then, probably a hideout for Jorge and the other men, far enough from Rock Run to remain undetected, and yet close enough that they could spy on the clan without actually stepping foot onto their territory.

Footsteps sounded. Jorge, his scent dark and ripe. Feral. His former mentor had finally gone over the edge, or as near as made no difference.

"You awake?" Jorge asked in Portuguese. He poked a toe into Tiago's still healing ribs.

Asshole.

"*Sim.*" Tiago struggled up to sitting.

"Good—now listen. I'm going to take the blindfold off, but if you're thinking of using your Gift on me, keep in mind we have your woman. If my men don't hear from me in twenty-four hours, their orders are to use her any way they want—and then kill her."

He dares... The beast awoke. *He dares threaten the mate, hold us prisoner. Let me out. Blood. Kill.*

No! Tiago returned. *First, I have to find out what he's done with Alesia. Then we'll attack. But if we kill him now, the others will hurt her. Understand?*

The beast snarled angrily, but to Tiago's relief, it subsided. So he hadn't imagined that moment last night when it had ceded control to him.

Jorge jerked off the blindfold. Tiago blinked and looked around him. As he'd guessed, he was in a cave, although it was larger than he'd realized—about the size of the entire ground floor of the Baltimore rowhouse that Jorge and his men had been using as a den. There were a few rough pieces of furniture and several piles of furs that Tiago assumed were bedding. The only illumination was a small kerosene lamp.

Jorge stood over him, legs wide and hands fisted on his hips, staring down at Tiago in a clear challenge. Tiago's hackles rose. He scooted back a couple of feet so that his back was against the wall and he had a better view of Jorge's face.

"Eyes down," the other man snapped.

Tiago instinctively curled his upper lip. Then he forced himself to drop his gaze as a wave of dizziness washed over him. For Alesia's sake, he had to placate the man. Besides, he couldn't do a fucking thing right now, injured and tied up as he was.

"Can I have some water?" he asked, obediently keeping his gaze down. It wasn't a trick; it had been hours since his last drink, and his mouth felt like it was filled with sand.

Jorge waited long enough to make a point, then picked up a canteen and walked out of the cave. Tiago moistened his lips, wondering if Jorge was really getting water or if this was a subtle form of torture.

But the other man returned in a few minutes and held to the canteen to Tiago's mouth. "Here."

He took a cautious sniff. It was only water, thank the gods. He wasn't sure he'd have been able to resist drinking even if it weren't. He swallowed greedily. The liquid slid down his parched throat, ice cold and reviving. He continued drinking until the container was empty.

Jorge set the canteen on a nearby table and returned to his post before Tiago.

Tiago risked a glance up at the grizzled, battle-scarred veteran. Even in the dim light Tiago could see that Jorge still carried the bruises from their battle two nights ago. In fact, he looked worse than Tiago, since he hadn't had the benefit of Cleia's healing energy.

He knew he shouldn't ask, but he was desperate to know. "The dryad? Where is she?"

"I told you. With Mys and Orius."

His men. Tiago must've been half out of it when Jorge had told him before because it hadn't sunk in. Jorge had left Alesia with the men who'd raped Marjani and who knew how many other women?

He growled and started to his feet. "*The hell she is.*"

Jorge aimed a deliberate kick at his bruised ribs. "Down."

Pain shot through Tiago. The air left his lungs in a whoosh and he froze halfway to standing, afraid even to breathe. He sank back to his knees and took a tentative inhale. It hurt like hell. But he made himself take another, then another.

By the time he could think again, Jorge had retied the blindfold around his eyes.

Tiago wanted to kill the man so bad he could taste it. He tested the thong binding his wrists, but the more he strained against the leather, the tighter it got.

"If you hurt her," he ground out, "if you even fucking *touch* her—you're dead. All of you. I will hunt you to the gates of Hades itself."

"Then do as I say."

Tiago's jaw tightened. "What's this about, Jorge?"

"Lord Jorge," he snapped back. "I'm alpha. My own den."

That's when Tiago realized that the man was speaking in short, declarative sentences like his animal would.

"Alpha," Tiago repeated neutrally.

"*Sim*. After Petros died—me next. We get females now. New clan."

"Fada that follow Dionysus and the old ways." Including men who believed women were inferior, good only as sexual toys and for bearing children.

"When Dion's father"—Jorge paused, clearly struggling to articulate, and then said in a burst—"banned the bacchas, anyone who disagreed had to suck it up or leave. Petros—he showed us we could break our clan ties. Start new clan."

"Hell," Tiago muttered. The man wasn't just feral, he was out of his fucking mind. With only two men left in his den, he had visions of starting a new clan? Unless—"How many of you are there?"

"Many."

But Tiago caught the uncertain tang. So there were just the three of them now—Jorge and the two Greek sea fada. He filed that away for future use.

"So you broke a sacred promise."

Jorge moved uneasily. "Dion forced us—promise. Not binding."

"I was there in the cave that day, remember? Forced or not, speaking your true-names bound you to your vow. I'm not sure how you broke it without making yourselves sick as a dog, but—" Tiago halted. "That's it, isn't it? It's why you all have the scent of ferals. Your animals can't take the pressure."

Jorge's jaw set. "I'm alpha. Lord Jorge." He made an agitated circuit around the cavern's perimeter.

Tiago shook his head. "You're fucking insane," he muttered, more to himself than to Jorge. "I'm nobody at Rock Run. A warrior, yeah, but low in the hierarchy. Why mess with me?"

The footsteps halted. Tiago heard the other man's breath

shudder in, and when he spoke, he sounded almost normal. "It bothers you, *sim*? That your brother doesn't help you more. Maybe he even keeps you down."

The words pricked, but Tiago forced himself to shrug. "I have to earn my place like anyone else."

"Still, you're impatient. That's how you were as a pup—always jumping into things with both feet. You must hate being the low man."

Tiago set his jaw but said nothing.

Jorge came closer. His ripe, unpleasant odor filled Tiago's nostrils. "You're stronger than him. You could be alpha—or my second."

Tiago kept his expression blank. He'd thought the same himself—that if he challenged his brother, he just might win—but it sounded a hell of a lot worse when voiced by another man.

"Dion is my alpha. I swore a warrior's oath to honor him as the head of my clan—and so did you."

"Bah." Jorge spat on the cavern floor. "You're as soft as the rest of them. But no matter. You'll do what I say or you'll die, along with your female."

"You're a *cabrão* to use a woman like that." He used the Portuguese word deliberately. It was a serious insult, meaning "asshole," but the literal translation was "goat," or worse, a man who'd been cheated on.

Jorge snarled. "Don't push me, boy. I left Orius to keep an eye on the dryad. But if you don't do what I ask, well—Mys likes to hurt women."

A black heat filled Tiago's head.

Deus, he wanted to kill the man. Behind his back, he flexed his hands. *If he could just get free...*

"What?" he asked, tight-lipped. "What do you want me to do?"

∼

A QUARTER MILE AWAY, Alesia crouched in another cavern, arms wrapped around her knees. The cave was small, with only a few yards between her and the two men sitting against the opposite wall. Its only entrance was a narrow passageway that had had her digging her fingernails into her palms to keep from whimpering as she'd inched her way through it.

Her home was the open branches of a tree, close to sun and sky. About the worst thing you could do to a dryad was force them into a dark, confined space, especially underground.

She eyed the two sea fada warily. Orius and Mys, they called each other. She recognized them from Petros Okeanos's den, although she'd never learned their names.

Orius was the large one, with a crooked nose and shoulders as broad as a door. Mys was shorter and whipcord lean, with cropped black curls and a look in his heavy-lidded eyes that made her want to curl into a tight little ball.

At least she and Tiago had gotten dressed before the men had attacked them. She was chilled from sitting on the damp ground, but it would be worse without the jeans and sweater. And being naked around these two men didn't bear thinking about.

Tiago. Please, please, let him be all right.

Jorge and Orius had rigged up a pallet for him from two poles and the picnic blanket and carried him, still unconscious, into the woods in the direction of the river. They'd refused to tell her where they were taking him. The back of his head had been smeared with blood and she'd begged them to at least let her clean it, but Jorge had bared his teeth at her and she'd shut up.

When they were gone, Mys had turned to her, his eyes a night-glow green in the dusk. Like Jorge and Orius, he was naked but seemingly impervious to the chill night air. She shivered at his silent appraisal.

Like he'd already claimed her and was examining his property.

He grabbed her arm and jerked his head. "This way."

They headed upstream in the opposite direction from which Jorge and Orius had taken Tiago, and across a field to another stand of trees.

The squirrels chittered worriedly as she passed by, and an owl hooted a warning. She knew they sensed her fear but didn't know how to help. And what could they do against a fada anyway? She could send them to Rock Run, but the base was across the river and several miles downstream. And Mys was careful not to allow her near enough to a tree so that she could escape.

Now would be a good time for Naomi to sense she was in trouble, but unfortunately, it didn't work like that.

By the time they reached their destination it was completely dark out. Mys ordered her into the cave first. When she balked, he gave a vicious snarl, and she hurriedly obeyed, groping her way along the wall in the narrow, pitch-black passageway. It couldn't have been more than ten yards long, but it felt as if it went on forever.

Inside the cavern, Mys lit a couple of candles and set them on a ledge. At least she wouldn't have to sit in total darkness. She slid along the wall until she was as far from him as possible, and then hunkered down in a corner. She wrapped her arms around her legs—for warmth, but for comfort, too.

And all the time Mys considered her with those dark, hooded eyes.

Not touching her. Not coming any nearer. Not even speaking.

But the look on his face made her skin crawl.

If only she could camouflage herself as bark. Not that Mys wouldn't know where she was, but there wouldn't be much he could do to a woman made of wood. But like her Gift of teleportation, it required her to be touching a tree, and trees were in short supply in an underground cavern.

Her tension ratcheted when Orius arrived. Now there were two of them. Men who looked on women as little more than sexual slaves. But at least Mys had someone else to turn that hot black gaze on.

Orius had returned with Tiago's messenger bag. He offered Alesia some of the food, and when she shook her head no, he and Mys polished off the cheese and bread and the last of the wine. They didn't speak much, and what they did say was in Greek, but Alesia could understand some of it. Like many dryads, she traced her ancestry to ancient Greece, and even though her family spoke English, Greek was still used in rituals. She understood enough to know that Tiago had been taken to a nearby cave.

She stored that information away. If she managed to escape, it gave her somewhere to start searching for him.

If she managed to escape. She eyed the two hard-faced fada and her heart sank.

She swallowed noisily. She *would* escape. Tiago's life might depend upon it.

At least they hadn't tied her hands behind her back like they had Tiago. But then, if she tried to run, Mys would be on her in the blink of an eye—and she had the feeling he'd love the chance to run her down. There was something off about him—sick. Orius, too. Their eyes were wild, their hair fell over their shoulders in shaggy manes and they smelled bad, like a dog with wet fur.

She'd never met a feral shifter. The fada kept things like that hushed up, but everyone knew that a feral was under his animal's control. If they were peaceful, they were allowed to live out the rest of their lives as their animal, and if not, they were quietly executed.

She shot another nervous look at Mys. He seemed calm, but something dark simmered beneath his composed exterior.

Stop imagining things, Alesia. Things are bad enough—don't make it worse.

Then Mys glanced at her and the darkness was there in his eyes. She couldn't help flinching, and he smiled.

She tightened her grip on her knees, then hated herself when he noticed. Her chin lifted. She would *not* let him intimidate her.

He reclined on one forearm, a smile playing on his lips. "You should join us, *glika*. We're founding a new clan. You'd be welcomed, treated like a princess."

Join them and become chief breeder for a den of renegades? She suppressed a shudder. "Thank you, but no."

Mys's face darkened. He strode the few feet to her and crouched down, taking her chin in a cruel grip. "So polite. But when you're mine, you'll learn I don't like to be told no."

She glared back. "I'll never be yours," she returned quietly but firmly. She would've liked to add that she was Tiago's, but something told her to be careful. The less they knew, the better.

"No? We'll see about that." Mys bared his teeth in a smile that was pure animal. The grip on her chin tightened.

She swallowed but refused to look away. Mys might think he could mate with her but it would be nearly impossible for him to father a child on her. Fae and fada rarely conceived outside the mate bond, and she was Tiago's mate—or as close as made no difference. Nothing could change that except his death.

That shook her. What if Mys and the others found out that Tiago had only to accept the mating for the mate bond to be complete? They might use it as an excuse to kill Tiago.

She dropped her eyes. Mys gave a satisfied grunt and returned to his place beside his friend.

She decided to chance a question. "Excuse me. Orius?"

The big shifter lifted a shaggy black brow. "What?"

"What are you going to do with Tiago?"

"Don't you worry about him," was the gruff reply. "As long as he cooperates, you'll be all right. If he does as he's told, you'll go free."

Mys growled a dissent and Orius sliced him a look. "The alpha commands it. Hurt her, and we won't have just Rock Run and the Baltimore shifters to deal with. The dryads will bring the fae down on us."

"So? We already have the sun fae after us. Tyrus's ward will protect—"

"Shut up," Orius snarled and Mys subsided.

Alesia blinked. Lord Tyrus was part of this?

Tyrus had tried to kill Merry Jones at least once. He was heir to the night fae prince. Merry was some sort of relation, and Tyrus was bent on wiping out all competition for his father's throne. Prince Langdon had protected the girl with a special ward to ensure Tyrus couldn't hurt her directly, but it would be just like Tyrus to make a deal with rogue shifters to kill Merry. The night fae lord was a snake in elegant clothing.

Alesia scrutinized Orius's broad face. He seemed more reasonable than Mys. She just hoped he could keep his friend under control. Orius gazed back unsmilingly, which reassured her more than a smile would have.

And it was true that hurting her would involve the fae. Her people were personally weak, but their Gift for making things grow meant the more powerful fae looked out for them, keeping them under their collective wing. Besides, most fada clans welcomed dryads with open arms, knowing how beneficial they were to the local ecosystem.

But these weren't most fada. They were wild, savage. Animals on two legs.

And they already had the Rock Run fada, the Baltimore shifters and the sun fae after them. What did they have to lose?

She felt a moan rising deep inside her. She bit down on her lip hard to stifle it. She glanced up to find Mys looking at her again, and hurriedly averted her eyes.

For a time the only sound in the cave was the two men breathing.

"Why Tiago?" Alesia blurted when she couldn't stand the silence any longer. "Is it because he's Lord Dion's brother?"

Orius grunted. "Jorge wants to challenge Dion for alpha."

"To challenge Dion? But what—"

"You take the brother, you get the alpha."

"So Jorge is using Tiago to lure Dion into a trap." It was starting to make sense now.

"Never you mind about that," Orius said maddeningly. He rummaged around in the messenger bag and found her candy, and proceeded to pop a whole handful of her precious chocolates in his mouth.

He offered the box to Mys, and they finished it off as she watched, openmouthed.

And then suddenly, she was burning mad. Because she'd waited five years for Tiago to get over Cleia. *Five freaking years.* And now that he had, she hadn't even had one whole day to enjoy it.

Her fists clenched. She set her jaw and boldly met Mys's unrelenting stare.

He started to his feet but Orius was faster.

"Out." Orius slapped a hand on the smaller man's chest and jerked his chin toward the entrance. "Now. Catch some fish. I don't know about you, but my belly's still not full."

Mys glared at the other sea fada for a tense few seconds, and then nodded and slipped from the cave.

Orius waited until he was gone and then crossed to Alesia. "Don't you know anything about fada, woman?" He lifted her by the shoulders as if she were a ragdoll and gave her a hard shake. "Staring into a man's eyes like that is a challenge. Don't do it unless you're prepared to accept the consequences. Understand?" He shook her again.

She gulped and nodded. "I'm sorry," she said, all the fight leaching out of her.

Orius shook his head and then threw her from him. She stumbled backward until she hit the wall and then slid to the ground, legs sprawled out, tears of humiliation burning her eyes.

She drew herself into a tight ball and pressed the heels of her hands to her face. She would *not* cry.

The cave fell silent.

Five or ten minutes had ticked past when something occurred to her. Whatever reason Jorge had had for kidnapping Tiago originally, he now knew about Tiago's Gift—and how dangerous he could be. After all, he'd seen him kill Benny.

Jorge knew how dangerous Tiago was, but still wanted him. Because of Dion.

A chill slid over her skin. She hugged her legs tightly to her chest.

What, exactly, did Jorge want Tiago to do?

22

"It's time." Jorge shook Tiago's shoulder. "Get up."

Tiago grunted. Beneath the blindfold, he blinked sleep-encrusted eyes.

Jorge wanted to challenge Dion. Jorge hadn't said why, but it didn't take a genius to connect the dots. Jorge sought revenge for having been banished to the Sahara, but that wasn't all. He wanted what Dion had—his woman, his clan—and as an oath breaker, he didn't have the right to meet the Rock Run alpha in a straight challenge.

So Jorge intended to use Tiago to compel Dion to accept his challenge. "And I'd better win," Jorge had growled. "For your dryad's sake."

At first, Tiago had been relieved that the other man wasn't ordering him to kill his brother outright, until he realized it didn't matter.

This challenge would be to the death—and it was Tiago's job to make sure that Jorge didn't lose. He'd nodded, but inside his mind was racing.

After that, Jorge left him alone. Tiago wracked his brains for a solution, but his head was pounding. He couldn't think straight. He must have passed out again.

All he knew was that he'd dreamt of Alesia being tormented by Mys and Orius while he looked on, helpless to come to her aid.

His mate.

Deus, he'd barely had time to take it in when she'd been stolen from him. He wasn't even sure if she knew they *were* mates; in fada, the males usually knew before the females.

In the dream, Alesia had looked at him with tortured eyes and whispered, "Help me." He'd nearly gone crazy trying to break free so he could get to her.

Now Jorge gave him another shake. "Up."

He struggled to sitting. His internal clock told him it was morning. His head still hurt, but it was nothing like the pain tugging at his chest, as if the mate bond were trying to literally drag him out of there and back to Alesia.

Jorge nudged him impatiently. Tiago stifled a groan. His entire body was stiff and his arms numb from being bound behind his back for so long. Just moving them was painful. He flexed his fingers, knowing he had to force some life into them or risk losing their use altogether. His wrists were raw and sticky with blood. He must have struggled in his sleep against the leather thong.

He saw again Alesia pleading for help. They were keeping her in a cave; he was sure of it—and she hated being underground. His chest tightened, the black despair threatening to descend again. He shook it off.

This was no dream. He was awake, and Alesia needed him.

"I'm going to cut you free," Jorge told him. "But remember, we have the dryad. Don't touch that fucking blindfold. You try anything and she's dead, *entende*?"

Tiago gave a short nod. "*Sim*." At least the man seemed lucid. Tiago would rather deal with his rational side than the feral.

Jorge slashed his knife through the leather binding Tiago's wrists. He clenched his teeth to keep from groaning aloud as blood rushed into the numb limbs, burning and prickling from his fingertips to his shoulders. Gingerly, he brought his hands forward to rest on his lap. His shoulders cramped in protest. It was agony just to move.

He forced himself to work through the pain: flexing his fingers, rotating his wrists and bending his elbows back and forth.

When he could move somewhat normally again, Jorge handed him the canteen, then took him outside so he could relieve himself. Before they returned to the cavern, he allowed Tiago to take a long drink from the stream and lift the blindfold enough to rinse the grit from his eyes.

As Tiago sat down again, Jorge set something on the ground before him. "Eat."

Tiago felt in front of him. It was a canteen and a bowl of food—fish, from the scent. His stomach growled. He grabbed them both before Jorge could change his mind.

There were no utensils so he used his fingers to scoop the fish into his mouth. It was a basic ceviche—chunks of raw shad cured in lemon juice and flavored with chili peppers—but as far as he was concerned it was the best meal he'd ever eaten.

The rest had cleared his brain. As he ate, he considered his options. Dion had put him on medical leave, so he wouldn't be missed for at least a couple of days. Even Rosana and Chico would figure he was out on the river somewhere, so chances were, no one was going to be looking for him.

At least that's what he prayed. He could let no one, especially Dion, near him until Alesia was safe.

Jorge crouched on the ground a few feet away, eating his own portion. "What do you see in her anyway?" he asked around a mouthful of food. "She's nothing compared to Cleia. A brown mouse of a woman."

Tiago's fingers tightened around the crude pottery bowl. Then he shrugged. "She's a good fuck," he said, deliberately crude, then had to listen as Jorge chuckled knowingly.

It was the truth—just not the whole truth. But hopefully, it would satisfy Jorge, because if he realized that Alesia was Tiago's mate, they were sunk. Jorge would know he could force Tiago to do anything—anything at all—to save her. His instincts would allow nothing else.

"Maybe I'll give her a try," the other man remarked slyly.

Tiago ignored him to take a swig of water from the canteen. But inside, he vowed that Jorge was dead.

When Jorge didn't get a reaction, he switched to grumbling about Cleia and Dion. "Why him?" he demanded. "I had her first. If I'd known a fae would mate with a fada, I'd have taken her myself—and then I'd be alpha of Rock Run."

Tiago moved a shoulder. He could've told Jorge it didn't work like that. The mate bond wasn't something you could will into being; it was as special and unpredictable as love.

"Is that what this is about?" he asked between bites. "You want to be alpha so that you can have Cleia?"

"I wouldn't say no to another round with her. But that's not the only reason. I'm as strong as Dion. He's only alpha because of the old lord."

"But if you wanted to kill him, why didn't you do that in the first place? Why take me and Adric's sister to that house in Baltimore?" Then he saw. "You were trying to set Dion and Adric at each other's throats, maybe even force one of them to challenge the other."

"Adric's strong," Jorge replied. "There's a chance he could kill Dion. If not, any fight between the two of them would still make things worse between Rock Run and the Baltimore shifters. Either way, it makes Dion weaker. If things got bad enough, Rock Run would welcome a challenge from me."

Tiago shook his head, then stilled as the abrupt movement

made his whole head tighten in pain. "You're an oath breaker. No one would follow you."

"They'll follow whoever wins the challenge," Jorge snapped back.

"You can't beat Dion. And even if you do, Rui would challenge you right after. There's no fucking way you'd beat them both."

"Then you'll have to make sure Rui loses, too."

Tiago set down his plate. "Like hell."

Jorge said nothing. But Tiago heard footsteps. He threw up his arms but Jorge's blow knocked him sideways. Tiago growled and started to his feet, hands on the blindfold.

But before he could remove it, Jorge grabbed his throat and shoved him up against the wall. "You killed my best friend. My mate." The older man's voice was raw with hatred. "So by *Deus*, you'll help me."

Benny was Jorge's mate? Fuck. He hadn't known that. But it wouldn't have made a difference.

"He attacked me, damn it."

He felt Jorge raise a hand to strike him again. Tiago's whole body went rigid. The beast flexed angrily. Tiago could swear he felt its claws scraping his nerves.

For a moment he forgot that these bastards had Alesia. "Try it," he invited through gritted teeth. "And I'll stop your goddamn heart."

Maybe he didn't need his vision to use his Gift. Beneath the blindfold, he narrowed his eyes and pictured a hand reaching for Jorge's heart, giving it a hard squeeze...

Alesia. The beast snarled and joined with Tiago, its primitive mind primed to kill. But then it halted. *No.*

It withdrew. Slowly and reluctantly, yes, but it still withdrew. *Find Alesia. Then—kill.*

Tiago pulled up short. It was the first time the beast had ever counseled patience, but it was right. Until Alesia was safe, Tiago had to take whatever Jorge dealt out.

He inhaled jaggedly, wanting so badly to kill Jorge that it was a harsh taste in his mouth.

But the other man could live. For now.

Jorge had no idea how close to death he'd come. "Then your woman will go to Mys," he snarled. "He'd love to play with her—but maybe she's likes it kinky, hm?"

Tiago's jaw clenched. "I'll cooperate."

"Good." The Greek fada shoved him toward the entrance. "Get going, then. I want to get to Baltimore during rush hour. Makes it harder for them to track us." He strode out ahead of him, knowing Tiago's keen hearing would enable him to follow through sound alone.

Tiago knelt and felt around for the plate and canteen and gulped down the last of the fish and water before following Jorge. At least he wasn't hungry or thirsty anymore. But unfortunately, he was no closer to a solution than he'd been last night.

As they left the cave, a smartphone pinged. Tiago's mouth went slack as Jorge answered it. *So he was working with the Baltimore fada.*

He listened as Jorge told a woman who sounded like Shania to get a message to Dion. "Tell him I have Tiago. I'll meet him at the Full Moon Saloon. Four p.m. And tell him to come alone or I'll slit his brother's throat."

He ended the call and grabbed Tiago's arm. "*Vamos.*"

23

Mys spent the evening watching Alesia with raw lust, no longer trying to conceal his impatience to have her.

It was clear he didn't give a damn that hurting her would only bring more trouble down on him and his friends.

The walls of the cave pressed in on her, her innate dislike of small, dark spaces made worse by Mys's unwavering stare. Every time she glanced at him, he was looking back with an expression that made her curl more tightly into herself.

She didn't dare fall asleep. But as the evening passed, she nodded off, then came awake, heart racing. The second time her eyelids drooped, she pinched her thigh to keep herself awake.

"Go to sleep," Orius growled at Mys. "I'll take the first watch."

Relieved, she curled up on the cavern floor, exhausted and terrified for both herself and Tiago. She tried to send him a message through the mate bond. There were a few seconds where she believed she'd reached him, but then the connection broke. A tear slid down her cheek. She sniffed miserably and shifted onto her other side, seeking a comfortable position on the damp ground.

By some miracle, she hadn't lost Tiago's necklace. Beneath the sweater, the pendant pressed against her neck. She took it out and fingered it.

She'd thought for a moment there in the woods that he'd realized that they were mates, but now she wasn't sure. But even if he didn't know, he'd let Jorge capture him rather than endanger her.

Please, she prayed as she closed her fingers around the delicate silver leaf. *Let me see him again. Give us a chance.*

Across the cave, Mys's breath slowed and deepened. Only when she was sure he was asleep did she relax. She must have drifted off sometime after that.

Now she came awake with a start, her heart slapping against her rib cage. Something had awakened her. She cautiously raised her head and looked around her.

The only candle still burning was flickering, about to go out. Nearby, Orius snored gently.

Something moved. A shadow, sliding along the wall where she'd last seen Mys.

Her heart stuttered. For a horrible few seconds she feared he'd tired of waiting. And then her panicked brain registered that the shadow was a large, cougar-sized cat. Its head swung in her direction, eyes glowing in the dark.

She scrambled backward until she hit the wall, then froze, her back to the stone, staring into those spooky eyes until the cougar swung back to Orius. She released her breath in a whoosh.

That's when she noticed the quartz pendant hanging from a cord around its neck.

Earth fada. But why was he—and she could see now the cougar was a male—here?

He crept toward Orius. The snoring stopped abruptly as the sea fada jerked awake. But he was too late—the cougar had him by the throat.

Alesia gulped and turned her face to the wall. Orius made a

brief, guttural noise, and then there were other sounds that she refused to identify. She pressed a hand to her mouth and tried not to wretch.

A shift in the air. And was that paws padding toward her?

Her throat dried.

Then a man said, "You can look now." He sounded amused, damn him.

She swallowed and forced herself to turn back. The earth fada had changed to his human form. It was too dark to see well, but she could tell he was of average height with a lean, hard body and hair that was blond at the tips.

She moistened her lips. "Lord Adric?" They'd never met, but her sister Dina had described him.

"And you must be Alesia." He reached out a hand to help her up.

She stared at it without moving. There was no blood on him—things like water or dirt or blood fell off your body during a shift. But she still couldn't bring herself to touch him.

She darted a glance at Orius. "Did you have to—?"

"Yes." When she still hesitated, he expelled a breath. "Damn it, woman, if I was here to kill you, you'd already be dead. Now are you coming or not?"

His impatience was somehow reassuring—and he had a point. He could rip her throat out in a heartbeat.

She came to her feet without taking his hand and glanced around for Mys. "There's another one," she said, low-voiced. "He may have been keeping watch."

Adric's nostrils flared, testing the air. "You sure? I don't scent him."

"He was here when I fell asleep."

"All right. Wait here while I look—"

"No," she interrupted. "I'll come too."

"You'd be safer in here."

"I can wait just inside the entrance." She darted a glance at

Orius. A black pool of liquid had formed under his body. She swallowed queasily. If she had to stay in this cave alone with a dead man, she just might lose her mind. "Please," she added. "I swear I won't be any trouble."

The earth fada alpha lifted his powerful shoulders in a shrug. "Hell. Come if you want."

The trip back through the tunnel seemed quicker this time, Adric leading the way with her close behind. As they exited, the sun was rising above the trees. It must be close to nine a.m.

She lifted her face, gulping in the brisk April air. If she never saw the inside of a cave again, it would be too soon.

Adric slanted her a look. "You okay?"

She squared her shoulders. "I will be."

His hard mouth quirked. "Good." He took a deep inhale and looked around him. "I don't smell him, but he could be concealing his scent. But I saw two water fada leaving with do Rio —he was probably one of them."

"You saw Tiago?"

"That's why I'm here. Now wait here while I make sure it's safe." He made a slow circle through the trees while Alesia watched.

Her skin prickled. Could Mys be somewhere nearby, watching them?

She eased over to a tree and put a hand on it. The trees here were too young and slim to climb; she'd have to go further into the woods to find one sturdy enough to use for teleportation, but just touching the trunk helped center her.

Adric returned. "There *was* someone else, but he left a couple of hours ago. Bastard." He turned his head and spat on the ground.

Alesia blinked. But then, these were the men who'd drugged and raped his sister.

"Get out of here." He jerked his head at her. "Go back to your island where it's safe."

"But Tiago—when you saw him, he was all right?"

"They had him in the back of an SUV. I only got a quick look as they drove off, but he seemed okay. Blindfolded, but he was sitting upright."

"That had to be them. There were two of them besides Orius. The man you—the man in the cave. Those two you saw must have been Jorge and Mys."

"Fuck." Adric's face sharpened so she could literally see the hunting cat beneath the skin. "I was so damn close. I tried to catch them, but they were already moving. My cat's fast, but it can't outrun a car—and my motorcycle is two miles away in the state park. But I contacted my people in Baltimore and gave them a description of the SUV. They'll be watching for it. I was heading back for my bike when I caught the scent of you and the sea fada and followed it here."

"Thank you." She touched his arm. "For helping me. You didn't have to do that. If I can ever do anything for you, please let me know."

"Just tell do Rio we're even."

"What do you mean?"

"He'll understand." Adric leaned closer to sniff her neck, and then rocked back, dark brows lifted. "You're his mate."

She shook her head. "He hasn't claimed me yet."

"He will." The earth fada smiled. "And come to think of it, there *is* something you can do for me. Invite me to your mate ball."

"Of course," she returned, although that smile made her uneasy.

"I'll hold you to that. Now go." He jerked his chin at the nearest large tree. "I'll keep watch until you're gone—just in case."

And he did. The last thing she saw was Adric shifting to a big, golden-brown cougar beneath the oak in which she perched. He was large and sleek and deadly. His lips stretched in another toothy grin, and then she closed her eyes, pictured her own oak, and a moment later, was home.

She took a minute to bolt down a couple of acorn cakes, and then settled against the trunk at an intersection of three branches. She focused inward. For a while, she'd lost Tiago, but now she sensed him again. He was somewhere south and east, awake now and feeling better. That was something, at least.

She hesitated, torn. She wanted badly to go straight to him, but common sense told her she needed help. She was no match for even a couple of fada, and Jorge and Mys might have others helping them. No, this was a job for Dion and his warriors.

Her mind made up, she touched the trunk and visualized herself downriver in a tree near the Rock Run marina. She felt a brief, pleasant tingle, and when she opened her eyes again, she was there. The sun streamed down on fada fishermen bringing in the morning catch on small white boats.

She threaded her way through the trees along the shore toward the marina. The workers there could get a message to Dion.

She'd only gone a few yards when a ripple in the river turned into an otter's sleek head and made a beeline in her direction.

"Fausto?" she asked.

He grunted assent and loped onto the shore.

"Oh, Fausto." She crouched down to run her hands over his fur, babbling in English. "Jorge has Tiago. We have to get help."

Fausto cocked his head at her.

She briefly closed her eyes. "You don't understand a word I'm saying, do you?"

Fausto moved his shoulders in a very human shrug. Then he nudged her, making it clear she should keep walking along the shore, while he trotted back to the river and dove in.

"I just hope you're going for help," she muttered.

He was. A couple of minutes later he popped to the surface

with Rui do Mar. She heaved a sigh of relief. She'd been dreading explaining this to an unknown sentry.

Rui rose from the water wearing nothing but a pair of shorts, big and broad-shouldered and safe-looking. She didn't know him as well as Tiago, but the Rock Run second had never forgotten her part in his mate and stepdaughter's rescue, and from time to time he'd visited the island to check on her. She wouldn't call him a friend, but he was the only Rock Run fada besides Tiago whom she trusted.

"Alesia," he said his deep voice. "What's the matter?"

"Oh, Rui." She dragged in a breath. "Tiago—he—they have him. Jorge—"

He muttered a curse. "Calm down, *querida*." He put a large, comforting arm around her shoulders. "Take it easy and tell me exactly what happened."

She nodded and then tried again. "Jorge and the two sea fada —Mys and Orius—they came after me and Tiago. There was nothing he could do—they had a knife to my throat. They split us up and then Lord Adric saved me and he said they had Tiago in an SUV and they took him somewhere. You have to find him, Rui. You have to."

"Take a deep breath. And don't worry, we'll get him back."

"They're going to make him do something—something bad. I know they are. We have to get to him before—"

"Hey, hey, little one." He squeezed her shoulders. "We won't let anyone hurt him. All right?"

Her breath shuddered out, but she nodded. Something about Rui do Mar inspired confidence. "All right."

"Good girl." He gave her another squeeze. "The first thing is to tell Dion. The land entrance is about a half-mile from here. You up for a run?"

When she said yes, he took her hand and started off at a jog through the woods that ran alongside Rock Run Creek. The entrance was hidden in a tumble of large rocks. She would've walked right by it if Rui hadn't been with her, and even then, the opening looked too narrow to fit his large body. But he turned sideways and slipped inside, pulling her after him.

They were in another tunnel. Alesia halted.

Rui frowned down at her. "What's wrong, *querida*?"

"I—" She shook her head and gamely continued forward.

But it wasn't so bad. The tunnel quickly widened into a passage large enough for a small vehicle to pass through, and it was lit by balls of soothing green fae lights. She could almost pretend she was in the forest at dusk. Almost.

The Rock Run base was a rabbit's warren of interconnected tunnels. She would've been hopelessly lost within minutes if not for Rui. They turned left, then right, then right again, passing what appeared to be a gym and a couple of smaller tunnels.

She was amazed at how large and elaborate the base was. It must have taken decades to carve it out, even working with the existing natural caverns. The walls were mostly a uniform gray stone, but here and there they were laced with veins of white or rust-colored minerals, and at one place the tunnel widened to accommodate a spectacular formation of calcite stalactites and stalagmites.

They turned into a passageway that was obviously occupied by families. Those clan members not out fishing were just beginning to come out of their apartments. They greeted Rui and nodded at Alesia in a friendly way.

At first Alesia was surprised, but when a chubby little girl toddled up to Rui and demanded, "Up, Papa," she realized she was still looking at the fada through Naomi's prejudiced eyes.

The fada might be an aggressive, warlike race, but they were also a people who loved: parents, mates, sons and daughters. You just had to see how Rui's stern face lit up as he swung the toddler into his arms and gave her a smacking kiss.

"*Bom dia, minha pequena.* And you, *querida*," he said as the toddler's mom arrived close on her heels.

"Noela," she scolded. "Papa's busy. Come here now."

Noela gave the smug smile of a child who knows her father is never too busy for her, and shook her head.

With a start, Alesia realized that the woman was Valeria. The last time they'd met, Valeria been bruised and shaking from the effects of the drug the Greek sea fada had given her. Now she glowed with happiness, her abdomen round with another child.

"*Mamãe*'s right." Rui planted a kiss on his mate's lips and handed over their small daughter. "I'm on my way to see Tio Dion."

Valeria slid Alesia a curious look. "*Olá*, Senhorita Alesia," she said in her pretty Portuguese accent. "It's a pleasure to see you again."

"And you. Peace to you and your daughters." Alesia nodded to her and the older girl who had come up alongside her.

The girl had to be Merry. She was the right age—about twelve turns of the sun—with wiry limbs and a thin, intelligent face, and she wore an earth fada's quartz around her neck.

"Peace to you and yours." The girl stuck out her hand with a shy smile. "I'm Merry."

"Nice to meet you." Alesia shook her hand.

"We're on our way to see Dion," Rui told Valeria. "Alesia has news about Tiago—and Jorge."

"*Ah, sim?*" Alesia could tell Valeria wanted to ask more but she just nodded and wished them a good day in Portuguese.

As Rui hurried Alesia down the hall again, she could hear Noela asking, "Is that *la dríade*?"

Rui took a right fork and they passed a large cavern filled with people—a mix of families and hard-eyed warriors who had the tired faces of men and women coming off night duty. The enticing scent of fresh bread and coffee filled the air.

Alesia's stomach rumbled and Rui sent her an apologetic look.

"*Desculpe-me.* I promise we'll feed you as soon as we talk to the alpha."

"Don't worry about me," Alesia said as he turned down yet another passageway.

And then finally they reached a heavy oak door, which was opened by the Rock Run alpha himself. Like Rui, Dion was dressed in loose cotton shorts, his big feet bare and dark stubble on his jaw. His heavy black brows lifted at the sight of Alesia, but he ushered them inside with a courtly bow.

"Welcome," he told her, "and peace to you and yours."

"They have Tiago," Alesia blurted out. Now that she'd finally reached Dion, she felt light-headed with relief.

"Calm down, *querida*." Dion took her by the arms and she realized she was shaking. "Tell me what happened so I can help."

He sounded just like Tiago. Alesia gave a little half-sob. "It's Jorge—he—"

"The *cabrão* has your brother," Rui told Dion in a hard voice.

The alpha's lips went white around the edges, but he nodded calmly. "Why don't you sit down," he told Alesia, "and tell me all about it?"

Taking a throw from the nearest couch, he wrapped it around her shoulders, and then guided her to the couch and sat down beside her. Meanwhile, Rui took a seat on a stone bench across from them.

Cleia, wrapped in a bright red-and-gold robe, entered from the bedroom. She yawned and stretched, and Alesia recalled that she was newly pregnant.

She saw Alesia and broke into a smile. "Why hello, Alesia."

Alesia gathered the throw around her and muttered an apology for bothering them. It was clear the alpha pair had been about to eat breakfast. A nearby table held rolls, fruit, cheese and a steaming pot of coffee.

The queen waved her apology aside. "It must be serious or you wouldn't be here." She offered Alesia a cup of coffee with a big dollop of cream, then poured a cup for herself that was more cream than coffee and settled into the big, comfortable-looking chair cattycorner to the couch.

"Now tell us. What's the matter, sweetheart?"

Alesia took a sip of the coffee. It was hot and milky, just the way she liked it. She wrapped her fingers around the warm cup.

"It's Tiago," she said, and launched into her story.

When she got to the part about being alone in the cave with the two sea fada, Dion took her hand in his big one. She sent him a shy smile and finished with what Adric had told her about seeing Tiago blindfolded in the back of an SUV.

"So you're saying," Dion said, "that Jorge and Mys have my brother and they're taking him somewhere south—probably to Baltimore."

She nodded. "Yes, but please—we have to do something. They hit him on the head. He was bleeding and they wouldn't let me help—"

Rui slammed his open hand down on the stone bench. Alesia jumped, and Dion shook his head at his second.

"Sorry," Rui muttered to her, but he came to his feet and started pacing. "You know why they want him, don't you?" he snarled at Dion. "They're going to force him to use his Gift against you. You should've let me go after him."

"*Por quê?*" The alpha released Alesia's hand and stood up as well. "So you could get your goddamn neck broken? As pissed off as you were, you'd have walked straight into a trap. How the fuck would I explain that to Valeria?"

The two men glared at each other. Alesia tightened her fingers around her coffee cup and glanced nervously at Cleia, who just shook her head.

"Dion. This isn't helping."

Her mate's chest heaved. Then he nodded shortly. "You're right. I'm just so—" He turned back to Alesia. "And you said Adric was there?" His tone was very calm and very cold. "That was...lucky."

"But not on Rock Run territory," Cleia pointed out. "On the other side of the river."

"But he was seen on our territory earlier that day."

"He *helped* me," Alesia emphasized. "I'd still be in the cave if it wasn't for him."

Dion blew out a breath. "Then it seems I owe him my thanks."

"There's something else," she added. "Mys said something about a night fae lord protecting them."

Cleia sat upright. "The night fae are involved? Who?"

Alesia traced Tyrus's name on an end table so she wouldn't have to say it aloud.

The queen's beautiful face turned frigid. She met Dion's eyes. "It's time we did something about Tyrus."

"Agreed. But right now, the important thing is to get Tiago away from these bastards. If only we knew for sure where they were taking—"

Alesia set her cup on the coffee table. "I can take you to him. Or at least pretty close."

Dion's head snapped around. "And how is that?" he asked in a soft, dangerous voice. "How do you know where to find him?"

"*Sim*," his second said, "I'd like to know myself."

At their combined stares, Alesia shrank back on the couch. "We're mates," she said in a voice barely above a whisper.

Their heads jerked back in unison. It would've been comical if it wasn't so serious.

"*Mates*?" Dion repeated. "You and Tiago?"

"Yes." She squared her shoulders and spoke more loudly. Because she was proud of it, damn it. "It's not official—I'm not even sure he knows about it—but the bond's there, connecting us. I can use it to trace him to wherever he is—not exactly, but close. It's how I found him yesterday. He was on the other side of the bay, but the bond led me to him."

Dion leaned forward and took a whiff of her scent. "Well, I'll be damned. A dryad and a fada."

"No stranger than a sun fae and a fada," drawled Cleia.

"If it makes you feel better," Alesia said, "my mother's not going to be any happier than you are."

Dion's hard mouth curved. "I'll bet she's not. A mating with a fada would be the last thing Naomi would wish. This will be interesting, *menina*. But don't get me wrong. I'm not unhappy—finding your mate is cause for celebration. And I have a feeling you might be just what Tiago needs."

"Thank you," she said and then blinked, a little overwhelmed, when he crouched on his haunches, took her by the shoulders and gave her a smacking kiss on both cheeks.

"This is good news, *querida*. The best." He gave her a squeeze and then released her. When he rose to his feet, his face was dead serious. "How soon can you put a squad together?" he asked Rui in Portuguese.

The rest of their conversation was too fast for Alesia to follow, but she understood enough to know that although Rui had told Dion he'd have a squad ready in fifteen minutes, he was insisting on going, too. "Valeria will understand."

"She's your mate," Dion said with a shrug.

Rui left, and Dion grabbed coffee and a couple of rolls and wolfed them down as he went into the bedroom to get dressed.

Alesia finished her own coffee and set the cup on the end table.

Cleia leaned forward and took her hands. "Don't worry, all right? Rui's one of the best trackers in the clan, and Dion is a Gifted hunter. They'll find Tiago, especially if you can get them within a few blocks. And this thing about you being mates is just wonderful. Tiago thinks the world of you. He'll accept the mating, I know he will. He's just been...preoccupied lately."

Alesia nodded. This close, the sun fae queen was overpowering. Not only was she one of the most beautiful women Alesia had ever met, she had charisma, too. You *wanted* to like her, even when you knew she'd tied your mate in knots for the last five years.

"I know." Alesia gently but firmly disentangled her hands. "He told me about his Gift." *But he was "preoccupied" with you, too.*

"He did?" Cleia appeared genuinely pleased. "Then he's closer to accepting the mating than I realized."

Alesia lifted a shoulder in a shrug. She was damned if she was going to discuss Tiago with Cleia.

Suddenly they heard a loud, agitated chitter.

"Fausto?" Cleia went to the door. The otter loped inside, planted himself in front of Alesia and let loose a frantic string of chirps, growls and grunts.

Alesia laid a calming hand on his shoulder. "*Qual é o problema?*" she asked him in careful Portuguese. "What the matter?"

The otter lifted on his hind legs and pursed his lips. "Go to Tiago," he said slowly and clearly in the same language. "Help."

"Who needs help?" Dion asked, coming back into the room. "Do you know where Tiago is?"

Fausto dropped back to all four legs and shook his head. "Help. Tiago."

"We know," Dion said. "Jorge has him."

The otter nodded vigorously. "Help. Alesia—go."

Cleia, Dion and Alesia looked at each other, baffled.

"But why?" she asked.

"I can handle Jorge," said Dion. "I just need to know where Tiago is."

Fausto shook his head, a look of frustration on his furry face. But before he could say anything else, Rui returned with the news that the operations room had just received a message from an earth fada female.

"She confirmed that Jorge has Tiago. Jorge wants you to meet him at the Full Moon Saloon at four o'clock. You're to come alone or he'll off your brother in front of you."

Dion muttered a short, vicious curse. "The hell he will."

Fausto planted himself in front of Dion. "Alesia," he said very clearly.

The alpha scowled. "She's going, all right? But I'm not letting her anywhere near that bar."

"Best case scenario," Rui interjected, "is to track down Tiago before four o'clock. But if we don't, we need a backup plan."

"*Claro*," agreed Dion, and the two men lapsed back into rapid-fire Portuguese.

Again, Alesia couldn't catch everything, but it ended with the two of them agreeing that they could only plant a couple of men in the bar without Jorge knowing.

"And it has to be men he doesn't know," said Rui.

Dion nodded. "Two of the younger men, then. And we'll have others in the streets nearby."

Cleia invited Alesia to help herself to some breakfast and then excused herself to get dressed. Alesia ate a roll and some cheese and then sat on the couch, forgotten, as the two men discussed weapons and tactics. It was clear that this time, Jorge and Mys weren't going to walk away alive.

Fausto hopped onto the couch. "Go to Tiago," he said.

She leaned forward. "I will," she whispered. "Just don't tell Dion."

He gave a satisfied nod, and then flopped onto his back and wriggled invitingly, shamelessly begging for a belly rub. She couldn't help a grin. Fausto was so blessedly uncomplicated. But she complied, combing her fingers through his soft, sleek fur.

She glanced at the two men, who were discussing something about Claudio and hidden entrances.

Life was strange. The two men were everything she'd been taught to fear—but she found herself fiercely glad they were on her and Tiago's side.

24

———

*J*orge and Mys shoved Tiago toward a vehicle, still blindfolded and with his hands tied behind his back.

Tiago balked. "Before I go anywhere, I want to see Alesia. How do I know your men haven't—"

A fist slammed into his belly. He doubled over, sucking in air.

"She's all right," Jorge growled. "That's all you need to know."

Tiago snarled back. Behind his back, he twisted his wrists back and forth, but the leather thong held tight.

"Keep it up and she's dead." Jorge's voice was a hoarse rasp. It was clear his animal occupied more and more of his brain.

Tiago gave a taut nod. He reminded himself yet again that he was the only thing standing between Alesia and these ferals.

"Move," Jorge barked.

Tiago moved.

On the ride to Baltimore, he wracked his brain for ideas. There *had* to be a way out of this. Damn it, he could talk to animals. If he couldn't draw on his Gift of compulsion, maybe he could use that?

But he didn't know any animals in the city, and just because you could talk to an animal didn't mean they'd help you. They were like anyone else—you had your kindhearted animals, but most wouldn't go out of their way for a stranger unless there was something in it for them.

When they reached Baltimore, Jorge had two men waiting. The men unlocked a door and hustled Tiago down rickety wood steps into a basement. He caught the scent of wolf and a big cat like a cougar. The men were earth fada—with Baltimore accents.

Hell. Did Dion know the Baltimore shifters were involved? And what about Adric? There was no way he'd have hurt his own sister—which meant these men had to be traitors.

Mys threw him up against a cold brick wall and ordered him to sit. Then Shania arrived, and things fell into place—Jorge had brought him to the basement of the Wildcat.

"Keep an eye on him," Jorge said, "and whatever you do, don't take off his blindfold. The man can kill you with his Gift."

"I can handle him," said Shania. "And if he gives me any trouble, Kelvin's here to back me up. You just do your part."

Jorge growled something and left with Mys and the cougar fada, leaving Shania and the wolf shifter—Kelvin—as guards.

Tiago waited a few minutes before testing the bonds again. But they were as tight as they'd been the last time he'd tried them.

Light, catlike steps approached: Shania.

He straightened. "So it was a set-up?"

"What do you think? You're cute, but—" Her voice held a sneer. "Our first choice was your sister, but Dion watches her like a hawk. You were the next best thing."

His jaw clenched. "You'd be dead if you'd taken her."

"Only if you caught me. But damn, if we'd had both the alphas' sisters..."

"Dion and Adric would've torn each other to pieces." He shook his head in reluctant admiration. Whoever was behind this, they were smart.

"I'm surprised Adric didn't kill you right then, that day at the hotel. Still, you and Marjani? That was almost as good as Rosana and Marjani."

"Glad to be of use," he muttered.

"If it makes you feel any better, it's not about you or Dion. It's Adric I want." Her tone was quietly venomous. "He's too strong—none of us could beat him in a challenge. But your brother just might be able to."

Footsteps approached. Kelvin muttered something to Shania and she assented.

"Here." She pressed a cup to Tiago's lips. "You must be thirsty."

And like an idiot, he drank. Blame it on the fact that he was still recovering from his injuries and, on top of that, preoccupied with escaping, but by the time the slightly-off taste registered, it was too late. He'd already swallowed a mouthful.

"More," Shania urged.

He clamped his lips shut and shoved her away with his knee. "Bitch. Get the fuck away from me."

She inhaled sharply but backed up a few feet. He felt both their gazes on him. Waiting.

When he got free, he'd... Beneath the blindfold, he opened and closed his eyes, dizzy. "What was in that, anyway?" His voice sounded oddly thick.

"Insurance. In case the blindfold isn't enough."

"You"—he shook his head—"you..." He forgot what he was going to say.

His eyes drifted shut. He forced them back open, but they closed again a minute later, and this time, it was too much effort to open them. His head felt as if a weight were attached to it. He rested his cheek against the brick wall.

Gods, he was a fucking idiot. Just because Jorge hadn't drugged him didn't mean the earth fada wouldn't.

When he came to, he was slumped to the side, head at an awkward angle. His inner clock wasn't as certain as usual, but he guessed it was around two or three o'clock. He was about to sit up when he realized Jorge and Mys were back. Jorge, Shania and another man were engaged in a hushed argument on the opposite side of the basement.

Tiago strained to hear them, but they were careful to keep their voices pitched too low for him to catch anything but a couple of names: Dion, Orius.

Jorge's voice rose. "Damn it, you said—"

"Everything will be fine," the man returned in a frigid voice, "if you don't lose your head. You get Dion there, and I'll make sure Adric hears about it. With any luck, all you'll have to do is sit back and watch them fight."

Fucking Baltimore fada. Tiago would've shaken his head if it wasn't at such an awkward angle. It figured they were using Jorge to take Adric down. The clan was a nest of rats.

"Four o'clock," the earth fada male said.

Tiago frowned. It wasn't the same man as before. The voice was different. So there were at least four Baltimore shifters involved: three men and Shania.

"I know," Shania replied. "I'm the one who contacted Rock Run, remember?"

The earth fada male left and Jorge crossed the basement to Tiago. "Wake up." He kicked Tiago's leg through the blanket.

"I'm up, I'm up." He pushed himself back up to sitting. "What time is it, anyway?"

"What time is it, *Lord Jorge*?" prompted the other man.

"What time is it, Lord Jorge?" he echoed in a flat voice.

"Afternoon. Your brother. Here soon. He was told to come alone, but I know the man. He'll bring others. But you—don't worry. We take care of them. You—control Dion."

"I'll do what I can, but he's strong. You know that."

"You must be stronger. I tell Orius—wait until midnight. If he doesn't hear from me by then, the girl is his."

Tiago's lips peeled back in a snarl. Jorge growled back and

Tiago tensed, but Shania approached and murmured something calming, and Jorge walked away without doing anything else.

Tiago rolled his neck, trying to get the kinks out. Jorge had explained what he was to do: control Dion without making it obvious so that his brother was forced to accept Jorge's challenge, and then make sure Dion lost.

Because otherwise, Dion would never let it come to a challenge. By breaking his vow, Jorge had made himself a pariah, outside *tradição*, the fada system of law. As alpha, Dion had the right to execute Jorge without following the rituals.

Tiago's mind churned, desperately seeking a way out.

If he used his Gift on Dion a second time, his brother would do everything he could to break him. Not even the fact that Alesia was Jorge's prisoner would exempt him. Dion simply couldn't let the clan know that Tiago had that kind of power. If Tiago could force Dion to obey him, then by *tradição*, Tiago was the dominant, and thus should be alpha.

And while Dion was distracted with fighting off Tiago, Jorge would make his move. And Tiago knew damn well he wanted Dion dead.

Jorge might not even let it come to a challenge—why risk a fight when he could kill Dion outright?

But if Tiago didn't help Jorge, Alesia would be at the mercy of these SOBs.

We'll take your woman and use her every way known to man, and then drop her in the deepest part of the bay.

It was an impossible choice. Tiago's claws sliced out. Behind his back, he tore desperately at the leather cord. He *had* to escape. But they must have set a spell on the leather because it remained stubbornly intact.

He ground his teeth in frustration.

Shania crossed the floor to him. "Just do as he says," she said in a hard voice. "Or your dryad is dead. Jorge would kill her in a heartbeat. You scented him, didn't you? He's going feral, and on top of that, he's half-crazed with grief. He and Benny were mates, you know."

"Then he should know how it feels to have someone he cares about threatened," Tiago growled. He shook his head. "How can you just stand by and let them hurt another woman like that? Maybe you don't give a fuck about Alesia, but Marjani? She's from your own clan."

"You think I care? I lost my mate five years ago."

"You were mated?"

"We hadn't celebrated the bond yet, but it was there. I could feel it here." He heard her tap her chest. "His name was Hunter."

"Hunter?" Tiago frowned. The name sounded familiar.

"He was there on the island that day with Jace."

"The bastard who tried to sell Merry Jones to the night fae."

Dion suspected that Hunter had been one of a small group trying to wrest control of the Baltimore clan from Adric, although the earth fada alpha wouldn't confirm it. But the next day, he'd sent Dion a curt, three-word message: *Hunter is dead.*

Shania grabbed a fistful of Tiago's hair and yanked back his head. "He. Was. Not. A bastard—or a traitor. He was just returning the girl to her people. She's dangerous—a quarter night fae. If they wanted her, why shouldn't we help them—and ourselves at the same time?" She slammed him into the wall and stalked away.

Tiago knew he should shut up, but he said, "Except that she's also one-half earth shifter. And anyway, she'd been with Rock Run for two years—she thought of Valeria as her mama."

"The night fae wanted her. Lord Tyrus is her uncle."

"And in return, Tyrus would've killed Adric for you." It was a guess, but Shania didn't disagree.

"He should never have made alpha," she shot back.

Tiago moved a shoulder. "That's your clan's business. But when you involve the night fae—"

"She's a mixed-blood," Shania returned.

"*Deus*," he said in disgust. "We're all fucking mixed-bloods."

"But in us, the fae blood is just a few drops. Merry Jones is one-quarter fae—and a night fae at that. Let them have her if they want her so bad."

Tiago shook his head. "She's just a kid. And you know damn well that Tyrus didn't want her because of any warm family feeling. He wants her dead."

Across the basement, Jorge gave a sharp, inhuman bark, then started to whine.

Shania immediately went to him and started talking in the same soothing voice she'd used earlier, but Jorge kept whining. It sounded as if he were crouched on the floor, rocking back and forth.

At that weird, high droning, the hairs on Tiago's nape lifted. The man was getting worse by the minute.

Lord, this was fucked. He and Alesia were at the mercy of two nearly-feral shifters and a woman out to avenge her lost mate. And that didn't count the other three Baltimore fada, including the one who seemed to be running things from behind the scenes.

Dion's strong, he told himself. Jorge wouldn't find him easy to control, even with Tiago's help. And Cleia would have her mate's back. Dion wouldn't let her within a mile of Jorge, but she'd probably asked her cousin Olivia, the sun fae's strongest spell caster, to set a protective ward on Dion.

But would that be enough? Tiago had never tested his Gift against a fae ward, but he suspected that together, he and the beast were strong enough to break it—especially if his own mate's life was at stake.

Shania must've somehow succeeded in calming Jorge, because Tiago heard him mutter that he was okay.

She returned to Tiago and told him that she was going to untie him so he could eat. "But first, I want your promise that you won't try anything."

"You've got it," he said immediately. His fingers had gone numb again, and there wasn't much he could do anyway, not with his eyes bound and them watching his every move.

"Turn around, then," she said, and when he obeyed, undid the leather thong.

This time, he expected the pain. He clenched his jaw and worked his arms and fingers until the pins and needles dropped to a bearable level.

When he'd regained use of his hands, Shania dropped a plastic bottle and a couple of energy bars onto his lap. He set the bottle aside without drinking it. He was dangerously dehydrated from the long hours without water and whatever they'd drugged him with, but he was damned if he'd fall for another one of their tricks.

She made an impatient sound. "It's only water. The bottle's never been opened—see for yourself."

He picked the bottle up and tested the cap. She was right; the seal was intact. Just to be sure, he unscrewed the lid and took a cautious sniff, but all he could smell was the plastic.

"Drink, already," she said. "Why would we drug you? We need you awake for this."

That made sense—and he was so dry, he was willing to take the chance. He drained the bottle and then wolfed down the energy bars.

After that, they left him alone. Shania even left his wrists unbound, after extracting a further promise from him not to move from the spot where he was.

He willingly swore whatever she asked. All he could do right now was let this play out.

But he used the time to go through his muscles one by one, stretching and then consciously relaxed them. His chance would come. He had to believe that.

The beast approved.

Yes. Wait. Chance.

Then—kill.

Tiago shook his head ruefully. He still wasn't used to his beast counseling patience, but for once the two of them were in complete agreement.

They'd wait—and then they'd make their move.

25

The Rock Run fada took motorcycles to Baltimore. While Dion and Rui finalized the details of who was going where, Cleia gave Alesia boots, gloves and a jacket in a buttery-soft brown leather, explaining they were to protect her from the iron.

"The bike body is encased in plastic, but you'll be on it for close to an hour—maybe more."

Dryads weren't as susceptible to the poisonous effects of iron as true fae like Cleia, but an hour was a long time to be in such close proximity to the metal. And iron was nothing to mess with —first it blistered the skin, and then the wound couldn't heal so that it festered or continuously seeped blood.

"And maybe you'd like a clean shirt, too?" The sun fae glanced at Alesia's sweater, gritty from her sleep on the cavern floor last night, and probably smelly as well.

Alesia shot her a grateful look. "If it's not too much trouble."

"No trouble at all." Cleia took her into the master bedroom and found her a bright red shirt

Alesia removed her sweater and put it on. The shirt was fae-tailored, with a sheen that intensified the red. As she buttoned it up, it fitted itself to her body as if it had been made for her and not the tall, curvy queen.

As she adjusted Tiago's necklace on top of the bodice, she caught a glimpse of herself in the mirror. *Holy mother.* She looked —hot. Sexy and confident, especially once she donned the trim jacket and cute little boots.

If only Dina could see her.

"Try not to worry," Cleia said as she handed her the leather gloves. The queen grimaced. "Sorry—how can you *not* be worried? But I'd like to help. May I give you some energy?"

Alesia hesitated, and then nodded. "I'd like that."

Cleia smiled broadly, as if Alesia were doing *her* a favor, and wrapped her arms around her. A warm glow filled Alesia from the inside out, and her anxiety felt more manageable somehow. She held herself stiff for a few moments, and then gave in and hugged Cleia back. The woman was impossible not to like.

And after all, Cleia *had* sent Tiago away when she'd found out how young he was. It wasn't her fault that the man had stubbornly refused to let go.

And then Dion was kissing Cleia goodbye and ordering her *not* to follow him or for that matter, interfere in any way—"And I mean it, *minha rainha*, this is Rock Run business"—and Rui was hustling Alesia out of the base and into a motorboat along with Dion and the four warriors who were going along with them to Baltimore. She knew Rock Run had women warriors, but this squad was all men in black leather jackets.

They gave her polite nods, and she caught a few surreptitious sniffs, but they were clearly not in the mood to chat. The youngest took out a knife and idly tested the blade with his thumb. She gulped, and the man looked up and caught her staring. He flashed her a smile and she realized it was Tiago's friend Chico.

She gave an uncertain smile back and then looked down at her hands, interlaced tightly in her lap.

It was a quick trip by boat up Rock Run Creek to the clan garage. Rui handed her a helmet—although she noticed he didn't use one himself—and made sure she had it on correctly before helping her onto the bike behind him. Together, the six of them roared out of the garage, Dion in the lead, and headed down the wooded country road that led to the interstate and Baltimore.

The morning commute was winding down, but this was I-95 between New York and Washington, DC, so there was still a lot of traffic on the road. The six fada formed a pack and stayed in the fast lane.

Alesia had been in a car perhaps four or five times in her life, and never on a motorcycle. The scenery flew past at a dizzying speed and the roar of the cycle vibrated through her whole body. She set her jaw, tightened her grip on Rui's waist and leaned when he did, determined not to do anything to slow them down.

The thirty-five-mile trip south took close to an hour. By the time they arrived in Baltimore, it was eleven o'clock and the streets were clogged with cars and delivery trucks. They entered Key Highway and headed toward the Inner Harbor, passing through a neighborhood of upscale condos and funky little restaurants.

They stopped at a traffic light and Dion looked at Alesia. "Where to?" he called over the rumble of six engines.

She concentrated. *There.* A tug to the northeast. "I think he's on the other side of the harbor." She pointed ahead and to the right.

"You sure?"

"No," she admitted.

For some reason that made him grin. "Okay, *querida.*" He looked around at his warriors and said what she guessed was the Portuguese equivalent of, "Let's roll."

They circled around the harbor past pricey-looking hotels and towering office buildings. Every few blocks, Dion stopped and asked Alesia whether they were going in the correct direction. They were, but it was frustrating—she couldn't pinpoint Tiago. Then he disappeared completely and for a terrible moment she thought he'd died.

But no, he was unconscious—a strange, dreamless unconsciousness.

"*Cabrãos* probably drugged him," Rui said when she described it.

They were in Fells Point now, a section of Baltimore that dated to the 1700s. Back then, it had been a working-class district of shipbuilders and factories, but now it was a picturesque neighborhood with a wharf, cobblestone streets, black iron lampposts and Federal-style rowhouses.

They drove up and down the narrow streets for another fifteen minutes, going further and further from the harbor, but Alesia couldn't narrow down Tiago's location any further.

"He's near here," she said with a helpless shrug. "I just don't know exactly where."

"Don't worry," Dion told her. "Near is good enough. We can find him now."

The six of them headed back toward the waterfront. There, they bumped down a cobblestone street that ran along the east side of the harbor and parked the bikes in front of a rowhouse owned by Rock Run.

Rui helped Alesia off his motorcycle. She took off her helmet and shook out her hair, her body still humming from the vibration of the engine.

A couple of men were watching them from across the street. Dion jerked his head at them in acknowledgment.

"Earth fada," Rui told Alesia.

She looked at them again. They stared back, unsmiling. They had Adric's tough, catlike body. They might not be as big as the Rock Run warriors, but she wouldn't want to meet either one in a dark alley.

"Don't worry," Rui said. "Dion has an agreement with Adric.

We have three days to take down Jorge and the others—then all bets are off. That's not going to stop them from dogging our steps, though."

They all trooped into the rowhouse. Rui took charge, deploying his warriors in various directions. In a few minutes he and three of the men had shed their leather jackets and donned various disguises, then slipped out through a basement exit that was apparently unknown to the Baltimore fada.

Dion went out the front door, having volunteered to search the streets nearby as himself. If the earth shifters wanted to trail him, so much the better.

Chico's task was to guard Alesia. He visibly swallowed his disappointment and ushered her to the front room, where they sat on denim-covered couches.

"So," he said with his most charming smile. "You're Tiago's mate, huh?"

She recalled the day Chico had visited her. She'd avoided him as she had all the Rock Run fada except for Tiago and Rui. When he'd finally coaxed her out of hiding, he'd given her that same easy smile, but she'd sensed a predatory edge beneath.

Now she could tell he was *not* happy to hear the news about her and Tiago. But the predatory edge was gone, too, which told her more than anything that he'd accepted it. No, Chico was in full protective-fada-male mode, questioning her about last night, asking if she wanted something to eat.

They ended up playing cards. Chico taught her blackjack and then staked her fifty dollars "to make it interesting."

She shrugged and went along. She might be a peace-loving, tree-hugging dryad, but she wasn't going to sit tamely by while they rescued Tiago. This was her mate's life at stake.

It wasn't just that Fausto had been so insistent that she should go. Her own gut said the same thing—that Tiago *needed* her there.

And so she would be—as soon as she figured out how to lose Chico.

26

———

*A*lesia gazed down at Fells Point from her perch in a scraggly street tree.

Across the narrow road, a small sign labeled a three-story rowhouse as the Full Moon Saloon. Everything about it marked it as a fada bar. The plain brick exterior. The dark plate-glass window. The howling wolf logo. And the bulked-up man with the shaved head guarding the front door.

So this was where they were bringing Tiago.

It was three-thirty; he'd be here any minute. It hadn't been hard to find the saloon. Tiago had awakened about thirty minutes ago, allowing her to pinpoint his whereabouts to within a block or two—and after that, she'd simply asked directions.

And in the end, it hadn't been hard to get away from the Rock Run fada, either.

Dion had returned to the rowhouse around two o'clock, his face somber. Alesia and Chico jumped to their feet, but he shook his head.

"Sorry, *querida*. The SOBs must be using some kind of magic to hide him. Cleia has her cousin Olivia working on it, but all she's been able to do is trace him to this general area."

"So what are you going to do?"

"I'm going to meet Jorge at the Full Moon Saloon at four."

Alesia had bitten her lip. "Can I speak to you in private?"

"Of course. Go outside," Dion told Chico. "Give those earth fada someone else to worry about. And then get yourself to the Full Moon by three-thirty. Jorge doesn't know you very well, but just in case, grab a jacket from a human store to disguise your scent. We're putting you and Eliana inside. She'll meet you there."

"Yes, sir!" Chico shot out the door.

When they were alone, Dion cocked a single black brow at Alesia. "Well?"

"You know Tiago's going to use his Gift against you. That must be what they want him to do."

"You think I don't know that? But he can't hold me. I'm his alpha—when it comes down to it, I'm dominant. He'll submit to me."

"Are you sure?" Her palms were sweaty. She rubbed them on her jeans. She knew what she had to do, but it was still hard to volunteer for what could turn into a full-out brawl. "Take me with you. If Tiago sees me, he'll know I'm—"

"No. It's too risky. What if Jorge and Mys get to you first?"

"I'll make sure they don't see me. If there's one thing I'm good at, it's blending in."

"*Sim*?" Dion looked unconvinced. "I don't think so, little one. I thank you for offering, but Jorge's sick—he's not thinking straight. Even with Tiago, he's not going to be able to control me."

"But what if you're wrong? What if Tiago *can* overpower you?"

"If it comes to that, my men have orders to knock him out. He can't use his Gift if he's unconscious. Now, here's what you're going to do: return to Rock Run. I need Chico at the Full Moon, and I can't leave you here unprotected. There's a ward on the house to keep intruders out, but wards can be broken. I want you safe at the base."

"But—"

"*Por favor*, Alesia." The alpha had held up a hand. "Indulge me, *sim*?"

She'd compressed her lips, and then nodded.

Rui had returned then and the two men had bundled her out the back door where a peach tree in full bloom presided over the tiny yard between the house and the harbor.

"It's not an oak," Dion had said, "but you can use it for transportation, yes? Now, promise me you'll go straight back to Rock Run."

"All right. I will."

"Good girl. Now, don't worry. I'm not going to let anyone hurt your mate."

He'd wrapped her in his arms and planted a kiss on each of her cheeks, and she gave him a shy peck in return. Rui gave her a hard hug, and then interlinked his fingers to boost her into the tree.

She swung herself up another few feet until she was at the tree's heart, surrounded by rose-pink blossoms. The peach practically quivered with delight at having a dryad in its branches. She murmured her thanks and a promise to return soon for a longer visit, and then with a wave to the two men, was on her way back north.

She hadn't lied to Dion and Rui. She had returned to Rock Run, where she went first to her island to pick up a few necessary items. Then she'd visited Dina before returning to Fells Point. All that 'porting should have been tiring, but she was running on adrenaline.

Now she narrowed her eyes at the bar's gritty exterior. Tiago was somewhere nearby, she was sure of it. But not inside the Full Moon.

She had the feeling he was underground—a basement or a shifter den. At least she could enter the saloon without him knowing.

She didn't have to be a mind reader to know Tiago wouldn't want her here. And Dion was *not* going to be happy to see her back in Baltimore.

A few days ago the thought of their anger would've had her scurrying back to her island, tail between her legs—but not anymore. She'd held her own with Mys and Orius, had even found the courage to stand up to Mys. She'd gone into the heart of a fada base and found they weren't all that different from her.

And if she and Tiago mated, he was going to have to accept that she had the right to make her own decisions. Otherwise he'd walk all over her and neither of them would be happy. Fada respected strength. Tiago wouldn't want a weak mate any more than she wanted to be one.

On the sidewalk below the tree, a herd of college students making an early start on their Friday night rumbled past. The scent of beer and cigarettes rose to her perch. She inhaled, nerving herself to leave the safety of the tree's branches.

She'd been in bars before, because hey, she might be a solitary, but that didn't mean she didn't have needs. Those bars, though, had been for humans and the occasional slumming fae, and she'd always been with at least one of her sisters.

Compared to those other bars, the Full Moon Saloon was quiet, with the music playing at a low level to accommodate a shifter's acute hearing. But that only emphasized it was a fada bar.

She glanced again at the forbidding exterior and flashed on Mys, gazing at her with eyes as cold and unblinking as a shark.

And Adric, tearing out Orius's throat in that silent, efficient way...

Her neck and shoulders tightened and her heart bumped against her rib cage. Who was she kidding? She was scared out of her freaking mind.

But Tiago needed her.

She was clinging to the tree like a monkey. She took a deep breath, released the trunk and leapt to the ground.

As she crossed the street, she donned Dina's large black sunglasses, concealing the most fae part of her. Dina had been dying to come with her, but Alesia had put her off by saying she had a date with Tiago. It wasn't a lie; she *did* have a date with Tiago. Just not the kind Dina assumed.

"Do Rio?" Her sister had grinned. "I *knew* something was up between you two."

Alesia had nodded. "Can I tell you a secret? You can't tell Mama—promise."

"I promise. Now what is it?"

"He's my mate."

Her sister's mouth fell open. "You're kidding."

"It's true."

And while Dina was taking that in, Alesia had borrowed the sunglasses and a pair of black skinny jeans, sprayed herself with eau-de-something-lemony to disguise her scent, and helped herself to a tube of bright red lipstick.

Now she walked up the short flight of steps. The big doorman had the yellow eyes of a wolf.

"I.D.?" he asked in a bored voice, clearly not realizing she was a dryad.

She let out a breath. First hurdle passed.

Fortunately, she'd obtained the correct card several years ago, and she had the fifty dollars she'd won from Chico tucked into her purse. She produced the driver's license with a flourish. He glanced from the card to her, taking in the tight black jeans and Cleia's ankle boots, and waved her inside.

She walked down a short hall into a room full of large fada males. Oh, there were a few females and humans, but most of the tables held men with a soldier's powerful body and stony eyes. She didn't see any of the men she'd come to Baltimore with, though; Dion and Rui must be keeping them out of sight.

Speculative male stares settled on her. Cleia's leather jacket nipped in at the waist, showing off her legs in the skinny jeans. She'd twisted her unruly hair into a braid that fell over one shoulder and put on the lipstick she'd borrowed from Dina.

Camouflage. Like she'd told Dion, she was good at blending in. Hopefully, no one from Rock Run would connect this woman with the shy, retiring dryad.

Keeping the sunglasses on, she headed for the long, polished-oak bar and ordered a beer. She took a sip and glanced around unsmiling.

She'd arrived early. Tiago wasn't at the bar yet, and neither was Jorge or Mys.

She glanced down the bar and froze. Chico, wearing a cap and a gray hoodie, was taking a seat at one end of the bar next to a pretty Latina with curly brown hair. He murmured something to the woman, who had to be Eliana.

Alesia turned the other way, giving them her back, and then strolled to the back of the bar where she found a dark corner out of their line of sight.

The music changed to a slow blues. Alesia was as susceptible to music as most fae. Her eyes drifted shut, her body swaying in time to the hypnotic rhythm. The man on the recording began to sing in a gravelly voice.

She opened her eyes to find a male—a human—propped against the wall next to her, a beer bottle in one hand. He slanted her a look. "The man rocks, doesn't he? John Lee Hooker."

The man was cute and blond, his eyes glazed with drink. Perfect. More camouflage.

"Yeah?" She leaned closer so that his body shielded hers from the rest of the bar and placed a hand on his arm. "I like it. Makes me want to move."

He smiled and tilted his head in the direction of the tiny dance floor. "Wanna dance?"

"Not right now." That would be like painting a bull's-eye on her back. "Maybe later." She lifted the bottle to her lips.

His gaze narrowed on her mouth, pursed around the brown glass neck. "Why don't we sit down then?"

She let her lips curve. "Good idea."

Placing a hand on the small of her back, he steered her to a booth. He waved her in first, and then sat on the bench beside her so that she was on the inside with him between her and the rest of the bar. Now she was concealed not only from the front door, but most of the other tables.

The only thing left to do was wait.

ALESIA'S new friend was named Sean. He'd been out of college for a few years and worked in IT.

He asked about her, and she responded with her usual cover. Humans were much more at ease with a forester named Lisa than a dryad.

Ten minutes passed, when suddenly, her heart gave a hard thump. She knew without looking that Tiago had entered the bar.

But not from the front. From the booth, she had a clear view of the short hall leading to the saloon's back door. Her eyes widened as Jorge strode toward her, followed by Tiago and Mys. She dove sideways so that she was hidden by the booth's walls.

Tiago couldn't find out she was here before Dion arrived. She had no idea how strong his Gift was, but Jorge and Mys had beaten him once. This time she was going to make sure the odds were on his side.

Jorge growled something at Tiago. She sneaked a peek from beneath the table. Jorge was herding Tiago in the opposite direction, toward the long wooden bar.

"Lisa?" asked Sean. "You all right?"

She sat up again. "Dropped my purse."

He nodded and took another sip of beer.

She waited until her heart stopped pounding before risking a look around Sean. Tiago stood at the bar with Jorge and Mys on either side. All three had their backs to her.

Tiago still had on the T-shirt and cargo pants from yesterday, but they'd found him a pair of canvas shoes and his shoulder-length hair was secured with a leather thong.

She leaned sideways so she could see his face in the long mirror behind the counter. Still bruised, but he seemed to be moving okay.

Thank the Goddess. At least they hadn't beaten him further, although Jorge and Mys looked like they'd been in a scuffle.

The bartender brought Jorge and Mys whisky, while Tiago stuck with water.

Sean rested an arm on the seatback behind her. His mouth moved and she nodded without hearing, all her senses trained on Tiago. He glanced around the room and she *felt* him searching for her.

Damn. She tamped down the mate bond and shrank down on the seat next to her blond companion.

She hadn't expected Tiago to sense her so quickly. Their bond was solidifying, something that would've thrilled her any other time.

The bar clock had a big white face with plain black metal hands. The long hand moved another notch. Ten to four.

Dion should arrive any minute now.

Across the room, Tiago took a sip of water before glancing around again. Chico and Eliana had taken a table across the bar. Tiago stiffened, but he kept his face expressionless and turned back to nod at something Jorge said.

A minute later he was scanning the room again, his worry and fear for her saturating their bond.

Alesia's stomach tightened. She ached to go to him, let him know she was all right.

You're doing the right thing.

Without her, Jorge had no hold on Tiago; nothing else would've brought him here. Once Tiago knew she'd escaped, he'd be free to fight back. But if Jorge found out she was here before Dion arrived, he or Mys would simply grab her again and they'd be back where they'd started.

And this time, she might not get free. She hadn't forgotten Jorge's threats—or the way Mys had seemed to like hurting her.

Then it occurred to her that unlike last night, today she had a squad of fada warriors backing her up. Her lips curved in a way that made Sean halt in the middle of a sentence.

She touched his hand. "You were saying?"

There was a stir at the entrance and Dion strode inside. Even Sean sensed the danger. He glanced over his shoulder and gulped.

The Rock Run alpha halted in the center of the bar and crossed his arms, large and lethal in the black leather jacket and weathered jeans. He looked exactly what he was—the most powerful male in a clan of warriors and assassins.

The room went silent. A couple of humans slipped out the door.

Jorge eyed Dion in the mirror. Then, moving so deliberately it was an insult, he finished his shot, set the glass on the bar and turned around, dragging Tiago with him so that he stood a little to the front and side of him.

Dion gave his brother an unreadable look and then raised a brow at Jorge. "I'm here. Now what?"

"I challenge you to a duel for alpha of—"

"No," Dion cut him off. "Challenges are to settle claims within the clan. You're an exile and an oath breaker. You have no right to challenge me."

Jorge's mouth opened and closed. He glanced around, confused.

Mys stepped to Tiago's other side. "Accept the challenge. We have your brother's woman. You might take a chance with your brother's life, but what about her? And maybe we won't kill your brother—just cut his spinal cord. Not even a fada can recover from that."

That's when Alesia saw in the mirror that Jorge had a knife to Tiago's spine.

Her lungs seized. Her fingers curled into her palms. She wanted so bad to do something, but interfering might make things worse

Then Rui stepped from the hall to the bathrooms, just ten feet away from the booth.

She smothered a gasp.

His nostrils flared and she knew he scented her, but he kept his eyes on the group at the bar. "Let do Rio go," he ordered Jorge in a cold-as-ice voice. "This is over. It ends here."

Jorge had recovered the ability to speak. He ignored Rui to sneer at Dion. "You were told to come alone, but apparently you're afraid to face me without your bully boy. What kind of alpha are you?"

"A smart one," Dion shot back. "I don't trust you worth a damn. But my second is right. Why bring Tiago and his woman into this? If you're so strong, come after me directly."

"Only a coward would use a woman like that," Rui added. "But then that's what you are. A goddamn fucking *cabrão* who preys on women and children."

"Maybe. But when this is over, your women will be mine." Jorge smiled, his gaze darting between Rui and Dion. "Both of them. And your pups, too."

"Like hell," Rui gritted and strode forward.

Dion flung out a hand to halt him. "Not yet."

Jorge gestured at Rui. "Kill him," he ordered Tiago. "Or the dryad dies."

A muscle in Tiago's cheek twitched, but he narrowed his eyes at Rui and muttered something.

Rui jerked and clutched his chest.

Dion started to go to his friend's aid, but Tiago growled, "*No. Stay where you are.*"

Dion's face was sorrowful. "Don't do this, *irmão*. Alesia—" He strained forward, his muscles bulging under the jacket as if he engaged in an invisible tug of war.

Meanwhile, Rui's face twisted in agony. He dropped to his knees a few feet from Tiago and Jorge, both hands to his chest.

The hell with it. Alesia jumped to her feet. She had to stop this. She was trying to squeeze her way past Sean when Dion spoke between clenched teeth.

"Tiago. Listen. Jorge—he doesn't have Alesia anymore. She got away. She came to us."

Tiago's gaze snapped to his brother. His focus must have broken because Rui inhaled harshly and released his chest. But he remained on his knees, struggling to breathe.

"This is true?" Tiago asked Dion. "You swear it?"

Before he could reply, Jorge snapped, "That's a goddamn lie. He'll say anything to save himself. Now kill do Mar, or the dryad dies—but first, my men get to play with her."

"*No*," Alesia said. "No, Tiago. *I'm here.*"

But Tiago had already turned to Rui, who had managed to come back to his feet. Tiago's hand shot out and Rui clutched his chest again. Tiago muttered something and the Rock Run second backed away, step by step, clearly trying to resist but unable to wrench control from Tiago. His back hit the wall next to Alesia's booth.

"Not. A lie," Dion gasped. "Orius is dead."

"Let me out." Alesia shoved Sean's shoulder. "I've got to stop this."

He looked at her as if she had straw for brains. "Are you out of your fucking mind? You know what these men are? *Fada.*"

"I know." She shoved his shoulder. "Now move."

He shook his head but rose to his feet, allowing her to slip from the booth. But instead of leaving, he hovered protectively nearby as she started toward Tiago. That was sweet, but stupid. The fada would crush him like a bug if he interfered.

She swung back to him. "Look, Sean. This is serious—fada business. It could come to a challenge. Do you understand?" She lifted her glasses so he could see the fae tilt to her eyes. "And I'm the dryad they're talking about."

"Holy mother of—" His mouth slackened. "Okay, okay. I'm out of here."

He hurried for the exit along with the other humans still present until the bar was empty save for the fada—and Alesia.

"Tiago?" She moved forward. "It's the truth. I'm okay. I'm right here."

His head snapped around. His focus broke, releasing Dion from the compulsion. With a roar, the alpha leapt forward.

At the same time, Tiago's face lit up with relief and something more. Something that made her heart contract. "Alesia?"

Jorge's jaw dropped. "Get her," he snapped at Mys, but Tiago twisted and did something behind his back and the knife clattered to the floor.

Dion was right there. He grabbed Jorge by the throat as Tiago shoved Mys into the bar. Mys swung around, but Chico and Eliana grabbed his arms. At the same time, the other three Rock Run warriors who'd come to Baltimore burst into the bar and converged on Jorge and Mys.

Her mate ignored them all to stride toward her.

"Tiago," she rasped, and ran toward him. They met in the middle and wrapped their arms around each other.

"Thank all the gods and goddesses," he said against her neck. He hugged her to him, lungs working like a bellows. "You're all right?" He ran his hands over her face, her shoulders. "They didn't—"

"I'm fine." She managed a smile. "Honest. I got away last night."

"But how?"

"Lord Adric helped me."

"Lord Adric? The earth fada alpha?"

She nodded. "He was looking for Jorge and found me instead."

"Well, damn." His big arms wrapped around her again. They clung to each other, his face buried in her hair. "I thought"—his breath hitched—"I thought they'd—"

She shook her head. "They didn't. But what about you? You're all right?"

"Of course," he said with fada arrogance.

Her lips curved. Goddess, she loved this man.

He gave her a last hug. This time when he lifted his head, he took in the lipstick, tight pants and cute little boots. His nostrils flared and she knew he'd picked up the lemon scent.

He quirked a brow. "What in Hades are you playing at, anyway?"

She lifted her chin. "Camouflage."

"*Deus*, woman." His gaze raked down her body. They were in a bar full of shifters one inch away from a full-out brawl, but damn if that hot, dark look didn't send a thrill shooting straight to her womb. "If that's camouflage, then I'm king of the faeries."

"It worked. No one recognized me."

"That's not the point. You—you're—" He waved a hand, then scowled at his brother. "What the fuck is she doing here, anyway?"

"Damn if I know." Dion narrowed his eyes at her. "She's supposed to be safe at Rock Run where Jorge and Mys can't use her as a bargaining chip. *Sim, menina*?"

Her smile was a shade guilty. "I *did* go to Rock Run."

Dion just shook his head.

"That reminds me." Tiago's mouth flattened. He pushed Alesia at Rui with a muttered, "Take care of her," and then swung around to where Dion was holding Jorge.

Jorge was still gaping at Alesia.

"You goddamned sonuvabitch." Tiago and slammed his fist into Jorge's grizzled face.

Something cracked. Jorge staggered backward into Dion.

Jorge brought his hand to his jaw. He blinked a couple of times, then snarled and shook off Dion to leap for Tiago. They fell with a crash onto a beer-stained table. The wood legs broke under their combined weight, and all hell broke loose.

27

———

Tiago had almost given up hope.

Jorge had a knife to his spine, and Shania and Kelvin were at a nearby table, ready to jump in if necessary.

Then Rui appeared, and Jorge shoved the knife a little deeper. Tiago stiffened, a cold sweat trickling down his nape. One wrong move and he'd be paralyzed for life.

Still, even then he wouldn't have tried to compel Dion. Not if it weren't for Alesia.

But he had no choice.

He was stronger now, the beast feeding him energy so that he could keep up the pressure and at the same time knock Rui to his knees. Dion fought hard, but Tiago kept at him, a steady, relentless pressure.

Then Alesia popped out of a booth and he saw his chance. He knocked the knife out of Jorge's hand and shoved Mys into the bar as hard as he could, and then practically flew the few steps to Alesia, afraid this was a dream and he'd wake up and find her gone.

All he could think was: *She's safe. She's safe.*

Behind him, Jorge muttered, "Fucking whore," in Portuguese.

Tiago snapped. His woman, *his mate*, had been kidnapped and spent a no-doubt terrifying night. He'd been drugged and forced to address this feral as "Lord" Jorge. And worse, he'd been compelled to turn on his own brother and alpha.

He handed Alesia off to Rui and smashed his fist into Jorge's face with everything he had. Jorge came back at him and they went down, but both of them were on their feet in an instant, claws fully extended. For a minute it was two furious animals going at it. Then Jorge twisted away and jumped to his feet.

Tiago started after him, then remembered Alesia. But Rui had hustled her to the side of the bar and was urging her under the table of the booth she'd just vacated. Meanwhile, Chico, bless him, had handed Mys off to another Rock Run man and taken up a stance in front of the booth to protect her.

With his mate safe, he turned back to Jorge.

The men in the bar were taking sides, the Rock Run fada lining up with Tiago and Dion, and Mys and the earth fada jumping in to help Jorge. Shania and Kelvin had disappeared like rats deserting a sinking ship.

A bottle flew toward Tiago. He ducked and it shattered against the mirror behind the bar. To his right, a table overturned. Rui shoved Tiago aside to grapple with Jorge himself. Tiago didn't have a chance to object before he was fighting an earth fada, back to back with Dion, who was fighting off two more.

Tiago's opponent was big and slow moving; he had to be a bear. He pulled out a knife and slashed viciously at Tiago's face. He bobbed and weaved, ducking under the knife and then slamming his fist into the man's belly.

His opponent hardly noticed. He came at Tiago again, slow but relentless.

Tiago drew back his arm and punched him in the jaw. The man blinked and then slid to the ground. Tiago turned in time to see Mys break free from the man holding him and dart across the bar to grab Alesia.

No fucking way.

He started toward them and then watched, stunned, as his shy little dryad grabbed a beer bottle and swung it at Mys's head.

But Mys had fada-quick reflexes. He ducked under the bottle, caught Alesia's arm and started dragging her toward the exit at the back of the saloon.

Tiago leapt into action. He was almost on them when a wolf shifter leapt in front of him. He shoved him out of the way, but the wolf grabbed him from the back. Tiago swore and tried to buck him off as Mys pushed a wriggling, cursing Alesia toward the rear exit.

She lashed out with the beer bottle, hitting Mys's temple with an audible clunk. Biting out something nasty in Greek, he grabbed her wrist and squeezed until she yelped and dropped it.

"You"—he grasped her braid and jerked her head back—"are going to be a pleasure to tame."

"Tiago!" she screamed. "Help!"

He growled and jabbed his elbow into the wolf shifter's ribs, then spun around and kneed him in the balls as hard as he could. The other man doubled over like a deflated balloon.

But as Tiago turned toward Alesia, the wolf pulled out a knife and lunged. Tiago jumped back, but the knife slashed through his T-shirt, slicing a line of fire down his chest.

Tiago snarled. "*Enough.*" He shot out a hand, fingers splayed. "*Freeze.*"

The wolf stilled in the middle of a knife thrust, his body angled forward and his arm out.

Tiago set a compulsion on him to stay where he was and turned toward Mys. "*Let. Her. Go.* And then don't move—not a single fucking muscle."

Mys went rigid but his fingers slowly opened. Alesia backed away as the sea fada watched her, his eyes alive with frustration.

Tiago looked around the bar. "Nobody move. Not a goddamn step. Freeze—all of you."

They all—river and earth fada—halted where they were, some still locked in each other's grip. Their chests heaved as they gulped for breath, but they remained in place as if glued to the floor.

Alesia blinked as the compulsion swept over her. He saw her glancing cautiously around. But he'd promised that he would never use it on her, and he'd meant it.

Working his Gift on so many people was a tremendous strain. Dion growled and fought to get free. Tiago gave up and released him—but only him. His instincts wouldn't let him release anyone else until he knew Alesia was safe.

Dion started toward Tiago, and then stopped. "What are you going to do, brother?"

"Watch and see," Tiago gritted. Sweat beaded on his forehead. His jaw clenched with effort. The beast rose up to add his strength to Tiago's.

Save. The mate.

He glanced at Alesia again. She'd picked up another beer bottle. She caught his eye and with a shrug, set it on the bar.

His eyes narrowed. She had a nasty scratch on her cheek and her shirt was torn open. She saw him looking and pulled the sides together. "I'm okay."

Tiago bit out a curse and started toward Mys. He was going to rip the man's throat out. But his focus had shattered and his grip over the room broke.

In an instant, the sea fada had his arm locked around Alesia's throat. "Let me go," he hissed, "or she dies."

"Like hell." Tiago shot his hand out and mentally squeezed Mys's heart with the energy like he'd done to Rui—but this time he meant it.

Mys jerked. His arm dropped to his side and he slumped to the floor.

The other fada moved. Tiago growled and ordered them to freeze again. This time, he focused on the Baltimore fada, allowing the Rock Run fada, including Dion and Rui, to remain free.

With less people, it wasn't as difficult, and the beast had caught on to what he needed. It fed him energy in a steady stream, easing the strain.

Alesia looked down at Mys and then back at Tiago.

He met her eyes. "He's dead," he confirmed, daring her to object.

Her throat worked. "Oh."

He looked around at the other fada, including those still frozen in place. "And if anyone else touches you, he's dead, too. Understand? Now listen, all of you. You have a choice—you can either leave or stay as witnesses. But the fight is over."

He flicked his fingers and released everyone else but Jorge. They cast wary glances at Tiago, but no one left. They shook themselves off and clumped into two groups—the five Baltimore shifters in one group and the Rock Run fada in the other, with Jorge in the center. Only Claudio remained separate, glaring at them all from behind the bar.

Jorge keened angrily. His face flushed a dark red and his body shook with the effort to free himself.

Tiago set his jaw. "You want a challenge, Jorge? You got it. But from me, not Dion. But you have to fucking wait until I make sure my woman is okay."

Jorge growled, but he stopped fighting the compulsion.

Tiago turned back to Alesia and held out his hand. "Come here, Lesia."

She twisted her fingers together and stared at him without moving.

So that's how it was. He brought his hand back to his side. His heart felt like it was caught in a giant vise.

Still, it was her choice. He wasn't going to force her to mate with a monster. This was who he was. If she wanted him, she had to accept his Gift. Otherwise she might as well take a knife to the mate bond right now.

Then she made a small sound and hurried toward him, arms out.

Tiago's breath released in a whoosh. His arms came around her like an iron band. But it wasn't tight enough. He wanted to take her inside of him, where she'd never, ever be in danger again.

"Alesia," he crooned. "Alesia." He buried his head in her hair, breathing her in beneath the lemon scent she'd drenched herself in. "You're my everything. You know that, don't you?"

She nodded against his neck. "I know. I know."

"*Deus.*" He rained kisses on her face. "I was so afraid that they —" He inhaled raggedly.

"I'm okay. They didn't hurt me."

Dion and Rui stepped forward. Tiago shifted Alesia to one arm, his gaze going to the two men, who had ranged themselves side by side in front of him.

Dion leaned in a little. "I believe I told you," he said between clenched teeth, "to never use your Gift on me again. The others— fine. But not me. I should break your goddamned neck." He flexed his fingers as if contemplating that very act.

Tiago growled low in his chest and Alesia whispered, "*No.*"

He gathered her closer and took a deep breath. "If you want to have this out, fine," he told his brother. "But back off. Alesia's had a rough time as it is, and I won't have you scaring her."

To his surprise, Dion looked abashed. He muttered an apology—to Alesia, not him, but that was fine with Tiago—and took a step back.

"As my alpha," Tiago continued, "you have the right to punish me—even banish me." Alesia caught her breath and he gave her a reassuring squeeze. "But know this. I did it for Alesia. I had no choice. Jorge was going to do to her what he did to Marjani—and worse."

Dion blew out a breath. "I know. And I wouldn't have respected you if you'd done anything else."

Tiago inclined his head. "Still, I beg your pardon."

This was important. Dion, Rui and the other Rock Run fada needed to know that he accepted his brother as his alpha. Because he'd learned something in the last ten minutes. His Gift might make him stronger in some ways than Dion, but Dion was his dominant. He had been fighting the compulsion with everything he had, and Tiago—and his beast—acknowledged his strength.

Because Dion had been winning.

He dropped his gaze submissively, waiting for his brother's answer. Inside, his beast did the same. Another first, and one which told him more clearly than anything that the beast had accepted his place—*their* place—in the river clan.

Dion jerked his chin. "You have it, *irmão*."

"Good." Tiago lifted his head and glared at Jorge, still frozen in place. "Then I, Tiago do Rio, challenge Jorge Teles to a fight to the death."

28

The room went dead silent.

Jorge's lip curled but Tiago tightened his mental hold on him. He was damned if the man was going to escape him now.

"Jorge Teles stole my mate," he stated to the rest of the bar, hard-voiced, "and scared the hell out of her with his threats—and he meant it. After he and his men were finished with her, he was going to throw her broken body to the fish. He also drugged me and kidnapped me—twice. His life is *mine*."

The older man's chest heaved but Tiago refused to let him speak.

Dion narrowed his eyes at Jorge. "You don't deserve such an honorable death. But if that's what my brother wants—"

"No," Rui growled. "I haven't agreed to it. My claim is as strong as Tiago's. *I'll* go first, then Tiago can have his turn. If there's anything left of the bastard." His gaze raked scornfully over Jorge.

Tiago held up a hand. "Remember five years ago when I helped rescue Valeria? You said then you were in my debt—that I could ask for anything, anytime. Well, I'm calling in that favor now. Jorge is *mine*."

"Damn you, do Rio." Rui scowled, then heaved a breath. "Fine. I cede you the right of first challenge."

"*Obrigado.*"

Dion's gaze swept around the bar. "You heard my brother. You all can stay as witnesses—or leave. It's up to you."

No one moved. The only sound was one of the earth fada muttering into his smartphone.

Tiago pulled Alesia aside for a quick kiss. "Goodbye, *querida.* I'll see you back at Rock Run."

"No." She set a hand on his chest. "I have the right to witness this."

He could tell from her expression that was a stab in the dark, but she was right. The fada had an intricate set of rules regarding mates' rights and interactions between males and females that kept the men from dominating the women too completely.

He trapped her face between his hands. "I'm not giving you a choice. This is going to be a fight to the death. If you don't want to return to Rock Run, you can wait at the clan's rowhouse. Eliana will go with you, right?"

Eliana rolled her eyes but said, "Sure."

Alesia's chin jutted. "No," she said, her heart-shaped face set in stubborn lines. "I'm staying."

He swore under his breath. "And I say you're going. *Now.*"

Dion spoke up. "Actually, she's correct, Tiago. As your mate she has the right to stay. Besides, this challenge is as much about her as you."

Tiago stilled. He'd just realized that nobody had seemed surprised when he'd claimed Alesia as his mate. "Dion knows, doesn't he?" he said to her. "So you knew, too."

She nodded.

"And you didn't tell me?"

"Apparently," his big brother interjected, "she was waiting for you to figure it out yourself, *idiota.*"

"I see." He leaned close and spoke for Alesia's ears alone.

"When this is done, baby, we're going to have a long talk, you and me—about why it's not a good idea to keep things from your mate. Understand?"

She licked her lips. "Yes."

His gaze followed that small pink tongue, and damn if he didn't want to forget Jorge and drag her to the nearest dark corner and sex her brains out.

But he needed to do this—for his own self-respect, but even more, for Marjani, Valeria, and most of all, Alesia. His mate would never be safe with Jorge alive. None of their women would.

"Fine," he told Dion. "Alesia stays. But you'd damn well better keep her safe." He gave her a nudge in his brother's direction.

"*É claro*." Dion draped an arm around her shoulders, and Rui took a position on her other side.

Tiago looked around the room. "The rest of you can remain as witnesses. But interfere and you'll die—and it won't be an easy death." His gaze lingered on the Baltimore shifters. "Is that clear?"

They nodded or grunted agreement and he said, "Good," before looking at Jorge. "It will be a fair fight," he promised, "no compulsion," and released him.

He sensed Alesia's worry. She had her fingernails dug into her palms, her lips moving as if in prayer. "*Please. Please.*"

Jorge stepped forward, his animal staring out of his eyes, the pupils a bright, unearthly green.

"Jorge Teles, I challenge you to a duel." Tiago spoke the ritual words. "To the death."

"I accept," the other man said in a thick, barely understandable voice. "*Tu estás morto.* I'll send you to Hades." He extended his claws and sprang at Tiago, aiming straight for his eyes.

Tiago lunged to the side, only just avoiding the long, wicked claws. Jorge stumbled forward, his momentum carrying him past Tiago.

There was a cry of outrage from the watching Rock Run fada.

In an instant, Rui had an arm around Jorge's throat. He snarled and tried to break away, but Rui hung on grimly.

"By *Deus*," he ground out, "you'll follow the rules or I'll put a knife in your liver right here and now." He pressed a stiletto to Jorge's back just under his ribs.

The entire room caught its breath. No one doubted Rui meant it. Tiago started to protest but the fada commander sliced him a look that made him shut his mouth.

Jorge snarled.

"Is that your answer?" Rui pressed the blade a little deeper.

They all waited, even Tiago. If Jorge was that far gone, there was no sense going forward with the challenge.

Jorge blinked and scowled. "No, damn you," he said in a more understandable voice. "Challenge rules apply."

"Swear it," Rui said. "And not on your true-name. On the god's name—the old god."

"I swear, on Dionysus's name."

"*Bom.*" With a curt nod, Rui released him.

The other fada in the room fell back, forming a ring around Tiago and Jorge. Alesia looked anxiously from Jorge to Tiago, but allowed Dion to position her a little behind him so she was shielded by his body.

"Get ready," Rui said. "Then wait for my signal."

Tiago nodded and stripped off his clothes as Jorge followed suit. It was a tradition that ensured neither combatant was concealing a weapon.

Rui raised a hand. "Challenge rules," he stated. "You're all witnesses. Neither man leaves the circle until it's over. Fight to the death."

Some challenges ended when the loser conceded, but no one expected Dion to let Jorge leave the Full Moon alive, even if Tiago lost.

Jorge was a dead man walking—it was just a matter of how many men he took with him.

Rui slashed his hand down, then stepped back into the circle next to Alesia.

This time Jorge was more cautious, waiting for Tiago to make the first move. *Smart.* Tiago suspected that first quick, vicious attack had been intended to rattle him.

They circled each other as the crowd watched in silence, save for the occasional grunt of encouragement or displeasure.

Tiago eyed his opponent. Jorge might be four times his age, his body marred with old scars and fresh bruises, but this wouldn't be an easy fight. Jorge was a master at hand-to-hand combat.

His words from long ago echoed in Tiago's ears. *Strike early and hard at whatever's closest. And don't be chicken-hearted. Aim to hurt your man.*

Tiago's foot lashed out, aiming at Jorge's knee. Jorge twisted out of the way but came back with a gut punch. Tiago jumped back and the blow glanced off his hip.

They resumed circling. Jorge feinted left and then aimed a flying kick at Tiago's balls. He turned aside just in time and Jorge's foot slammed into his thigh instead—against a still-healing bruise. Tiago registered the pain in some dim corner of his brain but ignored it to move in on Jorge.

They started fighting in earnest, exchanging brutal, no-holds-barred blows: punches, kicks, head-butts. The circle of men went silent, the sound the dull thud of flesh against flesh.

Tiago saw an opening and lunged, but Jorge was waiting for him. His hand chopped down on Tiago's neck just beneath his ear.

Stars exploded behind his eyes. He faltered and swayed on his feet. Jorge moved in with a flurry of blows and he spun away, nearly falling into the ring of fada.

Faces swung by like a bizarre merry-go-round: excited, grim, carefully neutral.

Dion muttered, "Stay on your feet, damn you." But Tiago saw the worry in his eyes.

He sucked in a breath and caught his balance in front of Alesia.

She was clutching Dion's hand, her other hand pressed to her mouth. She made a small sound of distress, her big, whiskey-colored eyes locked on his—and the mate bond chose that moment to snap fully into place. There was a wrenching pull from him to her, so intense his chest ached. At the same time, her love and worry poured back through the bond to him.

He blinked and staggered. Jorge shoved him from the side, sending him sprawling face down on the floor. The other man slammed onto his back like a ton of bricks.

Tiago's breath whooshed out. For a few seconds he was too stunned to move. Jorge shoved a knee into his spine and grabbed his chin, trying to break his back.

Alesia whimpered. Tiago instinctively tamped the mate bond down as low as it could go. He couldn't let her distract him.

He jammed an elbow into Jorge's ribs. He must have hit a sore spot because Jorge groaned and loosened his grip, enough so Tiago could twist onto his back.

Jorge growled and slashed open Tiago's cheek with his claws. The whites of his eyes were red, his face twisted into a feral snarl. He was losing control, his scent wild and all animal.

Tiago's beast rose in response. His first instinct was to resist, but he realized the beast was open to him, willingly adding his strength and cunning to Tiago's.

So Tiago grabbed at the beast's offering with both hands—because he'd suddenly realized how fucking stupid it had been for him to insist on fighting Jorge.

It didn't matter that Dion would defend Alesia to the death. If Jorge killed Tiago, she'd be subject to the living death of a person whose mate has died too soon.

Tiago had promised not to compel Jorge, but nothing said he

couldn't tap into the beast's strength and add it to his own, just as he'd used its energy before.

The beast must have shown in his eyes. Jorge snarled but his scent was acrid with fear.

Good.

Tiago caught Jorge's wrists and dug his thumbs into the pressure points between his tendons, using one of his own moves against him, until the older man was writhing in his grip, desperate to get away.

Tiago threw him off and jumped to his feet. Jorge rose too, more slowly.

Tiago waited until he was standing and then closed in, lashing him with a series of methodical blows—to his jaw, his solar plexus, his lower belly. Jorge slumped forward and Tiago saw his opening. He wrapped his arms around Jorge, getting him in a headlock.

Jorge bucked and twisted in his grip but it was clear he was tiring.

It was time to finish it.

He jerked Jorge's head sharply to the side and back. His neck snapped and he went limp. Tiago let him slide to the ground.

Breathing hard, he stared down at his former mentor. He waited for a surge of triumph but all he felt was a hollow sadness at the end of the man he'd once worshipped with all the intensity of a young boy.

His only consolation was that Jorge would've wanted it this way. He'd always said only a coward dies in bed.

The Rock Run fada were congratulating him and slapping him on the back. Only Chico and Eliana hung back. For once, Chico's handsome face was unsmiling, and Eliana was clearly hurt. Tiago knew he owed them an explanation, but right now Alesia was more important.

He nodded and muttered some response to the men congratulating him, but his gaze was on Alesia. She looked back uncertainly, but he could feel the love pouring through the bond.

Love for him.

Grabbing his T-shirt, he scrubbed the blood and sweat from his face and chest before tossing it aside and crossing to where she waited with Dion.

"You won," she whispered as his older brother discreetly faded back. "You—you're okay."

Tears filled her eyes. Her hands came up, stroking his face, his shoulders.

"Alesia. *Querida*. Please don't cry, baby." He cupped her face and swallowed noisily. His chest warmed, the hollow feeling melting away under the love emanating from her. "I'm sorry. So sorry you had to go through that."

"Hey." She touched his mouth, stopping his apologies. "I was the one who insisted on staying. But now I want to go home, okay?"

"Yes." He rubbed his lips over hers, breathing her in. His cock rose between them, pressing against her belly. He was too much a fada to be embarrassed by a hard-on, but getting her alone sounded like an excellent idea.

But how? Alesia could return to the island herself by jumping from tree to tree, but she couldn't carry him with her—and he was damned if she was going anywhere without him. Besides, she was exhausted; he could sense it through the mate bond. Too exhausted to 'port herself that many times.

He shot Dion a helpless look

"Here." His brother held out a key. "Take my bike. I'll ride with one of the other men. It's at—" He named a corner a couple of blocks away.

"Thank you." Tiago took the key gratefully. "For everything. And I'm truly sorry. I'll do whatever I can to make it up to you."

"We're clear," his brother said gruffly. "You only used your Gift to protect your woman. And when it came down to it, you didn't do me any harm except to my pride. As for Rui, as your commander he can decide on his own discipline. But we both know he'd be dead if your heart had been in it. You stayed in control—even during your duel. As far as I'm concerned, you've proved you can control your Gift."

Tiago swallowed convulsively. He was starting to believe that himself, but it meant a lot to hear it from Dion.

"Now get the hell out of here." Dion slapped him on the back. Tiago tried not to wince; with the adrenaline wearing off, he was feeling every single fucking bruise—both old and new. "Your mate's a tough little thing, but she's had a rough couple of days. Get her home and take care of her. She's the real gift."

"I know." Meeting Alesia's eyes, he mouthed, "*Love you.*"

She gave him a wobbly smile back and he sprang into action, releasing her to pull on his cargo pants and shoes. Claudio lent him a clean T-shirt with the howling wolf logo.

He turned to Alesia. She was trying to zip her jacket, but her hands were shaking.

His heart wrenched. His poor little fawn. Reaction was setting in. He needed to get her back to her island and her tree as soon as possible.

He brushed aside her hands and did up the jacket for her, then draped his arm around her shoulders.

"Let's go home," he said, and together, they walked out of the bar.

29

———

*D*ion scrubbed a hand over his head and watched Tiago and Alesia leave. His little brother—mated. And to a dryad. Who'd have thought it?

Rui had been helping Claudio direct the cleanup, but now he came over to Dion. "Hell," he muttered in Portuguese. "That was touch and go there for a while."

"*Sim*. But Tiago was holding back. Look what he did to Mys. That could've been us."

Rui rubbed his chest over the region of his heart. "Yeah. Remind me never to piss the man off."

Dion grimaced. Rui might've couched it as a joke, but it wasn't, not really. And if Rui, one of Rock Run's most dominant men and himself a former assassin, had that touch of fear, what about the rest of the clan?

"Bad joke," the other man muttered, reading Dion's mind like the old friend he was. "He'll be all right."

"I hope so."

He hoped like hell he'd done the right thing. But he'd meant every word he'd said to Tiago. He had a feeling that with a little work and a lot of encouragement, his brother would be an invaluable asset to the clan.

But this wasn't just about the clan—this was his kid brother, the pup he'd raised from the time he was ten. Dion wanted him to be happy—and if he had to knock a few heads together in order to make it happen, then he would. He'd be damned if he'd let Tiago be ostracized for his Gift.

"People like him," Rui said. "He'll win them over."

Dion nodded. "You'll keep an eye on him?"

"*Certo*. But that doesn't mean I'm not going to beat his ass in hand-to-hand the first chance I've got." Rui's lips curved in an evil smile. "It's good for discipline—and we can't have him getting too cocky, not with a Gift like his."

Dion cast his friend a grateful glance. "*Obrigado*."

Rui was a well-respected member of the clan, especially among the men. It would help a lot if he treated Tiago as just another warrior.

Claudio had softened enough to get everyone a round of beer. Rui accepted two foaming glasses and handed one to Dion.

Rui took a healthy swallow. "At least I knew you were never in any danger."

"What d'you mean?"

"Cleia. You had a protection ward, didn't you?"

"The hell I did. Is that what the men think? That I need my mate's magic to protect me?"

Rui raised a hand. "Sorry. So you're saying you didn't let her make you a ward?"

"Hell no. The day I need my woman to shield me is the day you can consign me to the water."

Rui shook his head. "You're a tough bastard, you know?"

Dion took a gulp of beer. It was perfect: dark, bitter and cold as an ice fae's heart. "That's why I'm alpha."

His friend chuckled.

They sipped their beers in silence for a minute and then Rui slanted a look at Dion.

"A dryad, huh?"

"Hell, if she'll take him on with a Gift like that, I'll welcome her to the family with open arms. And you know"—Dion rubbed his chin thoughtfully—"our vineyards still aren't producing like they could be. Even Cleia can't seem to get it quite right. Grapes need the right balance of soil, water, and sunshine."

His second nodded. "That island of hers is the lushest on the river. Looks like a damn jungle in the summer."

"*Exatamente.*"

They exchanged knowing smiles.

Dion glanced at Jorge and sobered. Claudio had unearthed a couple of sheets and he and a couple of the Rock Run fada were wrapping Jorge in one of them.

"I can handle this," he told Rui. "You have a mate about to give birth. Get back to the base before she has both of our heads."

"If you're sure—" His second was already turning to leave.

The front door slammed open and Adric strode into the bar. He looked around him, hands fisted on his hips. "What the *fuck* is going on?"

Rui swung back to stand beside Dion. "Who the hell called him?" he said out of the side of his mouth.

Dion shrugged. "It's his territory."

Adric halted a few feet away, his bronze eyes sparking blue fire. "This was Tiago's work?"

But they could tell he already knew the answer.

"Yes," Dion replied.

"Holy mother." The other alpha took in the dead bodies. "What the fuck *is* your brother?"

"That," Dion returned, "is none of your damn business. But you wanted these men? Here they are. The big one is Jorge, the man back there is Mys. But what I'd like to know is why the *hell* your men jumped in on the other side."

"They what?" Adric's spine went rigid. He turned to look at the four earth shifters other than the bouncer still in the bar.

The other three looked to the largest, a big bear of man with a shaved head who looked even younger than Adric. He gulped and shifted from foot to foot like an overgrown schoolboy.

"But, my lord...we thought since the river people harmed Lady Marjani, you'd want us to—"

Adric stalked the few feet between them and grasped the bear-man by the throat.

"Don't think, Beau," he said between his teeth. "That's my job." He thrust the man from him. "You assholes"—his gaze took in all four men—"it wasn't Rock Run who hurt Marjani. It was those men there—the dead ones." He jerked his chin at Jorge and Mys. "Lord Dion claimed the right to clean up his own mess, with my full agreement."

Beau winced. "Hell. I'm—I beg your pardon, my lord. We didn't know. I—Shania said..."

"Shania?" Adric's face sharpened. "She's part of this?"

The big man nodded. "Shania and Kelvin, they said that Rock Run was moving in on us, that we were needed. Shania told us to come to the saloon ASAP." He looked around, brow furrowed. "She was here a few minutes ago. Kelvin too."

"But why would you take the side of two water fada?"

"Shania said they were on our side."

"And you didn't scent a lie?"

"She contacted me through my crystal. But it made sense. She said it was for Marjani."

Jace Jones loped into the bar. Of medium height, with black hair and a cat's wiry build, he was Merry's uncle and one of Adric's top lieutenants. He took in the carnage, then glanced from Adric to Dion as if expecting to find the two of them at each other's throats.

When he saw they were just discussing things, he visibly relaxed.

"You heard about Shania and Kelvin?" he asked Adric. When the alpha nodded, he said, "We've got them. There were another couple of men, but they're gone."

"Who?" Adric gritted.

"They're not saying."

"No? We'll see about that." The earth fada's tone was cold, but Dion scented the anger coming off him in hot waves.

Jace glanced at Dion, but Adric jerked his chin. "Talk," he ordered. "They took Tiago prisoner and tried to use him to bring down Dion. Whatever you found out, it involves Rock Run, too."

"Sounds like you already know most of it," the lieutenant replied. "Shania and Kelvin were helping Jorge and his men. Luc heard some talk and decided to check it out. When he realized what was going down, he called me in as back up. We caught Shania and Kelvin in Sandtown, but the others must've realized something was up and they went to ground."

Adric's nostrils flared, but all he said was, "Good work."

"What about Shania and Kelvin?"

"I'll deal with them," was the terse reply. Adric turned to Dion and jerked his head at Jorge and Mys. "Need any help with these two?"

"Thanks, but no. We'll take them out into the bay, return them to the elements."

Adric nodded and looked at the four earth fada. "As for you men, I'll talk to you later. For now, just get the fuck out of my sight."

The men inclined their heads and hurried out the door.

"Lord have mercy," Adric muttered. "I want my people to think for themselves, but..." He shook his head.

Dion's lips twitched. "It's a balance."

"Yeah?" Adric shot him a look. For a second, his cocky exterior slipped and Dion glimpsed a young, in-over-his-head alpha. Then his face hardened and he looked at the dead men, both enshrouded in white sheets now.

"Thank you for this." Adric inhaled slowly, scenting them. "Feral?"

"Yeah. Or as near as makes no difference."

"Then they needed to be put down," was the flat response.

Dion nodded. That was one thing they could agree on.

"Give your brother my thanks," Adric added. "I'll make sure Marjani knows. She'll sleep a little easier tonight."

"Hell, you don't owe us any thanks. I'm just sorry your sister got dragged into this. If there's anything we can do for her—anything at all—contact me. All right?"

"Thanks," Adric said, but Dion could tell he was just being polite.

The other alpha dragged a hand through his spiked-up hair. "Look, I have to know—the deal's still on with your mate?"

"That's between you and the queen. But you need to get your house in order. I don't care what deal she cuts with you, I'm not letting you within ten miles of either of our territories if you're not in full control your clan."

"Fair enough." Adric stuck out his hand. "I know you don't want my thanks, but you have it anyway."

"*De nada*." Dion shook his hand firmly.

Rui waited until Adric had left before setting his empty glass on the bar. "Think we can trust him?"

"Last week I'd have said no way in Hades. But now?" He moved a shoulder.

His friend's green eyes narrowed. "I'm thinking Tiago's going to want to stay close to the base now that he's mated. At least for the next year or so. You know how newly mated men are."

"And?"

"Luis and I were talking, and if this deal between Baltimore and the sun fae goes through, we'll need someone to supervise the men assigned to guard the Baltimore miners. Your brother would be perfect. Not only will our men obey him, when what happened here gets out, the earth shifters would be idiots if they tried to pull anything."

Dion nodded slowly. "That's not a bad idea."

"Tiago's alpha material. He'll be happiest if he's in charge of something. And with his Gift, the Baltimore fada will think twice before messing with him. Adric, especially. Word is he can hypnotize you almost instantly with that quartz of his."

"So I hear. But if he tried it on Tiago, he'd stop him in his tracks."

"And it would prove to Tiago that he has your complete trust."

They exchanged a look.

"Clever." A corner of Dion's mouth lifted. "This is why I keep you around. Now get the hell out of here and back to your mate."

30

———

Outside the Full Moon Saloon it was still daylight. Tiago blinked. It felt as if hours had passed since he'd first entered the bar, but it was actually only a little after five.

The Friday-night crowd gave him and Alesia a wide berth. Tiago caught sight of himself in a window and saw why. He looked like a boxer on a bad day—battered face, a bloody gash across his left eyebrow and his hair a tangled mass around his shoulders.

Ah, well. He was never going to be a cuddly sort of man. But Alesia didn't seem to mind—although for a few moments there, she'd had him worried.

He gave her a squeeze. "You know I'd never hurt you, don't you?"

"I know." She pressed a kiss to his neck. "Back there in the bar, I wasn't afraid of you. And I know you had to kill Mys—or he'd have killed me. It's just that...this isn't easy for me."

"Alesia." He turned and took her by the shoulders right there in the middle of the sidewalk, uncaring of the passersby. "I promise it won't touch you. That's clan business. I won't bring it home."

"Oh, Tiago." She touched his cheek. "I don't think the mate bond works like that. I'll deal with it. As long as you promise to think long and hard before unleashing your Gift on anyone—even a plant or an animal. I think maybe we're mates for a reason. I need your strength and you need my—"

"Peace," he finished for her. "You're peace to me. Everything good and green and growing."

They kissed then, a slow, sweet mingling of breath and promises, and Tiago fell a little deeper in love with her, if that were possible.

They turned as one and started down the street again, fingers intertwined.

Alesia pulled up short. "Uh-oh," she said under her breath.

Tiago followed her gaze to the couple seated on a bench under the largest tree on the block—Naomi, and a man who had to be Alesia's father. Tiago looked at the man curiously. Male dryads were rare. Many dryad families were polygamous because of it, with one man having several mates, although he couldn't see Naomi sharing her man with another female.

The man had the lean muscles of a dancer and the pointed ears of a fae. Like Alesia, his hair was golden brown where Naomi's was black, and he had heavy dark brows and chiseled features where his mate's were more delicate, but the two of them could've passed for Alesia's older sister and brother.

"Mama—and Dad." Alesia released Tiago's hand to hurry forward. "What are you doing here?"

Tiago squared his shoulders and followed her. This wasn't the time and place he'd have chosen to meet Alesia's father, but hell, there was probably never going to be a good time to announce to her parents that she'd mated with a fada.

The dryad couple rose to greet their daughter. They tried to draw her to one side, but she shook her head at them and turned to Tiago.

"You already know Tiago, Mama."

Naomi nodded, her expression set.

"And this is my dad, Danaus."

Tiago inclined his head respectfully to them both. "Peace to you and yours."

"And to yours," Danaus returned. He crossed his arms over his chest and looked Tiago up and down.

He accepted the inspection, hands loose at his sides. These were his mate's parents, after all. He owed them deference.

"There was a fight," Alesia rushed to say, "but it wasn't Tiago's fault. He was trying to help me."

Naomi was wearing a forest-green tunic over black leggings. She made an impatient movement, and the jagged green hem fluttered like leaves around her legs. "I hear some river men kidnapped you. So they think you're fair game now?"

Alesia sighed. "No, Mama. The men weren't from Rock Run. They're the ones who kidnapped that Rock Run woman five years ago. Tiago tried to stop them and they knocked him out. He—"

Tiago caught her hand, halting the spate of words. "The important thing is they won't be bothering your daughter anymore."

Danaus raised a brow. "They're dead?"

"Yes."

Naomi frowned, but Danaus just said, "Indeed," in neutral tones.

Tiago took a subtle sniff. Naomi was clearly agitated, but the dryad male's scent was as neutral as his voice.

Danaus turned to Alesia and his face softened. He smoothed a hand down her hair. "You're all right, little one? These men, they didn't hurt you?"

She shook her head. "I'm fine. They didn't touch me."

Danaus briefly closed his eyes. "Thank the gods."

Alesia tightened her grip on Tiago's fingers and took a deep breath. "We have something to tell you. We're mated."

"Oh, Alesia." That was Naomi. "With a fada?"

Alesia's chin lifted. "Yes."

Danaus narrowed his eyes at Tiago. When he just gazed calmly back, Danaus gave a little half-smile and slid an arm around his mate's waist. "Congratulations. We're happy for you, aren't we, love?"

Naomi expelled a breath. "Yes, of course. But how could you be mated without the ritual?"

He and Alesia looked at each other. "It just happened," Alesia said.

"But you'll have the mate-bond ritual."

"Of course," Tiago replied. "I want everyone to know that Alesia is mine."

Naomi nodded tightly and then put out her hands to her daughter. "Congratulations."

Alesia stepped forward and Naomi pressed her a sedate kiss on each cheek—and then the two of them were laughing and crying and hugging each other. Well, Alesia was laughing and crying and gripping her mother around the waist, while Naomi patted her awkwardly on the back—but Tiago thought he saw the sparkle of tears in her black eyes. Meanwhile Danaus waited his turn with a wry smile.

The two older dryads wanted to hear exactly what had happened between Alesia and the sea fada. Alesia explained in a few short sentences, glossing over the part about Tiago's Gift to his relief. Time enough to explain that their daughter's mate had the power of compulsion. Instead, in Alesia's telling, Tiago was a hero who had defied everyone, including his own brother, to save her.

When the women moved on to discussing the when and where of the mate-bond ceremony, Alesia's father pulled Tiago aside.

"You do know," he said, "that a dryad can't leave her oak for more than a day or two at a time."

"I do. But we'll make it work. Her tree is in Rock Run territory, after all."

"I'll be frank," Danaus said, "you're not who I'd have chosen for my daughter, but the chances of her finding a mate among us was very small. But she'd better be happy, or I don't care if she's your mate, you won't see her for more than a few days a year. Dryads are solitaries. We don't have to live with our mates."

Like hell. Tiago wanted to bare his teeth, but all he said was, "She's my mate. Do you think I won't do everything I can to make her happy?"

Danaus scrutinized him, then gave a decisive nod. "Good. Then you have my blessing."

"Thank you, sir." Tiago turned to where Alesia was finishing up with her mother. "We'll be in touch about the ceremony," he told Naomi, "but you're both invited, of course. And Alesia's sisters, too."

"We'll be there," said Danaus.

"I'll stop by in a couple of days to see how you're doing," Naomi said. It sounded like a warning, but she lifted her face for Tiago to kiss.

He set his lips to each of her cool, unlined cheeks, and then watched as they scaled the tree they'd been sitting under and winked out of sight.

Alesia blew out a breath. "That went...better than I expected."

"Hey, you can't expect them to be overjoyed." He slanted her a grin. "But don't worry, I'll turn on the charm. It worked with you, didn't it?"

She grinned back. Then her smile faded. "You're bleeding." She touched his lip. "Let's go home."

Home—with Alesia. He liked the sound of that.

Dion's bike was just up the street. As they strolled toward it, Tiago set his hand on Alesia's lower back, and from there his hand found its way to her ass. He could feel the muscles moving through the tight jeans. He gave them a good squeeze.

She shot him a wide-eyed look, her painted lips making a

perfect, round O. He grinned back even as his groin tightened.

She was *his*. His mate.

He was still absorbing the wonder of that. His mate, and he'd fought for her honor and won. Both man and animal wanted to shout it aloud to the world—and claim their reward.

He nuzzled her neck, marking her with his scent, then nipped —just hard enough to leave a slight pink imprint.

She made a small sound of arousal that vibrated up the mate bond. How the hell was he going to wait until he had her back home? But she was exhausted. The quickest way to restore her energy was to get her back home to her oak.

But he couldn't resist another squeeze of that round ass. She blinked and turned those big fawn eyes on him.

His breath hitched. "When you look at me like that..."

"What?" She raised her brows as if she didn't have a clue, but he sensed her mirth. This mate-bond thing was going to have some advantages.

"Bad girl." He smacked her butt. "Keep it up"—he jerked his chin toward a nearby alley—"and you're going to find yourself up against the wall, taking my cock."

"Sorry," she said, but underneath she was still laughing.

He leaned close and husked, "Consider yourself warned."

She chuckled and pulled him down the street to the bike. As they reached it, Eliana and Chico strode up beside them.

Tiago pushed Alesia behind him. "What do you want?"

Chico scowled. "If you think I'd hurt your mate, you're even more fucked up than I thought."

Hell. Tiago really didn't need this. Not right now.

"I'm sorry," he said without letting up on his protective stance. "But I still need to know why you came after us."

"To escort you back to Rock Run, you asshole. Your brother's orders."

"Yeah?"

Eliana sent Chico an exasperated glance. "What he means is,

we *volunteered* to escort you, and the alpha agreed. We wanted to make sure you were all right, and that you and your mate got safely home."

"Thank you." Tiago relaxed a little. Alesia appeared at his side, looking from Chico to Eliana curiously.

Chico was still scowling. "So. You have another Gift."

"Yeah. So?" Tiago crossed his arms and stared back at his best friend, daring him to say something.

Chico put his fists on his hips and leaned forward, practically vibrating with fury. "I understand you didn't want to tell the clan, but us? We're your fucking friends. At least I thought we were." He shook his head in disgust.

Tiago let out a long breath. "You're right. I should've told you. I'm sorry."

"Damn right you should've. So why didn't you?"

Tiago moved a shoulder. "When it first appeared, I told myself I had to learn more about it. That it was best to hide it until I understood myself what I could do with it."

"And then—?"

"And then"—Tiago dragged a hand over his hair—"I don't know. You've heard the stories—about men getting banished from their clans. I was afraid to let anyone know."

Chico growled at the same time Eliana said, "Oh, Tiago."

"You think I'm afraid of you?" the other man demanded. "This is me, Chico." He thumped a fist against his chest. "I know you, Ti. There's no way in hell you'd ever hurt anyone in the clan. You're fucking going to be an alpha someday, Tiago, and alphas don't use their Gifts to hurt others."

"Yeah?" Tiago said.

Eliana nodded emphatically, her dark curls bouncing. "You know we'd follow you anywhere, Tiago. Not now, but someday, if anything ever happens to the alpha—or if you decide to start your own den. And before that, when you make squad leader, I'm going to be first in line to be one of your warriors. Not just because you have a badass Gift, but because you'd die before you'd let anyone in your squad down. You think we don't know that?"

Tiago's cheeks heated. He felt humbled and bemused—and almost as good as when he'd realized Alesia loved him. "Thanks," he muttered.

Alesia slipped her arm around his waist. "And thank you from me as well," she told them. "Tiago's going to need you."

They nodded. Eliana said, "We already told Lord Dion that Tiago has the support of our whole cohort. And we'll make sure the clan knows Tiago's got his Gift under control."

"Thanks," he said again. "I don't"—he swallowed noisily —"I—"

Chico saved him by wrapping him in a bear hug. "Asshole," he muttered again. "But we've got your back, *entendes*?"

"Yeah—and right back at you, *irmão*."

He and Chico pounded each other on the back. Eliana got in on the action and dragged Alesia in too for a group hug. Then his friends jogged off to get their motorcycles.

Tiago glanced at Alesia. She appeared a little shellshocked.

"Alpha?" she asked.

He shrugged. "Not if it means I have to challenge my own brother. But I'd make a damn good squad leader. And I could see starting my own den someday—with you."

"Whoa." She raised a hand. "Let me get used to mating with a fada first."

"Take all the time you need. Because I'm going to be around for a long, long time." He dragged her into his arms.

She squeaked and then grinned at him. He kissed the grin right off her face. That kiss turned into another, then another. By the time the two of them came up for air, Eliana and Chico had zoomed up on their bikes. They waited as he and Alesia mounted Dion's motorcycle.

Alesia set her hands carefully on either side of his waist. "I'm not hurting you, am I?"

Hell, he hurt everywhere. But he'd heal—and he craved her touch.

He placed a hand over hers. "Keep them there. I like it."

He disengaged the clutch and pushed the start button, and the engine growled to life. Putting the bike into gear, he pulled out into traffic, flanked on either side by his two best friends.

He smiled the whole way up I-95.

BY THE TIME they reached the road to the base garage, the sun was setting. They followed the narrow country road along Rock Run Creek through the darkening woods, the headlights picking out the trees against the navy-blue sky. The air was clear and cool. Tiago took a deep, contented breath.

Alesia rested her head on his back and he felt how tired she was.

"Almost there, love." He patted her hand, and she nodded against his back.

There was no bridge to her island, so he stopped near an oak tree. Chico and Eliana gave them a thumbs up and zoomed past to the garage while he gave Alesia a leg up into the oak promising to follow as soon as he could.

She nodded and shimmied up the tree. Even exhausted, the woman moved like an acrobat. The boots didn't even slow her down.

He waited, enjoying the view of her ass in the snug jeans, until she turned and blew him a kiss. "See you soon."

He grinned and sent her a kiss back. The air around her glowed a pale green, and then she was gone.

Tiago left the bike in the garage, dropped his clothes in a bin left for that purpose and went out the back door. It was only a few steps to the creek.

Chico and Eliana were already in the water as their dolphins. He changed to his dolphin as well and headed downstream to the Susquehanna, taking his time, letting the icy water cleanse his cuts and soothe his bruises.

The two of them stayed with him until he reached Alesia's island, then with a flip of their tails, sloped off to return to Rock Run as he strode onto shore.

He didn't bother with clothes. At forty-five degrees, the air temperature wasn't cold enough to affect him—and he'd just be removing them anyway.

Tiago jogged along the dark path. The oak came into sight and he blinked. It was lit up with pink and yellow and purple fae lights like one of those silly human Easter trees.

He grinned and stopped at the base. "Alesia?"

The only answer was a chuckle.

His grin widened. So she wanted to play? She must be feeling better. He grabbed a branch and swung himself into the tree.

She didn't make it easy. Instead of being near the top like usual, she'd concealed herself at the end of a low-hanging branch. He passed her and then had to double back down. By the time he located her, he was swearing under his breath.

He hunkered next to her on the branch and nudged one of the shining balls of light closer so that it cast a warm glow over her hard gray form.

"Change."

He could feel her smile inside but she obeyed immediately. It was still too slow for him.

He waited impatiently as her skin gradually infused with color. She'd taken off the jacket but was still wearing the boots, jeans and fire-engine red shirt. She was posed like a pinup model: hands on the branch behind her, legs outstretched along its length and a single braid falling over one shoulder.

He went instantly hard. He ran his hands down the sleek muscles of her legs, brought his hands to those small, sweet breasts. He was already picturing himself sinking deep inside her while she wrapped those long legs around him—preferably wearing the boots.

He fingered the collar of her shirt. "I don't know where you got these clothes, but I like them."

"Yeah?"

"Oh, yeah." The top button had been torn off, but he popped the next one open. "You about started a riot in that bar."

"That wasn't me," she protested. "It was you fada."

"Mm?" He was only half-listening, his focus on her buttons. He popped another one open, revealing the inside curve of her breasts. And was that a black bra she was wearing? He swallowed a groan.

He nuzzled each soft swell and then reluctantly pulled back. Alesia might be used to dancing along the branches like a gymnast, but he preferred something a little wider. "Let's go up to the main level."

She nodded and led the way up to the large, spreading branches where she did most of her living. He nudged her to sit on a branch with her back to the trunk, directly under another fae light, this one a pretty rose-pink. He wanted to see every soft, ivory-skinned inch of her.

Crouching down, he took her arms and raised them above her head, pressing the wrists against the trunk behind her. "Now, *mate*—"

Holding onto her wrists with one hand, he undid the shirt's next button.

She drew a slow breath. His gaze dropped to her mouth and he recalled those lush lips wrapped around his cock. He swallowed and stopped unbuttoning her shirt to run his thumb over her lower lip.

The air between them seemed to quiver. "Tiago?" Her tone was questioning but she was squirming on the branch, she was so turned on.

She was enjoying this.

Damn. The blood pulsed in his groin, slow and heavy. He was already hard, but knowing she was as aroused by their play as him had his whole body tightening.

He leaned closer and licked her lips. Soft and easy. Because they had the entire night before them...and all day tomorrow. Hell, Dion and Rui wouldn't say anything if he didn't return for a week.

"Yes, baby?"

"I—I—you were saying—"

"Was I?" he rasped against her mouth.

"Yes," she said more firmly. "About us being mates. I'm sorry if you're angry, but—"

"No." He drew back at that. "How could I be angry about that?"

"But in the bar—"

"Ah, Alesia." He cupped her face and rested his forehead against hers. "I'm sorry. So damn sorry."

Her delicate brows drew together. "For what?"

"For being such a stupid ass all these years. I think deep down I knew, but I couldn't let go—"

"Of Cleia." She grimaced. "I know."

"She was never mine except in a boy's fantasies."

She gave him a wry smile. "I know."

Her eyes shimmered. Lord, she wasn't going to cry, was she? But he could feel her pain through the bond.

His chest clenched. "Lesia—"

"It's just I didn't think you'd ever—"

He put a finger over her mouth, stopping her. "It was always you. You're the one I came back to, not her. It never really felt like I was back home until I saw you."

"Honest?"

"You know I'm telling the truth."

She gulped and then pulled him close for a long, open-mouthed kiss.

Desire slammed down his spine. He wrapped his arms around her but let her take the lead, accepting what she gave him.

When she pulled back, he blinked at her and drew a deep breath. She smiled dazedly, equally affected.

His lips curved. She was going to be so fun. She might have ten years on him, but she was so damn innocent. A woman couldn't fake that bemused expression.

With an effort, he brought his racing pulse under control, then gave her as stern a look as he could manage.

"Now, *mate*"— he twisted her braid around his palm, loop by slow loop—"we're going to have that talk I promised you. About why you don't keep things from your man—your *mate*—unless you want to find yourself in trouble. Deep trouble."

Her grin was sly. "What if I like that...being punished, I mean?"

He gave her hair a little tug. "I'd say you were a smart mate."

She made an outraged noise and he smothered a grin. He finished looping her braid around his palm, then drew her head back until her throat was open to him.

Her eyes drifted shut. She waited, her breath coming in fast pants.

He nipped the soft, vulnerable skin of her throat. Her pulse beat beneath his mouth in quick, excited beats. He breathed deeply, reveling in her fresh, woodsy scent.

"*Amo-te*," he murmured thickly.

Her eyes drifted shut. "I love you, too."

With his free hand he unbuttoned her blouse and tossed it to one side. She was indeed wearing a black bra, a silky scrap of material that had him humming his approval. He nuzzled her cleavage, then took hold of the bra with his teeth and pulled it lower, exposing her nipples.

There was a soft flush of arousal on her breasts. He was on top of her now, his knees on either side of her hips, his hand still controlling her through her braid. He rubbed his cock against her bare belly, slid it between her cleavage.

She moaned and lifted her breasts, rubbing against him like a cat in heat.

Stones, he needed her. He grit his teeth against the overpowering urge to slam his cock into her, to ride her hard and fast.

"Look at me." He gave her hair a small tug.

Her lids opened partway, the pupils dark and sultry beneath gold-tipped brown lashes. "What, Tiago?"

"You're mine. Understand? Forever."

"You know I am. That's what being mates means."

But it wasn't enough. She still didn't understand. He had to know that she was his completely, body and soul.

His fingers fumbled with the button of her jeans. He pulled down the zipper and shoved them down her legs. She was wearing tiny black panties that matched her bra. He drew in a breath at how they framed her hips. He smoothed a finger over the silky black material.

"Another gift from Dina?"

"No. I did some shopping last month when you were away. Just in case."

"Yeah?" His lips quirked. "I never had a chance, did I?"

Her smile was downright wicked.

He chuckled and jerked the panties down her hips. Someday he'd take the time to enjoy how they looked on her, but right now he ached to take her. He nudged her legs open and slid his fingers into her hot, wet cleft.

"Damn," he breathed, "I want you. I'm going to fuck you until you're screaming that you're mine."

She gazed up at him, panting softly. Somehow he found enough control to stroke her for a minute. She tried to move but he placed a hand on her hip, holding her still while he teased her with his fingers.

"Tiago," she moaned. "*Please.*"

"That's it, baby. I want you begging. I need you begging. Now stay where you are—understand?"

She hesitated, then gave a small nod. He released her hair to remove her boots and undress her the rest of the way. When he had her naked, he gazed down at her body. Her nipples were tightly furled, her stomach taut. She had one knee bent up so he could see her flushed center, pink and pretty as one of her flowers.

Her need pulsed through the bond linking them. He groaned and came between her legs, opening them further. She clutched his shoulders and pulled him closer.

He lowered his head and licked her, slow and easy. Then he did it again...and again. She was everything hot and good.

"Mm," he said against her slick flesh.

Her thighs flexed.

He slid a finger inside her and groaned. She was so wet and tight. He licked her again, toying with her swollen little clit while he teased her inside with his finger. She bucked and tensed around him.

"No," he warned. "Not yet."

"Tiago."

"It will be better that way, trust me."

She nodded vigorously. "I do. I do."

Ah. He took that as a challenge. He settled in to lick and stroke her. Unconsciously, he'd opened himself fully to the bond, and he could tell exactly what to do to bring her pleasure.

He brought her close to climax. Once, then a second time.

And when he had her wound so tight she was sobbing with desire, he came up over her and thrust inside her. A long, slow slide that seemed to go on and on for both of them.

She moaned his name and came.

But he could tell she wasn't finished.

"More," he said.

"Yes."

Together, they moved their hips, joining their bodies and their minds. Pleasure shot from her to him and back again. The sensation was incredible, sizzling and sparking through his nerves like lightning. He set his jaw and moved slowly in and out, determined to make this last. The beast rose up in him, but only to wonder at the pleasure at being one with their mate.

Then she wrapped her legs around him, urging him on, and he was lost. His balls drew up and he pounded into her, hard and fast and so deep his dick touched her womb.

"Look at me," he gritted at her. "Tell me. *Now*."

She knew what he wanted. She dug her fingernails into his back and he felt her surrender.

"I'm yours," she sobbed out. "I'm yours."

"And I'm yours." He brought his hand between their bodies to rub her clit.

She writhed beneath him. "Ah, Goddess," she breathed. "It feels so good...so good."

And then she gave a small scream and tightened around him, squeezing him hard as she came in a wild rush that nearly blew his mind.

He closed his eyes and thrust in and out—once, twice, three times—until he followed her over the edge.

When he came back to himself, he was on top of Alesia, pressing her into the hard branch.

He muttered an apology and levered himself off her, turning so his back was against the trunk, Alesia cuddled in his lap. He felt too satiated to move, and the beast was curled up inside him like a contented pup.

She petted his chest, tangling her fingers in the wiry hair, tracing a finger around the Celtic knots encircling his left bicep. Gradually, their breathing returned to normal.

Alesia traced a dark smudge on his lower ribcage. "That's a nasty bruise. You're not hurting?"

"A little. Why don't you kiss it and make it better?"

She chuckled, a low, musical sound. "All right." She swung a leg over his and straddled him.

She started at his head and moved down, kissing each bruise with deliberate care: the gash on his eye, a scrape beneath his jaw. Then moving to his ribs and down to his thighs, ignoring his rapidly growing erection. She even found a bruise on his shin that he hadn't known he had.

On the way back, she stopped at his groin. Her mouth was so close he could feel her breath, hot on his straining flesh.

"Alesia," he groaned. "Take me in your mouth. Now."

She cupped his balls and slanted him a look. Her golden-brown eyes had never looked so fey. "Is that an order?"

"Yes. No. Whatever." He'd been teased by some experienced women, but this one had him forgetting his own fucking name.

She flicked her tongue out and sensation lashed through him.

"*Deus*," he groaned. "That's it."

She wrapped her hand around the base, closed her mouth around him and moved leisurely up and down. Tonguing him. Sucking him. He shut his eyes so he could better enjoy it.

Warm. Wet. Friction.

His balls tightened and she hummed against his cock. She lifted her head. "I can feel you," she said wonderingly. "Like you're in me. When we were having sex, did you—?"

"Yeah. It was wild."

"Wow." She went to take him into her mouth again.

"The hell with it," he muttered, and grabbing her shoulders, pulled her back up and guided himself inside her.

After the last time, he wouldn't have thought it could get any better.

But it could.

And it did.

By the time Adric got home, it was almost midnight. He found Marjani in the kitchen, toying with a bowl of cereal.

He scowled. It was way past dinnertime. She must be starving —and her cat needed meat to heal.

"I'll get you something to eat," he said.

She looked up at him, her gaze so flat it was like looking into the eyes of a corpse. "I'm not hungry."

"But you'll eat."

She moved a shoulder. "Whatever you say."

He clenched his fists, helpless and hating it.

"Shania and Kelvin are dead." He'd texted her an update on his way to where Luc was holding them in Kelvin's Sandtown den.

"Are they?" She stirred the cereal. "How?"

"Shania killed herself right before I arrived." There'd been nothing Luc could do; she'd used her own quartz, turning its energy against herself before Luc could stop her. "And I took care of Kelvin."

Kelvin he'd executed himself after a long interrogation that hadn't revealed anything Adric didn't already know, other than that the night fae had apparently been helping from the sidelines —providing wards and magic dust that they'd used to hide in full sight.

It had been a quick, clean death—not that Kelvin had deserved it after what he'd set Marjani up for. But Adric was alpha, and after what he'd seen during the Darktime, he was damned if he'd operate outside the bounds of justice.

Kelvin had protected his co-conspirators until the end. Maybe he'd been incapable of giving their names up; Adric wasn't the only person in the clan capable of working mind tricks.

But Kelvin had let slip the leader was another wolf shifter.

"So that's it?"

He hesitated. "There was another man, but I don't know for sure who it was."

Marjani glanced at him. Something sparked in their dull depths and he held his breath, but she just nodded and then went back to stirring her cereal, the spoon making slow, aimless circles.

She knew as well as him that it was probably Corban. But there was no proof, and without proof, Adric couldn't confront his cousin. Things were still too dicey. If it were anyone but Corban, he could just demand the truth. But Corban had his own following. If he refused to answer, there would be nothing Adric could do except kill him—and that could very well set off another civil war.

Either way, Adric was fucked. In fact, he wouldn't put it past his wily cousin to have engineered it that way.

But he could take a leaf from Corban's father's own book, though, and send his cousin on an assignment to the other side of the world. The ice fae king, Sindre, had a job he wanted done.

Leaving Marjani in the kitchen, he went to his bedroom and shut the door. He took out his cell phone and tapped Corban's icon.

His cousin's handsome face came on the screen. "What's up?"

Like the sonuvabitch didn't know.

Adric kept his expression neutral. "Nothing I can't handle. But that's not why I called. Start packing—I have a job for you. You're leaving for Delhi on the first flight tomorrow."

"Delhi?" Corban repeated incredulously. "Delhi, India?"

"Yeah. Sindre's got a rogue female that's gone to ground in the mountains north of Delhi. We need a good tracker to find her."

Corban's jaw clenched, but all he said was, "You're the alpha."

Adric's anger got the better of him for a moment. "Just see you fucking remember that." Then he drew a breath and continued, "And Corban—you're to go alone, and use an alias. Our employer doesn't want this connected with him in anyway."

He explained that the ice fae king wanted the female captured unharmed, finishing, "Say it, Corban. I want your oath that you'll go alone and that you won't return until you've delivered her to Sindre in Iceland."

"Like hell."

Adric just stared at him.

The seconds ticked past, and then Corban exhaled and sullenly spoke the words binding him to see the job through to its finish.

Adric gave a curt nod, and then forwarded the ice fae female's photo to Corban before cutting the connection.

With any luck, she'd lead his cousin on a merry chase for months—or even better, take him out, saving Adric the trouble. The woman had eluded three previous attempts to bring her in— and all of her pursuers were now dead.

That settled, Adric ordered a couple of fat, juicy burgers from a nearby bar and made Marjani eat every bite of hers. When they were finished, he told her to get some sleep, but she shook her head.

"I slept most of the day. I'll just lie by the fire."

She went into the bathroom to get ready and when she came

out she'd already shifted to her cougar. She padded past him into the living room.

"I'll be there in a minute," he said, because he wasn't about to leave her alone. Not when she was like this. She and Shania had been good friends. This had to hurt.

He paid a visit to the john himself and then joined her as his own cat. She was curled up on the rug in a tight ball, staring into the fake fire.

He lay down beside her, offering her the comfort of touch. It was all he could think to do for her right now. But it must have helped because her body went lax and she fell asleep.

He rested his head on his paws and stared into space. Two more gone. Three if you counted his cousin.

Corban he'd never trusted, and even Shania he'd kept a wary eye on, but Kelvin had seemed happy to accept Adric as his alpha.

How many others were there? Lord, he was sick unto death of trying to hold this fucking clan together. Some days he'd give his right arm to chuck the whole thing and head out West to roam the Rocky Mountains as a solitary.

Marjani whimpered in her sleep, reminding him of why he stayed in Baltimore. And not just for his sister, but for all the other members of the clan who counted on him to keep the peace.

He rumbled comfortingly, and she sighed and settled back down.

Exhaustion rolled over him. He put the whole mess from his mind; he'd worry about it tomorrow.

His last thought as his eyes shut was of pretty Rosana do Rio and the promise he'd extracted from the dryad.

As a guest at Tiago and Alesia's mate ball—and an honored guest at that, because hell, he'd saved the woman's life—Dion would have to let him dance with Rosana at least once.

A corner of his mouth twitched up, and then he fell asleep.

SEA DRAGON'S HUNGER

A FADA SHAPESHIFTER STORY

Chapter 1

The fae were closing in.

Cassidy's entire body prickled. She dragged a hand over her cropped hair and stared out the grimy motel window. But the parking lot was empty save for a few cars.

She unconsciously rubbed the scab on her right calf. The center was a starburst with lines snaking around her leg, a souvenir of her last encounter with the fae. The bastards had hit her with a fae ball.

A small hand touched her hip. "What's wrong, Mam?"

"Nothing for you to worry about, love." She swung Rianna into her arms and planted a kiss on her worried little face. "How about a swim?"

At three, her daughter was still easy to distract. "Yes!" She pumped a fist.

Setting her down, Cassidy moved swiftly around the room, stuffing clothes and other necessary items into a waterproof rucksack. She'd have to leave whatever didn't fit behind at the motel, but there was pitifully little, anyway. She and Rianna had been on the run for three weeks, crossing the Atlantic from Ireland and then zigzagging across America from Maryland to California.

Making their way toward Nic.

She scowled, because she'd sworn she'd never ask him for anything. But she had no choice. Besides, Nic *owed* her, damn it. Big time.

"Let's go." She pulled on the rucksack and took Rianna's hand.

The motel was a half mile from the Pacific. The two of them raced down the narrow road toward the beach. A human child wouldn't have been able to keep up, but Rianna had a shifter's strength. She ran alongside Cassidy, her sturdy little legs pumping. When her energy flagged, Cassidy swung her into her arms and continued running.

Her injured calf started to burn. It should have healed by now, another worry. Normally fada shapeshifters healed quickly, but the fae ball had left an angry scab that still hadn't healed.

The sense of impending doom increased. Her heart pounded in her ears.

Hurry, hurry, hurry…

Cassidy drew a sobbing breath and picked up speed. Their pursuers were closer than she'd realized. She raced down the road and darted across the Pacific Coast Highway.

Above them, heavy gray clouds rolled in—a storm was on its way. On the TV in their room, the forecast had been for a near-typhoon. Between that and the fact that it was Thanksgiving Day —a big American holiday, apparently—they had the beach to themselves.

Cassidy halted on the edge of the sand, her breath scraping in and out of her lungs. But there was no time to rest. Setting Rianna down, she shrugged out of the rucksack and tore off both their clothes. She shoved everything into the pack and sealed it back up.

Donning the rucksack again, she crouched down, her back to Rianna. "Climb aboard."

The little girl wriggled into the special straps Cassidy had sewn onto the rucksack for her.

"All set?"

"Yep." Small arms wrapped around Cassidy's neck as she rose to her feet.

Hurry, hurry, hurry...

A jeep screeched to a halt on the side of the highway.

Cassidy sprinted into the ocean. Icy water slapped her naked legs.

"Stop them!" someone shouted. A bullet pinged into the surf to their right.

Rianna flinched and whimpered. A blinding rage gripped Cassidy. She knew it was only a warning shot—they wanted the little girl too badly to shoot directly at her.

But bullets could go astray, and even if they didn't, they'd scared her baby. At that moment, if the arse with the gun had been any closer, Cassidy would've ripped his bloody throat out.

A chill blue wave towered above them.

"Take a breath," Cassidy shouted to Rianna—and dove into the wave's center.

A mother and child on the run. A dad who craves a second chance. And the powerful fae who's after them all...

ALSO BY REBECCA RIVARD

THE FADA SHAPESHIFTERS

Stealing Ula: A Fada Shapeshifter Prequel (Nisio & Ula, set in Ireland)

The Rock Run River Fada

Seducing the Sun Fae (Dion & Cleia)

Claiming Valeria (Rui & Valeria)

Tempting the Dryad (Tiago & Alesia)

Sea Dragon's Hunger (Cassidy & Nic)

The Baltimore Earth Fada (The Darktime Trilogy)

Saving Jace (Jace & Evie)

Charming Marjani (Marjani & Fane)

Adric's Heart (Adric & Rosana)

Fada Shapeshifter Short Reads

Lir's Lady (#3.5—Lir & Isleen)

Shifter's Valentine (#3.6—Jenny & Chico)

Find out more and read exclusive excerpts: https://rebeccarivard.com/shapeshifters/

The Vampire Syndicate Romances

Pursued (Gabriel)

Craved (Rafael)

Taken (Zaquiel)

The Vampire Blood Courtesans

Ensnared: Star (Star and Remy)

Compelled: Cerise (Cerise & Bard)

Find out more: https://rebeccarivard.com/vampires/

Join *Rebecca Rivard's newsletter* to stay informed and be eligible for giveaways and sneak peeks. As a thank you, Rebecca will gift you with a steamy short story!

Sign up at rebeccarivard.com or go to this link: Rebecca's newsletter

ABOUT THE AUTHOR

USA Today bestselling author Rebecca Rivard read way too many romances as a teenager, little realizing she was actually preparing for a career. She now spends her days with dark shifters, sexy fae and other magical creatures—which has to be the best job ever. When she's not writing, she walks, bikes and kayaks in the Chesapeake Bay area with her guitar-playing, storytelling husband.

Five of her novels have been awarded the coveted Crowned Heart Review from *InD'Tale Magazine* and the FADA SHAPESHIFTER SERIES was voted Best Shifter Series in the Paranormal Romance Guild Reviewer's Choice Awards.

Her books have also won the prestigious PRISM Award (*Charming Marjani*) and the PRG Reviewer's Choice Award (*Saving Jace*), and have finaled in both the RONE and the HOLT Medallion.

www.ingramcontent.com/pod-product-compliance
Lightning Source LLC
Chambersburg PA
CBHW021809110726
47902CB00006B/1710